Kate Ellis was born and brought up in Liverpool and studied drama in Manchester. Keenly interested in medieval history and archaeology, she lives in Cheshire with her family. *The Shroud Maker* is her eighteenth Wesley Peterson novel.

Kate has been twice nominated for the CWA Short Story Dagger and her novel, *The Plague Maiden,* was nominated for the Theakston's Old Peculier Crime Novel of the Year in 2005.

Visit Kate Ellis online:
www.kateellis.co.uk
www.twitter.com/kateellisauthor

Praise for Kate Ellis:

'A beguiling author who interweaves past and present'
The Times

'[Kate Ellis] gets better with each new book'
Bookseller

'Kept me on the edge of my seat'
Shots magazine

'Ellis skilfully interweaves ancient and contemporary crimes in an impeccably composed tale'
Publishers Weekly

By Kate Ellis

A High Mortality of Doves

Wesley Peterson series:
The Merchant's House
The Armada Boy
An Unhallowed Grave
The Funeral Boat
The Bone Garden
A Painted Doom
The Skeleton Room
The Plague Maiden
A Cursed Inheritance
The Marriage Hearse
The Shining Skull
The Blood Pit
A Perfect Death
The Flesh Tailor
The Jackal Man
The Cadaver Game
The Shadow Collector
The Shroud Maker
The Death Season
The House of Eyes
The Mermaid's Scream

Joe Plantagenet series:
Seeking the Dead
Playing With Bones

THE
SHROUD
MAKER

Kate Ellis

piatkus

PIATKUS

First published in Great Britain in 2014 by Piatkus
This paperback edition published in 2014 by Piatkus

5 7 9 10 8 6

Copyright © 2014 by Kate Ellis

The moral right of the author has been asserted.

*All characters and events in this publication, other than those
clearly in the public domain, are fictitious and any resemblance
to real persons, living or dead, is purely coincidental.*

All rights reserved.
No part of this publication may be reproduced, stored in a
retrieval system, or transmitted, in any form or by any means, without
the prior permission in writing of the publisher, nor be otherwise circulated
in any form of binding or cover other than that in which it is published
and without a similar condition including this condition being
imposed on the subsequent purchaser.

A CIP catalogue record for this book
is available from the British Library.

ISBN 978-0-7499-5803-9

Typeset in Baskerville by M Rules
Printed and bound in Great Britain by
Clays Ltd, St Ives plc

Papers used by Piatkus are from well-managed forests
and other responsible sources.

MIX
Paper from
responsible sources
FSC® C104740

Piatkus
An imprint of
Little, Brown Book Group
Carmelite House
50 Victoria Embankment
London EC4Y 0DZ

An Hachette UK Company
www.hachette.co.uk

www.littlebrown.co.uk

For the people of Dartmouth

Prologue

She loved this time when the town was still half-asleep. The time before the cacophony of a thousand alarm clocks dragged people from their beds.

At this hour the shops were shut and silent and there were no drinkers spilling from the town's pubs, glasses in hand, puffing with desperate concentration on half-smoked cigarettes. This was her time, when she could be alone with the memory of the flames.

She walked along the quayside slowly, watching the diving, shrieking gulls. Anybody who saw her would probably wonder what she was doing in her long velvet gown carrying her battered black instrument case. But there was nobody around to see; it was just her and the gulls. And the fishing boats chugging back up the river, bringing in the night's catch.

Suddenly she sensed that she was being watched but when she turned her head there was nobody there, although she thought she saw a slight movement in the bushes fringing the Memorial Gardens; there for a second, then gone. Probably the breeze blowing in off the water.

She stared out at the river, at the hordes of boats bobbing at anchor. She had spent her childhood on the water and it had once felt so safe. Until the day that still haunted her nightmares, the time of destruction and loss.

She shut her eyes and was back there, running along another waterfront, running home. Then the world had exploded in a flash of red fire and she had stood there, shaking, unable to scream, unable to weep, unable to feel, as all that had been precious to her was destroyed.

When she opened her eyes again the sun had emerged from behind the clouds, dazzling her momentarily, making her squint. Shielding her eyes, she focused on the boat. No, she hadn't been imagining it.

She wasn't sure what made her do it. Curiosity? Revenge? A desire for the truth? Or some unacknowledged longing for death? Further along the quayside she quickened her pace as the flight of narrow stone steps came into view.

She hooked up the sweeping skirt of her velvet gown in trembling fingers and began to descend into the world of the unknown.

Chapter 1

As DCI Gerry Heffernan observed in the CID office on Saturday morning, even though John Palkin had been dead six hundred years, the old bugger was still causing trouble.

At last year's Palkin Festival there'd been a mass brawl of drunken lads from Morbay, who'd at least had the decency to join in with the spirit of the proceedings and dress as medieval peasants. Two visiting yachtsmen had been mugged and a girl from London had vanished, never to be seen again. The cells had been full on that occasion and this year it looked as if history was set to repeat itself.

Gerry had just emerged from his office, scratching his head. His grizzled hair looked as if it hadn't been combed and one of the buttons on his shirt had given way under the strain, leaving a glimpse of pale torso peeping through the gap.

'Anything new on our knight in shining armour?' he asked. Even after so many years in Devon, he hadn't lost his Liverpool accent. 'Is the victim's statement any help?'

One of the young detective constables sitting by the window shook his head. The festival had only been going for a couple of days and he already looked tired. Last night a woman had been robbed at a cashpoint in the centre of town, the perpetrator dressed as a medieval knight. So much for chivalry, Gerry had lamented when the report came in.

The Palkin Festival was a matter of civic pride and the chief superintendent was concerned that the upsurge of crime it brought with it didn't reflect well on the town. The fact that Jenny Bercival had disappeared without trace at the last festival had irked the team for a year. The last thing they needed was for yet another incident to cast a pall over the event.

The phone on Gerry's desk began to ring so he hurried back into his office. After a short conversation he returned to the main office, heading for the desk of a man in his late thirties with dark-brown skin, warm eyes and a fine-featured, intelligent face. The man turned in his seat as Gerry approached.

'Fancy some fresh air, Wes?' Gerry looked at his watch. It was ten thirty and a beautiful day outside.

DI Wesley Peterson stood up, as though he was eager to go. He was taller than Gerry by a couple of inches, and considerably slimmer around the waist. 'Why? What's up?'

'That call I've just had. It's someone we need to see.'

'Who?'

'I'll tell you on the way.'

As Wesley followed the DCI out of the police station the church bells started ringing. But they had competition in the form of distorted pop music blasting out from the fair-

4

ground rides in the central car park. The heady aroma of hot dogs had begun to scent the air. Gerry pulled a face and muttered something about feeling hungry. Wesley, who had grave misgivings about the hygiene standards of the hot-dog stalls dotted around the town for the duration, couldn't share his boss's weakness.

The crowds were gathering, meandering along the streets, many in improvised costumes. Some had made a real effort but most had just donned an approximation of medieval garb and hoped for the best.

'So are you going to tell me where we're going?' Wesley asked.

'George Street. To see Jenny Bercival's mother.'

Wesley had been on a course in Exeter when Jenny disappeared but he remembered the case all right. And he remembered the newspaper headlines. *Where is Jenny? Puzzle of missing London girl. Have you seen Jenny?* The missing persons inquiry had dominated the papers for a week or so until the press, both local and national, became weary and moved on to something fresh.

'I thought the mother owned a holiday place in Millicombe.'

'Maybe she's sold it.'

Gerry said no more as they passed the boat float and headed down the High Street where tall half-timbered buildings shaded the pavements. George Street was steep and narrow and led upwards from the little square dominated by St Margaret's Church. Here the upper storeys of the pale stucco cottages jutted out over the thoroughfare. Anyone foolhardy enough to take a car up there would have a difficult time.

They reached number thirty-two, a pretty white cottage,

smaller than its neighbours with the slightly soulless look of a holiday let. There was no bell so Gerry used the large cast-iron knocker.

The woman who answered was unhealthily thin with a helmet of immaculate blonde hair and a face that, despite a thick layer of make-up, couldn't conceal the fine lines caused by age or maybe by a year of grief and anxiety.

Gerry stepped forward, his face suddenly sympathetic: the caring side of the police force.

'Mrs Bercival. Can we come in, love?'

The woman closed the door behind them, plucking nervously at the silk scarf she was wearing, then stood with her back to the door, looking from one man to the other.

'This is DI Wesley Peterson, by the way,' Gerry began.

Mrs Bercival gave Wesley an absent-minded nod but said nothing.

'You said you wanted to speak to me?'

For a while she stood in silence. Then the words came out in a rush. 'Jenny's still alive.'

Gerry stared at her for a few seconds, stunned. 'What makes you think that, love?'

'Last week I received a letter saying she's here in Tradmouth. I've come here to find her. I thought I'd better let you know.'

Wesley saw a film of tears forming in her eyes, as though she found it painful to believe that her daughter was alive and hadn't made the effort to contact her.

'What did the letter say exactly?' Wesley asked, careful to keep his voice soft and unthreatening. The last thing this woman needed was to feel she was being interrogated.

She took something from the handbag that stood on the coffee table – an envelope with a typewritten address. Her

6

hand was shaking as she passed it to Gerry who took it and studied it as if memorising every word.

Before extracting a sheet of paper from the envelope Gerry donned the crime scene gloves that he kept in his pocket. He read it and then held it up for Wesley to see.

The single sheet had five words written on it in bold letters. JENNY'S STILL ALIVE IN TRADMOUTH. There was no other information and no signature.

Gerry turned to Mrs Bercival. 'I'm sorry, love. I don't really think this helps us much.'

He glanced at Wesley, who gave her a sympathetic smile. 'You were here with Jenny last year when she went missing?'

She nodded. 'I thought at the time that perhaps her father walking out on me had unsettled her. She's in her twenties but they still feel things like that very deeply, don't they? And Jenny was fragile. She needed certainty.' She shook her head and sniffed. 'If she is still alive I need to find her.'

'Extensive inquiries were made at the time,' said Gerry. 'But there was very little evidence so we drew a blank. Can you remember anything that might help us? Anything she might have said or anyone she might have mentioned?'

Mrs Bercival sat up, her back ramrod straight. Even her daughter's disappearance hadn't robbed her of some degree of self-assurance. 'Over the past year I've been over and over every detail, trying to remember anything that might help make sense of what happened.' She paused. 'Jenny did say something shortly before she ... disappeared. I wasn't taking much notice but—'

'What was it?'

'She said she'd met someone from the past and that she

7

was going back in time. I presume she meant someone she knew from school or university.'

'Possibly,' said Wesley.

'And then there was the tattoo. That was completely out of character, not the sort of thing I thought she'd do at all. But she was an adult so I felt I couldn't say too much.' She frowned. 'Did I mention that at the time? I don't remember.'

'Yes, you did tell us, love.' Wesley saw Gerry lean forward. 'Wasn't it a ship tattooed on her shoulder?'

'That's right. An old-fashioned ship. Medieval. Like that one on the waterfront.' She looked at Gerry with hope in her glistening eyes. 'I couldn't really understand it because she'd never shown any interest in that sort of thing. I asked her what it was but she wouldn't tell me. Do you think it's important?'

'It might be,' said Gerry.

Wesley knew she was clutching at any possibility, any clue as to why her daughter had vanished on that late May evening a year before. When he'd returned from his course he recalled Gerry saying that the girl was probably dead, fallen in the river after having a few too many drinks during the Palkin Festival and swept out to sea by the River Trad's lethal currents. The anonymous letter had raised the mother's hopes. And he wasn't entirely sure whether that was a good thing.

Mrs Bercival continued: 'When she disappeared I searched for her phone but she must have had it with her.'

'The phone never turned up,' said Gerry gently.

'But that's good, isn't it. It means she still has it.'

'It's been switched off. Impossible to trace. I'm sorry.'

Mrs Bercival didn't seem to have heard. 'She knew

several people in Millicombe but no one in Tradmouth, as far as I'm aware. But that doesn't mean she hadn't met someone here, someone she went off with. Oh, I wish to God she'd confided in me.'

Gerry looked down at the envelope in his hand. 'I see you still live in London?'

'My former husband allowed me to keep the house in Hampstead but the holiday home in Millicombe had to go. That's why I've had to rent this place,' she added with a hint of bitterness. 'I need to find my daughter.' She looked Gerry in the eye. 'I know you failed last time but now we have this letter ... Will you help?'

Gerry bit his lip and Wesley knew he was torn between uttering comforting words and spelling out the truth. 'We'll do our very best, love, but I can't promise ...'

'She's still out there somewhere, Mr Heffernan. I know she is.'

The small inflatable dinghy bobbed in the shadow of the cliffs. At first it had floated near the river-mouth for a while, weighed down by its grim cargo. But now, with the tide turning, the currents had started to transport it out into the open sea.

The young woman had been laid out with some reverence in the bottom of the flimsy craft, her hair in a halo of auburn curls around her head and her wide, unseeing blue eyes gazing upwards at the cloud-specked sky and the circling gulls. In a short time the birds might gather the courage to peck at those eyes but for the moment they wheeled around the boat, keening their mourning song.

Her blue velvet gown was neatly arranged and her hands were folded across her breast. If her face hadn't been contorted in agony and her tongue hadn't protruded from her cyanosed lips, she might have come from a Tennyson poem – the tragic lady floating away to some distant Camelot. But this death had nothing to do with poetry; it had been savage, the cruel curtailment of a young life.

The dinghy floated smoothly past the cliffs, out into the cold, frightening world.

Chapter 2

Many say that John Palkin was Tradmouth's greatest son. Three times mayor and buried before the altar of St Margaret's Church in the heart of the town, he presided over one of the most prosperous periods in Tradmouth's history, revered in life and honoured in death.

However, I have found no evidence that John Palkin was a good man. In fact it was said of him during his lifetime that he sold his soul to Satan for riches and a fair wind to carry his ships back to port.

His symbol, later to feature on his coat of arms, was a cog, the ship that was the seaborne workhorse of the medieval period, used in the port of Tradmouth to carry cargos to France and return with fine wines from Bordeaux. Cogs had a large square sail and a rudder attached to the stern post. They were also built up at bow and stern into 'castles' where sailors could take shelter to shoot arrows during the sea fights that were so frequent at that turbulent time. Palkin was the owner of a number of such vessels and they brought him the wealth that enabled him to control the town in the late fourteenth and early fifteenth centuries.

John Palkin married the daughter of another prosperous merchant in 1375. Her name was Joan Henny and they had a son, Richard. Joan died in childbirth as was common in those days, and the fact that John failed to marry again until many years later at a time when custom dictated that, after a respectful wait of a year, a wealthy man would be bound to seek another wife, may indicate that he held her in some affection. Richard himself was to die tragically at the age of eighteen leaving John's brother, Henry, as sole heir to the Palkin business interests.

Throughout his life Palkin had a reputation for an almost supernatural amount of good fortune in business. While his rivals lost ships to French privateers and the merciless storms that blow up around the Devon coastline, John Palkin's cargos always arrived safely in port and his wealth grew.

Perhaps it was because of this that he was habitually surrounded by dark tales. But, in the opinion of one who can claim descent from the great man, I consider that verdict does him an injustice. John Palkin was a genius.

From 'The Sea Devil – the Story of John Palkin' by Josiah Palkin-Wright. Published 1896

The coastguard received the call from a yachtsman who'd spotted the body of a woman floating in a dinghy near the mouth of the River Trad. By the time the Bloxham lifeboat was scrambled, along with a rescue helicopter, the tide had caught the tiny craft and was carrying it out into the English Channel.

When the youngest member of the lifeboat crew was

attaching a towing line to the little boat, he caught sight of the dead woman's twisted features. He stared for a moment at the pecked-out eyes, the bloody holes in a face that had once been beautiful, before leaning over the side to vomit into the calm grey water.

As Wesley and Gerry walked back from George Street to the police station the crowds were pouring into Tradmouth, dropped off by the park-and-ride buses that were working overtime for the festival, shuttling to and fro between the town and the car park. When Wesley had first moved down to Tradmouth from London, the festival had been a half-hearted affair. But over the past three years or so more people had made the effort to dress up in costume, especially the teenagers – just the group he would have expected to avoid anything that smacked of the uncool. And it wasn't just the locals and the organisers who seized any opportunity to do so; people whose accents and behaviour marked them out as tourists, outsiders, joined in with equal enthusiasm.

Some of the young people were wearing badges – a black medieval-style ship on a white background – and Wesley wondered fleetingly if they belonged to some sort of society. But he had other more pressing things on his mind, like the meeting with Mrs Bercival. He asked Gerry what he made of it.

Before the DCI answered he sidestepped around an overweight couple and their two corpulent children who were licking large ice creams with studied concentration. 'I find it hard to believe that Jenny Bercival would have disappeared of her own accord without telling anybody,' he said once he was back on the pavement.

'Her mother said she was in a fragile state.'

'But even if she was upset by the break-up of her parents' marriage, surely she'd have let her mum know she was safe. According to Mrs Bercival Jenny had always been a considerate girl.'

'Parents usually think the best of their kids. Maybe Jenny Bercival wasn't the paragon of thoughtfulness her mum liked to imagine she was.'

Gerry shook his head, as though he couldn't quite bring himself to believe it.

'She'd had a tattoo; her mother thought that was out of character too.'

'Lots of people have tattoos,' said Gerry. 'It's probably irrelevant.'

'Jenny was a student, wasn't she?'

'She'd left London University the year before she disappeared. She'd studied English and she'd been hoping to go into publishing. She'd done an unpaid internship but nothing had come of it so she'd taken a series of temporary jobs in bars and cafés, filling in until something came up. Back then her family still owned a holiday cottage in Millicombe where they spent every summer and she'd come down to join her mother there a couple of weeks before she vanished.'

'Not short of a bob or two if they can afford a second home in Millicombe.'

'Mr Bercival was a banker who traded his wife in for a younger model about six months before Jenny went. He must have had a conscience because the wife got the house in London, even if she wasn't allowed to keep the holiday cottage.'

'Remind me what happened on the night she disappeared?'

'She'd arranged to meet some friends at the Palkin Festival on the Friday evening.'

'What friends?'

'A few rich kids who spent most of their summer holidays at their parents' second homes in Millicombe. Jenny hung around with them but, according to Mrs Bercival, they weren't particularly close. Jenny was crazy about the whole Palkin thing and went to the festival every year. She borrowed her mother's car to come over to Tradmouth and she left it in the park and ride. There was some kind of rock concert at the boat float and once it was over she parted from the friends and made her way back to the bus stop. But she never got there. And the car was still in the car park the day after.'

Wesley frowned, puzzled. 'But the park-and-ride stop is almost next to the boat float and there must have been crowds of people about. Surely someone saw her.'

'That's the thing that doesn't really add up, Wes. A witness saw her walking towards the market square. What she was doing there, I've no idea. That was the last sighting though.'

'Who was the witness?'

'A lad who'd just finished his shift serving behind the bar at the Tradmouth Castle Hotel. We put an appeal out at the time and he answered it because he recognised her. She'd been in the hotel bar earlier that evening with her friends. She was in costume – a green dress. Quite distinctive.'

'He was sure it was her?'

'He seemed pretty sure at the time but who can say.'

'Any chance he might have had something to do with it? Saw her, fancied her, tried his luck and things got out of

15

hand?' Wesley sometimes regretted the fact that his years in the police force had caused him to think the worst of his fellow human beings.

'Immediately after he saw her he met some mates in the Porpoise by the market. Stayed there with them till after midnight and staggered home with a couple of them. His story checked out.'

They had just reached the police station. Wesley glanced up at the hanging baskets decorating the façade that some wit had created out of old-fashioned policemen's helmets. The chief super had considered it a good PR stunt. Showed the force had a sense of humour.

As he made his way up the stairs with Gerry trailing behind him, he tried to visualise Jenny Bercival's journey. To get from the boat float to the market square Jenny would have had to make a detour past the Memorial Gardens and then take the side road past the Butterwalk up to the market. If she was supposed to be heading to the park and ride it didn't make sense, unless she'd arranged to meet someone there.

He stopped on the stairs and waited for Gerry. 'Were the friends from Millicombe eliminated?' he asked.

Gerry halted to catch his breath and it was a few seconds before he spoke. 'Oh yes. They all went off for a drink immediately after the concert. One lad we talked to had known Jenny for years because their families were always down here at the same time, and to give him his due, he did offer to walk her to the park-and-ride stop and wait for the bus with her but she refused.'

'He didn't know if she'd arranged to meet someone else?'

'She didn't mention it. But he did say she'd been acting

strangely, as if she had a secret. I think she was up to something.'

'A man?'

'Possibly. If you ask me, she was good at keeping her cards close to her chest. When she didn't arrive home that night, Mrs Bercival thought she'd probably spent the night with friends – or a boyfriend – so didn't report her missing till the following evening. An appeal was put out and a few witnesses came forward but, apart from the sighting near the market, there was nothing much to go on and no useful CCTV once she'd left the town centre. The market area was searched and we made house-to-house visits to all the properties in the streets round about but we drew a blank, Wes. It was as if she'd vanished into thin air.'

When they reached the CID office they stopped by the door.

'So what do you think happened to her?' Wesley asked.

Gerry sighed. 'Suicide maybe. She'd been fragile since her dad left home so she might have chucked herself in the river or she might have fallen in by accident and her body never turned up. As you know, it happens from time to time. The currents are lethal around here.'

Wesley hesitated. 'Of course she might have been abducted.'

'Or she might have chosen to disappear. Trouble at home and all that. What do you make of the anonymous letter?'

'Could be someone playing mind games. Some sick people get a thrill out of things like that.'

'I don't know how her mother thinks she'll find the truth at this bloody festival. Only thing she's guaranteed to find here is a load of drunks and show-offs who like dressing up and making fools of themselves. And the sailing of course. The regatta attracts the crowds.'

'But I can understand why she's grasping at any glimmer of hope,' said Wesley. 'She'll want to feel she's doing something.'

They entered the office. DS Rachel Tracey was sitting at her desk and as soon as she saw them she stood up, an eager look on her face, as though she'd been waiting for them with important news. She'd lost weight recently and now she was slim, almost to the point of thinness, and her dark trouser suit and recently cut fine blonde hair gave her a businesslike appearance. Wesley had preferred her hair long, although he hadn't commented on her new style. At one time there'd been a frisson of attraction between them. But he was a married man and the diamond solitaire ring on Rachel's wedding finger announced to the world that she was engaged, although her enthusiasm for the wedding arrangements had hardly reached bridezilla proportions. Wesley briefly found himself wondering why he found her apparent lack of interest in her forthcoming nuptials so gratifying.

'I was just about to call you,' Rachel began. 'Bloxham lifeboat's been called out to a dinghy drifting near the mouth of the river. It contained the body of a young woman. Looks suspicious.'

'Where's the body now?' Wesley asked, looking at Gerry.

'The lifeboat's towing the dinghy round the headland to Bloxham. In view of the Palkin Festival they thought it'd be best to avoid Tradmouth.'

Wesley nodded. In normal circumstances, Tradmouth would have been the obvious destination but the lifeboat crew had shown initiative. 'We'd better get over there,' he said.

'Just hope we can get on the car ferry,' Gerry said with uncharacteristic pessimism. 'Good job this bloody festival only happens once a year. Robberies, disappearances, dead women in dinghies. What next?' he added to nobody in particular.

Wesley caught Rachel's eye and she gave him a coy smile. He almost asked her how Nigel, her fiancé, was. However, the discovery of a body made social chit-chat seem somehow inappropriate.

As he drove out of town with Gerry in the passenger seat, the crowds were thronging on to the embankment to watch a rowing race on the river, the participants in an approximation of medieval clothing. A couple of the vessels had painted dragon prows more in keeping with Viking longboats. But the festival spirit allowed a few historical mix-ups.

'Wonder where they get all these costumes from,' Wesley pondered, steering the car away from the thronging river. 'And what are these black-and-white badges people are wearing?'

'No idea,' Gerry replied as they passed another park-and-ride bus crammed with passengers.

'Shouldn't be hard to find out.' Wesley frowned, concentrating on the crowded road. 'Medieval ships. Mrs Bercival said Jenny had a tattoo in the shape of a medieval ship. Might be worth looking into.'

'Might be, Wes. I'll leave it to you. Did you know there was a special service at St Margaret's yesterday evening – I was singing in the choir. A thanksgiving to commemorate the life of John Palkin. I reckon an exorcism would be more appropriate. The old bugger still haunts the place, bringing all sorts of trouble with him.'

'We don't know that this body in the dinghy has anything to do with the festival.'

'If I was a betting man I'd put good money on Palkin being involved somewhere along the line.'

The queue for the car ferry wasn't as bad as feared and they were soon driving past fields and woods down the network of narrow lanes that led to the fishing port of Bloxham. He'd been told that the pathologist, Colin Bowman, had already been summoned, along with the crime-scene team. Once the body had been photographed and carefully removed to the mortuary for the postmortem, the inflatable dinghy would be minutely examined in the hope that it might yield some useful information.

When they arrived in Bloxham they found that the lifeboat had towed the dinghy to a quiet part of the harbour, well away from the fishing boats and the bobbing yachts. Normally tourists would be milling around the waterfront but the Palkin Festival had lured everyone away into Tradmouth, leaving the quayside almost deserted. This wasn't a bad thing because gawping sightseers would have impeded the work of the team gathered around a wooden jetty that had been sealed off with police tape, most of them wearing what Gerry described as snowman suits.

The lifeboat was tied up at the end where four lifeboatmen in bright orange clothing were standing around talking to a trio of uniformed officers who'd been assigned to take their statements, glancing nervously at the crime-scene team a few yards away. They were used to dealing with danger, and occasionally death, but Wesley sensed that what they'd just witnessed was new to them.

Gerry, the experienced sailor who'd served in the merchant navy before joining the police, strode down the jetty ahead of Wesley who trailed behind. The salty tang of sea-weed hung in the air mingled with the smell of fish from that day's catch, and the gulls cried overhead like lost souls as the police photographers went about their work, capturing every detail from every conceivable angle.

Before Gerry and Wesley could get to the focus of all the attention, they were handed their white suits. In his, Gerry's expanding middle gave him the look of a plump goose as he waddled amongst the assembled CSIs. When he reached the edge of the jetty he stopped and stared ahead. The high tide had raised the dinghy almost level with the landing stage and Wesley, standing beside the DCI, felt that if he wanted, he could squat down and touch the dead woman in the boat.

The first thing he noticed about her was her dress. It was blue velvet with a high waist and squared neckline and its voluminous folds had been neatly arranged. She had been laid out with apparent reverence, her hands crossed over her chest. Her long auburn hair was carefully spread out like a halo around her head. She wasn't particularly tall and she fitted perfectly in the dinghy. On her feet she wore fashionable black leather ballet pumps, the kind you could see in any high-street shoe shop, the dead woman's only concession to the present day.

Lying there in the bottom of the boat, she might have conjured a romantic image if it wasn't for her face, gull-pecked and contorted in agony. Her neck too told of violence and bore the angry mark of some kind of ligature.

'Whoever killed her took some trouble to arrange her like that,' Wesley said.

Before Gerry could reply Wesley heard Colin Bowman's voice calling a hearty greeting. The pathologist, tall and thin with a freckled face, receding hair and a genial expression, made his way down the jetty carrying the bag which contained the mysterious tools of his trade. Wesley knew that Gerry was relieved to see him. There'd been a chance that his colleague Dr Jane Partridge might have turned up in his place – and she and Gerry had never really seen eye to eye.

As always with Colin, social pleasantries had to be exchanged before he got down to the serious business of examining the corpse. So, after inquiring about the detectives' respective families and commenting on the popularity of the Palkin Festival, he donned his crime-scene suit and stooped to make his preliminary examination.

He asked whether the photographers and CSIs had finished, and after a while permission was given for the body to be moved on to the quayside so he could carry out his task more thoroughly. Getting the dead woman out of the small, rocking craft proved a challenge but eventually she lay like a sunbather on the wooden planking. At last Colin could work unimpeded and his preliminary verdict came as little surprise. The woman was in her early to mid twenties and his initial conclusion was that she'd died of strangulation. He would be able to tell them more after the postmortem which he would perform first thing the following morning.

The discreet black van was waiting in front of a quayside pub to take the dead woman away and Wesley watched as the stretcher was placed carefully in the back. He bowed his head. They didn't know who she was yet – the CSIs had found no identification on the body – but her costume had been rich and elaborate, chosen with care. And she was somebody's daughter, somebody's lover: surely she would be missed.

*

Rosie Heffernan rarely told anybody what her father did for a living. She'd discovered long ago that being label-led a policeman's daughter created some kind of invisible barrier between you and your fellows. Not that her friends and colleagues had any criminal connections – but there were always the minor transgressions; the smok-ing of the occasional spliff; the purchase of the latest phone at an unfeasibly cheap price in a pub; or some swapped responsibility for a speeding ticket. It was useless protesting that her dad was a DCI dealing with serious crime and was unlikely to concern himself with such rela-tively minor sins. It was easier not to mention his job at all. If anyone asked, she told them he worked for the local council.

The school half-term holiday had just begun and she'd grabbed the chance of the break from her job teaching music at Morbay Comprehensive School – now renamed Morbay Academy, a specialist arts college – to embark on a musical adventure of her own. Medieval music had always interested her and she'd been flattered when she'd been asked to join Palkin's Musik, the ad hoc group formed espe-cially to perform at the festival.

If it had rained, they would have played in the main marquee in the Jubilee Park but as that evening was forecast to be fine they would perform on the floating stage that had been built on the boat float for the festival. Palkin's Musik was headlining that evening, entertaining the revellers with music from the Middle Ages played on replicas of original instruments. Angelus and Virginem, a jaunty pop tune from the age of Chaucer, and swirling Italian dances from the time of Boccaccio. She liked the catchy melodies and bouncing rhythms that set audiences tapping their feet whenever they performed. Sometimes they even danced, swinging around like barn dancers.

Dan Hungerford had assembled the group by using his contacts – a mixture of former music students and those with an interest in early music. Rosie had met Dan when he'd visited her school to give a talk on the benefits of studying music and she'd found his single-minded enthusiasm infectious. This same enthusiasm united the clashing personalities that formed Palkin's Musik.

Rosie herself played the recorder, which made a change from her usual range of instruments but presented her with no particular problem. Then there was Kassia on viol, Ursula on rebec and lute, Harry on shawm and sackbut and Dan himself on percussion and hurdy-gurdy. Kassia also sang. She had a lovely voice, pure and angelic, a voice that Rosie envied, as she did the attention Kassia's beauty brought with it. If pushed, she might have confessed that she didn't much like Kassia, but for the sake of musical harmony she'd kept her mouth shut.

It was time for rehearsal. Like most other people taking part in the Palkin Festival she'd dressed up for the duration. So many people had made the effort with costumes this year that she would have felt a little out of place in her everyday clothes – like a teetotaller at a boozy party. She wore a high-waisted brown gown – plain, not like Kassia's princess outfit. During performances she donned a conical headdress, a hennin to give it its proper name, with a gauzy veil billowing from the back, like a puff of smoke from a chimney. It was a clichéd accessory, like something from a pantomime. Dan had said it looked right, though, so she didn't argue.

Before the rehearsal Harry had picked her up from her

flat in Morbay. He drove a battered and unreliable Skoda but, as she had no transport of her own, she had little choice but to trust herself to the vagaries of the ageing vehicle. Fortunately they had reached the rehearsal venue just in time: St Leonard's Church Hall on the edge of Tradmouth, available to them between the morning's toddler group and the evening's pensioners' whist drive.

When Rosie had first arrived she'd feared they were slightly late – then she'd realised that Kassia wasn't there and felt a frisson of satisfaction that she'd put a foot wrong.

Dan Hungerford was looking at his watch anxiously, asking everyone whether they'd heard from Kassia. Someone said the traffic was bad and she might have been delayed. But when half an hour later Kassia still hadn't shown up, people began to worry.

Neil Watson was used to taking part in digs that were accessible to the general public, digs where he had to field the same questions over and over again. So when he'd received the phone call out of the blue inviting him to excavate the site of John Palkin's house, he hadn't much liked the idea of being on display during the Palkin Festival. Too many tourists. Too many idiots in fancy dress. Too many potential drunks and ignoramuses around who might interfere with his precious excavation.

However, it turned out that he'd misunderstood. This particular dig was strictly private. The owner of the site, Chris Butcher, had made his fortune from the internet – Neil was vague as to the details – and had bought a bungalow on the edge of the river as a second, or maybe even a third, home: a pied-à-terre in one of the most eye-wateringly expensive spots in the West Country.

The bungalow itself stood in a large and neglected garden that led down to the water's edge, hidden behind a tall stone wall. The place had been built in the late 1940s and was in sore need of renovation.

As soon as the builders began digging the foundations for the proposed extension, they'd uncovered the remnants of some stone walls and Butcher, having a keen interest in such things, had started to research the history of the site. He'd been unable to contain his delight when he'd discovered that John Palkin's house and warehouse had stood on that very spot so he'd halted the building work for the time being and called in the County Archaeological Unit to conduct an excavation. He was funding the whole thing himself and Neil couldn't quite believe his good fortune. Many wealthy men he'd come across in the course of his career would have instructed his builders to destroy the medieval walls and carry on so he'd found himself liking Chris Butcher before he'd even met him. Especially now that recent budget cuts had placed the Unit's future in jeopardy.

Neil pushed his fair hair behind his ears. Most of his contemporaries had tidied up their appearance years ago, but Neil still regarded his worn combat jacket and stained cargo pants as a badge of office. Maybe in a couple of years he'd adopt an Indiana Jones hat, just to complete the look, he thought as he trowelled the soil away from the remnants of a wall.

He could hear music in the distance, drifting over from the fairground on Tradmouth's main car park. He'd experienced the Palkin Festival in previous years and knew it was an event to avoid if possible; full of kids in fancy costumes using Tradmouth's most famous son as an excuse for overindulgence.

'I think I've found a cobbled floor surface – could be medieval.'

Neil looked round and saw his colleague, Dave, squatting on his haunches a couple of yards away, a frown on his face and the trowel in his right hand poised in midair. Dave was a large man with a prominent beer gut. Like Neil, he wore his hair long, only Dave's was thinning on top which gave him the look of a dissipated monk.

Neil straightened himself up and walked over to have a look at Dave's discovery. 'All the documentary evidence points to this part of the site being Palkin's warehouse so a cobbled floor would make sense. The house would have been nearer the road – probably where the present bungalow stands.'

Dave scraped away more soil. 'Looks as if it would have been a good dry floor in its day,' he said. 'But if he was a merchant bringing in wine from France, he'd have wanted a decent warehouse to store it in. It must have been tacked on to the back of the house.'

'People lived over the shop in those days.'

Dave nodded, adjusted his kneeling mat and returned to work. The other diggers, a couple of PhD students and a trio of undergraduates glad of the experience, were working away nearer the bungalow. The late May weather was being kind to them and so far things were going well.

Neil spoke again. 'I saw Chris Butcher going out before, all dressed up in his medieval finery. They really go for this Palkin thing round here, don't they.'

'Any excuse for a party,' Dave said dismissively. 'Have you seen that ship moored on the embankment? It's a replica of Palkin's flagship the *Maudelayne* apparently.'

'I know. There were bloody great queues to go on board earlier or I might have treated myself.'

Neil stopped digging and felt a twinge of pain in his back. Perhaps, he thought, it was nature's way of telling him to be a little less hands-on. Some retired archaeologist had once said that when middle age begins to creep up, you should retreat to a nice warm office to carry out desk-based assessments, write reports, process finds and dispense your expertise to your devoted followers. Trouble was, Neil lived for the thrill of the dig and devoted followers were thin on the ground. Still, there was always the option of paying a visit to an osteopath.

'Wasn't Palkin supposed to be some sort of pirate?' asked Dave.

Neil looked out over the river, teeming with yachts and pleasure craft. Sailing as a leisure pursuit would have been unthinkable back in Palkin's day. Handling a ship with its rigging and sails, pitting yourself against winds and storms, wasn't something to be taken lightly.

'That's one way of looking at it,' Neil replied. 'He made his fortune from trade then he was licensed by the King as a privateer, attacking the vessels of enemy countries and getting a share of the proceeds.' He paused. 'And he was supposed to have sold his soul to the Devil in return for great riches.'

Dave smirked with disbelief, shrugged his broad shoulders and focused on uncovering the cobbled floor. These were tales to scare the gullible.

Chapter 3

John Palkin was the son of Ralph Palkin, himself a well-to-do Tradmouth merchant who first appears in the town records in 1338. Ralph Palkin and his wife, Alice, were granted a piece of land on the shore between Baynard's Quay and Battlefleet Creek where he built a quay for use by his trading ships, a house referred to in contemporary documents as Palkin's Hall. There was also a warehouse on the site where he could unload and store his lucrative cargos.

Ralph Palkin's cogs sailed up the River Trad to Neston where they would load up with woollen cloth before sailing across the Channel to sell the cloth in France and return with a rich cargo of wine from Bordeaux. It was a lucrative trade and when Ralph died in 1358, John inherited the house and ships and the enterprise flourished.

However, John's younger brother, Henry, resented his brother's success. He too worked in the family business, in charge of the ropeworks, a vital but workaday part of the enterprise. How

Henry's bitterness towards his older brother must have grown and festered as John prospered.

From 'The Sea Devil – the Story of John Palkin' by Josiah Palkin-Wright. Published 1896

An incident room had been set up at Tradmouth police station and Wesley had sent a team of officers out to make inquiries amongst the festival crowds. Others trawled through missing persons reports and attempted to trace the origin of the dinghy that had served as the dead woman's floating coffin.

It took less than an hour to confirm that no one answering her description had been reported missing. And so far nobody with a boat moored in Tradmouth had admitted to missing a dinghy, a common type stowed aboard many of the vessels in the harbour.

The yachtsman who'd reported the body had been interviewed but he'd come upon it by chance and could tell them nothing more. By seven thirty Wesley was becoming impatient for some snippet of useful information to come in. A dead woman in full medieval costume cast adrift in a flimsy boat. If the yachtsman hadn't seen her when he did, the dinghy would most likely have carried her out to sea where it would have capsized, taking her down into the depths with it. He was as sure as he could be that this had been her murderer's intention; only she had been spotted before this convenient disposal could take place.

There was nothing much they could do until the team's inquiries began to bear fruit so Wesley seized the opportunity to acquaint himself with the Jenny Bercival case. Ever since the dead woman had been discovered so soon after their visit to Jenny's mother, the two cases had become entwined in his consciousness and he couldn't banish the thought that the dead woman might be Jenny. After all, the physical description was similar.

He spent ten minutes comparing the latest crime-scene pictures with photographs of Jenny: a smiling graduation picture provided by her mother and a more casually posed holiday snap. When he'd finished he walked into Gerry's office. The DCI looked up from the reports he was reading and his eyes lit up, as if he was grateful for the company.

'Do you think our dead woman's Jenny Bercival?' Wesley asked as he sat down.

Gerry frowned. 'To tell you the truth, Wes, it's the first thing that occurred to me. I've sent Rachel to tell Mrs Bercival that a body's been found. I didn't want her to hear about it on the news.'

'So you do think it's her?'

Gerry looked uncertain. 'There is a resemblance but ... '

'Is it worth getting Mrs Bercival to identify her? Or maybe a DNA test would be better. Then we'll know for sure without the poor woman having to go through the ordeal of viewing the body.'

'Good idea, Wes.'

'I'll arrange it tomorrow.'

'What's come in so far?' Gerry asked.

'Nothing much but it's early days. It'll be on the TV news tonight so someone might come forward with information.'

'Either that or tomorrow we'll have every nutcase and timewaster in the West Country queuing up at the door.' Gerry gave a loud yawn. 'Why don't you get off home, Wes, and we'll make an early start in the morning?' He glanced at his watch. 'I've got to leave at nine anyway 'cause it's Rosie's performance tonight.' He gave a coy smile. 'She said she didn't want me there but … Well, you've got to show your support, haven't you.'

'What is it she's doing?'

'She's in an early music group. Palkin's Musik they call themselves. Musik spelled with a "k". It's medieval music played on original instruments. Sackbuts and hurdy-gurdies, that sort of thing.'

Wesley could tell that the boss was brimming with pride in his talented daughter. 'Enjoy yourself,' he said, edging towards the door. He'd already rung his wife, Pam, to say he'd be late and she'd sounded resigned rather than annoyed; then again she'd had long and bitter experience of his working hours during a murder investigation. There were times when he was afraid her patience would run out, though that was something he tried not to think about.

He often walked back home up Albany Street so retracing Jenny Bercival's last journey wouldn't take him out of his way. As he left the police station he wove through throngs of festival-goers, all dressed as if it was the year 1400. Wives, maidens, jesters, merchants, knights, peasants and kings and a fair few portly bearded Palkin lookalikes. The whole of medieval life was there in Tradmouth and on every street corner buskers played the greatest hits from the Middle Ages on strange and ancient instruments.

The crowd appeared to be making for the waterfront where there was entertainment and an ale marquee and Wesley noticed large groups of teenagers with black-and-white ship badges pinned on to their elaborate costumes. He had assumed that the most enthusiastic participants in the Palkin Festival would be the type who were into real ale and morris dancing and this lot didn't fit his mental stereotype at all.

Once he'd reached the market and pushed past the drinkers spilling out of the Porpoise, he made for the flight of old stone steps that led up to Albany Street, the old packhorse route into Tradmouth with its wide, shallow steps leading up to St Leonard's Church at the top of the town. Jenny Bercival had last been spotted near here by the off-duty barman. But where had she gone? She might have cut down the back street leading back to the waterfront or she might have retraced her steps into the town centre. Without witnesses there was no way of knowing. And if it was Jenny in that dinghy, where had she been in the intervening year?

As he walked up Albany Street he found himself looking at each small, pastel-painted house. Had Jenny visited one of them? Many were let out as holiday homes so the population was transient and when house-to-house inquiries had been made nobody had admitted to seeing her. But why had nobody except the barman spotted her that night a year ago when the festival had been in full swing? Where could she have gone?

Pondering the possibilities made the journey home pass quickly and before he knew it he'd arrived at his modern house at the top of the town. It was almost dark and Pam had switched the front-room lights on but hadn't yet drawn the curtains. The scene inside looked warm and inviting. And he was hungry.

Pam greeted him with a quick absent-minded kiss. She was wearing a short cotton skirt and a pink vest top, dressed for good weather although as sunshine had been scarce so far that year her bare limbs were pale.

She pushed back her shoulder-length brown hair and

took his arm. 'I heard about the body in the boat on the news so I wasn't expecting you back so soon,' she said as she led him into the kitchen. 'They said it was suspicious. How did she . . . ?'

'Colin's doing the PM first thing tomorrow but all the signs are that she was strangled.' He took her hand and squeezed it. 'There wasn't much we could do tonight until more information comes in but it'll be a long day tomorrow.'

She didn't try to hide her disappointment. 'This would have to happen when I'm off work for half term. You couldn't have arranged it better.'

He gave her an inquisitive look, unsure whether this was a joke or a rebuke. 'Where are the kids?'

'Michael's staying the night at Nathaniel's and Amelia's round at your sister's cooing over her new cousin. She wanted to stay the night and Maritia said it was fine by her. Mark'll bring her home in the morning.'

Wesley sat down at the table. All was well and he felt a warm glow inside. His sister, Maritia – a GP and the wife of a local vicar – had recently given birth to a baby boy called Dominic who, during his short life, had managed to charm all around him, including Wesley's nine-year-old daughter, Amelia. Spending the night in such close proximity to the object of her devotion would be a major treat for her. Wesley's son, Michael, seemed to have got over the rocky patch he'd gone through last term when he'd been the victim of bullying and had had a slight brush with the law. Pam approved of Michael's friendship with Nathaniel and she was delighted that the two boys would be going to the same school next term. The jagged rocks of negative peer pressure had been narrowly avoided this time. As a teacher she'd seen many a child come to grief on those rocks in the past.

'Just the two of us then,' he said.

'You hungry? I've made a chilli.'

He caught her hand and stood up. 'I can eat later.'

She grasped his meaning at once and began to lead him out into the hall. With the children out of the house it was almost like old times, and as it was the school holidays Pam was a different woman to the stressed-out, snappy creature of termtime when juggling child care, teaching, and paper-work took its toll. During the holidays their marriage seemed solid but in termtime Wesley sometimes felt things were more fragile. Pity retirement was years away.

They reached the foot of the stairs and kissed, first ten-tatively, then with more passion.

The doorbell rang. Pam swore under her breath.

'Don't answer it,' Wesley said.

'We can be seen through the glass in the door. Besides, it might be important.'

She wriggled out of Wesley's arms, kissing him lightly on the lips. The moment was lost. When she opened the front door he saw Neil standing there on the doorstep, grinning.

'Hope I'm not disturbing anything.' There was a sugges-tion in Neil's voice that told Wesley he'd picked up on the situation. However, he'd known Neil since they'd studied archaeology together at Exeter University, long enough to dispel any embarrassment.

'I wasn't expecting to see you. I've only just got back myself,' he said as Pam stood aside to let Neil in. 'Have you eaten?'

'Yeah. But I wouldn't say no to a drink. I was in town earlier. Word has it some woman's been murdered.'

'Her body was found in a dinghy floating out to sea. We're treating it as suspicious.' Wesley felt like changing the subject. When he turned and made for the kitchen Neil and Pam followed.

Wesley fetched his food and a bottle of Rioja. He needed it. Pam had already eaten but she sat at the table, taking charge of the wine glasses.

'What are you doing in Tradmouth?' Wesley said before he took his first mouthful. 'I thought you'd be in Exeter.'

Neil leaned forward, as if about to share a confidence. 'We've started working on the site of John Palkin's house and warehouse. Down by the waterfront beyond Baynard's Quay. There's a bungalow there now and it's just been bought by Chris Butcher, the internet millionaire. He's going to renovate it and he's letting us stay there while the dig's on. It's hardly the lap of luxury but it's better than a lot of places I've stayed in, believe me. We're getting as much digging done as we can before his patience wears thin and he tells the builders to get started.'

'What's Chris Butcher like?' Pam asked.

Wesley excavated a forkful of chilli con carne from his plate and listened to Neil's reply with interest. He'd heard a lot about Butcher too and he was curious.

'He's in his fifties but he looks a lot younger. Very charming. Charismatic, I guess you could call it. Mind you, money helps. He must have made a bloody fortune from his websites. He had a go at digging yesterday. Not that he stuck it out for long. Got bored when nothing turned up in his trench.'

'What have you found so far?' Wesley asked.

'The foundations of a substantial building – probably a grand town house, although we think some of it must be under the bungalow. And we're pretty sure we've found the site of Palkin's warehouse nearer the water. There's a section of cobbled floor that could be medieval.'

Pam took a long sip of wine. 'Is Butcher married?'

'Yes. His wife watches him like a hawk whenever she's there and shoots him dirty looks if he talks to any of the girls.' He smirked. 'I get the feeling she's had trouble with him in the past, if you know what I mean.'

'Where are the Butchers staying until the house is finished?' Wesley asked.

'They've got a house in London but they spend a lot of time down here. Butcher mentioned that his wife has relatives nearby so that's probably why. They're living on board his yacht until the house is finished; not that that's much hardship 'cause it's a bloody great gin palace parked by the Marina Hotel. Butcher's mad on medieval history and he comes down here every year for the festival.'

'Why is Palkin still such a big noise in Tradmouth?' To Wesley, the life of John Palkin was still a mystery. During his years in Tradmouth he'd been aware of the festival – it was hard to avoid it – and he'd heard snatches of his story here and there. But he was vague about the details.

'Apparently he made his fortune from exporting cloth to France and bringing back cargos of wine. He was Mayor of Tradmouth three times and he built fortifications up by the castle to defend the town against the French during the Hundred Years' War. He also attacked and robbed foreign merchant shipping with the backing of the King, so he was probably little better than a pirate gone legit. He's buried in St Margaret's. Posh tomb in the chancel.' He tilted his head to one side. 'I imagine him as a cross between a dodgy businessman and a Mafia boss.'

'No saint then,' remarked Pam, draining her glass.

'Doubt it,' Neil said as he watched Wesley finish his meal. 'I've been researching him in various local history books but I'm trying to get hold of a book by a nineteenth-century historian called Josiah Palkin-Wright which went out of print decades ago.' He paused. 'I did hear one odd local legend, although I haven't found anything to support it.'

'What's that?'

'It's said that he murdered two of his wives and when he died they dug him up and drove a stake through his heart.'

The audience applauded enthusiastically but Rosie Heffernan felt that the performance had been a shambles. Kassia had let them down badly by not appearing.

Rosie had spent the entire day in the closed bubble of rehearsal and performance. She had seen or heard nothing but the music, and the concentration required to take in Dan's changes to the repertoire to accommodate Kassia's absence meant that the group was oblivious to the rumours flying around the town about the discovery of a woman's body on the river. Even if she had heard, she probably wouldn't have associated the discovery with Kassia. Every year the Palkin Festival seemed to bring trouble of some kind in its wake. And the fact that Kassia irritated her meant that she didn't automatically cast her in the role of victim. She was a flaky madam who'd most likely not turned up because she had a better offer.

All the members of Palkin's Musik apart from Dan Hungerford went for a drink after the concert. Tradmouth's pubs were packed but they'd managed to find an unoccupied corner in the Star next to St Margaret's Church – usually a locals' pub but now filled with people in costume in search of refreshment after a long day at the festival. Rosie didn't feel like making the effort to get back to Morbay; besides, she'd had a bit to drink so she was planning to stay the night at her father's house on Baynard's Quay which couldn't be beaten for convenience. She'd left a message on his voice mail earlier to say she'd be there at some point but she hadn't been specific. She just hoped that Joyce, his girlfriend – if that was the right word for a woman of her father's age – wouldn't be there.

She left the Star, pushing her way through the drinkers, cradling her recorder case carefully against inadvertent bumps and shoves. The sudden change of temperature from the fuggy pub to the chilly May night made her shiver. Once outside in the narrow street, she hurried past a small knot of smokers hovering around the door, intent on their shared vice, and made her way down the street past the crooked quaintness of the Angel, also heaving.

A flight of steps ran beside the little half-timbered pub, leading to the street below. Tradmouth was a town of crazy levels, a builder's nightmare, and with the dark passages and hidden stairs there were shadows, unlit places where a lone woman was wise not to venture at night. But Rosie had been raised here and familiarity quashed any fear of the unknown. She picked up the hem of her skirts and tiptoed down the steps with the confidence of one who knew the geography of the town as well as she knew her own flat. It wasn't till she was halfway down the steps, caught between the Angel on one side and the side wall of a souvenir shop to the other, that she heard footsteps behind her ringing on the stone, getting closer. She speeded up but so did the footsteps.

She felt the hand on her shoulder and the adrenalin

coursed through her body as she prepared for flight. Then she turned, breathless.

'I've already told you I don't want this anymore,' she whispered. 'Leave me alone.'

When Wesley left home the next morning Pam told him she was thinking of taking the children down to the festival later. It was Sunday so things might be quieter. Wesley suspected this was optimistic.

He walked into the town with some trepidation. Colin would be performing the postmortem first thing and he and Gerry were obliged to attend. Some people he knew became hardened over the years, but however much he tried, Wesley could never detach himself from the proceedings, never forget that the thing on the slab was a human being who had lived, loved, laughed and cried like he did. Some mother had borne and loved him or her. He or she had been to school, made friends, taken lovers, maybe had children of their own. Each was an individual.

Then there was the press. They'd got wind of the story the previous day, before Gerry and the press officer had had the chance to make a statement. Wesley knew that once word got out that the victim was wearing a medieval gown and had been cast adrift on the river like some tragic heroine from an ancient poem, they'd be besieged by slavering journalists in pursuit of the story of their careers.

There was no sign of Gerry when he arrived at the CID office. Normally when they were due to witness a postmortem he was there at his desk bright and early, raring to go. He asked Rachel if she'd seen the boss. She answered in the negative and returned to her computer to check through all recent missing persons reports, as though she wasn't in the mood for talking. She hadn't come up with any potential names for the dead girl yet, apart from the obvious one of Jenny Bercival.

When Gerry finally arrived he looked distracted. And as he marched straight into his office he didn't greet his underlings with his usual repertoire of Liverpudlian witticisms, Wesley knew something was wrong. He followed Gerry in and sat down in the visitors' chair, noticing that his boss's eyes were bloodshot as though he hadn't slept.

'Something the matter, Gerry?'

Gerry sat down heavily in his swivel chair and put his head in his hands. After a few seconds he looked up. 'I don't know.'

Wesley waited for an explanation. Eventually it came.

'Rosie took part in that concert last night at the boat float. I went to watch her.' He lowered his eyes, suddenly sheepish. 'Stood near the back of the crowd so she wouldn't see me. I mean, I didn't want to put her off, did I. Anyway, she'd rung home around teatime and left a message on my voice mail to say she was planning to stay the night 'cause she was going for a drink with some of her mates after the concert. Only thing is, she didn't turn up. I've tried to call her mobile but there's no answer. I've left messages but . . . '

'She might have decided to go back after all, or to stay with a friend, and she didn't think to let you know.' He couldn't say he knew Rosie Heffernan well but he had the impression that she wasn't the most thoughtful of daughters.

'You're probably right, Wes.' Gerry let out a long sigh and Wesley could sense he was trying hard to conceal a niggling worry, the sort that burrows like a worm in your mind, impossible to get rid of. 'Joyce was going to stay at mine last

41

night but she changed her mind because she didn't want to upset Rosie. You know how things are.'

Wesley knew all right. He also knew the animosity was one-sided. Joyce, a plump middle-aged divorcee who worked at Morbay's register office, had made every effort to be Rosie's friend. But for some reason, perhaps out of loyalty to her dead mother, Rosie had seemed intent on making the woman's life awkward. Her brother Sam got on well with Joyce. Sam, a vet, had inherited his father's easygoing nature. Rosie, on the other hand, was highly strung and temperamental – not a comfortable person to be around. Wesley sometimes wondered what his own children would be like as adults. But he knew that it was hard to predict these things.

'I'm sure she's fine,' Wesley said with as much reassurance as he could muster. He looked at his watch. 'Time for the postmortem. Colin said nine thirty.'

Gerry stood up. Wesley could see the signs of strain on his face; the deepening of the lines around his mouth and the shadows beneath his eyes. However old your kids are, you still worry. Think the worst.

They walked to the hospital along the esplanade. The cog was still in port, tied up by the quayside. Her timbers and rigging looked quite new, just as the originals would have looked way back in the Middle Ages. A gangway had been placed between ship and shore and a small queue was forming; couples with children as well as people in costume. Gerry stopped to look at it and Wesley almost cannoned into him.

'Fine replica,' said the experienced sailor. 'She was built in Bristol, so I've heard.'

Wesley said nothing. Maritime matters were more

Gerry's territory than his and besides, if they didn't hurry, they'd be late for the postmortem. But he guessed Gerry was right. Whoever had built the *Maudelayne* had taken great pains to ensure the vessel's accuracy. The one thing that surprised him was the noise, the loud creak of the timbers as the ship rocked gently on the water. For a moment he visualised the medieval harbour when the quayside would have been packed with wooden ships, scuttling to and fro from France and returning to unload the rich cargos that had made Tradmouth wealthy at that time. The sound of creaking wood must have been deafening. All that trade had brought prosperity with it, however, so Wesley doubted if anybody would have complained about the noise.

Gerry walked on and Wesley saw him take out his mobile and check it for messages. Rosie still hadn't been in touch. Wesley, tempted to tell him that there was probably nothing to worry about, knew the words would sound trite and unconvincing so he said nothing.

They arrived at the mortuary and made straight for Colin's office. He was waiting for them, writing up notes. When Gerry greeted him he smiled.

'You managed to navigate your way through the crowds then.'

'It's not as bad out there as it was yesterday,' replied Gerry.

Colin looked straight at Wesley. 'What do you make of our strange customs?' His expression suddenly changed, as though he'd realised the question might have been construed as racist. 'Coming from London, that is,' he said quickly. 'You must think all this business about John Palkin's a bit . . . ' He searched for a suitable word. 'Obsessive.'

Wesley hadn't taken offence. He recognised racism when he encountered it and he knew that was the last thing on Colin's mind. 'It brings a lot of visitors into town,' he said. 'Bit of a nuisance for the locals though.'

'You can say that again,' Gerry muttered.

'I'm just amazed at how the young people enter into the spirit of the thing,' Colin continued. 'Some of them make a real effort with the clothes. I include our corpse in that, by the way. Her dress seems elaborate, to say the least. It must have been expensive. I take it we haven't got a name for her yet?'

'Not yet,' said Wesley.

Colin stood up. He was already wearing a green surgical gown, half-prepared for his gruesome task. They followed him out of the office, down the corridor to the postmortem room. Unlike the new facility at Morbay Hospital a few miles away, there was no glass screen here to shelter behind. Nothing to separate them from the reality of what was going on, from the smells and sounds associated with Colin's painstaking dissection of the body on the table.

The dead girl had been undressed and her blue velvet gown lay on a nearby steel trolley, packed up in a large paper evidence bag. According to reports, Jenny Bercival had been wearing a similar green gown when she'd vanished. If this was Jenny, perhaps she owned two. Wesley examined the packages. One for the gown. One for the shoes. One for the underwear; through a clear window in the bag he could see a black lacy bra and matching pants which looked decidedly twenty-first century.

'There's a label in the gown, by the way,' said Colin as he watched Wesley pick up the package. 'A company called Bygone and Sons, theatrical costumiers.'

'Thanks,' said Wesley. 'I'll get someone on to it.'

Colin turned his attention to the woman on the slab and began to speak into the microphone which dangled above her body. He made his first observations. A well-nourished young woman in her early twenties. As for distinguishing features, there was a tattoo on her left shoulder blade which was about two inches across and appeared to be a depiction of a medieval ship.

Colin nodded to his assistant who slid a gloved hand underneath the shoulder and lifted it for Wesley and Gerry to see. It was a ship all right, almost identical in shape to the cog moored not a hundred yards from the hospital entrance.

Wesley's heart began to beat a little faster. 'Jenny Bercival had a tattoo like that.'

Gerry nodded and Colin gave him an inquisitive look.

'A girl went missing last year at the last Palkin Festival. According to her mother, she had a tattoo exactly like that on her shoulder,' said Gerry.

Colin raised his eyebrows. 'You think this might be her?'

Gerry frowned. 'I spent hours staring at that girl's photo when she vanished last year. I admit the hair's similar and she's the same physical type but ... ' He hesitated. 'I can't be sure.'

'Even if this isn't Jenny Bercival, the tattoo suggests there must be a connection,' said Wesley.

'I've seen a lot of people around during the festival wearing badges with a similar image,' said Colin. 'I did wonder about their significance. Whether it was some club or ... '

'It shouldn't be hard to nab someone and ask them what it means,' said Wesley. 'If we don't manage to do it on the way back to the station, I'll get someone to check it out today.'

If nothing else, it was a starting point. If this wasn't Jenny – and in spite of Gerry's misgivings, he felt pretty sure that it must be – this dead girl might still be connected to her in some way.

'Do we have a time of death, Colin?' asked Gerry.

'Early on Saturday morning. Probably about five to seven hours before she was found.'

Colin began to study the angry line around the dead woman's neck where the ligature had been pulled tight. 'Whoever killed her came up on her from behind. He must have put the ligature over her head and crossed it over at the back like so.' He raised his hands and performed a demonstration using gestures.

'What do you reckon he used?' Gerry asked.

Colin examined the area closely with a magnifying glass. 'Not a rope. Something flat and smooth and just over an inch wide judging by the mark on her neck. There are tiny traces of something that could be leather on the flesh but I'll send them off to the lab for analysis. If I'm right, it could be a belt or some kind of strap.'

Wesley thought for a few moments. 'If this does turn out to be Jenny Bercival, where has she been for a year?'

'And who with,' said Colin. 'Find that out and you're halfway to finding her killer.'

Chapter 4

There is no doubt that John Palkin made enemies throughout his life and perhaps these enemies are responsible for some of the more colourful stories that have been passed down over the centuries.

In the town records of Tradmouth there exists a letter written by Palkin complaining of the machinations of someone called the Shroud Maker, although the accusations are not specific. It has been surmised by historians that this shroud maker was most likely his younger brother, Henry Palkin, a rope maker who equipped Palkin's ships, shrouds being the ropes that support the masts. Tradmouth's lengthy rope walk is still just visible in a wooded terraced area above the town and the manufacture of rope for shrouds and other rigging was a major and essential industry during the port's heyday.

It may be that John Palkin had some dispute with his brother, and yet on the death of Palkin's only son, Richard, Henry became his sole heir.

**From 'The Sea Devil – the Story of John Palkin'
by Josiah Palkin-Wright. Published 1896**

It felt good to be digging there on the bank of the river on a fine day, watching the boats as the small white clouds scuttled across the blue sky. Neil didn't mind working through the weekend. On a day like this he loved his job, although over the past couple of years when he'd been stuck in a muddy trench in driving November rain that love had begun to lose its lustre. But you can't be a fair-weather archaeologist in the British Isles. He'd accepted that long ago.

He adjusted his kneeling mat and started to tease away the earth again. Dave had just opened up a new trench a few yards away in what Neil had calculated to be the interior of the warehouse, the very place where all that Bordeaux wine had been stored all those centuries ago.

The diggers worked silently now, intent on each new discovery, and the only sound Neil could hear, apart from the lapping water and the vociferous seagulls, was the scraping of metal trowels on the newly uncovered stones.

'How's it going?'

Neil looked up. Chris Butcher was standing at the back door of the house. He had abandoned his medieval costume today and was wearing shorts and a polo shirt. His greying hair was tousled by the breeze blowing in off the water and the tan on his face and limbs suggested a recent holiday somewhere with plentiful sunshine. The look was one of effortless prosperity, as though he'd been sprayed with some invisible golden lacquer.

Neil stood. 'We think we've found the floor of Palkin's warehouse.' He pointed at the spot where a female student was digging. 'In a few places you can still see the old cobbles and the position of what's left of the walls indicates that this is an interior space rather than a courtyard.'

'That's fantastic,' Butcher said enthusiastically, like a child with a brand-new and exciting toy. 'How do you know it's the warehouse and not his house? Weren't they next to each other?'

'A very early map of the town actually shows the building. The structure just here jutting out from the main house is labelled as "Palkin's warehouse". Besides, the warehouse would be nearest the river so the goods could be hoisted in from the ships. Not dressing up for the festival today?'

Butcher shook his head. 'I'm going later. Astrid wants to visit a gallery in Tradmouth first. She's seen a picture that she says would be perfect for the house when it's finished.' He nodded towards the run-down bungalow that would soon, no doubt, be transformed into a palace of luxury and good taste, and gave Neil a conspiratorial smile. 'Between you and me, she doesn't share my enthusiasm for all things Palkin.'

'You're really into all this Palkin business, aren't you?' Something about the man's zest for the subject intrigued him.

'Absolutely.' He sounded like an old-fashioned schoolboy discussing the latest comic. He wondered if Butcher, like many people, had a rose-tinted view of the violent and foul-smelling past. But Butcher was paying for the excavation so he smiled back indulgently. Never let cold facts get in the way of someone's harmless passions.

After a brief discussion of the dig's latest finds – several large sherds of medieval pottery and a coin dating to the reign of Edward II – Butcher left Neil to resume his work.

As he returned to his trench he noticed that Dave had stopped work and was staring at a newly uncovered section of bare earth with a frown on his face.

'How's it going?' he called across.

Dave turned to look at Neil. 'It looks as if the soil's been disturbed in this area. But I guess it might have been done when the bungalow was built.'

Neil stood up and squinted at the place where Dave was digging. The ground certainly looked different here, and as it wasn't particularly near the bungalow he found it rather puzzling. He tilted his head to one side and stared at the ground. 'It'd liven things up a bit if we find a body,' he joked.

Dave rolled his eyes and carried on digging.

Neil looked round. Near the boundary with the next property the wall between the garden and the road was lower and from time to time passers-by stopped to watch them at work. The old man with the weather-beaten face and the old Breton cap had been there on and off since the start, watching, staring as if he was waiting for something. But as soon as he saw Neil looking in his direction he vanished like a ghost.

If you're looking for something, you can never find it even if you've seen it hundreds of times before. So it was with the black-and-white ship badges. As Wesley walked back to the police station by Gerry's side, he scanned all the people he passed but none of them was wearing the badge. He'd thought it would be easy but now it turned out that there was nobody to ask.

They returned to the station via the waterfront and as they walked the postmortem was still on Wesley's mind. According to Colin, the victim's stomach contents revealed that she hadn't eaten since the evening before she was found. But she'd been drinking whisky around five to six

hours before death and she'd also had sex, probably con-
sensual as there were no signs of violence. Samples had
been taken and now it was a case of hoping for a DNA
match. Wesley could tell by Gerry's expression that he was
optimistic about identifying the lover who might also be her
murderer. If his DNA wasn't on the database, though,
Wesley knew they might have a struggle.

Rachel had been sent to get a DNA sample from Mrs
Bercival, assuring her that it was just routine. Mrs Bercival
had refused to believe that the dead woman could be Jenny,
but Wesley wondered if she was deceiving herself.
Sometimes the only way to deal with pain is to deny that it
exists.

They turned left to walk through the Memorial Gardens
where craft stalls were crowded into the little square by the
bandstand. People were hovering around them like wasps at
a picnic, examining the colourful goods for sale: paintings,
ceramics, cushions, preserves, jewellery, driftwood sculp-
tures – the usual items on the tourist wish list. The stalls
held no interest for Wesley and Gerry so they strode past;
the police station was in sight now and they needed to get
back.

Apart from complaining that he needed a strong coffee,
Gerry had been uncharacteristically quiet. Wesley guessed
he was preoccupied by Rosie's lack of contact and he felt
for him.

They had just passed the last stall when Wesley heard a
familiar voice calling his name. This was all he needed.

He was torn between the temptation to ignore Pam's
mother, Della, and his ingrained belief that any greeting
demanded a civilised response. He blamed his upbringing
and his parents who had always insisted on good manners,

whatever the situation. Nurture got the better of him and he stopped and turned round.

Della was standing behind one of the stalls, an array of garishly coloured pottery ranged in front of her, most of it hideous. She was waving enthusiastically. Wesley always felt uneasy when Della was enthusiastic.

'I'll go on. Don't be long.' Normally Gerry would have made some witty comment but he sounded serious. Before Wesley had the chance to reply Gerry had gone, weaving his way through the crowd.

He walked over to Della, trying his best to hide his impatience. She was in costume but the overall impression was more tavern wench than medieval lady. She wore a long black skirt and a black bodice tightly laced over a white blouse, low cut to reveal a crinkled cleavage.

'You skiving off? No wonder there's so much crime,' Della said in a voice that was all too audible to anyone passing by.

'I've just been attending the postmortem of a murder victim.' He hoped this answer would shut his mother-in-law up. He'd only been with her a minute and she was beginning to irritate him.

'Not the woman in the boat? "The Lady of Shalott" the papers are calling her. Know who she is yet? If she's a tourist it won't be good for the festival. I mean—'

'Sorry, Della, I've got to get back to the station,' Wesley said.

'Suit yourself. I'm just looking after this stall for a friend. I was thinking of calling round tonight to see my grandchildren. They'll be in, I take it?'

'Why don't you ring Pam and find out?'

He'd been so anxious to get away that he hadn't been

looking at her closely. Only now did he notice it – a small black-and-white badge pinned to the front of her bodice. A black cog sailing on a stark white sea.

'That badge you're wearing . . . '

'What about it?'

'Does it have any significance?'

He could see distrust in her eyes. Why did he want to know? What was he after? She taught at a further education college and prided herself on her right-on credentials, which didn't include getting cosy with a member of the police force. When she'd found out her daughter's black, archaeology-graduate boyfriend had joined the Met, she'd been horrified.

'What's it to you?' she asked.

'I'm just curious. I've seen a lot of people wearing them.'

She touched the badge protectively. 'It's just something my students are into. It's called Shipworld. It's an online blog. Fantasy, that sort of thing.'

'What sort of fantasy?'

She shrugged, as if she couldn't be bothered to explain. But Wesley persisted and repeated the question.

'It's a story set in a medieval port. There's merchants and pirates and invaders. The usual sort of thing.'

Wesley looked at her expectantly, waiting for her to continue. As Della had never been able to resist filling a period of silence with chatter, she obliged.

'There's a character called Palkin. Must be based on the real one; the one the festival's about. He's in charge of Shipworld. He raises an army and sends out the ships. Then there's the Lady Morwenna – she's the beautiful young wife of the old Lord of Shipworld, the one usurped

53

by Palkin, but I don't think she really existed. There's also a dark figure called the Shroud Maker – he's really bad news.' She hesitated. 'If you want to know more I suggest you have a look at the website yourself.' She looked down at the gaudy wares on her stall. 'Look, I haven't got time to stand here chatting even if you have.'

Wesley ignored the rebuke. She was right. Shipworld was something he could discover for himself. But he still had another question to ask. 'So the Palkin Festival is a big event for Shipworld fans?'

'Oh yes. The whole thing's gone viral. A lot of my students are into it. There's talk of someone publishing the blog as a book. Ready-made fan base, you see.'

Wesley glanced at his watch. 'Have any of the fans had tattoos of that ship symbol?'

'Wouldn't surprise me. Some of them are quite obsessive about it.'

'That badge of yours – where did you get it?'

She looked down at the badge as though she was almost surprised to see it there. 'Someone gave it to me.' She looked at him defiantly. 'And before you ask, I can't remember who it was. And I'm not sure I'd tell you even if I could. I wouldn't want to get anyone into trouble.'

Wesley resented Della's assumption that he was a representative of some oppressive state, intent only on persecuting the innocent, but he kept his expression neutral. He was only glad that Pam hadn't inherited her mother's myopic nature.

Della's eyes lit up. 'So why are you asking all these questions? It's about the Lady of Shalott, isn't it? She was wearing one of the badges, wasn't she?'

Wesley didn't answer; confiding the details of the case

54

was several steps too far. He gave his mother-in-law an insincere smile and walked away.

They were awaiting the results of the DNA tests and until they proved otherwise, Wesley knew they had to consider the possibility that the victim was Jenny Bercival. Had she lain low somewhere for a year, only to return to Tradmouth for the Palkin Festival? Or perhaps she'd been in Tradmouth all the time, maybe living under an assumed name. An e-fit picture of the victim in the dinghy had been produced and given to the local and national press and Wesley had to admit that the image didn't look much like Jenny, although science would confirm it one way or the other.

DC Trish Walton was going through all the missing persons reports to see whether the dead woman matched any descriptions. There was also a team out making door-to-door inquiries, hoping someone would recognise her as a neighbour or friend, and the chief super had persuaded Gerry to make a statement on the local TV news that evening which, it was hoped, might persuade someone to come forward. Until they knew the victim's identity for sure and learned about her life and her last movements, Wesley felt they were working in the dark.

He brought up the Shipworld website on his computer and spent ten minutes scrolling through pages of elves, ethereal maidens and dashing knights. Fantasy had never really been his thing. His search was interrupted when Gerry emerged from his office, still with the careworn look of a man with major worries. He'd been trying to contact Rosie since he got back and had had no luck.

'I've managed to contact one of the people in this early

music group Rosie plays in,' he said as he sat down by Wesley's desk.

'And?' Wesley wondered what was coming.

'It's a girl called Ursula Brunning. She hasn't seen or heard from Rosie since the concert last night. But the group are rehearsing at St Leonard's Church Hall at one thirty so I'm going along. Either she'll be there or one of them might know where she's got to.'

Wesley had an uneasy feeling that Gerry was overreacting. From what he knew of Rosie, she was unpredictable and, in Wesley's opinion, this was probably the kind of stunt she'd pull. But perhaps he was judging her too harshly.

Gerry paused for a moment then he spoke again. 'This Ursula told me that another girl in the group's gone missing. Her name's Kassia and she never turned up for yesterday's rehearsal or the concert last night. That's worth checking out, isn't it?' He looked at Wesley eagerly as though willing him to agree.

'Did you get her description?'

Gerry shook his head and Wesley guessed he had been so concerned with Rosie that he'd forgotten.

'We'll ask when we go up to the church hall later.' Wesley's mind was working overtime. The dead girl had been wearing an elaborate costume, the sort a professional performer might wear rather than some improvised outfit like Della's. He looked at Gerry and felt a sudden pang of sympathy. No amount of reassurance, no repetition of the fact that most people who go missing turn up again within a short time, can calm the fears of a parent. He was one himself. He knew.

The two men had lunch in the office, a sandwich brought

to the desk by one of the DCs drafted in from Neston to help out. They worked on, allocating jobs, receiving reports and examining any statements the junior officers thought worth bringing to their attention. A huge whiteboard took up one wall of the office. On it were pictures of the dead woman and the dinghy which had served as her floating hearse. Gerry had scrawled lists of things to action: missing persons reports; house-to-house inquiries; interviews with local and visiting yachtsmen and anybody else who used the river. Someone must have seen something.

One of the detective constables had been given the task of contacting the theatrical costumiers who'd made the victim's gown but it was Sunday so there had been no answer. Wesley told her to try again tomorrow.

Gerry didn't fancy walking up the steep hill which led to St Leonard's Church Hall so they drove there in one of the pool cars. Gerry said nothing during the short journey. Rosie hadn't even been gone for twenty-four hours; officially, it was far too early to start worrying. But since there was a killer about, a killer who had already strangled a young woman and set her dead body adrift on the river, Wesley understood his concern. In spite of outward appearances, he knew Gerry was as vulnerable as the next man. Perhaps more so at times like this because, since his late wife Kathy's death, he already knew what it was to lose someone he loved.

They arrived at the church hall just before the rehearsal was due to start. It was quiet up there at the top of the town, away from the throngs of people and the boats jostling on the crowded water. When they emerged from the car all they could hear was birdsong and faint traffic noise from the main road nearby.

The double doors of the church hall were unlocked and Gerry went ahead and pushed them open impatiently. Wesley knew he was hoping Rosie would be there, perhaps a little annoyed that her father was making a fuss. But when they stepped inside there was no sign of her, only a pile of instrument cases lying on a long table and three people – two men and a small young woman with unruly dark curls – sitting at the far corner of the room by an open refreshment hatch. They looked as though they were waiting for something. Or someone.

The doors swung closed behind the two policemen and the people in the corner looked round.

'Can I help you?' The man who spoke was in his forties, older than the others, tall and athletic with thick steel-grey hair; he wore a striped shirt and chinos and an air of effortless authority. His dark eyebrows were raised inquiringly. It was obvious he thought these intruders would apologise and leave, but they were about to disappoint him.

Wesley walked into the room, holding out his warrant card. 'We're looking for an Ursula Brunning.'

The dark-haired girl stepped forward, giving the older man a nervous glance. 'That's me. Have you come about Kassia?'

Before Wesley could answer the question, Gerry posed one of his own. 'Has anyone heard from Rosie Heffernan?'

Wesley could see his professional shell was cracking. He was looking at the group anxiously, willing them to come up with the answer he wanted.

'Not since last night.' The older man looked at his watch. 'She should have been here by now.'

Gerry hesitated. Then he drew himself up to his full height. 'I'm her dad. She was supposed to be staying at mine last night but she never turned up.'

The man's lips curved upwards slightly. 'She probably had a better offer. She is a grown woman.'

Wesley saw Gerry's body tense, as if he was fighting the temptation to land a punch. Knowing it was up to him to calm the situation, he touched the boss's back gently. 'I don't know whether you've heard but a young woman was found dead yesterday. We're treating her death as suspicious.'

The group exchanged looks.

'Kassia's been missing since yesterday.' Ursula sounded anxious. 'She never turned up for rehearsal. Or for last night's concert.'

Wesley addressed the man who was obviously in charge. 'What's your name, sir?' He made a great show of taking his notebook from his pocket.

'Dan Hungerford. I'm the musical director,' he answered, more subdued now that things were on an official footing.

Wesley turned to Ursula. 'When did you last see Kassia? What's her full name by the way?'

Ursula looked at him gratefully, as though she was glad someone was taking her seriously. 'It's Kassia Graylem. And we last saw her at the opening concert on Friday night.'

'She's let us down badly,' said Hungerford quietly.

'Has Kassia done anything like this before?'

The group shook their heads, as if in unison.

'Did she mention that she might be going somewhere? Meeting someone?'

It was the young man who answered. He had fair hair that flopped over his forehead and looked like a relic of the 1920s in his cricket jumper and corduroy trousers. 'I'm Harry Treves by the way. To be honest we don't know Kassia that well.' He looked at Hungerford accusingly. 'You took her on, Dan. Wasn't she a student of yours?'

All eyes were now on Dan Hungerford. Wesley usually tried to keep an open mind; he of all people knew the downside of prejudice. Nevertheless there was something about Hungerford he didn't like. An arrogance maybe, or perhaps it had been his sneering response to Gerry's questions about Rosie.

Hungerford cleared his throat before replying. 'I teach music and music history at Morbay University. But I've never actually taught Kassia. In fact I spotted her when she was busking in Neston. She was playing a viol, which is unusual to say the least. I was looking for musicians for Palkin's Musik at the time and I persuaded her to audition. She's never studied music formally but she has a remarkable talent and a good voice.'

'Do you have an address for her?'

'She lives outside Neston,' said Harry. 'In a squat. Not sure of the exact address.'

'How do you contact her?'

It was Hungerford who answered. 'She gave me a mobile number but it's not hers. Belongs to someone else in the squat, she said.'

'A boyfriend?' Gerry asked.

Hungerford shrugged. 'I only rang it once and a woman answered.'

'Have you been trying it?'

'Of course. But there's no answer.'

Wesley looked at Ursula and Harry. 'What about you? Do you know anything about her?'

The question was greeted with blank looks.

'Are you students?' Wesley asked.

Ursula shook her head. 'Not any more. I did study music but now I work in the box office at the Morbay Hippodrome.'

'I teach music,' said Harry. 'Brass and woodwind. Dan got in touch when he was forming Palkin's Musik. I've always been interested in old instruments so . . . '

'Can you tell us anything else about Kassia?'

'Not really,' said Ursula. 'She keeps herself to herself and she's always rather vague about her background. She's a bit of an enigma, if you ask me.'

'You wouldn't have a photograph of her, by any chance?' Wesley said, looking from face to face hopefully.

Dan Hungerford sighed. 'There's a publicity shot of Palkin's Musik in the festival programme. Hang on.'

He delved into the depths of his brown leather briefcase which lay on the table beside the instrument cases and brought out a glossy booklet. Wesley had seen quite a few of them around but he hadn't been inclined to look at any, taking the attitude of many Tradmouth residents that the festival was mainly for the tourist trade.

Hungerford found the page and passed it to him. The group had posed in costume, holding their instruments. Rosie Heffernan was at the front on the left, a large recorder half raised to her lips. Harry stood at the back with Dan Hungerford in the centre. Ursula was on the right and sitting on the ground at Hungerford's feet was a young woman with tumbling auburn curls wearing a familiar blue velvet gown.

Wesley stared at the picture for a while, overwhelmed by a feeling of deep sadness. It was her all right: beautiful and bubbling with life. And now she was lying in a refrigerated drawer in the mortuary.

He passed the programme to Gerry. They had a name for the victim. Next it was a question of finding out who had ended her life.

Wesley was about to ask whether anybody was willing to identify the body when the doors to the church hall opened with a crash.

'Sorry I'm late,' said Rosie Heffernan as she stumbled in carrying a long, black instrument case.

It was then Wesley noticed the bruising around her left eye – and the look of fear on her face.

Chapter 5

When John Palkin married his first wife Joan Henny, the match increased his wealth and allowed him to pay for the construction of four new cogs for his expanding fleet. However, Joan died giving birth to their son, Richard, leaving John a widower of considerable means. Strangely, some eighteen years after Joan's death, shortly before the untimely death of their son, Joan's father, Thomas Henny, wrote a will leaving his entire fortune to his grandson, his only living relative.

Some two months after the will was made, Thomas Henny was murdered. According to the coroner at the time, he was set upon by footpads while riding home from visiting Tradmouth (he lived eight miles away in Neston). The footpads – a pair of runaway servants – were caught and hanged. These were men outside the law, branded as wolf's heads by the authorities for stealing from their master and badly beating a fellow servant who tried to stop them. But they protested their innocence, claiming they'd never set eyes on Thomas Henny, let alone murdered him. At the time Henny had been carrying a

purse of gold coins which was found on his body. Which begs
the question, were the servants innocent? And if they were, who
was responsible for the death of Thomas Henny?

A short time after Palkin's son Richard inherited his grand-
father, Thomas's, fortune, he too died at a tragically young age
leaving his father, John Palkin, an extremely wealthy man.

From 'The Sea Devil – the Story of John Palkin'
by Josiah Palkin-Wright. Published 1896

When Gerry asked Rosie about her injuries, her answers
were evasive. She claimed she'd bumped into something
and that everything was fine, even though it didn't take a
detective to know she was lying.

Wesley had asked Dan Hungerford to identify Kassia's
body. As he was in charge it only seemed right that he took
the responsibility. The man had been reluctant at first but it
was something he couldn't wriggle out of.

Once in the mortuary, Hungerford had seemed
detached, speaking in a monotone and showing no emotion. Wesley suspected that this was the man's way of
dealing with the horror of the situation. But he'd made a
positive ID. The dead woman was Kassia Graylem all right.

They'd made arrangements to interview the group later
down at the police station. Wesley, of course, would be the
one to speak to Rosie and he wondered whether she would
reveal where she'd been the previous night. Somehow he
doubted it.

After arranging for a patrol car to drop Hungerford back
at the church hall, Wesley and Gerry returned to the
incident room where Gerry assembled the team and called
for attention before making the announcement. The dead

woman had been identified as Kassia Graylem, aged twenty-two.

The phone number Hungerford provided had already been tried but there'd been no answer. All they knew about Kassia was that she was a busker who lived in a Neston squat and Wesley asked Trish Walton to find an address for her so that they could interview her fellow squatters and trace her family. He hardly liked to think of her unsuspecting parents receiving a visit from some hapless police officer who'd been told to break the bad news, stumbling for the right words and feeling like the Angel of Death. He'd done the job himself in his time but now he tried to delegate it to others. Sometimes this made him feel like a coward.

Wesley asked Rachel to call on Mrs Bercival to tell her the news. Then he followed Gerry back to his office where he asked the question that had been on his mind since Kassia's body had been discovered.

'Do you think Kassia's death is connected to Jenny Bercival's disappearance?' he asked as Gerry sat down. 'I can't get over how alike the two women are. And the tattoos . . .'

Gerry looked at him. 'You think we might have a serial killer who targets redheads? The press is going to love that. And it'll do the hair dye industry no end of good.' Gerry sounded tired, as though his day of worry about Rosie had taken its toll and he was longing to go home and get some sleep. It was, however, only four o'clock so they still had hours of work stretching in front of them, and the positive identification of the victim had just given the investigation a fresh boost.

'What if Jenny was killed in the same way but her body was never recovered? After all, it was only chance that the dinghy was spotted before it capsized. You know all about tides, Gerry. What do you think? If that was the case would Jenny's body have been washed up on a beach somewhere? Or is there a chance it could have been carried out to sea and lost?'

Gerry considered the question for a moment. 'Bodies have been lost never to resurface so it's quite possible. It would depend on the prevailing tides and currents at the time.' He paused. 'But there's no need to mention that to Mrs Bercival, not till we know anything for certain.' He picked up a sheet of paper from his desk. 'This is the forensic report on that anonymous letter she received. Nothing found.'

Before Wesley could answer, there was a token knock and DC Paul Johnson poked his head round the office door.

'Something you might be interested in, sir,' he began, stepping into the room. Paul was tall and had the lanky frame of a keen athlete.

Wesley looked up at him. 'What's that?'

'There's been a call from a lobster fisherman. He was bringing his catch back into Tradmouth yesterday morning around ten thirty when he noticed a yacht moored up at the mouth of the river beyond the castle, not far from where the lifeboat found that dinghy. Someone on board was leaning over the side as if they were trying to fish something out of the water and he reckoned they ducked down when they saw his boat passing. He thought it was odd at the time and when he heard about the murder on the news he decided he'd better report it, just in case.' In his hand Paul had a sheet of paper which he placed on Gerry's desk.

Wesley turned it round. Below the fisherman's details

was a name. The *Queen Philippa*. 'This the name of the yacht?'

'That's right. I've been in touch with the harbour master and she's moored here in Tradmouth. Belongs to a Dennis Dobbs. London address.'

Gerry looked up. 'Don't tell me he's sailed off to God knows where.'

Paul grinned. 'No. The boat's still moored up not far from the Higher Ferry. Want me to go down and have a word? I could take Trish.'

Wesley caught Gerry's eye. Paul and Trish had once gone out together but had broken up some time ago. However, that didn't stop Paul angling to work with her at every opportunity. If Paul hadn't been such an uncomplicated, straightforward young man, it might have been interpreted as stalking. Not that Trish had ever made any complaint.

Gerry looked at his watch. 'Ta, Paul, but I think I'll have a word with this Dennis Dobbs myself.' He stood up, looking at Wesley. 'It's about time we got some fresh air.'

Wesley followed him out of the office. Some people didn't mind being stuck behind a desk directing operations once they reached the rank of detective chief inspector, but Gerry liked to speak to suspects and witnesses himself, saying it was the only way to get a feel for the truth. At this stage he liked to follow his instincts and only when they had the culprit was Gerry happy to hand them over to be interviewed by specially trained officers who would dot the i's and cross the t's for the Crown Prosecution Service.

It was a fine day and Wesley was glad to be outside, walking down the quayside, shading his eyes from the sun as he peered at the vessels moored on the river. The Palkin

Festival and its attendant regatta had brought visiting boats from all over. He spotted a couple with French flags flapping on the stern and one sporting the Stars and Stripes. But most boasted the usual Red Ensign of British-registered vessels. Gerry himself was a keen sailor who'd restored a thirty-foot yacht called the Rosie May after his daughter who'd been eleven at the time and the apple of his eye. She was moored over the river at Queenswear because the fees were cheaper. Several times he'd invited Wesley to go sailing with him when they'd had a rare free weekend. Wesley had always made an excuse. He suffered from seasickness and knew his limitations.

They found the *Queen Philippa* moored at the end of a long wooden jetty that protruded into the river not far from where the new car ferry plied to and fro across the water. She was larger than her immediate neighbours and when Gerry spotted her he muttered his admiration. The *Queen Philippa* was a nice vessel.

'Must have cost a pretty penny.'

'You jealous?' said Wesley with a smile.

Gerry snorted his disdain and walked off ahead down the jetty, halting by the bobbing yacht with its gleaming white hull, neatly furled sails and spotless deck. He cupped his hands and shouted: 'Anyone aboard?'

Wesley caught up with him and stood beside him as he repeated the question, a little louder each time, disturbing the seagulls which increased their volume in reply. For a while there was no sign of life. Then the cabin door opened and a head popped out.

The man was in his mid twenties with an open face, bare torso and sun-bleached hair which fell in soft waves to his shoulders.

'What can I do for you?' He sounded confident, almost cocky.

'Dennis Dobbs?'

'Who's asking?'

'Police,' said Gerry, flashing his warrant card.

The young man's cockiness suddenly vanished. 'Den's gone into town.'

'And you are?'

'I just crew for him.'

He jumped up on to the deck with almost feline grace. Wesley could see he was endowed with muscles most men would envy and a deep tan that hinted at time spent in sunnier climes. If it weren't for his public-school accent he might have been mistaken for an Australian surfer.

Gerry asked him his name and he hesitated before replying. 'Jason Teague. Look, if Den's in any sort of trouble . . .'

'No trouble,' said Wesley smoothly. 'We're making routine inquiries concerning the murder of a woman whose body was found near the mouth of the river yesterday.'

'I heard about that. It's terrible.'

'Can we come aboard?' said Gerry, sick of having to conduct the conversation from the jetty.

'Be my guest,' Teague said with casual confidence.

Gerry stepped on to the deck and Wesley, after a moment's hesitation, did likewise. Gerry put out a hand to steady him as he climbed aboard. Once safely on the deck, Wesley took a deep breath. Boats made him uncomfortable. Even when he took the short ride across the river on the passenger ferry, he was only too pleased to get off at the other side.

Jason led them down into a spacious cabin, comfortably furnished with all modern conveniences: plush seating, a

TV, a sound system and a well-stocked drinks cabinet. He invited them to sit, casting a nervous glance at the clock.

'I take it you were aboard yesterday morning around ten thirty when this boat was seen sailing out of the river?' said Wesley.

Teague shook his head. 'No, I wasn't. Den told me on Friday that he wanted to take her round to Bloxham for a short run yesterday morning. Said he wasn't going far so he wouldn't need me.' He smiled. 'Think he went under power – he isn't the world's best sailor.'

'So where were you while he was chugging round the headland?' Gerry asked.

'I spent Friday night with a friend then I had business to attend to the next morning so I didn't get back till yesterday lunchtime. She was here at her mooring again by then.' He shrugged.

Wesley looked at Gerry for guidance. He'd know whether the story was feasible if anyone did. Gerry said nothing so Wesley assumed it was.

'So what about this friend you were with while Mr Dobbs went on his solo voyage?'

'It was someone I met at the festival. A girl.'

Wesley took his notebook from his pocket. 'She lives in Tradmouth?'

'She's got a flat up near the market. Then yesterday morning I went to see an old mate here who wants a partner to help with his yacht charter business. We met at his office.'

'How long have you worked for Mr Dobbs?'

'Only a few weeks. I met up with him in Antibes. I'd been crewing for an American guy and Den said he needed someone to help him sail the *Queen Philippa* back to

Blighty. She's a nice craft,' he said, looking round appreciatively.

'You've worked a lot in the South of France?'

'Yeah. All around the French coast.'

'But you're planning to settle in Tradmouth if your mate's job offer works out?' Gerry sounded genuinely interested.

The man shrugged his shoulders. 'I guess so and if it doesn't work out there are a lot of yachts in Tradmouth for this Palkin Festival so if Den doesn't need my services any more, I won't have any trouble getting another berth.' He smiled.

'Is that what you do for a living ... bum around on yachts?'

The smile widened to a grin. 'It's nice work if you can get it. And so far I've never had any trouble.'

'What can you tell us about Dennis Dobbs?' Wesley asked.

Teague's manner suddenly became guarded. 'Den's OK.'

'How does he earn a living?' This was a question Wesley would have liked to ask many of the yacht owners who turned up in Tradmouth each year. He suspected that not all the flashy vessels moored in the river were paid for by honest graft.

Jason rolled his eyes. 'In my line of business you learn not to ask too many questions. I do my job and I do it well. That's it.'

'Where does Dennis Dobbs live when he's not on his yacht?'

'London as far as I know.'

'What time is he due back?'

'Not till this evening. And before you ask, I don't know where he's gone or who he's seeing. I'm just the hired help. He doesn't confide in me.'

'You said you'd heard about the woman who was found floating in an inflatable dinghy yesterday.'

'Can't avoid it. It's the talk of Tradmouth. How did she . . . ?'

'She was strangled.'

Jason frowned. 'Bad business.' He looked away, avoiding Wesley's eyes.

'A fisherman saw this yacht anchored near the entrance to the river yesterday, about half an hour before the call came in to report the body.'

'Like I said, Den took her out on his own.'

'Do you have an inflatable dinghy on board?'

'Sure. But I can assure you it's still where it should be.'

'You're certain about that?'

'Course I am. Have a look if you like.'

Gerry caught Wesley's eye and stood up. He wasn't taking Jason's word for it that the inflatable dinghy was still there. He followed Jason out on to the deck while Wesley waited below.

Wesley hadn't been aboard many boats and was pleasantly surprised at how comfortable this one seemed, although he guessed that comfort came with a hefty price tag.

He decided to stretch his legs so he walked around the cabin, looking out of the portholes at the river, bustling now with the extra traffic caused by the clement weather and the Palkin Festival. The water looked so crowded that he was surprised there weren't more collisions. But what did he know about maritime matters?

Gerry returned after a few minutes, a look of disappointment clouding his face. Wesley guessed that the dinghy had been exactly where it should be. But Dennis Dobbs had been seen acting suspiciously near the spot where the body had been found. They needed to speak to him as soon as possible.

Neil knew that the signs of disturbance in the soil didn't necessarily indicate anything sinister. The builder of the bungalow might have buried a sewer pipe in there. Or some rubbish. Or a pet dog, or anything, come to that. It was hardly worth mentioning to Chris Butcher.

Dave was impatient to get on with the digging but Butcher had just arrived and Neil would have preferred to wait until he was well away from the premises. He wasn't quite sure why this was, just some nebulous feeling that if it turned out to be something interesting he didn't want the house owner breathing down his neck.

As they trowelled away the soil from the section he was starting to think of as the warehouse wall his eyes kept being drawn to the anomaly in the neighbouring trench; a definite edge where the shade of the soil changed subtly. The sight teased and tempted him to plunge in and satisfy his curiosity. But any excavation has to be done systematically, scientifically. It isn't just a case of taking a spade and shovelling the earth away until something interesting turns up.

From where they were working he could see that the bungalow's front door was ajar. Butcher had gone inside earlier, too preoccupied to say hello, which wasn't like him as he usually stopped for a chat whenever he visited, wanting chapter and verse on each new find, however run-of-the-mill. This time he'd marched into the house and when his wife Astrid had arrived ten minutes later she hadn't even glanced in the direction of the trench. She had never been the friendliest of women, usually cool and aloof with her dark hair pinned in a neat French pleat. But today she looked as if she was boiling with pent-up rage. Maybe Chris had done something she disapproved of and she was gunning for a row. There were times he was glad he'd stayed single.

He stopped digging and stood up, intending to see how the students were progressing, when he heard voices coming from the direction of the house. A high-pitched female voice raised in anger and a man's, quieter, appeasing and almost inaudible.

Standing still he could just make out what the woman was saying.

'It's her, isn't it? The one you've been seeing.'

Butcher answered although Neil couldn't catch what he said, only the tone of his reply: calm and unemotional. The voice of reason.

The woman spoke again. 'It's all your fault ... just like it was last time.'

When the door opened Neil bobbed down, trying to look inconspicuous. Dave caught his eye and winked.

Astrid emerged from the house, her face ash-pale. And she was crying.

Wesley had asked Jason Teague to report to Tradmouth police station to make a statement but Dennis Dobbs still hadn't turned up.

Teague arrived at the front desk surprisingly promptly but his statement was of little help. He'd never met Kassia Graylem. Never even heard of her. Den said he was taking the *Queen Philippa* down the river on the morning in question but as the boat was at her mooring when Teague returned from his meeting, he couldn't confirm whether he'd kept to his plan. The whole thing was a complete mystery to him.

On the night Kassia vanished he'd stayed the night with a girl called Kimberley who worked as a chef in the kitchens of the Tradmouth Golf Club Hotel two miles outside the town. It had been Kimberley's evening off and he'd gone back to the flat near the market she shared with two other girls and spent the night with her. He knew she'd vouch for him but he didn't know the exact address of the flat, although he was sure he could find the place again. He'd left Kimberley's around nine thirty the following morning to go straight to the meeting with his mate about the yacht charter business. Then he'd looked around the town before having lunch at the Angel, not setting eyes on the *Queen Philippa* again until about one. Wesley had asked someone to check out both stories. There was always a chance Jason was lying.

He'd arranged for Kassia's fellow musicians to report to the station to make formal statements and Dan Hungerford was the first to arrive. As he and Gerry had already spoken to Hungerford when he'd identified Kassia Graylem's body, Wesley sent Rachel and Trish to speak to him in the interview room, hoping a fresh approach would produce more information. He wasn't too optimistic; the man looked as if he wouldn't give much away.

The other members of Palkin's Musik turned up half an hour later as requested and officers were assigned to take their statements.

When the call came to say that Rosie had arrived at the front desk Gerry looked unusually anxious. Rachel had just finished with Dan Hungerford and Wesley knew she'd be the ideal person to conduct the interview as he could rely on her not to be swayed by the fact that Rosie was the boss's daughter. He told Gerry what he was planning and the DCI nodded agreement. The other members of the group had claimed that they hardly knew Kassia Graylem – something that would be checked and double-checked in due course – but there was always a chance that Rosie might know more.

Wesley felt a little apprehensive as he made his way downstairs with Rachel walking slightly behind him. Besides being the boss's daughter, Rosie was an intense young woman who made him feel awkward whenever they met. When he reached the interview room he paused for a second before pushing open the door.

Rosie was sitting there waiting for him. Gerry had often said that she looked like her mother. He had never met Kathy Heffernan but he'd seen photographs of her in Gerry's house and he could see the resemblance. No wonder the fond father always forgave his daughter's shortcomings. She was all he had left of Kathy.

Rosie looked up. 'Where's my dad?' She sounded nervous.

Wesley smiled at her and sat down. 'Afraid he's busy. You've met Rachel, haven't you?'

Rachel gave her a cautious nod, as if she found the situation uncomfortable.

'Yeah. Hi.' Rosie began to fidget with the empty coffee cup on the table in front of her. 'Look, we've got a gig tonight so I'd be grateful if we could get this over with as soon as possible. Kassia dying has caused us major problems so . . .'

'Not as many problems as it's caused her,' said Rachel quickly. Then she fell silent, as though she regretted the sharpness of her words.

Rosie bowed her head, realising that what she'd said had been insensitive. The bruising on her eye was still visible, even though she'd tried to conceal it with make-up. She was still insisting that she'd done it by accident and Wesley couldn't help wondering if she was telling the truth.

'We've spoken to everyone else in the group and they all claim that they didn't know Kassia very well.' Wesley paused. 'What was your relationship with her?'

'Well, we passed the time of day and talked about the music but I wouldn't have said we were bosom pals.' There was a hint of defiance in her voice.

'Do you know who her friends were? Did she mention any names? It's important that we find out everything we can about her life.'

'She never mentioned anyone in particular. She didn't talk about herself much.'

'Did she say anything about her family?'

'I asked her about them once and she said they were dead. She clammed up after that so I think the subject upset her. The only thing I know about her is that she lived in a squat in Neston.'

'Did she ever talk about the people she shared with?'

'I think there was someone called Pixie but that's all I know.'

'Would you say she was secretive? As if there were things she didn't want you to find out?' Rachel asked.

Rosie thought for a few seconds. 'Yeah. That'd be about right. It was odd. Almost as if she hadn't had a life before she joined Palkin's Musik. Like she'd been beamed in from outer space.'

'We haven't found her things – a bag or a mobile phone.'

'She didn't always carry a bag and I don't know if she had a phone – never saw her with one.' She paused. 'But she would have had her instrument – her viol – in a battered black case. Have you found it?'

'Not yet. Did you ever see her with anyone?'

Rosie hesitated before answering. 'When we were rehearsing on Thursday she was very jumpy. Then she disappeared when Dan wanted to get on with the rehearsal. He got a bit annoyed with her if you must know. He told us to take a break so I went out for a ciggie.' She leaned forward. 'For God's sake don't tell Dad I've started smoking again. He thinks I've given up. He'd go mad if ... His dad died of lung cancer, you see, and ... '

Wesley uttered the necessary assurances. Gerry would never learn her unhealthy secret. 'So where did she go?'

'I saw her in the churchyard talking to someone. And before you ask, I don't know who it was 'cause I didn't see him.'

'How come?'

'He was in the church porch, in shadow. I couldn't see who it was or even if it was a man or a woman to be honest. But I did hear some of what she said. She told this person she'd see him or her later. And she said she was sure she was right. I couldn't hear what the other person said but Kassia sounded a bit, I don't know, excited maybe.'

'Do you know anything about the tattoo she had on her shoulder?' Wesley asked. 'It was a ship. A medieval cog?'

'Like the Shipworld logo?'

'Yes. Was she into Shipworld?'

'She never mentioned it. But lots of people are. I've seen the badges all around at the festival. Not that I'm into it, of course. All that John Palkin stuff and the Shroud Maker.'

Rachel raised her eyebrows. 'Who?'

'The Shroud Maker. The dark force who controls Shipworld. Palkin's his enemy. Or is he his puppet? You see, I know all about it even though I'm not a fan. Can't avoid it,' she added dismissively. She looked at Wesley, her head tilted coquettishly. 'Can I go now, Wes? I've told you everything I know. Honest.'

He glanced at Rachel. 'Fine. But if you remember anything else that might help us, you'll let us know, won't you?'

'Sure,' she said. She bent down to retrieve her denim bag from the floor and stood up.

'Is something bothering you, Rosie?' Wesley asked.

'Is that any of your business?' Rosie muttered before hurrying out of the room.

'She's hiding something,' said Rachel as Rosie disappeared off down the corridor.

Wesley didn't answer.

When Wesley returned to the incident room Gerry summoned him to his office.

'How did you get on with Rosie? Is she OK?' Gerry was trying to sound casual but Wesley detected anxiety behind the question.

'She seems fine,' Wesley said as he sat down, pushing aside the paperwork piled up on the boss's desk.

If Gerry was worried about his daughter, he felt bound to bring some reassurance. 'She overheard the dead girl talking to someone in St Leonard's Church porch a couple of days before she disappeared but she's no idea who it was. She's given a full statement.'

He looked at Gerry expectantly but there was no reaction. Then after a few seconds Gerry spoke. 'She didn't mention me?'

'Not really. Why?'

'No reason.' Gerry gave a heavy sigh. 'I just wonder if she didn't turn up at mine because of this thing she has about Joyce.'

'Did she give an explanation?'

'She just said she'd met a friend and decided to go back to her flat after all. Says her mobile battery wasn't charged so she couldn't let me know.'

'And you don't believe her?'

Gerry shrugged. 'I don't know. I thought things were OK between her and Joyce for a while and that she'd accepted the situation but recently ... If she ever sees Joyce she's downright rude to her and ...'

Wesley said nothing. In his opinion Rosie was a grown woman and should have got over teenage tantrums by now.

There was a knock on the open office door. Wesley turned to see Trish standing there, and he could tell by the eager expression on her face that she had news.

'The *Queen Philippa* was bought with cash in the South of France a few weeks ago. And the address Dennis Dobbs gave is false.' She looked from Wesley to Gerry, gauging their reaction to the news. 'Do you think we're talking money laundering? Or something more sinister?'

Chapter 6

Written at North Lodge, Upper Town, Tradmouth this 10th day of January 1895

My dearest Letty

You have not replied to my last letter and I long to hear from you. Why do you not write even a word to me? Is it that my last letter disturbed you? If this is the case, my dearest sister, please consider my feelings and my increasing fear.

Josiah speaks little to me. Rather he keeps to his study working on his book, his mind focused solely on the life of his illustrious ancestor. In Josiah's absence on Monday night, after ensuring Maud Cummings was lying drunk and snoring in her bed, I sneaked like a thief into

*his study. There I perused the notes my husband
has made for the book he claims to be writing
and I found the contents most distasteful. If
Josiah's writings are to be believed John Palkin
was a man who cared nothing for man or God
and it is small wonder that he worships him as a
hero for he is cut from the same cloth.*

*I do not like Maud Cummings for she seems to
wield a power over my husband inappropriate
for a mere housekeeper. I would dismiss her but I
dare not for fear of Josiah's temper.*

*The records of St Margaret's Church reveal
that John Palkin was a great benefactor. But
how can this be if he was as wicked as my
husband claims? I wish I could discover more but
Josiah forbids me to leave the house
unaccompanied.*

*I beg you, Letty, please reply to this. I am
now and always your loving sister,*
Charlotte

As they couldn't get hold of Dobbs, Gerry decided that the
next best thing was to come down heavier on Jason Teague.
He'd been with Dobbs, cooped up on board a boat for a
couple of weeks. Wesley found it hard to believe that you
wouldn't get to know somebody pretty well in those circumstances. If anything untoward was going on, surely
Teague would have been aware of it.

In the meantime Wesley was becoming more and more
intrigued by Kassia Graylem, possibly because, as Rosie
had said, she seemed to have been beamed in from outer
space. A girl with no baggage, no family, no past. Or maybe

it was the fact that her body bore the same ship tattoo as that of the missing Jenny Bercival.

He sat at his desk, going through the statements taken from the members of Palkin's Musik. When Trish had interviewed Ursula Brunning, she'd asked her where Kassia had got her blue velvet gown from. But Ursula had no idea. Kassia had simply turned up in it for a rehearsal and when Ursula had admired it and inquired about its origins, Kassia told her she'd been given it by a friend. She hadn't elaborated, much to Ursula's chagrin. It was obvious, Trish had observed, that she'd been envious of Kassia's costume.

Someone had already been in touch with the theatrical costumier Bygone and Son and their records showed that the gown had been bought two years ago. They still had Kassia's measurements and details of the design and fabric but the dress had been paid for in cash and the only name they had was Kassia's and an address in London that was being checked out. Trish wondered how a girl who lived in a squat and busked in the streets could have afforded such a rich garment. And why she'd gone to the trouble of having it made.

While Wesley was mulling over these questions he saw DC Nick Tarnaby approaching. When he was a few feet away he hesitated, as though unsure of his welcome. Nick was hard work and Wesley sometimes wondered whether his wariness was due to some suppressed racism or whether in the past he had offended him in some way without realising it.

Wesley looked up expectantly. 'Did you want a word, Nick?'

'We've found the squat where the victim was living,' the man said without enthusiasm.

'Where is it?' Wesley felt as if he was coaxing a stubborn child.

'Big old place just outside Neston. Three of them live there. We should send some uniforms down. See what they're growing,' he added meaningfully.

'No. I'll speak to her housemates myself,' Wesley said, heading off disaster. If Tarnaby had his way the interview with Kassia's fellow squatters could turn into a raid. Hardly the best way of prising information out of people who probably harboured an instinctive mistrust of the boys in blue.

Wesley made for Gerry's office to break the news. Gerry immediately pushed his paperwork to one side, and Wesley could tell that he was eager to be doing something constructive again.

They drove out to the address Nick Tarnaby had supplied. It was a substantial Georgian house in its own grounds, too small to be a stately home but too large for the average family if they didn't fall into the millionaire category. The name Bolton Hall was painted in Gothic lettering on a flaking wooden sign next to a pair of rusty gates that would have been impressive in their heyday. The rest of the property was similarly dilapidated. The grounds were overgrown and the grass of what had once probably served as a croquet lawn was almost waist height. The original sash windows had been left to rot and the stucco of the elegantly proportioned façade was badly stained and falling away in places to reveal the brickwork beneath.

The half-rotten front door was firmly shut and the cheap plastic doorbell which had long ago replaced the elegant bell pull had dwindled to a pair of wires protruding from a cracked rectangle. Gerry rapped on the door but when there was no answer Wesley suggested they try round the back.

Soon they found themselves in a large paved yard filled with clucking chickens and fringed by raised vegetable beds containing small plants which, with luck, would triple in size come the height of summer. Their arrival had disturbed the chickens and a young woman emerged from the back door to see what was causing the commotion. Her hair was bunched into mousy dreadlocks and a long patchwork skirt draped itself over her skeletal body. In Wesley's opinion she didn't look well.

He stepped forward to speak to her holding up his warrant card and her eyes widened in alarm. 'My name's DI Wesley Peterson and this is DCI Gerry Heffernan. We've been told that a Kassia Graylem lives here.' He hoped she'd guess from his solemn expression that they were there to bring bad news.

The woman seemed to catch on fast. 'Yeah. But we've not seen her for a couple of days. We were getting a bit worried, to tell you the truth. Has something happened?'

'I'm afraid Ms Graylem was found dead yesterday. We're treating her death as suspicious. I'm very sorry,' Wesley said gently. He waited a few moments for the news to sink in.

'Is there somewhere we can talk?'

The girl looked uncertain.

'We're not interested in any dodgy plants you might be growing. We just want to find out what happened to your friend,' said Gerry. 'What's your name, love?'

'Scarlett. Scarlett Derringer.'

'Who owns this place, Scarlett?'

'I do. I inherited it from my grandparents.' There was a suggestion of proprietorial pride in her grey eyes as she glanced towards the building. 'It needs a load of work. Pixie's quite handy so he does the odd essential repair but ... You'd better come in.'

'So it's not really a squat then,' said Wesley.

Scarlett shook her head. 'People make assumptions, don't you find?' Her eyes met his and she smiled. When she smiled she looked beautiful.

She led the way through a dingy kitchen out into a hall-way where the plaster was falling off the walls in places, revealing the laths beneath. The proportions of the large room they ended up in were stunningly perfect and the large sash windows in the semi-circular bay afforded what would have been a breathtaking view of the gardens and the countryside beyond. Wesley looked round at the splintering floorboards and the peeling wallpaper, once grand red and gold but now faded to a muted pink. Perhaps one day somebody would love this place and restore it to its former glory. If they had the cash.

Scarlett sat down on a dusty velour floor cushion of indeterminate colour and invited the two policemen to take a seat on the sagging sofa opposite. Avoiding the horsehair stuffing springing from the seat, they did their best to make themselves comfortable.

'I know this must have come as a shock,' said Wesley. 'But can I ask you some questions?'

Scarlett sniffed and nodded.

'What can you tell us about Kassia? Any boyfriends for instance?'

The woman looked as though she was making a decision. Eventually she spoke. 'I think there was someone. Not that she said much about him. She wasn't that kind of person. How did she ... ?'

'She was strangled. You've not heard about the body found in a dinghy not far from Tradmouth Castle?'

A look of horror flashed across her face for a moment then she shook her head vigorously. 'We don't have TV here . . . or radio or newspapers. Was that her? Was that Kassia?'

Before Wesley could answer the door opened. A man marched in and stopped to stare at the newcomers. He was in his twenties, with long, dark straggly hair, several facial piercings and a pasty complexion. He wore a faded grey T-shirt and drooping washed-out jeans.

'Who's this?' The question was hostile, as though he'd found Scarlett entertaining a pair of con men, bent on getting her to sign over the house.

Scarlett struggled to her feet. 'They're from the police. Kassia's dead. She was murdered.'

The man froze as if he couldn't quite believe the news. 'When? How? Do you know who did it?' The words came out in a rush.

'She died early on Saturday morning. She was found floating in a dinghy at the mouth of the river. She'd been strangled.'

The man slumped down on a plastic garden seat next to the sofa and stared ahead. Scarlett introduced him as Pixie and he gave a small nod of acknowledgement.

Once the news had sunk in, Scarlett and Pixie were models of cooperation. They wanted the bastard who killed Kassia caught and put away. Wesley considered that a good start, although something about the inappropriately named Pixie's reaction perplexed Wesley – the way he kept asking for details of how Kassia had been found, as if it was the manner of her death that worried him. Still, that could have been his imagination.

Wesley asked them to tell him everything they could about Kassia and her life, and anyone she might have been afraid of. Had they heard Kassia mention a Dennis Dobbs? Or a Jason Teague? In each case the answer was a definite no.

'Did she mention if she was planning to meet anybody? On a boat perhaps?'

The pair shook their heads.

Scarlett's tantalising mention of a possible man in Kassia's life had captured Wesley's attention and he couldn't quite believe that these people knew nothing about him. There must be something, however small, that she'd let slip even if they weren't aware of it. 'Please think hard. It could be very important. This man she was involved with: can you remember anything she said about him? Anything at all?'

Scarlett and Pixie exchanged looks, as if each was wondering if the other was in possession of some secret knowledge. It was Pixie who finally broke the silence.

'Remember when I went into Tradmouth with her a couple of days ago?'

Scarlett nodded.

'We were walking down the High Street and she dodged into a side alley. She said there was someone she didn't want to see. When I asked her about it she said she thought she'd seen someone from her past.'

'Was it a man?' Wesley asked.

Pixie shrugged. 'She just said someone she knew once. Could have been a woman, I suppose. I really don't know.'

'When was this?'

'Last week ... Thursday maybe. Come to think of it, she did seem a bit jumpy after that.'

'Was it the man she was involved with, do you reckon?'

There was a flicker in Pixie's eyes, something Wesley couldn't read. 'Sorry. No idea.'

'What about her family? Do you know anything about them?'

Scarlett shook her head. 'She said they were dead. She never talked about them.'

'How long has she lived here?'

'About four months. Someone left and we put an advert on the noticeboard of the wholefood supermarket in Neston. She was the first to answer and we liked the look of her.'

'You didn't check her out? Get references?'

Scarlett gave him a scathing look. 'We like to trust our instincts.'

'What did she tell you about her life before she came here?'

'She said she'd lived in London for a while and that she'd dropped out of uni. She decided to come down here and try her luck busking in Neston.'

'Anything else? Anything at all?'

'I think she said her grandparents came from up North,' said Scarlett. 'She might have mentioned Manchester but I'm not sure. She was always vague about details. Evasive.'

Pixie nodded in agreement.

'Does she have a computer here?'

'I won't allow computers in the house. Don't believe in them,' Scarlett said piously.

Pixie's face went red and Wesley suspected he might have disobeyed the house rule. But that was hardly a crime.

'What about a mobile phone? Did she own one?'

'No,' Pixie said. 'We've got one between us, a sort of house phone. She used to give people that number if they needed to get in touch with her and whoever answered it would pass on the message. Once she'd joined this early music group we got a few calls from the man who led it – Dan his name is – arranging rehearsals and all that.'

'Nothing else?'

'No.'

'Dan says he's been trying to get in touch but there's been no answer.'

Scarlett sniffed. 'We can't always get a signal here. That's probably why.'

Wesley thought it unusual that this young woman should be so dismissive of modern technology but he assumed her rejection of the modern world was a matter of principle. He couldn't help feeling a small twinge of sympathy with her stance.

Gerry stood up. 'We'll send someone round to take your statements and ask where you were at the time of Kassia's death. Don't worry, it's just routine.'

'Can we have a look at her room before we go?' Wesley asked.

Scarlett led the way up a once-magnificent staircase which wouldn't have taken a great deal of effort to polish up and restore to its former glory. Kassia's room was near the top of the stairs and Scarlett opened the door reverently.

'Nobody's been in here,' she explained. 'We take our privacy very seriously.' She looked around as she stepped into the room, as though the surroundings were unfamiliar to her.

Wesley stood behind her in the doorway, taking in the

scene. It was a large and perfectly proportioned room with stained floral wallpaper and a four-poster bed in the centre. The bed drapes were tattered red velvet, ripped in places to reveal a grubby lining. In spite of this the bed was neatly made, a modern brown cotton duvet looking rather out of place amongst the shabby grandeur.

'It was my grandmother's bed,' Scarlett explained. 'She actually died in it. Not that I told Kassia that.'

When her comment was greeted by silence, Scarlett seemed to get the message and left them to it. As soon as she'd gone Wesley and Gerry began to investigate, opening the massive oak wardrobe. It wasn't crammed with clothes as Wesley had assumed it would be, just the basics: long skirts; jeans; trainers; a couple of pairs of ballet pumps similar to the ones she'd been wearing when she died. As expected there was no computer and the books on the dusty mahogany shelves in the corner were an eclectic mix of fantasy fiction, romantic novels and classics. They included a set of Dickens and the complete works of Shakespeare as well as two volumes of Sherlock Holmes stories – Wesley's own adolescent favourite.

A big mahogany chest of drawers stood in the corner. The top drawers contained clothes and underwear, but the bottom one was filled with papers. Wesley took out the drawer and when he placed it on the bed he saw Gerry rub his hands in anticipation.

There was a birthday card on top, a reproduction of a French impressionist scene, and when Wesley opened it he saw that it was from someone called Lisa who had been thoughtful enough to scribble a note on the back and an address in Didsbury, Manchester. The note just said that Lisa had been trying to get in touch with her and that she'd moved and was letting Kassia know her new address. She ended the note by asking why Kassia hadn't been in contact.

Wesley saw a pink photograph album covered with over-cute pictures of prancing kittens nestling underneath the card. As he flicked through it he saw that it was only half-full and the photographs all seemed to date from around the same time, summer by the look of the weather. They were taken at a harbour, a beach, or aboard a boat and a suntanned couple, probably in their late thirties, featured heavily. The round-faced woman favoured long skirts and washed-out T-shirts and her fair hair cascaded around her shoulders. The ponytailed man looked as if he spent a lot of time out of doors and wore the same outfit in each picture, a khaki T-shirt and shorts, and he sported a single earring. In one of the photographs the couple stood with a younger Kassia, the man's arm draped casually around her shoulder. They had the relaxed look of a family on holiday together. A unit.

Kassia had written captions neatly underneath each picture. *Me with Mum. Me and Dad. Dad and Mum on board the* Sally Jane. One photo, Wesley noticed, appeared to be missing but the words were still there printed neatly beneath the empty space: *Me, Dad, Mum and R.*

He replaced the album and continued his search. There were letters in the drawer from University College, London dated a year ago. Official stuff and terse communications about why Kassia hadn't turned up for her exams. Then the offer of pastoral advice, the final warnings and the last judgement. As Wesley read them he had a feeling he was learning her story, that of a life and potentially comfortable future careering downhill. But there was no clue as to the cause. He discovered two brown envelopes at the back of the drawer, both posted in Tradmouth and bearing the Bolton Hall address. According to the postmarks, they'd both been sent over the past couple of weeks. It was Gerry who opened them first. Then, saying nothing, he thrust them into Wesley's hand.

Wesley read them one by one. The typed words had the sharp, clear look of something churned out on a laser printer. Untraceable.

> I'LL BE WAITING FOR YOU TOMORROW. DON'T
> BE LATE. I NEED YOU. PALKIN NEEDS YOU. YOU
> MUST NOT BETRAY HIM.

The second was dated a week later.

> COME TO ME ON WEDNESDAY AT TWO WHEN
> THE LIGHT IS AT ITS BEST. PLEASE DON'T LET
> ME DOWN. IF YOU DO, I'LL COME AND FIND
> YOU.

Wesley held them at arm's length, as though he feared they were contaminated.

'Is that a threat, I wonder? We'd better get these bagged up and sent to Forensic. The mention of Palkin fits in with the clothes she was wearing.'

'And the group . . . Palkin's Musik.'

'We need all the available CCTV in Tradmouth and Neston examined.'

'It's already being done for the area around the water-front.'

'I know, Gerry, but I think we should extend it. If by any

93

chance this character's been following her, he might show up on the footage.' He looked at the letters. 'What's this about the light being at its best?'

Gerry didn't have an answer for that one.

It was almost the end of the day and Neil hadn't seen Chris Butcher since his spat with Astrid. The woman had marched off without glancing in the archaeologists' direction and Neil would have dismissed it as just another domestic if it hadn't been for Astrid's accusation. 'It's all your fault ... just like it was last time.' The words rang in his head as he opened a new trench nearer to the house. 'It's her isn't it? The one you've been seeing.' Sometimes he envied his friend Wesley's ability to ask questions and use the force of law to get answers, like legalised snooping.

A couple of the diggers had had to leave early to go up to Exeter and Neil had decided to save the excavation of the disturbed area of earth until their return. On the other hand he couldn't help asking himself whether something might be buried there. In the end his curiosity got the better of him and he began to dig. It would do no harm to carry out some preliminary investigation before they started in earnest tomorrow.

After a few minutes' work he saw it, standing out pale against the dark earth. It was obviously bone. Possibly part of a butchered animal, or part of a human femur. He needed to dig further to find out.

Neil had imagined that after the row with Astrid Chris Butcher would have left the bungalow and made straight for his yacht, so he was surprised to see the man emerging from the back door. Butcher was in costume but instead of looking ridiculous, as many did, the clothes seemed to endow him with an air of authority. Perhaps it was because he wore them with the confidence of a Shakespearean actor. Confidence, Neil knew, could conquer most things.

He walked over to the edge of Neil's new trench and stopped, staring down at the soil. Eventually he spoke. 'What's that?'

Neil looked up. 'It's bone. Could be human,' he added, half joking.

Butcher froze for a few moments. Then he leaned forward confidentially and lowered his voice. 'To tell you the truth, Neil, I'd prefer it if things weren't delayed too much. The builders are waiting to start and ... Any chance you can forget what you've just found and close the trench? I know something like that creates lots of bureaucracy so you'd be doing me a great favour.'

And before Neil could answer, he strode away.

Scarlett and Pixie had sworn that they hadn't a clue who the letters were from or what they meant. But Wesley had them sent off to Forensic because he had a feeling they might be important.

When Wesley and Gerry returned to the police station, there was a message on Gerry's desk. Mrs Bercival wanted to see him urgently because another letter had arrived in that day's post. He called her back, saying they'd be round as soon as they could. Wesley thought he sounded excited as if he hoped they might be on the verge of a breakthrough.

While Gerry made some further calls Wesley strolled over to his own desk and placed photographs of Jenny and Kassia side by side. The two girls were certainly the same physical type. And then there were the tattoos on their shoulders. The more he considered it, the more certain he was that the two cases were linked. But he needed proof.

Gerry emerged from his office and paced up and down the incident room, staring at the noticeboard with its photographs of the victim and some of the main players – the members of Palkin's Musik, Jason Teague and now Scarlett Derringer and Pixie. None of them was known to the police, which left Dennis Dobbs, the man who'd given the false address – an address which, according to the Met, didn't even exist. As yet there was no picture of Dobbs so all they had was Teague's description of him.

A search of the *Queen Philippa* had failed to turn up his passport, which meant he had it with him so he could easily have left the country by now. The possibility of their main suspect slipping through their collective fingers had put the DCI in a bad mood but the prospect of another meeting with Mrs Bercival had seemed to raise his spirits a little.

When they arrived at the cottage on George Street Mrs Bercival greeted them eagerly, as if the newly received letter had given her fresh hope. She led them through to the kitchen where the radio was tuned to a play on Radio Four, the sound of human voices providing the illusion of company. An Ordnance Survey map of Tradmouth and the surrounding area was spread out on the pine dining table under the living-room window as though she was planning a walk. But she was dressed for town rather than a hike in the countryside.

'I was just getting a feel for the lie of the land,' she said after inviting them to sit. 'I wanted to see if there was anywhere Jenny might have gone . . .'

As she began to fold the map Wesley could see tears forming in her eyes. She took out a tissue and wiped them away, seemingly annoyed with herself for yielding to negative emotions.

'You said you'd received another letter,' said Gerry gently.

'It was here when I got back. I've been walking round Tradmouth looking for her.'

She gave a brittle smile and pushed an envelope across the table to Gerry. He took a pair of crime-scene gloves from his pocket and drew out a sheet of paper. It looked identical to the earlier letter, the one saying that Jenny was still alive. The address on the envelope was neatly printed and the first-class stamp was franked with a Tradmouth postmark.

'Whoever sent this not only knows your address in London but also where you're staying here in Tradmouth.'

'He must have followed me here. He must be watching me,' she said, her eyes wide with panic.

Gerry unfolded the paper and began to read. "'JENNY IS STILL ALIVE AND WELL. SEEK AND YOU SHALL FIND.'" He pursed his lips and exhaled. 'Short and sweet.'

'What does it mean?'

Gerry didn't answer.

'Have you seen that ship?' she said. 'The old one.'

'You mean the *Maudelayne*, the replica medieval ship moored at the embankment?' said Gerry.

'It's just like Jenny's tattoo.'

'Yes,' said Wesley. 'You mentioned the tattoo.' He hesitated, wondering how to introduce the subject of Kassia. There was a long silence and he realised he couldn't delay the moment any more. 'Someone came round to tell you about the body that was found floating in a dinghy on the river.'

97

The woman nodded.

'We've discovered that her name was Kassia Graylem and that she was a musician. She had a similar tattoo to Jenny's so we ...' He searched for the right words. 'We were wondering whether there might be some sort of connection. Have you heard the name before?'

'No. I'm sure I haven't.'

'Is there anything, anything at all that you can think of that might help us? Something that might have seemed unimportant at the time?'

She shook her head in despair. 'I wish I could help but I've told you everything I know.'

'What about Jenny's friends?'

'All her friends were spoken to when she disappeared. But ...' Her voice sounded tentative, as though she wasn't sure it was something she should mention.

'But what?'

'Well Jenny used to be close to her cousin, Karen. She moved to Canada a few months before Jenny went missing but they kept in touch.'

'How? By e-mail? Phone?'

'E-mail. After Jenny went missing the police looked through her e-mails but they couldn't find anything relevant. But I remember Jenny rang Karen during the week before we came down here. I don't think I mentioned it to the police at the time because I didn't think it was important.'

'Have you asked Karen what Jenny said?'

'I called her after Jenny ... left, but she didn't say much and I'm wondering now whether there was something she didn't want me to know. I can't be sure though. You imagine all sorts. Grasp at any possibilities.'

'I understand,' said Wesley. Karen's caginess might have been in Mrs Bercival's imagination but it was worth the effort of a long-distance phone call. They had nothing to lose.

After providing Karen's contact details, Mrs Bercival showed them to the door, looking as though all the ills of the world had descended on her shoulders. Kassia had been murdered so if the two cases were linked, the chances that Jenny was still alive were looking slim. And there was something about the letters that bothered him. Something that didn't quite ring true.

On the way back to the police station Wesley passed several knights in chain mail, a gaggle of surprisingly clean peasants and several gentlemen of ample proportions wearing tights, tunics and floppy velvet hats that had been the height of style in the fifteenth century. All preparing for another evening of festivity.

The festival would last until the following Sunday and he was sick of it already. But the news Rachel Tracey had for them on their return to the incident room cheered him up no end. As soon as she spotted them at the door she left her desk, bristling with untold information. Wesley knew that whatever she had to say was important. Rachel wasn't the sort to fuss about nothing.

'There's been a development,' she said. 'Alf Higgs who runs the castle ferry had been having engine trouble so he was checking the boat out at the embankment at quarter to six on Saturday morning before he was due to start work. The ferry ties up about seventy feet away from the jetty where the *Queen Philippa*'s moored.'

'Yes, I know,' said Gerry who was only too familiar with

the little red clinker-built ferry with the outboard motor which plied between the town and the castle from spring till autumn. And, in common with most long-term residents of Tradmouth, he knew Alf Higgs. The ferryman was in his sixties and had been born and brought up in the town. His outdoor life had wizened his skin and his constant encounters with humanity had bestowed on him an air of world-weary amusement. The general consensus of opinion was that Alf was a wise man ... especially after several pints of best bitter in the Star.

'Alf says he saw the victim walking along the embankment. He noticed her particularly because of her dress. And the fact that she was carrying a violin.'

'This was quarter to six in the morning?'

'Give or take ten minutes or so.'

Wesley looked at Gerry. 'Her viol hasn't been found. I presume that's the "violin" she was seen carrying.'

'There's a CCTV camera on that part of the embankment,' said Gerry with a hopeful gleam in his eye. 'Get all the footage checked to see if anyone else was around at the time. This could be the breakthrough we need.'

Chapter 7

Written at North Lodge, Upper Town, Tradmouth this 25th day of January 1895

My dearest Letty

Why do you not respond to my letters? Have I offended in some way, my sweetest sister? If so, I beg forgiveness.

All is not well here. I am aware that in law a wife and all she owns are her husband's property but I had not thought to believe it in my heart. Josiah uses me like a chattel, a possession with no sense or feelings. Yesterday I attempted to leave the house but he forbade it, saying there was no need as I had no friends to visit nor any provisions to buy as Maud Cummings assumes all domestic duties necessary for the running of the household. I am held here like a prisoner in a cage of rich fabrics decorated with aspidistras and grand furniture. I am trapped as surely as if I were incarcerated at Princetown Jail.

I wrote also to Mama but I have received no reply. It may be that she is afraid to offend Josiah. I overheard the veiled threats he made to her when he claimed my hand and my fortune, threats to reveal our late papa's secret, whatever that may be. I am sure, dearest sister, that our papa had no secrets. He was not a man to commit a shameful deed. Mama is eccentric, I grant you, but last week Josiah spoke of committing her to an asylum for her own protection and I feared for her. If our papa were alive all would be different but wishes will not restore him to life.

My sweetest sister, please say you will visit me. I am in sore need of comfort and company. There is a locked room at the top of the landing where I am forbidden to go. If you were here, I might gather the courage to discover its secrets. For I am sure that within lies something that, were it discovered, would be the ruin of my husband.

Have you had word of the Reverend Johnson? I think often of his kindness and the memory gives me strength.

For pity's sake write to me, my dearest one.
Your loving sister
Charlotte

With both children occupied with their respective friends and Wesley not expected home till late, Pam Peterson wasn't sure how best to take advantage of her freedom. Should she do something improving and uplifting? Or should she fritter away her time on idleness and relaxation? She decided on the latter.

She turned on her computer. There was something she wanted to look at, something Della had mentioned when she'd phoned for a chat that morning. Something Wesley had been asking about. She typed in the word Shipworld and perused the results. When she was satisfied that she'd found the right website, she brought it up on her screen.

The first thing that struck her was how colourful and lavishly presented it was. She soon found herself reading a story but, because the characters were unfamiliar, she scrolled backwards, trying to pick up the narrative.

Palkin was there. Controlling Shipworld and thwarting his adversary, the Shroud Maker, a shadowy figure wearing what looked like a white ski mask, a faceless monster who lurked in the background of the story making mischief for Palkin and his followers. Palkin himself appeared to be a cross between Falstaff and a superhero – a jolly ale-swilling sea captain with miraculous powers, the scourge of enemy shipping and upholder of all that was good in Shipworld. She read on and discovered that some of the content was fairly violent, describing torture and gruesome murder in a detail she could have done without.

It bore all the usual hallmarks of fantasy fiction. There were strange sea creatures, malevolent elves who inhabited caves in the cliffs below the castle and wraith-like maidens who had died and went to inhabit the realm of the half-dead, eternal prisoners of the Shroud Maker and his minions. She was a little disappointed to see that, apart from the main character sharing his name with a real person, it bore no resemblance whatsoever to the genuine history of Tradmouth.

After a while she began to find the whole thing tedious and at that point even checking her e-mails seemed more attractive. She was just about to log out of Shipworld when something caught her eye: the Death of Alicia. She clicked on the relevant words and a picture came up, a florid and professionally executed illustration, filling the screen.

A young woman with flowing auburn locks was lying in the bottom of a boat, her blue gown artistically arranged about her slender body. The boat appeared to be floating on open water and she stared upwards at the stars, an expression of desperate sadness on her flawless features. Around her neck a rope was pulled tight, crossed over at the front. The woman was clearly dead, strangled like the victim in Wesley's investigation.

Printed beneath the picture in bold lettering were the words 'Alicia has betrayed the Shroud Maker. She has entered the Realm of the Dead where the Birds of Morven shall peck out her lovely eyes.'

Pam picked up the phone and dialled Wesley's number.

There was to be another rehearsal that night. Rosie Heffernan thought it unnecessary but Dan Hungerford reckoned there'd been too many mistakes in Palkin's Musik's last performance. They'd managed to cover for Kassia's absence but only just.

Rosie was beginning to wish she'd never got involved with Palkin's Musik. She'd thought it would be fun to create music again rather than trying to teach the rudiments to recalcitrant kids – but she hadn't reckoned on Dan being so exacting. She wished she was spending her half-term holiday mooching around and going out with her mates instead.

She returned to her flat in Morbay, wondering how she was going to get through that evening's rehearsal without saying something she'd regret. She let herself in the front door of the large Victorian villa that had once housed one prosperous family but was now divided into eight small flats. Hers was on the ground floor at the back overlooking the garden. She loved the view but she liked even better the fact that she now had a place of her own, especially since her dad had taken up with Fat Joyce, that simpering woman who always tried far too hard to be her friend. She knew Fat Joyce was trying to take her mum's place but she never could. Sam might be soft but Rosie wouldn't allow it. Never.

She opened her post box in the hall only to find two items of junk mail and a bank statement. She tore the latter open and stared at the numbers. More bad news. Then she fumbled for the right key and let herself into her flat. There were three hours before Harry was due to pick her up for the rehearsal. Time to put something mind-chilling on the TV, make herself something to eat and relax.

Once inside, she flung her shoulder bag down on the floor with relief. She was home.

All the doors leading off the tiny hallway were closed so it was dark. But instead of reaching for the light switch she put her hand out to open the living-room door. As soon as that door was open, daylight would flood in to overwhelm the darkness. Everything would be as it should be.

She pushed it open, expecting light, only to find the curtains were shut. And she remembered quite clearly flinging them open that morning.

The creak of her bedroom door's unoiled hinges was unmistakable. It was something she hardly noticed during the day although she heard it every night when she went to the bathroom. The door was opening slowly, moved by an unseen hand, and although she knew she ought to rush out into the entrance hall and call for help, her body was paralysed by fear.

This couldn't be happening. Not in her own home. Her refuge.

Wesley stared at the picture of the dead Alicia in her floating coffin which had appeared since he'd last looked at the Shipworld website. Pam had been right about the similarity to Kassia Graylem's murder. The only difference was that the illustration on the website was a sanitised image. The dead woman lay neatly in the clinker-built boat, her face serene and beautiful, as if she was merely sleeping, quite unlike the twisted, contorted face of the real victim. Apart from this, it was a fairly accurate depiction of the truth. Which meant it had to be a lead.

Wesley was the first to admit that investigating the origins of websites was beyond him, but he knew somebody who could get to the heart of the mystery. He put in a call to Tom from Scientific Support and left it with him.

Sam Heffernan had just finished a day's work. It had been an especially tough one. In the morning he'd had to inform a heartbroken owner that her beloved Labrador had an incurable tumour, and in the afternoon he'd had to break the news to a farmer that three of his prize cows had tested positive for TB. He was glad the day was over.

And now he'd arrived home to find his sister, Rosie,

sitting on the doorstep of the cottage he rented in the village of Stokeworthy, hugging her knees to her body. She looked like a sulky child. But to Sam, who had inherited his father's naturally sunny disposition, she had always seemed like a bit of a drama queen.

As soon as she saw him get out of his Land Rover, she rose to her feet.

'What's up?'

She didn't answer. Instead she waited until he'd unlocked the door and followed him inside. He shared the cottage with his girlfriend, Freya, who was a junior doctor at Tradmouth Hospital but he didn't expect her back until later because she was on duty that evening. Rosie looked round nervously as though she was afraid they might be interrupted, but he assured her that they were alone. This was obviously something she didn't want Freya to overhear and as the moments went by he was becoming more intrigued.

He led her into the low-beamed living room and offered tea but it was refused.

'How did you get here?' Like his father, his sister didn't drive.

'Taxi. Can you put me up for a few nights?'

He hesitated, unsure whether Freya would welcome the intrusion. 'What about Dad's?' He frowned. 'You'll really have to get over this thing about Joyce. She's the best thing that's happened to Dad in ages and—'

'I don't want to involve Dad. Please.' She looked at him with pleading, puppy-dog eyes. As a vet he could never resist the charms of puppies, or for that matter kittens either.

'OK. Don't see why not.' Family was family after all. 'What is it you don't want Dad to know? Don't tell me

107

you've done something illegal. You're not on the run are you?' he asked with a grin.

His smile wasn't returned. Rosie looked deadly serious. And scared.

'What is it? Tell me.'

She stayed silent for a while, as though she was searching for the right words. Then she spoke. 'I'm in a bit of trouble. There's this bloke ... '

'You're not pregnant are you? Am I going to be an uncle?'

Rosie looked at him with weary disgust and as soon as the words had left his mouth, he knew he'd said the wrong thing.

'If you're not going to take this seriously ... ' She stood up and began to make for the door.

He grabbed her arm and gently pulled her back. 'What's wrong. Tell me.'

She sat down again. 'I've been seeing someone. He was really good fun at first but now he frightens me.'

'In what way?' He wished she'd be more specific.

She shook her head. 'Maybe I'm just being stupid.'

'Who is he? And does Dad know you're seeing him?'

Her eyes widened in horror. 'For God's sake don't tell him.'

'Why? Dad's usually OK about your boyfriends. Apart from the odd interrogation but that's probably force of habit in his job. What's wrong with this bloke?'

'He's a bit older than me for one thing.'

'How much older?'

She looked away. 'About ten years.'

'That's hardly a crime. There's something else, isn't there?' he guessed, watching her face.

There was a long pause. Sam waited, wondering what was coming next.

'I think he might have known Kassia,' she said, lowering her voice. 'He said something about finding a violin and her viol's missing. The police are looking for it.'

'Finding it? How do you just "find" a viol?'

'I don't know. And when I asked him he told me to mind my own business.'

'Is he responsible for that bruise on your face?'

She didn't answer. Sam had known his sister had got herself into scrapes in the past but this beat the lot. 'You've got to tell Dad.'

'No way.'

'Why not?'

'Because you know what he's like. He'd go in all guns blazing. Make it official.' She bowed her head. 'I'm probably overreacting. Promise you won't mention it.'

Sam, a rotten liar, turned his head away so that she couldn't see his expression. 'OK. Have it your own way.'

When Wesley arrived at his desk on Monday morning he found a message from Mrs Bercival asking whether they'd made any progress on the new anonymous letter. It had been sent to Forensic for examination and it would be a while before they came up with anything, even if there was anything to find.

He was more interested in the report that was waiting for him, tucked underneath the message. It hadn't taken Tom long to come up with the information Wesley needed. By tracing back a variety of links he'd come up with the name of a company. Further detective work had produced the name of the individual behind the Shipworld website. Chris

Butcher, who'd made his fortune from a variety of internet enterprises. It seemed almost too convenient that the man was actually there in Tradmouth for the festival. Wesley smiled to himself. Someone up there was looking after him.

He hurried to Gerry's office to break the news. The DCI was deep in paperwork but as soon as he heard about Tom's discovery, he rose from his seat and reached for his jacket on the coat stand near the door. After learning earlier that the CCTV camera on the embankment wasn't working and nothing relevant had been found on any of the others, he needed something to cheer him up.

They decided to walk to Butcher's house. Or rather his second home, still to be made habitable. Of course it was always possible that he was aboard his yacht moored at the marina but Wesley preferred to try dry land first. Besides, he knew Neil would be there excavating the area around the house for evidence of John Palkin's former home.

Gerry insisted on taking a detour along the embankment. As Wesley suspected, his motive was to take a closer look at the *Maudelayne*, still tied up there, bobbing gently on the incoming tide. It was only nine thirty in the morning so there was no queue to look round the ship. Wesley could tell that the boss was itching to set foot on board.

They walked up the road, past the line of exhaust-belching vehicles waiting to be transported over the river on the car ferry, and climbed the flight of steps leading to the road above. After a hundred yards they came to a wooden gate bearing a battered wooden sign with the words Palkin House written in dirty white lettering. Wesley noticed an elderly man with the look of an ancient fisherman standing on the pavement watching them, leaning on his walking stick. As soon as he saw Wesley looking in his

110

direction he began to walk away, his stick tip-tapping on the pavement.

Gerry pushed the gate and it opened with a loud creak. No doubt it would be replaced with something smarter once the renovations were completed. The bungalow lay below them beside the glistening water. From where they stood they were level with the roof and a flight of stone steps led down to the front door. The pebbledashed walls, once pristine white, were now stained and flaking after years of exposure to the maritime weather and the window frames were showing signs of rot. Of course Chris Butcher's renovations would take care of all that and more. The position alone made it a desirable property with a hefty price tag.

Wesley spotted a familiar figure in the garden near the entrance, standing in a long trench. When Neil looked round Wesley raised a hand in greeting before making his way down to join him.

'Chris Butcher about?' he asked.

Neil shook his head. 'Haven't seen him yet today. But he usually calls in every morning to see how we're doing. He's very keen.'

'You can say that again.' Dave stood up from his kneeling position, stretching out his back. 'He's been a bit of a pain in the arse, if the truth be known,' he said. 'Mind you, it's his property so I suppose we're lucky he called us in. And he's letting us stay here in the house so ...'

'And he's funding the dig,' said Neil. 'So we're being especially nice to him.'

Wesley heard a snort from Dave's direction. There was something they weren't telling him.

'What have you found?' Gerry asked. He'd been

watching from the top of the steps but now he'd joined them and was peering into the trench like a nosy neighbour.

'John Palkin's house and warehouse stood on the site and we've found lots of medieval stuff.'

Wesley saw Neil exchange a glance with Dave, full of a meaning he couldn't quite catch. He focused his eyes on the ground. At the bottom of the trench he could see a scattering of cobbles, probably part of some ancient floor, and at one end he could see the remnants of a wall which looked medieval, some stones bearing the signs of fire.

'There's been a fire at some point.'

'According to records the place burned down in sixteen seventy-five, long after Palkin's time. Then there was nothing on this land until the bungalow was built – apart from an old wooden boathouse which was probably constructed some time in the nineteenth century.'

Neil climbed out of the trench. 'Come and have a look at this.'

He led the way to another trench covered with a large tarpaulin. With the help of some of the other diggers who were working on a third trench nearer the water, he peeled aside the covering and stood beside Wesley looking down. The trench was about three feet deep and eight feet square. Wesley wondered why it had apparently been abandoned. He waited for Neil to enlighten him.

'The corner of the original house is over there where Dave's working and we think this was part of Palkin's warehouse. It stood by the water so he could unload his ships directly into the storage area. Now there is a sewer pipe nearby so the earth might have been disturbed when the bungalow was built. Or it might have been done more recently. It's hard to tell.' He paused. 'We found a bone.'

From the way Neil said the word, Wesley could tell there was more to come.

'It looks very like a femur to me but I'll need an expert to confirm it.'

'So when are you going to resume work on this trench?'

'I've been asked not to.' The words were loaded with meaning and Wesley was intrigued.

'Who by?'

'Chris Butcher. I joked that it could be a grave and he took me seriously. Said we were to leave it because he has the builders standing by and he doesn't want any holdups.'

'So that's what you're doing?'

Neil shrugged his shoulders. 'He's paying. But I'm itching to find out what's down there.' He looked Wesley in the eye. 'Now if the police suspected an illegal burial and ordered us to dig, there'd be nothing much he could do about it, would there.' He paused. 'I presume you and Gerry aren't paying him a social visit. What's he done?' He looked meaningfully at the disturbed earth and Wesley knew he was putting together a few pieces of the flimsiest of evidence and constructing a murder case.

'He hasn't done anything as far as we know. We just want a word with him.'

Neil looked as though he didn't quite believe it. But that wasn't Wesley's problem. On the other hand, from what he now knew about Butcher's connection with the Shipworld website – and the fact that Jenny Bercival had been missing for a year – he would have been neglecting his duty if he didn't take action.

He lowered his voice. 'Would it be possible to excavate without Butcher finding out? Keep the tarpaulin over the trench and backfill quickly if you don't find anything.'

A wide grin spread across Neil's face. 'Anything to help the police with their inquiries. Me and Dave can be very discreet when we want to be. Some of the others are working on the trench near the gate so they can warn us if—'

'You've no idea when Butcher'll be back?'

Neil shook his head. 'He had a row with his wife yesterday. Then he issued his edict about the trench and we haven't seen him since.' He paused, as though he was making a decision. As Wesley waited for him to continue he heard Gerry's voice, exchanging amiable small talk with Dave. It wouldn't be long, he knew, before the DCI's patience would wear thin and he'd want to be off.

Then Neil spoke again. 'When Butcher and his missus were arguing I couldn't help overhearing.'

'And?'

'Well Astrid said something a bit odd. Something like: "It's her isn't it? The one you've been seeing. It's all your fault just like last time." What do you make of that?'

Wesley looked round. Gerry should really be in on this conversation. 'Why didn't you tell us this before?'

Neil looked a little sheepish. 'People say all sorts of things when they're having a row, don't they, and I didn't think it was worth bothering you as you were in the middle of this murder investigation. I take it you still want us to dig this trench?'

Wesley nodded. 'Better get on with it.' If the bone Neil had found had only been a source of curiosity before, now he'd heard what Astrid had said, the matter had taken on a new urgency. Or was he reading too much into her ambiguous words?

When Wesley beckoned Gerry over and explained, the DCI looked at Neil expectantly. 'Think it's a burial then?'

'We're getting a bit ahead of ourselves,' Neil replied. 'It might just be an animal bone.'

Gerry looked mildly disappointed. And, reluctantly, they left Neil and Dave to it. As Wesley climbed the steps back up to the gate he turned his head and saw that they were removing the tarpaulin from the trench. It had just started to drizzle so their timing was rotten, but in spite of this Wesley wished he could have stayed to watch. However, they had things to do. He put in a call to Rachel back at the station to ask her whether Butcher's name had come up in any past inquiries.

At least that would start the ball rolling.

Jason Teague sat in the Tradmouth Arms staring at his pint of lager. Kimberley had sounded pathetically pleased to hear his voice when he'd called to arrange to meet her again. She wasn't really his type but he'd go along anyway.

Dennis Dobbs still hadn't turned up and, if it wasn't for the opportunity to get involved in the charter business – an option he was seriously considering – and the fact that the police had said they'd probably need to speak to him again, he might have cut his losses and gone off somewhere where the weather was more predictable. With his crewing skills he was always in demand and he liked the itinerant life, existing in the moment free as the seagulls that wheeled overhead.

Den had promised everything would be straightforward but now he knew it had been a mistake to go along with his plans. He'd been too trusting and now he'd learned his lesson. Men like Dobbs always lead you into trouble.

His mobile phone was on the table in front of him and when it started to ring he looked at the caller display. At last

Dobbs had deigned to return his calls. He answered with a hushed 'Where the hell have you been?', glancing round the bar to make sure nobody was taking too much interest.

But Den didn't answer the question. Instead he asked one of his own. 'Have the police gone yet?'

Pub walls, he knew only too well, are often bristling with ears so he answered simply, 'No.'

There was a long silence at the other end of the line. Then Dennis Dobbs spoke again. They needed to meet to sort out their unfinished business once and for all.

Wesley and Gerry found Chris Butcher aboard his boat, a gleaming white forty-foot cabin cruiser called *Palkin's Beauty*. The name caused Gerry to raise his eyebrows and mutter something about everyone being obsessed. As soon as Gerry called Butcher's name the man emerged on to the deck and Wesley sensed that he wasn't pleased to see them. But after a few moments he rearranged his features into the standard expression of the helpful citizen and invited them aboard, asking how he could help them and trying his best to sound sincere about it.

They were led down into a plush cabin, complete with leather upholstery and a bar, and Butcher offered them a drink. Gerry refused and Wesley did likewise. They weren't there to socialise.

They sat down, sinking into the soft feather cushions that had been neatly arranged on the seats. No wonder Butcher felt he could live aboard while his house was being reno-vated; it was far more comfortable than many hotel rooms Wesley had seen.

'We've just found out that you're responsible for the Shipworld website,' Wesley began. 'It's very popular, I believe.'

'Fantasy fiction is a big growth area. We have a great following.'

'Where did you get the idea for the site?'

'From a book about John Palkin. It was written by a Victorian descendant of his called Josiah Palkin-Wright. The man was a typical Victorian scholar.' He smiled as if he was enjoying some private joke. 'Or some people these days would say obsessive.'

'Do you think up the stories?'

'I had the initial idea for Shipworld but now the story-lines are developed by someone else.'

'Who?'

There was a moment of hesitation. 'Sometimes fans contribute but most of the recent stuff has come from someone called Palkinson.'

'Palkinson?'

'That's what he calls himself. His nom de plume.' He tried to smile but didn't quite succeed.

'Ever met him?'

Butcher looked away. 'That's not how it works. It's anonymous.'

'But traceable.'

'I expect you've got the resources for that sort of thing,' Butcher said, trying his best to sound casual.

Wesley made a mental note to get someone on to it. He wanted to know who Palkinson was. And how, in the case of Kassia Graylem, he'd managed to make fiction fit with fact so accurately.

'Does Palkinson provide the illustrations as well?'

'No. Some are provided by fans, like the copy, but it's hard to get material that's good enough so a professional illustrator does most of them. He lives here in Tradmouth.'

'We'll need his name and address,' said Gerry.

Chris Butcher looked uncomfortable as if he feared he'd land his illustrator in some sort of trouble. Nevertheless he recited the details; most of the Shipworld illustrations were done by a Miles Carthage who lived there in Tradmouth. Gerry made a great show of writing down the name and address in his notebook.

'The young woman who was found dead was called Kassia Graylem. Did you know her, by any chance?' Wesley drew the picture taken from the festival programme from his pocket and passed it to Butcher. He saw that the man's hand was shaking a little as he gave it back, as if he feared it was contaminated and he wished to get rid of it.

'No. I don't know her.'

'Are you sure about that?'

Butcher gave an almost imperceptible shake of his head but Wesley knew he was lying. 'Where were you around six o'clock on Saturday morning?'

'I was here.'

'Can anyone confirm that?'

He hesitated. 'No. My wife was in London that night.'

They thanked Butcher for his time and as they stepped ashore Wesley glanced back. Butcher was watching them. And he looked worried.

'I'm going to have a word with Miles Carthage. Want to come with me?' Wesley said, looking at his watch.

Gerry shook his head. 'Our new chief super wants to be brought up to date with the Kassia Graylem case.'

Wesley caught a hint of uncertainty in Gerry's voice. Over the years he had reached an understanding with Chief Superintendent Nutter, who had recently retired.

Gerry hadn't reckoned much to Nutter as a copper but, on the other hand, he hadn't interfered too much and Gerry had liked it that way. But CS Noreen Fitton was a new broom brought in from HQ over Gerry's head. He wasn't sure of her yet so he was treading warily. Wesley wondered how long he could keep it up.

In the end Wesley decided to take Rachel with him to Albany Street. As they cut through the winding back streets, avoiding the festival crowds, the drizzle was trying its best to turn into rain. They emerged on to the market square where shoppers browsed amongst the vegetables, clothing and bric-a-brac while the stallholders attempted to erect makeshift awnings against the wet.

'How are your wedding preparations going?' he said to Rachel as they walked. He thought it polite to ask.

'OK.'

He waited for her to elaborate but when she stayed silent he got the message that she didn't want to discuss the matter. He couldn't help feeling curious about her reticence, wondering if her farmer fiancé, Nigel, had transgressed in some way. From what he'd seen of Nigel he seemed a good, reliable man. It was Rachel rather than her colleagues, though, whom Nigel had to impress.

They climbed the steps up to the street above, steadying themselves on the metal handrail attached to the wall. When they reached the top Rachel set off ahead of him, striding upwards, her steps shortened a little by the tightness of her skirt. Wesley followed, examining the house numbers as they made their way up the hill and eventually they reached number forty-eight, a tall, whitewashed double-fronted house, larger than its neighbours, with bay windows to the ground floor. An oval painted sign told them that this was North Lodge and two bells beside the glossy black front door indicated that the building was divided into flats. There was also a circular plaque to the right of the door informing the passer-by that between the years 1888 and 1918 the building had been home to local historian and author Josiah Palkin-Wright. Miles Carthage's name was printed neatly beside the upper bell. Wesley reached out and pressed it.

After a minute or two the door opened a crack, as though the occupant was preparing to slam it shut. When Wesley announced himself it opened a little wider. And when they held up their ID cards, the man in the hallway made a great show of examining them. He was a wiry man, dressed entirely in black, and his skin was pale, suggesting he rarely spent time out of doors. His dark, almost black curly hair was neatly cut and there was an intensity in his pale eyes that Wesley found a little disconcerting.

When Rachel asked if they could come in and have a word, he hesitated before standing to one side to admit them. He led them up the central staircase and through an open door to their left into a spacious room, brightly lit by a tall window. The centre of the room was dominated by a large table covered with paints, paper and a half-finished picture; a work in progress.

Glass cases of the type normally found in museums stood around the walls. Wesley could see they contained specimens of moths and butterflies, the small corpses pinned there for eternity.

'I see you're a collector,' he said.

'I inherited them. But, as an artist, their beauty fascinates me.'

'They're more beautiful alive,' said Rachel.

Carthage gave a mirthless smile. 'I can't say I agree. These specimens are over a hundred years old and if they'd lived their natural lifespan, they would have rotted to dust many years ago. Now they're immortal.'

Wesley's eyes were drawn to the half-finished picture on the table. Something about art had always fascinated him. Perhaps because he had no talent in that direction himself, the ability to capture scenes and people on paper seemed like some sort of miracle.

It was the image of a group of women in flowing medieval robes, stylised, almost Art Nouveau in browns, greens and gold. The women were all beautiful with fluid curls and perfect feline features but somehow they lacked character – and humanity. They were images from another age, expertly executed but hardly original. There were knights too, strangely androgynous and as beautiful as the women.

'You're an illustrator I believe?' In Wesley's experience artists, with their fragile egos, can never resist talking about their work.

'Yes.' He spoke with a slight lisp that made him sound almost childlike. 'These are for a new book about King Arthur.' He swept a hand towards the pictures on the table.

Wesley noticed that Rachel was examining some canvases piled up against the far wall. From time to time Carthage glanced over his shoulder at her, as if he was afraid she was going to vandalise his life's work. The only time Wesley had seen anyone so jumpy was when they had something of a seriously criminal nature to hide. He carried on talking. If Carthage was preoccupied with what Rachel was doing, he probably wouldn't be able to concentrate on thinking up convincing lies.

'We've been talking to Chris Butcher. He says you do illustrations for the Shipworld website.'

'That's right.'

'You've heard about the woman who was found dead in the river? She was cast adrift in an inflatable dinghy.'

'I don't know anything about that.' The denial sounded unconvincing, like a child trying to wriggle out of some discovered petty wrongdoing. *It wasn't me. I never did it.*

'She was wearing a blue velvet medieval gown.'

They hadn't been invited to sit so the three of them were standing, Carthage by the table facing Wesley and Rachel behind, out of Carthage's line of sight. She'd finished her cursory examination of his work and Wesley could see a look of suppressed triumph on her face, as if she'd discovered something interesting. They had no search warrant, so she was being discreet.

She had something in her hand. A sketch book. She made her way over to Wesley and passed it to him. What he saw made his heart beat faster: it was a picture of a cog, just like the tattoos on the shoulders of the dead Kassia and the missing Jenny Bercival.

Wesley placed it on the table and took the picture he'd printed of Alicia dead in the boat from his pocket. 'Did you draw this?' He handed it to Carthage who stared at the picture for the few moments before answering.

'Yes, this is one of mine. The story was that Alicia had betrayed the Shroud Maker so he strangled her and placed her on a boat to voyage to the Realm of the Dead where the Birds of Morven pecked out her eyes as punishment. It's all there in the narrative. I go by the text and illustrate it as best I can.'

Wesley picked up the sketch book and flicked through the

pages: the cog had been drawn time and time again from many angles, the rigging lovingly depicted, accurate to every fibre of the rope. Carthage had clearly been aboard the *Maudelayne* because he had drawn the deck and the interior of the cabins. Then further on there were figures in medieval dress, men and women, young and old, wealthy and humble.

When he came to the next to last page he saw something that made him freeze. It was definitely her: Kassia Graylem in her blue velvet gown, although in the pencil sketch you couldn't see the colour. In one picture she was standing, eyes shielded as if she was gazing out to sea, and in the other she was walking, her delicate fingers lifting the hem of her gown off the floor. The artist had captured her vitality, her grace of movement. And for Wesley, who had only seen her in death, he had made her human.

Wesley held it up in front of Carthage's face.

'Why didn't you tell us you knew the dead woman?'

He was silent for a while, as though his mind was working hard to come up with a valid explanation. 'I didn't know her. She was just a musician I saw performing at a concert. I decided to draw her. I draw lots of people and . . . ' His voice trailed off.

'Did you speak to her?'

'No.' Something about his denial didn't ring true.

'Where were you around six o'clock on Saturday morning?'

Carthage looked confused. 'Here in bed asleep. Where else would I be?'

'Any witnesses?' Rachel asked.

Carthage shook his head. To Wesley his answer had sounded spontaneous and truthful. But he'd still drawn the victim. There had been a point of contact.

'You're into all this Palkin stuff?' There was something dismissive in Rachel's question.

Carthage seemed relieved at the change of subject and the light of enthusiasm suddenly appeared in his eyes. Perhaps more than enthusiasm: obsession. 'His biographer, Josiah Palkin-Wright, once lived here. He was a descendant of the great man.'

Wesley returned his attention to the sketch book. 'These pictures of the ship. They resemble a tattoo on the dead woman's shoulder.'

Miles Carthage's face clouded. 'I'm not a tattoo artist,' he said with a hint of disdain. 'I know nothing about that.'

The rain would have put even the hardiest of swimmers off taking a dip in the unheated outdoor pool at Newlands Holiday Park. So, as the current residents of the park liked their comforts and there was a newly built indoor pool, it lay unused, enclosed behind its seven-foot-high white concrete walls, stained here and there with green moss that really should have been dealt with before the start of the season.

The wrought-iron gate, painted white but rusted in places, was shut for safety because it would never do for a young child to wander in there and fall into the water. And as none of the children spending their half-term holidays at Newlands were unaccounted for, nobody had ventured near the pool that day to check. That was why the body had floated there on the azure water for an hour or so before it was discovered.

The corpse was wearing a business suit. It was hard to tell the quality of the dark, pinstripe cloth because immersion in that much chlorinated water would have rendered even the dearest Savile Row tailoring shiny and shapeless. He was wearing a dark tie too, which floated out like a rope designed to pull the body ashore. Ties were hardly the garb of the typical Newlands Park holiday-maker so he looked strangely out of place there in the pool, even for a dead man.

Chapter 8

*Written at North Lodge, Upper Town, Tradmouth
this 31st day of January 1895*

My sweet Letty

 *Josiah is gone from the house to do business in
Truro and leaves me in the care of Maud
Cummings who watches me as a prison wardress
watches her charges. She is an odious, slovenly
woman and there are times when I find her
manner threatening. Her insolence to me is
intolerable but Josiah will not countenance any
criticism of his protégée.*

 *How the days pass slowly when I am without
company. I long to go out into society but Josiah
forbids it. He says I am delicate, that
misfortunes would befall me were I to venture out
into Tradmouth. He has said it so often that I
begin to believe it myself.*

Before my marriage I became lost in the town and I happened upon the houses of Tradmouth's poor. I passed houses built centuries ago for rich merchants that had now become filthy tenements crowded with many families. Mama told me they housed the kindred of coal lumpers who were obliged to dash out day or night to coal the steamers on the river. It grieved me to see the thin, ragged children and the women with their tawdry clothes and bold stares. I think perhaps some of the women sold their bodies to the wealthy men of the town but Mama would not speak of such horrors.

Today when Maud Cummings was out of the house, I went into Josiah's study. I touched nothing for I fear that he would know at once if anything was disturbed, even in the slightest degree. I stood by his desk and studied the papers that lay thereon and saw that they all concerned the object of his obsession, John Palkin. Palkin is buried in the chancel of St Margaret's Church and I have seen Josiah standing by the painted rood screen after Sunday service, staring through at Palkin's brass like one worshipping an idol. I am forbidden to speak to anyone after the service. He instructs me to wait in my pew while he undertakes his devotions. Sweet sister, how long can I endure this?

Your loving sister
Charlotte

When Gerry returned to the office after his meeting with CS Noreen Fitton, two items of news awaited him, neither of which was particularly enlightening. First, Jason Teague's alibi had been confirmed and, second, the owner of a yacht moored close to the *Queen Philippa* had arrived in Tradmouth that day to find his inflatable dinghy missing. To begin with the man had been annoyed, thinking he'd been the victim of a theft, but when he'd learned about the murder he'd become subdued; the model of cooperation.

So far they'd had no luck tracing Kassia's family and Greater Manchester Police were still trying to contact her friend, Lisa. Gerry complained that there seemed to be brick walls everywhere and shut himself in his office, only to be disturbed by DC Paul Johnson.

'A body's been found at Newlands Holiday Park, sir. Uniform have just called it in. They want CID there.'

Gerry, who'd just started to study a report on his desk, looked up. 'Is that because it's suspicious or is it a straightforward heart attack and the buggers are too idle to do the paperwork?'

'The first, sir. Body was found floating in the swimming pool.'

'Accident?' Gerry asked hopefully.

'Possible. But on the other hand it might not be.'

Gerry looked at his watch. He'd already called Joyce to tell her he'd be late. He'd thought about calling Rosie too, just to see how she was doing, but he knew she'd only accuse him of fussing. In theory, you had to stand back and leave daughters to their own devices. In reality it was difficult.

'I suppose I'd better get over there and see what's going on. Where's DI Peterson?'

As soon as the question had left Gerry's lips Wesley appeared, carrying a plastic cup from the drinks machine in the corridor filled with some brown liquid that might have been tea, or coffee. It was hard to tell.

As Paul hurried away, Wesley stopped at Gerry's door, sensing something was happening. 'Just the man I want to see,' said Gerry. 'How did you get on with Carthage?'

Wesley gave a quick account of his visit before Gerry reciprocated by bringing him up to date with the new developments in the Kassia Graylem case. Not that there were many.

He saved the news about the body at the holiday park till last, knowing Wesley would share his frustration. They needed to find Kassia Graylem's murderer and a drowning in a swimming pool was an unwelcome distraction.

As he was speaking Trish appeared in the doorway. 'I've been on to the Met, sir. They're checking to see whether Chris Butcher's name's come up in any inquiries.'

'Good. Anything else?'

'I've managed to speak to Karen Gregson, Jenny Bercival's cousin in Canada. She told me that Jenny was involved with a man. She said he was older and married and Jenny hadn't told her mother about him. Karen had the impression that he was very controlling – said she had to dress a certain way and all that. Karen told Jenny to ditch him but she wouldn't. Karen said she despaired of her.'

'Any names mentioned?'

'He was called William.'

'No surname?'

'Afraid not.'

Wesley looked at Trish. 'What do you think? What kind of man could persuade a woman to behave like that?'

Trish's cheeks reddened. 'An extremely rich one?' She gave a little giggle, as though she was embarrassed by her flippancy. 'Or a charismatic one perhaps. Or perhaps she just accepted it. Low self-esteem maybe.'

Gerry rested his chin on his hand, a wistful expression on his face. 'Charisma. Now that's something we'd all like to have.'

'But is it something money can't buy? Or does having a few million in the bank help?' said Wesley.

Gerry smiled. 'You're probably right there, Wes.'

'I'm sure there's a connection between Kassia Graylem's murder and Jenny's disappearance.' He thought for a moment. 'Could that be what Butcher's wife meant by last time?'

'It's worth bearing in mind, Wes.' Gerry stood up. 'I suppose we'd better show our faces at Newlands Holiday Park.'

Wesley put down his half-finished drink and went to fetch his jacket.

It didn't take long to reach the holiday park which stood, surrounded by fields, on the main road out of Tradmouth. Wesley swung the car through the wide gateway and drove between the rows of neat white chalets. The rain had stopped and there were lots of people about: families with young children valiantly making the best of the British weather. In typical fashion, the drama caused by the arrival of police vehicles seemed to be causing stranger to speak to stranger, sharing speculation about what was going on up near the swimming pool. Crime was often a wonderful icebreaker.

They drove on and saw a trio of police cars parked up

near the white wall that enclosed the open-air swimming pool. A constable was standing by the wrought-iron gate set into the wall and when he saw Gerry he stood to attention.

'Hope we've not been called out on a wild goose chase. What have we got?' Gerry asked with a hint of impatience. Behind him Wesley tried to peer through the gate. Inside he could make out the unnaturally blue water of the pool and dark uniformed figures gathered around something on the ground.

Wesley looked about. 'Dr Bowman on his way?'

The constable nodded. 'The dead man was floating face down in the pool when he was found. Could have been drunk and fallen in.'

'Any ID on him?'

'There's a wallet and a mobile in his pocket. And he's wearing a suit.' He said this as though a suit was some kind of exotic costume.

Gerry rolled his eyes and looked at Wesley. 'Suppose we'd better make sure there's not a dagger sticking out of his back.'

The constable opened the gate for them to enter the pool area. It opened with a sinister creak and banged shut behind them.

The dead man was lying on the concrete paving slabs and Wesley noticed that the uniforms of two of the officers standing nearby were as sodden as the corpse's dark suit. They had clearly gone in to retrieve the body. He was just glad he hadn't had to do it – but then it was one of the advantages of rank that you could delegate that sort of thing.

'Could have been an accident.' The constable had followed them in and was hovering anxiously behind.

'We'll wait for Dr Bowman's verdict on that,' said Wesley.

The waterlogged contents of the dead man's pockets were lying near the corpse in a clear plastic bag. Wesley put on his crime-scene gloves and picked it up, slid out the wallet and took a look inside. The contents were wet but still perfectly recognisable

Apart from sixty pounds in notes, there were three credit cards in the name of Eric Darwell. An inner pocket contained a driving licence bearing a photograph of the dead man and a Manchester address.

He found some other items snuggling in the inner recesses of the wallet: two supermarket loyalty cards and a library card. There was also a photograph that had been protected by being in a sealed section of the wallet; it was of a smiling woman with a rather prominent chin who appeared to be in her thirties and wore her dark hair short. Another picture showed the same woman with a toddler, a boy, and one more was of the dead man with them both, the three of them smiling happily against a background of a tall Christmas tree. He turned the photo over and saw 'Christmas 2011' written in ballpoint pen on the reverse. He handed it to Gerry.

'Looks as if he's a family man.'

'Greater Manchester Police'll send someone to the address so we'll soon find out.'

'Rather them than me,' Gerry muttered. Wesley knew how he felt. Breaking bad news was something every police officer dreads.

Wesley turned to the constable. 'Does anyone know what he was doing here?'

The constable nodded eagerly. 'I spoke to the girl on

reception and she says he was staying in one of the chalets near the road. She was keeping an eye on him because he's here alone and she thought that was a bit odd. I mean there's a lot of kids here and you can't be too careful, can you.'

'Indeed you can't,' said Gerry, staring down at the body.

'He claimed he was down here for a few days on some sort of business,' the constable chipped in. 'Said he couldn't get a hotel or B&B because of the festival so he asked if they had a vacancy. But Siobhan on reception didn't believe him.'

'Why not?' Wesley asked.

'She didn't say.'

They heard a voice greeting the officer guarding the gate, a good-natured greeting, positively hearty. Colin Bowman had arrived to a fanfare of creaking hinges as the gate was pushed open.

Gerry straightened himself up. 'Hello, Colin. Looks like we've got a drowning. We're busy with this murder down in Tradmouth so if you confirm he fell in the pool by accident after having one over the eight, I'd be eternally grateful.'

Colin donned his surgical gloves and calmly placed his case on the ground. He stood beside Gerry gazing at the body for a while before kneeling down to make his examination. He spent a lot of time loosening the tie and unbuttoning the shirt so that he could assess the neck and chest and then carefully rolled the body on to its side and studied the head. There were a few sighs and tuts as he worked. Wesley and Gerry stood perfectly still awaiting the verdict.

It was five minutes before Colin stood up and took off his gloves. His face was serious.

'You'd better get the area cordoned off as a crime scene, Gerry. Our friend here's had a nasty blow to the back of the head, although it probably wasn't enough to kill him. I won't be able to say anything for certain until I get him on the slab but, in my opinion, it could be suspicious.'

'Better get the team down here then,' Gerry said, nodding to Wesley who proceeded to make the necessary calls.

They left Colin to go about his business. The CSIs and the whole panoply of forensic investigation would be arriving shortly but they had things to do.

The reception office was their first port of call. There they found a young woman with unnaturally black hair and a figure which suggested a passion for junk food. There was a half-eaten doughnut sitting on a plate beside her like an inflated half-moon. Dressed from head to toe in mourning black, she looked up through heavy false eyelashes as they entered.

It was Wesley who did the talking. As the girl, who introduced herself as Siobhan, turned the sign on the glass door to Closed and pulled down the blind, she looked nervous but, in Wesley's experience, a lot of people did when questioned by the police.

'You told one of our officers that the man found in the swimming pool was staying here and that his name was Eric Darwell.'

Siobhan nodded.

'Is there anybody here who'd be willing to identify the body?' Wesley spoke gently. 'The park owner or . . . ?'

'As far as I know he never met him.'

'Did Mr Darwell have a car?'

She consulted a ledger and nodded. Yeah. Here's the

number. Cars for that chalet should be left in car park two, just near the site entrance.'

Wesley called the search team. Someone would have to examine the dead man's car in case he'd left anything in there that might provide information. When he'd finished, he addressed the receptionist.

'Who found him?'

Siobhan swallowed hard. 'I did. The woman in chalet seventy-three lost her purse and I was looking for it. She'd been at the pool yesterday, you see, and I said I'd look in the changing room 'cause it's locked today because of the weather. Anyway, I went into the pool area and there he was just floating there. I've never seen a dead body before and ... Then I ran back here and called the police.'

'Did the dead man always wear a suit?' Gerry asked.

'Yeah. I thought it was a bit odd. But he did say something about being down here on business. And every time I saw him he was carrying a briefcase.'

'Would you be willing to identify him?' he said. He felt reluctant to put the girl through the ordeal but the sooner they had a positive ID the better.

'You don't have to do it if you don't want to, love,' Gerry added. 'But it would be a help.'

Siobhan looked from one policeman to the other, her eyes wide with panic. 'I don't think I could. Can't you get someone else to do it?'

Wesley felt sorry for her and asked if anyone else would be likely to recognise him. The answer was no but she still couldn't bring herself to look at him again. They'd have to rely on the ID from his pocket until the next of kin were informed.

'I believe you've been keeping an eye on Mr Darwell,' said Wesley.

'How did you know that?'

'The constable up at the pool told us. He said you had your suspicions about him.'

'Not suspicions exactly,' she said, twisting the large silver ring she wore round and round nervously on her finger. 'I just thought it was a bit odd. I mean, a man here on his own. We usually get families or couples. Or sometimes groups of friends. And it's half term and the festival so there's lots of kids and ... '

'You didn't believe his story about not being able to find other accommodation? You thought he might have been a paedophile.' Wesley caught Gerry's eye. If this was the case they might be looking for a vigilante or a vengeful parent. Either way, the culprit shouldn't be difficult to find.

'I don't know. I never saw him looking at kids or anything like that but ... '

Wesley understood. In this day and age the public saw child molesters behind ever bush. But if Eric Darwell's tastes lay in that direction, there was sure to be evidence somewhere. And the best place to start was his chalet.

Siobhan showed them the way, walking a little ahead. When she arrived at the small, whitewashed chalet she unlocked the door with her spare key and pushed it open, standing aside so the two detectives could enter. Wesley thanked her and said they could manage.

Before they looked round the dead man's chalet Wesley put in a request for the team to interview everyone in the holiday park in case they'd seen anything. The Manchester address the dead man had provided when he rang to book a week previously matched the one on the driving licence and Gerry made a call that would set the ball rolling with the police up there. All the routine stuff was dealt with. Now it was time to find out all they could about Eric Darwell's life.

The chalet consisted of a compact lounge with a small kitchen area in the corner. There were two bedrooms, one with bunk beds and one with a double, and a tiny bathroom with a bath, basin and lavatory. No shower. The place clearly hadn't been modernised since the 1980s apart from newish floral curtains and a grey cord carpet. It was cheap accommodation for families on a budget. Those who desired luxury went elsewhere.

'No sign of a briefcase,' Wesley observed.

'Killer might have nicked it. Was a chalet key found in his pockets?'

Wesley nodded.

They took a look around the living room but discovered nothing there of a personal nature. The bedroom, Wesley imagined, would be the place he'd keep anything important he'd brought with him. He looked in the small built-in wardrobe, which revealed three clean white shirts as well as a couple of polo shirts and a pair of chinos, presumably for his off-duty hours, making Wesley wonder what the nature of the man's business had been.

Wesley searched through the drawers, pushing underwear aside to examine the furthest recesses.

He reached up and lifted down a suitcase that had been placed on top of the wardrobe. When he laid it on the bed and opened it, he could see something inside. A small box containing a wad of business cards and a few A5 fliers, all bearing the same details.

ED Associates. For all your
confidential investigation needs.
Your confidence is our business.
Reasonable rates.

Wesley's mobile phone rang – a tinny rendition of Mozart's overture to *The Marriage of Figaro*. It was one of the search team and he had news. A rock had been discovered in a herbaceous border just outside the swimming-pool enclosure: a rock that bore traces of blood and hair.

The others had departed at five o'clock, leaving Neil and Dave to their clandestine excavation. They worked quickly, prepared to abandon the trench at the first sign of Butcher's return and pull the tarpaulin over to hide their activities if necessary. But he still hadn't turned up, which was unusual as he called in most days to keep an eye on his investment. At six they took a break to fetch fish and chips from the town because neither of them worked well on an empty stomach, though Neil had wolfed them down so fast that now he had the beginnings of indigestion. He tried to ignore his churning stomach as they dug deeper.

So far they hadn't come across any more bones, nor had they found any pottery or coins that might provide useful dating evidence. In spite of this Neil was determined to carry on until they reached the natural.

'Hey up.'

Neil raised his head. Dave was sitting back on his heels, pointing his trowel at the ground.

Neil hoisted himself upright and shuffled to the other

end of the trench. When he saw what Dave was pointing at, he bent down to get a closer look. Something smooth stood out against the soil, stained yellow-brown like the walls of some old-fashioned pub before the smoking ban came in. The rest of the object was hidden beneath the surface but Neil already knew what it was. He retrieved his trowel and began to help, carefully easing the soil away until the thing was recognisable as a human skull, grinning up at him with empty cavities where the eyes had once been.

'Definitely human,' said Dave. 'We'll have to notify the coroner and the police.'

Neil nodded. He knew the rules only too well. 'Chris Butcher won't be pleased.'

'It might have been found when the builders started digging the foundations for the extension. We've just beaten them to it.'

Neil looked around. The greater section of the garden was still unexcavated. What if there were more graves? What if Chris Butcher had wanted to close the trench down because he'd already suspected what they might find in it?

He took his mobile from his trouser pocket, but before he could make the call he heard the gate open. It was Chris Butcher and he looked worried. More than worried, angry. Neil positioned himself in front of the trench, blocking Butcher's view.

'Something the matter?' Butcher asked.

'You told us not to dig where that bone turned up. Why was that exactly?' said Neil with a new-found boldness, born of having the law on his side.

For once Butcher looked unsure of himself. 'I told you.

I didn't want any holdups. Why? Have you found some more?'

'See for yourself.'

Butcher walked to the edge of the trench slowly, almost reluctantly and stared down at the skull. For a few moments he stood in transfixed silence.

'Did you know it was down there?'

'Of course not.'

'I'll have to report it, you know. It's routine procedure whenever human remains turn up unexpectedly during an excavation.'

Chris Butcher seemed to deflate like a pricked balloon before their eyes. 'Astrid's fed up with the delay already. She's saying I should never have called you in. Can't you pretend you haven't seen it?'

'Sorry, can't do that. And by the way,' said Neil. 'The police were here before, looking for you.'

'They bloody found me,' he said. Butcher left without another word, slamming the gate behind him.

It was almost eight when Wesley called Pam. He hadn't needed to tell her he'd be late; she'd guessed that already. He said he'd be back as soon as he could.

He had been trawling through the witness statements gathered from the Newlands Holiday Park. Predictably nobody had seen anything suspicious, although one or two people had noticed a man in a suit and assumed he was some visiting salesman or something to do with the holiday park's financial side. Nobody had paid the dead man much attention, apart from one particularly observant guest who'd seen him near the car park carrying a black briefcase. The briefcase that hadn't been found either at the scene of his death or in his chalet or car.

Wesley knew that Gerry had already rung Joyce to cancel the meal they'd planned for that evening and that he'd also called Rosie, just to see if she was all right. The call hadn't lasted long and Wesley, who hadn't been able to help overhearing, sensed she'd been short with her father, impatient with what she'd probably interpreted as fussing.

Gerry had received word from Greater Manchester Police that Eric Darwell's widow had been informed. He'd told them they'd travel up tomorrow to speak to her. Darwell's postmortem had been booked for ten o'clock the following morning but they'd have to delegate that to someone else in the team and await the verdict. Wesley was relieved to escape a trip to the mortuary. A long drive north seemed attractive in comparison.

They'd finally managed to contact Kassia Graylem's friend, Lisa, in Didsbury and while Wesley was up in Manchester he planned to pay her a visit. It was about time they made some more progress on that investigation and speaking to someone who knew her might give them the lead they needed.

Gerry emerged from his office and told him to get off home.

Wesley didn't need telling twice. He left the station before Gerry could change his mind.

As he walked home past the Porpoise he thought of Jenny Bercival. The anonymous letters received by her mother were being examined but Forensic were taking their time. He climbed the steps up to Albany Street and trudged up the steep hill. As he passed North Lodge he could see that a light was on in Miles Carthage's first-floor living room. The blind had already been pulled down but Wesley found himself wishing that he could see into the room beyond. He was sure Carthage knew more about Kassia Graylem than he was letting on.

He was halfway up the street when his mobile began to ring. The call was from Neil, and from the urgent note in his voice Wesley knew he had important news.

'Dave and I have found a body.'

Wesley stopped walking and shut his eyes. This was all he needed. 'Tell me more,' he said, dreading the answer. The possibility that the disturbed area of earth in Chris Butcher's garden might be Jenny Bercival's last resting place had already flashed briefly across his mind and his heart started to beat a little faster.

'About three feet down we found more bones, including a skull,' Neil continued. 'I'm calling it in. The coroner's been informed.'

'How long would you say they've been down there?' Neil was used to dealing with ancient skeletons. After all this time he was bound to have a feel for these things.

'Hard to say.'

Wesley was frustrated by the answer. Still, he knew it was often hard to be exact without further tests and detailed examinations.

'There aren't any fillings in the teeth if that's any help. I'd say the skull's female. Probably in her twenties. And, judging by the leg bones we've found, I'd estimate she was about five feet two, give or take an inch or so. We still haven't uncovered the pelvis.'

Wesley did a swift calculation in his head. Jenny Bercival had been five feet four so it was still possible. As for fillings, he'd have to check. Her mother was bound to know.

'I usually like to lift the bones as soon as possible but it's getting dark so we're leaving them in situ tonight. We'll be sleeping in the house so it should be safe enough. I guess your lot might want to take some snaps and send your Forensic people over. I've been on to Sacha Vale, the forensic anthropologist. She'll be here first thing in the morning to have a look.'

'That name seems familiar.'

There was a pause. 'Yeah. They wheel her out on TV when they're trying to bring a touch of glamour to some crumbling bones. You must have seen her. Long red hair. Always simpering at the camera and flirting with the presenter.'

'I know who you mean.' He'd often seen the woman on archaeology programmes and although she seemed to know her stuff he found her irritating, as did Pam. 'Are you still at Butcher's house?'

'Yeah. Fancy coming over to have a look at the bones?'

Wesley hesitated. Pam was expecting him back. On the other hand, a swift look at Neil's discovery wouldn't take long.

He retraced his steps, hurrying down the flight of steps and past the place where Jenny Bercival had last been seen, wondering whether he was finally about to come face to face with her, buried in the cold earth on the banks of the river.

The next morning Wesley awoke at five o'clock, trying not to disturb Pam who appeared to be fast asleep beside him. But as soon as he placed his bare feet on the floor, her eyelids flicked open.

'What time will you be back tonight?'

'We might have to stay over in Manchester. I'll let you know.' Wesley wasn't too pleased about the prospect of spending the night in some soulless chain hotel. He knew exactly what would happen. Gerry would drag him out in search of a decent pub with a bit of character and some beer that hadn't been processed in a chemical works. Then they'd both end up drinking too much and Gerry would get maudlin and start talking about his late wife Kathy and the problems he'd had with Rosie since her mother's death. They'd get to bed far too late and he'd wake up the next morning with a thumping head in a strange bed in a strange room.

Pam, knowing there was nothing she could say, turned over and closed her eyes again.

Wesley hadn't slept well. His mind had been racing, thinking about Neil's discovery. By the time he'd reached Chris Butcher's house the previous evening the light had been fading and when Neil had lifted the tarpaulin aside and shone a torch at the ground the bones had stood out, glowing against the soil in the artificial light. Just before his arrival, Dave had uncovered a pelvis which seemed to confirm the gender. The woman was probably young and approximately Jenny Bercival's height but nothing had been found in the grave to date the burial. No coffin or corroded shroud pins and no convenient pottery or coins in the surrounding soil. It was a clandestine interment which suggested that the woman, whoever she was, was most likely a murder victim. She might have lain there for over six hundred years, or she could have been buried last year. Without dating evidence only science would provide the answer. But science took time and the signs of disturbance in the ground didn't bode well.

After grabbing a slice of toast for breakfast he packed a holdall with a few overnight essentials and as he walked down to the centre of the town the sky was bright, promising a fine day. Tradmouth hadn't yet woken up and the only activity on the river was a pair of homecoming fishing boats chugging upstream laden with lobster pots. Kassia Graylem had died at around this time that Saturday morning, a time when most people wouldn't venture out unless they had work to do. Kassia had last been seen performing at Friday night's Palkin's Musik concert. What had she been doing between then and the time of her death?

Gerry greeted him on his arrival in the CID office. He wore an eager expression as he picked up the small, well-used canvas holdall by his feet.

Wesley told him about Neil's discovery, experiencing a pang of regret that he wouldn't be there to witness Sacha Vale's examination of the bones. Gerry's first question was whether it might be Jenny Bercival but when Wesley replied that they wouldn't know until a battery of tests had been performed, he seemed to lose interest.

'We'd better get off right away, Wes. GMP said that the widow's expecting us around lunchtime. I suggested that we bring her back with us.'

Wesley said nothing. The prospect of a long awkward journey with a grieving woman, minding every word they said, was hardly appealing but it had to be done.

Setting off at seven thirty, Wesley estimated that they should be in Manchester before one. Then just as they were about to leave Gerry received a phone call. He wasn't one of those people who could hide his feelings; like a child, his every emotion showed on his face as he spoke, and today's emotion was disappointment.

He put down the receiver. 'The new chief super wants a meeting. I told her about the Manchester trip and she said you should go with someone else. Sorry, Wes, I really wanted to be in on this but ... '

'No problem,' said Wesley. He looked around the office. Rachel had arrived early and she was already sitting at her desk going through statements. Routine stuff.

'Look, why don't you take Rach with you and I'll be able to attend Darwell's PM with Paul?' Gerry said. 'She might fancy a night in the fleshpots of Manchester.'

Some quiet inner voice, a tiny bat squeak of caution, made Wesley hesitate. Gerry, though, had got the bit between his teeth. 'A break from all this wedding stuff will do her good. She's been looking peaky recently. Probably the stress.'

Gerry strode out into the main office and Wesley watched as he stooped to speak to Rachel. Although it was difficult to gauge her reaction, he saw her nod her head as she began to tidy the papers on her desk.

She said very little as they walked out into the car park to pick up the pool car. She seemed preoccupied and Wesley hoped she might enlighten him during their long journey. He stopped off at the cottage she shared with Trish Walton so she could pack some essentials in case they didn't make it back to Devon that night. The cottage stood down a lane just outside the boundary of the town, near the sign announcing to drivers that they had arrived in Tradmouth. It was whitewashed and pretty but instead of a border of hollyhocks and roses around the door, the tiny front garden was paved over for convenience – the only sign that it was a rented property. After she'd announced her engagement, he'd wondered whether she'd move in with her fiancé, Nigel, whose farm was just outside Neston, hardly far away. As she'd been raised on a local farm, she was accustomed to the agricultural life.

He watched from the driver's seat as she emerged from the cottage, giving the front door a push to ensure that it was locked. She climbed in beside him and gave him a businesslike smile.

'Everything OK?' he asked, more for the sake of something to say than as a genuine inquiry.

'Fine.'

He put the car radio on. Classic FM. Not being sure of her musical taste, he asked her if she'd like something else. But again she said it was fine.

They drove on in silence, stopping only once at the services. Wesley bought a *Guardian*. Rachel used the time to study some case notes.

After Stoke on Trent her silence was beginning to unnerve him.

'Everything organised for the wedding?'

'More or less.'

He hesitated. 'You don't sound too enthusiastic. Most brides get excited at this stage.'

'I'm not most brides.'

'Not having second thoughts?'

She didn't answer; and she didn't speak again until they reached Eric Darwell's semi-detached house in the Manchester suburbs.

Eric Darwell had been stripped of his sodden suit but the faint scent of swimming-pool chlorine still lingered in the air around his body.

Colin Bowman studied the corpse for a while before making his first incision, speaking into the microphone suspended above the table, recording his observations.

Gerry watched as he began to cut into the pale flesh, keeping up a commentary as he always did, happy to answer any question Gerry cared to put to him. Not all pathologists, Gerry knew, were so obliging.

DC Paul Johnson stood by Gerry's side, his six-foot frame towering over his boss as he watched in silence. He didn't avert his eyes as Gerry had expected. Instead he wore an expression of polite concentration, as though he feared Colin would take offence if he wasn't paying attention.

When Colin had finished his work, he gave his verdict. 'As far as I can tell he was stunned by a blow to the head and then he was pushed or he fell into the pool. He was definitely alive when he went in. His lungs are full of water. Poor chap drowned.'

Gerry raised his eyebrows. 'A rock was found with blood and hair on it. It's undergoing tests but we're presuming that's what his attacker used to stun him.'

Colin stood back a little, staring at the dead man's head while he considered the question. 'Unfortunately the water's washed away any small traces the weapon might have left in the wound but a rock would certainly fit with the injuries. As for the stomach contents, he ate something that looks and smells remarkably like a hot dog with mustard a couple of hours before death. And something pink and gooey as well. Could be candyfloss. I'm thinking of the fair at the Palkin Festival.'

'Thanks, Colin. That means he probably went down to Tradmouth shortly before he died. We'll see if we can find him on someone's CCTV.'

'And by the way, he wasn't the healthiest of specimens.

In a few years' time his arteries would have silted up like blocked tunnels. That's what you get from a lifetime of dedicated junk food consumption. If he didn't mend his ways I'd say he would have been dead in ten years at best.' He gave Gerry a meaningful look, as if he wanted him to take his words as a warning.

'Poor sod,' said Gerry with a sigh. He glanced at Paul and saw he was nodding his head in agreement, as solemn as an undertaker on duty.

Gerry's phone rang and he muttered an apology to Colin. After a short conversation he ended the call, an enigmatic smile on his face.

'Everything OK, Gerry?' Colin asked.

'I think so. Remember that girl who went missing last year? Jenny Bercival?'

Colin nodded.

'Her mum's had a couple of anonymous letters claiming that she's alive. I had them sent to Forensic and they say they've come up with something interesting.'

Colin returned to his work. At that moment, with the dead man lying on the table in front of him, missing girls were low on his list of priorities.

Wesley and Rachel arrived at the small red brick semi with the curved bay window. It was a suburban street, slightly run-down with an array of wheelie bins lined up on the pavements. The Darwells' house had clean net curtains at the windows and a neat front garden, still grassed over unlike those of most of the neighbours who'd replaced their tiny lawns with paving.

Wesley recognised Julie Darwell at once from the photograph in her husband's wallet. She was being comforted by a neighbour who told them in hushed tones that the police had been to break the news the evening before. The neighbour was a sensible-looking woman in her sixties with steel-grey hair cut severely short. But her round, plump face was kind and Wesley felt thankful that someone was looking after Eric Darwell's widow who had the devastated look of a woman whose entire world had just collapsed around her. Julie's son, the neighbour explained, was with a friend who had a child the same age. Luckily he was too young to realise what was going on. To him it was just another sleepover.

Rachel sat down beside Julie and Wesley left it to her to break the ice. Somehow she always seemed to find the right words. It was something he'd always admired about her, although he'd never dream of telling her.

He'd seen the same scene so often in the course of his career and it got to him every time. The woman – distraught wife or, worse still, mother – perched on the edge of a sofa, tissue in hand, numbed by shock and grief. Julie Darwell was no exception. The neighbour sat next to her with a protective arm around her shoulder, and before the questions began she shot Wesley a warning look. Be gentle. Don't prod away at wounds that are new and raw.

'I'm so sorry about your husband, Mrs Darwell,' he began. In his mind's eye he could see Eric Darwell's body lying beside the azure pool, his saturated suit draped around him like melting wax. 'You'll understand that we have to ask you a few questions, just so we can get a picture of what Eric was doing down in Devon.'

Julie looked up. Her eyes were bloodshot with crying. 'He went down there for a client.'

'Do you have a name for this client?' Wesley asked, his voice soft, unthreatening. The last thing he wanted was to add to this woman's troubles.

Julie shook her head. 'Sharon'll know. She's his secretary. She deals with all that.'

'ED Associates?'

Julie stared at him, surprised. 'That's right.'

'We found some of his business cards. I take it he's a private investigator.'

'Yes. His office is about a mile away in Didsbury village.' Her eyes began to fill with tears again. 'He said he might be away for a few days. He told me it was just a missing persons inquiry. Routine.'

If the inquiry had led to his murder, it couldn't have been that routine, Wesley thought. But he said nothing. After asking more questions about Eric's life, he looked at his watch. By the time they'd spoken to Sharon at ED Associates and paid Kassia Graylem's friend, Lisa a visit, it would be too late for the long drive down to Devon with Julie. They'd spend the night in some convenient hotel then start back in the morning.

When he offered to take Julie back to Devon she nodded gratefully. She didn't drive, she said, so she'd been worrying about how she was going to get down there. Her friend had offered to have her son, Craig, for as long as necessary so she didn't have to worry about that.

They promised to pick her up the following morning and took their leave before heading for Didsbury; just a short drive down a wide road of council properties and then a right turn down the road leading to the village. From what he'd gleaned many of the Manchester suburbs seemed to be referred to as villages. Once, long ago in the mists of time, they would have been, only to be devoured by an Industrial Revolution that had swallowed the bucolic settlements like a hungry, smoke-belching giant bringing riches to some and despair to many.

ED Associates' office was above a delicatessen on the main street. Wesley saw Rachel stop and gaze at the colourful window display. Cheeses he'd never even imagined existed as well as foods from around the globe. He recognised Caribbean spices and ingredients his mother and grandmother used in their cooking. And the smell wafting from the door reminded him of childhood visits to his parents' native Trinidad, transporting him back for a few short moments to those warm, innocent days.

'Very cosmopolitan,' Rachel said, almost in a whisper, as though she feared the natives would overhear and take her for some country bumpkin.

Wesley didn't answer. In spite of the heavy traffic and diesel-belching buses, this was a pleasant, prosperous suburb. It probably attracted young professionals and academics from the university – people in a hurry – and it reminded Wesley of where he had been brought up in London. And of why he'd chosen to abandon a promising career in the Met's Art and Antiques Squad to make the move to Devon.

At the side of the shop was a glass door etched with the name ED Associates. When Wesley pressed the entryphone they were buzzed in immediately and they climbed a steep, carpeted staircase to the first floor.

Wesley had somehow imagined that a private investigator's office would be a little seedy. Perhaps he'd read too much Raymond Chandler in his youth – a literary phase that had followed his early enthusiasm for Sherlock Holmes. However, here he found no smoke-filled shabby office with a Scotch bottle on the desk; just an overweight middle-aged woman with a floral frock, glasses and a motherly manner. When Wesley asked if she was Sharon she smiled pleasantly as she asked if she could help them. And when Wesley told her what had brought them there her mouth fell open in horror.

Sharon invited them to sit and offered coffee, although she looked as if she could do with something stronger. They sat on a pair of tweed-covered office chairs while she fussed with the filter coffee machine, making a meal of it as if she needed something to occupy her hands while her brain raced ahead.

'I can't believe he's dead.' She sounded stunned. 'Was it an accident?' she asked once the coffee was served.

Wesley caught Rachel's eye. 'We're treating his death as suspicious.'

She gasped. 'No. That can't be right. He was such a nice man. He hadn't an enemy in the world.' Wesley could see tears forming in her eyes. 'How did he . . . ?'

Wesley knew the facts because Gerry had called earlier to deliver Colin's verdict. It was just a case of phrasing it tactfully. 'He was found in a swimming pool at a holiday park near Tradmouth in South Devon. It appears that he was stunned then he fell into the water and drowned. He was staying in a chalet at the holiday park.'

'Yes. I found it for him on the internet. It was the only accommodation available. There's some sort of festival on, I believe.'

Sharon stood up and walked over to the filing cabinet. Her bulk meant that she didn't move fast. She drew out a file and as she passed it to Wesley, he saw that her hands were shaking.

He opened it and saw a photograph of a girl he recognised immediately as a younger Kassia Graylem and his heart lurched. He showed the photograph to Rachel and saw her raise her eyebrows.

'Her name's Kassia Graylem and after her parents died she went to live with her grandmother for a while until she went to study down South. She dropped out of university and there was some sort of argument and they lost touch. Her grandmother discovered that Kassia had moved down to Devon but she didn't know her address so she hired Eric to find her.'

'How did she find out about Devon?'

'I think she met a friend of hers who told her she'd moved there.'

'Is this friend's name Lisa, by any chance?'

'I'm sorry, I don't know. Eric had all the details of the case with him. He always keeps his notes and all that in his old briefcase. You'll find everything in there.'

'His briefcase is missing.'

Sharon shook her head, as though she couldn't quite believe it.

'You've no idea what was in the briefcase? You don't keep copies of documents in the office?'

'That's not how Eric likes ... liked to work.' She thought for a moment. 'He would have had all the notes he'd taken during his interview with Mrs West – that's the missing girl's grandmother – and a copy of the photograph she gave him along with any notes he made about his findings. I'm sorry, I don't know exactly. Eric kept things close to his chest while he was working on a case – until it was time for me to type up the final report. And the invoice, of course. But he did call to say he'd managed to locate the girl and that he was staying on in Devon for a few more days. He didn't say why.'

There was something Wesley had been dying to ask. 'He was wearing a suit when he was found. Did he by any chance mention that he'd arranged a meeting or . . . '

'Eric always wore a suit when he was working. He said it made him feel professional. It was just one of his things.' Sharon smiled fondly. 'Casual clothes make for casual minds, he used to say. He was old-fashioned in some ways but that's not necessarily a bad thing, is it. He was always a gentleman.'

'I'm sure he was,' said Wesley. The tears had begun to roll down Sharon's full, flushed cheeks and she dabbed at them with a crumpled tissue.

'Where does Kassia's grandmother live?'

'Not far from here.'

'Can we have the address?'

'Of course.' Sharon delved into the file and passed them a sheet of paper bearing a neatly typed address. Wesley thanked her and asked if there was anything else she could tell them, however trivial it seemed.

She thought for a while before replying. 'Mrs West was quite anxious to be reconciled with her granddaughter. Perhaps you can help her find Kassia now that Eric's . . . '

Wesley caught Rachel's eye, wondering whether to tell Sharon the truth about Kassia's death. But he decided against it for now. Sharon had had enough shocks for one day.

'How's Julie?' Sharon said suddenly.

'As you'd expect,' said Rachel. 'We're taking her down to Devon tomorrow to make a formal identification of her husband's body.'

Wesley expected a pious comment, an expression of sympathy for the boss's widow. But instead Sharon made a harrumphing sound and looked away.

'I think she's jealous,' Rachel said as they left, letting themselves out of the glass door into the street.

'You mean she fancied Eric Darwell?'

'I reckon it's a classic case of the secretary having the hots for the boss. He probably didn't reciprocate though – not if he was such a gentleman.' She smiled and Wesley was glad she'd lightened the mood. 'Where to now?'

'We'll have a word with Kassia Graylem's friend Lisa first. See what she has to say.'

He took the *A to Z* he'd brought with him from his pocket and opened it at the appropriate page. He found Lisa's address and calculated that it was only five minutes' walk away. 'Kassia's an enigma and we need to find out more about her,' he said. 'All we know about her past is that her parents are dead, she lived with her grandmother for a while then she dropped out of university and ended up in South Devon.'

'You think she was running away from someone or something?'

'Jenny Bercival was involved with a controlling man, according to her cousin. And she and Kassia had the same tattoo. It's possible that they were both killed by the same man. This William maybe?'

Rachel's eyes lit up. 'And don't forget those letters you found in Kassia's room. If she was being threatened maybe Jenny was too.'

They'd rung ahead and when they arrived at Lisa's small red-brick terraced house in a narrow side street she was waiting for them. She was a pretty young black woman who wore her straightened hair long, and as she invited them in she gave Wesley a nervous smile.

Wesley assumed that Lisa didn't know about Kassia's murder so it was up to him to break the news. He had expected her to be shocked; to cry or to react with stunned disbelief. He was surprised when she seemed angry.

'I warned her about him. I bloody warned her. When you find him I hope you'll lock him up for good.'

Sacha Vale was every bit as glamorous in the flesh as she was on the TV screen and Dave appeared to be awestruck at being in the company of a celebrity. Neil, however, was determined to treat her like any other colleague. She might pout and order the other diggers about but he wasn't impressed. In his opinion, she wasn't the best forensic anthropologist he'd worked with. His old colleague Margaret was much more thorough. And Margaret didn't have an attitude that got up his nose. He said as much to Dave when they were alone but Dave jokingly accused him of being jealous. Sacha had the attention, and she was paid more money for her TV appearances in a year than most archaeologists could expect to earn in ten. As well as that, the media hung on her every word. What was there to be jealous of?

They'd excavated around the bones, dislodging them from the earth with a leaf trowel, then Neil had lifted them carefully while Dave and some of the others had begun to extend the trench.

He watched as Sacha examined the bones they'd already found, her russet hair hidden beneath the hood of her protective white suit. After several minutes she looked up at him, a challenge in her wide blue eyes. 'Adult female.

Possibly in her twenties. No dental work. It looks as if she's been in there a long time but sometimes conditions can . . . ' She tilted her head to one side. 'I'll be able to examine the bones more closely in the lab but there are signs of staining on the skull that might suggest asphyxiation. As to when she died, I'll need to take samples for dating. And I'll take a tooth so we can pin down where she grew up.'

She stood up and once she'd walked away from the trench she took down the hood and shook her tresses loose like a model in a shampoo advert.

'Any chance she could be a recent murder victim?'

'Did you find any dating evidence in the trench?'

'The ground's been disturbed at some point but that might have been done when the bungalow was built. There are other areas of disturbance too, probably where services have gone in over the years.' It pained him to admit it, but he hadn't a clue.

He heard Dave calling his name just as the gate creaked and then crashed shut. When he looked round he saw Chris Butcher standing there, his eyes fixed on Sacha, devouring her. He saw her give a nervous half-smile. It was hard to tell whether the pair knew each other but if they didn't Neil guessed that Butcher would soon rectify the situation. He watched as Butcher led her to one side and began to speak to her, too softly to be overheard, and he could see that her cheeks had reddened a little. If Astrid had come in at that moment, Neil thought, she definitely wouldn't have been pleased.

Dave called his name again with a hint of impatience and Neil hurried over to join him.

'Think Butcher's starstruck or what?' he said quietly

when he reached the extended section of the trench where Dave was standing, gazing at the ground. When he didn't answer Neil noticed that the other diggers were staring at the same spot. Neil looked down and saw why. The unmistakable orb of a human skull was starting to emerge.

'Looks like we've found another one,' Dave said.

Chapter 9

Written at North Lodge, Upper Town, Tradmouth this 15th day of February 1895

My sweetest Letty

How your silence disturbs me. It may be that you are unwell. I pray not for I cannot bear the thought.

Josiah is gone from the house again, this time to Exeter to visit the archives there. He does not confide in me but I suspect he searches for documents concerning John Palkin, his great obsession.

Before he left he came to me in my chamber and spoke to me in a way he never has before. He seemed strange, almost bewitched, as he recounted what had befallen John Palkin's first wife Joan Henny. She died in great agony, he said, giving birth to his son. He described how the child was torn from her body and told me to thank the Lord that I have never been with child. His words frightened me for he has never attempted to do that which Mama told us was the duty of a husband towards a wife. Rather he prefers to bind me and hurt me with blows and such delicate cruelty that I am cold with fear whenever I hear his footsteps outside my chamber.

Do I shock you, dear sister? Did you not suspect there was something strange and unnatural about the husband who confines me here like a prisoner?

Maud Cummings watches me still. How I hate her. Oft times I wonder what she is to my husband for I believe she is more to him than just a servant.

I heard noises from the attic last night and saw Cummings climb the little staircase bearing a tray but I could not see what was on it. She did not see me but I am afraid. I suspect she wishes me harm.

Your most loving sister
Charlotte

Wesley saw Rachel listening attentively as though she feared any slight movement would break the spell and render Lisa silent.

'Who do you mean, Lisa?' Wesley said softly. 'Who did you warn her about?'

He could see fury in Lisa's eyes. And frustration, maybe

directed at a friend who hadn't listened to sense and had paid with her life. 'His name was William de Clare. He was quite a bit older than her and she fell for him in a big way.'

'William?'

'That's right.'

'You didn't approve of him?'

'No. I didn't.'

'Why was that?'

'Because she changed when she met him. She became ...' She searched for the word. 'Cowed. As if she was afraid of putting a foot wrong. I used to see her when she came back from uni. Go out for a drink or meet for coffee.'

'What do you do?' Rachel asked.

'I'm at the university here doing a doctorate. Economics. I'm from Manchester originally and I decided to come back.'

'How did you know Kassia?'

'After her parents died she moved in with her gran and we were in the sixth form together. Then I went to uni in Leeds and she went to London. She was studying history. Medieval history.'

'She didn't study music?' Wesley asked.

'No but she was heavily into it. She was a really talented violinist.' She smiled. 'She made quite a bit from busking during the vacations actually and when she was in London she joined an amateur orchestra. She had an old instrument which had belonged to her dad – a viol she said it was. I often wondered why she hadn't opted to go to music college but she said it was more of a hobby.'

'Just before she died she joined an early music group down in Tradmouth in Devon.'

Lisa nodded. 'She would have loved that.'

'When were you last in touch with her?' said Wesley.

'It must be about five months ago. When it was her birthday last November I sent a card to the last address I had for her in London. I let her have this address and asked her to keep in touch and I did get a card on my birthday in January with a note saying she was about to move to South Devon and that she'd let me have her address once she'd settled in. But I never heard from her again after that.'

'That's how we found you. She kept the birthday card you sent her – she must have taken it with her when she moved.'

A slight smile appeared on Lisa's lips, as though the thought touched her. Then the smile vanished.

'I was worried about her.'

'Why?'

'Because she changed when she met William. I sometimes went down to London in those days and we'd meet up. But once he'd really got his claws into her she kept putting me off. I've heard some men like to take women away from their friends so they can have them to themselves. Control them.' She shuddered.

'And you think that was happening to Kassia?'

'Yes. I saw it once with someone else I knew. It made me angry. I suppose I was annoyed with Kassia for letting it happen.' She shrugged her shoulders. 'But there was nothing I could do about it. In the end it was her choice.'

'Did you say anything? Try to make her see sense?' Rachel asked. Wesley could sense her disapproval.

'Of course I did but she wouldn't listen.'

'So she dropped out of university after her second year?

Do you know what she did between then and the time she moved to Devon?'

'I'm afraid not. We lost touch for a while. In fact I'm surprised my card got to her. I thought she might have moved in with William but I could be wrong. If she'd sent me her new address in Devon I would have written and tried to catch up but . . . '

'Did you ever meet William de Clare?' asked Wesley. If this man was responsible for Kassia's death, a decent description would help them no end.

But Lisa shook her head. 'I wouldn't know him from Adam. Do you think he killed her?'

Wesley didn't answer the question. 'Do you know what he did for a living?'

'I've no idea but I think he was well off. Maybe that's what she saw in him. Although I wouldn't have said she was the mercenary type.'

Wesley knew from long observation of human nature that even the least materialistic of souls can have their heads turned when the realities of wealth sink in. The comfort of good hotels, the ease of first-class travel, all those tempting trappings that one wouldn't necessarily miss until they were gone. Kassia was probably no exception, although there was no evidence that she'd benefited in that way, not while she was living at Bolton Hall with Scarlett and Pixie.

'I take it he had a car. Did she mention what kind?'

'No. She wasn't really into cars. She didn't really say much about him at all, come to think of it. Just how wonderful he was. Not that I think the way he treated her was very wonderful. Creepy if you ask me. If any guy treated me like that . . . '

'What do you mean?' Rachel asked. Wesley could tell she was preparing to bristle with feminist indignation.

'He used to insist she wore clothes he'd chosen. He even bought her this gorgeous medieval gown – blue velvet. She was really thrilled with it. Tried it on for me once. That must have been the last time I saw her, just before she dropped out of university,' she said. 'It was made properly, like a theatrical costume.'

'She was wearing it when she was found,' Wesley said softly.

Lisa said nothing for a few seconds. Then she looked Wesley in the eye. 'Look, I'm really sorry I can't tell you more but, like I said, she kept him well away from me. I think he was one of those guys who didn't like his woman having any life of her own. He wanted to own her.'

'Maybe the relationship turned sour,' said Wesley.

'It probably wouldn't have taken much with someone like that.'

Wesley saw the gleam of nascent tears in her dark brown eyes.

'What do you know about her family?'

'She lived with her gran but I don't think they got on too well.'

'What about her parents?'

'They died in some sort of accident when she was fifteen. She never spoke about them.'

Wesley caught Rachel's eye. This matched Scarlett Derringer's story.

'You don't know why she decided to move to Devon?'

'She used to talk about the Southwest sometimes. Said she'd been happy there when she was a kid. I asked her how long she'd lived there and she said she hadn't really lived anywhere. I thought it was a funny thing to say.'

'Did she ever mention Tradmouth? Or the Palkin Festival?'

Lisa pulled a tissue from her pocket and dabbed her eyes. 'The name Palkin rings a bell. Maybe it was something this William was into. I wish now that I'd taken more notice of what she told me. But, to tell you the truth, I was disgusted with the whole situation so I tried not to pay much attention to what she said about him. I'm sorry.'

'Quite understandable,' said Wesley. He knew it was natural to blot out the unpalatable, to ignore the sordid details of a friend's path to self-destruction.

Lisa stood up and went to a cupboard by the fireplace. She opened the cupboard door and took out a photograph album. After selecting a page she placed it in Wesley's hand. 'That's us, me and Kassia.'

Wesley looked at the photograph. Two laughing teenage girls, arms linked, standing in a sunny pub garden, raising their glasses to the unseen photographer. The image made Wesley feel unbearably sad. The last time he'd seen that face, those generous lips had been contorted in pain and the smiling eyes had been pecked at by hungry gulls.

'I hope you find who killed her, I really do,' Lisa said in a whisper.

Wesley handed the album back to her. It was time to visit Kassia's grandmother.

Wesley was glad that Rachel was there beside him as he steered the car towards Mrs West's house. She was good with grieving relatives; calm and sympathetic. He himself was dreading the encounter, and yet he was interested in why grandmother and granddaughter had lost touch. However, he'd given up wondering about the strange ways of families years ago.

From Didsbury village they drove down a wide road lined with large Victorian villas, mostly converted into flats. The area where Mrs West lived had clearly been prosperous in Manchester's heyday when cotton had been king, but in recent years it had become the haunt of students after cheap rented flats. There had been an effort to make the district vibrant and Wesley noticed an array of bistros, galleries and takeaways on the main street.

Mrs West lived down a side street of tall Victorian terraced houses but her house was one of a pair of 1960s semis squeezed between their loftier neighbours.

They climbed out of the car and a few seconds after Wesley rang the doorbell, the glazed front door opened to reveal an elderly woman with dyed black hair showing grey at the roots. She wore a trouser suit that would have been fashionable in the 1980s and her pencilled eyebrows and heavy make-up only served to emphasise the deep lines on her face.

She peered at Wesley over her glasses and as soon as he introduced himself her eyes focused beyond him on the car. 'You haven't come in a police car. How am I supposed to know you're who you say you are?'

Wesley held out his warrant card. She took it from him and examined it closely, comparing the photograph with Wesley's face. She didn't bother with Rachel's.

'You'd better come in,' she said after a while. 'What's this about?'

'Can we sit down?' Rachel's voice was soothing. The voice she used to break bad news.

The first thing Wesley noticed about Mrs West's living room was that it was surprisingly modern with sleek, pale furniture and a large abstract rug on the wooden floor. The pictures were frameless canvases, close-ups of flowers. A perfumed candle burned on the sideboard giving off a heady odour that made the room oppressive. There were no photographs. No memories of Kassia.

Mrs West invited them to sit and sank down on the chair opposite, her head tilted slightly as she waited for them to speak. Wesley allowed Rachel to explain why they were there. He watched the woman's reaction, surprised when, after an initial gasp of shock, she swiftly rearranged her features into an emotional blank.

'Thank you for telling me,' she said formally, staring ahead.

'I'm very sorry for your loss, Mrs West,' said Wesley. 'Would you like us to contact anybody or —'

'I'm quite all right, thank you.'

Wesley waited a few moments before asking the next question. 'You hired a private investigator to find your granddaughter?'

The woman looked a little sheepish, as though Wesley had spoken of some embarrassing weakness. 'I thought I'd better try to trace her. We'd parted on bad terms and . . . '

'Why was that?' Rachel asked.

'She'd left university. Never finished her degree. It was such a waste. She'd become involved with some man, not that she ever told me anything. She was wasting her life. Throwing away her opportunities. I wish I'd had her chances, I really do.'

Wesley listened to her chattering on in the same vein for a few minutes, almost as though she hadn't taken in the enormity of the news.

'I blame my daughter,' she continued. 'She went off with that Jake, sailing round on that boat like a pair of gypsies. Kassia never went to a proper school until she came up here to live with me.'

'Do you know anything about the man Kassia was involved with?' Rachel asked.

'Only that she met him in London when she was at university. I don't think he was a student. I think he was older. But she never confided in me. We were never really close.' Wesley detected a wobble in her voice, as if the shell was beginning to crack. 'Did she suffer?'

'I don't think so,' Wesley lied. The truth seemed pointless.

'Do you know who did it?'

'Not yet. But we will. I believe her parents were killed in an accident. It must have been a terrible time for you.'

She bowed her head. 'I'd just lost my husband and the last thing I needed was a difficult teenager about the place, staying out late and worrying me sick.'

There was an awkward silence. Then Wesley asked a question. 'What was Kassia like?'

Mrs West looked up, as though his voice had shocked her out of a trance. 'She liked to wear her hair like the girls in those Pre-Raphaelite paintings in the City Art Gallery. Didn't live in the real world if you ask me. But that was how she'd been brought up. All that airy-fairy hippy stuff.'

'What about her parents' accident? Can you tell us what happened?'

'There was a gas leak on their boat. Jake and Linda – that's my daughter – went on board and they think Jake lit a cigarette. That was typical of him – always smoking, he was. There was an almighty bang and ... '

169

'You blame Jake for what happened?'

'Of course I do. I don't know what Linda saw in him. But she was stubborn. She wouldn't listen to sense.'

'And Kassia came to you after her parents were killed?'

'I had to take her in. She had nobody else. She was in a terrible state. I didn't know what to do with her for a while.'

'Did the private investigator, Mr Darwell, report back to you at all?'

She nodded. 'He said he'd found her. He'd seen a picture of her in a programme for some festival.'

'Do you know if he actually met her?'

'If he had, he hasn't mentioned it to me.'

'Did he tell you anything else?'

'Only that he was following a new lead and that he'd be in touch as soon as he knew more.'

'Any idea what this new lead might have been?'

'I've no idea and I'm still waiting to hear from him. I wonder what he's playing at.' She looked at Wesley accusingly. 'You haven't spoken to him, have you?'

Wesley caught Rachel's eye. There was no avoiding the truth. 'I'm sorry to have to tell you that Mr Darwell was found dead yesterday,' he said gently.

Mrs West's hand went to her mouth. 'Oh no. Poor Mr Darwell. He was such a nice man.'

Wesley waited for the news to sink in before speaking again.

'Do you mind if we talk about Kassia? You said she was musically talented. Before she died she was playing the viol in an early music group.'

'Jake was a musician.' She wrinkled her nose at the mention of Kassia's father, as if she found the memory of the man distasteful. 'It was him who chose her name. Kassia of

170

Constantinople was a ninth-century female composer – a Byzantine nun. I thought it was a bit pretentious myself. He used to take her busking with him. Begging for money,' she added with distaste.

'How did you know she was in Devon?'

'I met an old school friend of hers in Didsbury village. Lisa. Nice girl. She said Kassia had written her a note saying she intended to move to South Devon. That's all I had to go on.'

'Have you ever heard the name William de Clare?'

She shook her head. 'Is that him? Is that the man who killed her?'

'We don't know that.'

Wesley could see that her eyes were glazed with tears. 'I know we had our differences but she's my only grandchild.'

The veneer of control broke and she began to sob, her shoulders shaking as tears and mucus ran down her face, mingling with her foundation and eyeshadow to form rivulets of colour. Rachel hurried over to sit on the sofa beside her, placing her arm around the woman's shoulders and handing her a wad of tissues from the padded box on the side table. 'Is there anyone who can stay with you? A neighbour or a relative?'

She gave the name of a neighbour, another widow who lived a few doors down. Another survivor of the old days before the street had become home to a transient population. Wesley left Mrs West with Rachel and went to the hall where he found an address book by the telephone. Luckily the neighbour answered after the second ring and said she'd be round right away. Wesley was glad she hadn't asked too many questions.

Before they left Rachel asked Mrs West if she wanted to

171

travel down to Devon with them and Mrs Darwell the next morning. She declined, saying she couldn't face it.

Wesley didn't blame her.

After Wesley's call came in, Gerry Heffernan sat at his desk contemplating the news. Kassia Graylem's friend, Lisa, had said she'd been involved with a man called William de Clare. It sounded like a name from a medieval tale. Or the Shipworld website. Wesley had reminded him that, according to Jenny Bercival's cousin, she too had been involved with somebody called William. It was a tenuous connection, but even so it was one.

He asked one of the DCs to trace anyone of that name who might fit the bill and he'd also asked her to find out whether it was the name of one of the Shipworld characters. It was worth checking.

Wesley had also mentioned that he'd had a call from Neil to say that more human remains had been found during his excavation next to the house recently purchased by Chris Butcher; Chris Butcher whose company ran the website that appeared to have inspired Kassia's killer. The coroner had been informed about the bones and a couple of DCs had gone down there to deal with it. But Gerry could tell that Wesley was itching to get back from Manchester and see for himself. He had heard the disappointment in Wesley's voice. Gerry hoped the two sets of bones wouldn't add to their workload.

Gerry was frustrated that there was still no sign of Dennis Dobbs. All patrols were on the lookout for him and he had to be somewhere; Gerry just wished he knew where. Perhaps they should put more pressure on Jason Teague, he thought. But when he'd sworn that he didn't know where Dobbs was, somehow Gerry had believed him.

He looked at his watch. Five o'clock. The day was still young. He was already hungry and he began to wonder which takeaway he was going to patronise that night. In the meantime, he had a problem; something he'd put off dealing with because he wasn't quite sure how to go about it. He'd received a call from Forensic earlier that day while Colin had been conducting Eric Darwell's postmortem, to say that when they'd examined the anonymous letter received by Mrs Bercival they'd found that it bore the indentations of another letter written on the sheet of paper above it on the writing pad. An hour later they'd e-mailed the results over.

He'd asked Trish to print out the e-mail for him. When he read it, the contents were quite unexpected; however, the more he thought about it, the more it made some sort of sense.

He was just contemplating the dilemma when his phone rang again. When he answered it he heard a man's voice, the accent European, possibly Spanish. The caller introduced himself as Captain Garcia, the master of the *Maudelayne*. Something had been found on board the cog, something that might be linked to the death of the girl in the dinghy.

Gerry thanked him and said someone would be round as soon as possible. The captain hadn't been specific but for him to take the trouble to call, whatever it was must be important.

He surveyed the CID office, which was still buzzing with activity. The team were working to trace Dennis Dobbs and eliminate every William de Clare who fell into the right age group and might conceivably have been in London at the appropriate times. No wonder everyone looked overworked and harassed.

He rose from his seat and made his way over to the noticeboard where he called for attention and spouted what he considered to some inspiring words of encouragement to his troops before leaving the office. He would pay the *Maudelayne* a visit, then after that he'd call on Mrs Bercival and pick up some fish and chips on the way back. Nobody could say it wasn't an efficient use of police time.

When he reached the embankment he saw the cog bobbing at anchor, timbers creaking with each movement of the tide. The gangplank was still in place and a dozen or so visitors were waiting in line to go on board to take a look around. Gerry had been eager to board the vessel ever since she'd sailed into port with her great square sail raised to catch the breeze. Today the massive sail was neatly furled away and the supporting rope shrouds ran taut from the deck to the top of the great mast like the well-ordered webs of some monstrous spider.

In Tradmouth's heyday, the quayside would have been crammed with vessels like this, loading and unloading their cargos. And in times of war, the purpose of the cogs would change and they would bristle with the arms needed to take on their French counterparts which prowled the Channel, concealed by banks of fog, waiting to slip into the river and attack the town.

Gerry took his warrant card from his jacket pocket. What was the use of having the might of the law behind you if you couldn't jump the queue? There was a fair-haired young man on the deck dressed as a medieval sailor, guarding the rope barrier and ensuring that only a few visitors were allowed on at a time. He looked the clean-cut type, more at home on the sports field than strutting around in tights. Gerry wormed his way to the front of the queue, apologising good-naturedly. 'Sorry, love. Sorry, mate. Police. Can I just . . .'

When he reached the foot of the gangway, he shouted up, displaying his warrant card like a shield. 'Police. I'm here to see Captain Garcia.'

The rope barrier was unhooked and Gerry clambered aboard, taking in every detail of the rigging with undisguised admiration. Whoever had built this accurate replica had performed a labour of love.

'Sure. If you'd like to come this way.' The young man's accent was American, which surprised Gerry slightly.

'You been on crowd control all day then?'

The man looked puzzled. 'Pardon me?'

Gerry nodded towards the queue of people, some of whom were watching intently, hoping for a vicarious sniff of drama.

'Only a couple of hours. Captain's cabin's this way.'

Gerry was led below deck, bowing his head to avoid the low ceiling. It smelled of new wood down here, even though the ship was at least ten years old and the claustrophobic darkness was relieved by flickering candles. At first Gerry thought they were real then he realised they were electric imitations to limit the risk of fire.

Here and there visitors stumbled around, the children silenced by the gloom, the adults speaking in hushed voices as if they were in a church. The creaking was louder here and the deck shifted rhythmically beneath their feet. But Gerry felt quite at home.

The captain's cabin was at the aft of the ship. The

American knocked and after a few moments the door opened.

The man standing there was probably in his forties with black hair that was turning white at the temples, and he had something that the DCI recognised immediately: authority, a presence that couldn't be ignored. When Gerry introduced himself the man held out his hand. 'Sebastian Garcia,' he said. 'We spoke on the phone earlier.'

'Good to meet you, Captain,' said Gerry, shaking the man's hand heartily. 'You said you'd found something?'

'That's right. The police came on board asking if anyone had seen anything of that poor girl whose body was found in the dinghy. Nobody had but ... ' He paused and made his way over to a cupboard that had been built in beneath the tall bed. From here he took out a case, black and somewhat battered and slightly larger than a violin case. He passed it to Gerry.

'The news bulletins said she was a violinist and that her instrument was missing. One of my crew found this pushed into the bushes near the public lavatories by the Memorial Gardens. He took it and hid it in his cabin but the man he shares with found it and brought it to me. I've already had a word with him,' he added ominously. 'I suppose you'd like to see him.'

Gerry nodded and the captain poked his head out of the cabin door and shouted to some unseen person to tell Andre Gorst he was wanted in the captain's cabin. Now.

As they sat down and waited Gerry began to talk about the ship, modestly outlining his own sailing credentials. Garcia related how the *Maudelayne* had been built in Bristol to celebrate the Millennium and travelled around the coast for events throughout most of the year and how the Palkin Festival had been a regular booking since 2010. Garcia had been involved in the project from the beginning and had taken over as master in 2008. The cog was his life, he said. A dream come true.

After about ten minutes there was a knock on the cabin door and a young man burst in. 'I can't find Andre. Someone said he went ashore earlier. Must have been just after I found that violin.'

The captain stood up, looming over Gerry. 'He's supposed to be on board.'

The young sailor gave an apologetic shrug, palms upward. 'I've looked everywhere. He hasn't come back.'

'Do you know where he was on Saturday morning first thing?' Gerry asked.

'He was on shore leave,' Garcia replied. He looked at the sailor. 'You share a cabin with him. Have you any idea . . . ?'

He shook his head. 'I don't know. I spent the night ashore too – my family live in Morbay.'

Gerry turned to Garcia. 'Tell me about Andre Gorst.'

'He's been with me three years but I wouldn't say I know him well. I've heard he's one for the ladies. Likes his shore leave.'

'Girl in every port?'

'He's certainly got one here at the moment,' the cabin-mate said with a nervous glance at the captain. 'Keeps slipping off to meet her.'

'Did he say anything about the instrument case you found?'

'I asked but he told me to mind my own business. I heard the police were looking for it so I took it to the captain. Haven't seen Andre since.'

Gerry produced a picture of Kassia and handed it to the sailor. 'Recognise her? Ever seen her with Gorst?'

'Sorry. No,' he said. Gerry gave it to the captain who shook his head.

'You say you've been here for the Palkin Festival for the past few years,' Gerry said as Garcia handed the picture back. 'That means you were in port last year when a girl called Jenny Bercival disappeared.' He watched the captain's face carefully. All the animation had vanished, to be replaced by a blank expression that was impossible to read.

'Yes, we were in Tradmouth then. But the name means nothing to me.'

'Was Andre Gorst here too?'

'As I said, he's been a member of my crew for three years.'

'I need a photograph of him. And as soon as he comes back you call me or one of my team. Day or night.' He handed the captain his card. 'Where are you headed when you leave Tradmouth?'

'London. St Katharine Docks. We spend a lot of time there. The *Maudelayne*'s a great attraction.'

'Thanks,' said Gerry, his mind working. 'And as well as the picture of Gorst can you give me a list of all the present crew members who were with you when you visited Tradmouth last year. I'll send someone round to get it and pick up the viol. And we'll need the fingerprints of everyone who's touched it for elimination purposes.' He gave the captain a businesslike smile which wasn't returned. A hint of annoyance appeared in the man's eyes but, like most sensible people, he was wise enough to suppress it in front of a police officer.

As he left the cog and headed inland to Mrs Bercival's

rented cottage, Gerry experienced a fresh thrill of hope. They now had a suspect who'd been in possession of Kassia's missing instrument and surely it wouldn't be long till he was found and brought in.

Gerry hadn't called ahead so Mrs Bercival wasn't expecting him. When she opened the door and recognised him, her lips parted with a half-formed question, her eyes shining with hope. He felt bad about what he had to do.

'Can I have a word, love?'

'You've found Jenny?'

'Sorry, love. No news yet. But we're doing all we can.' It was the most reassuring phrase he could come up with on the spur of the moment.

The hope in her eyes vanished and she stood aside to let him in, her head bowed in disappointment.

He made himself comfortable on the sofa in the small living room and she sat down opposite him, perched on the edge of the armchair, nervously twisting the wedding ring she still wore round and round.

'Our Forensic people examined that last letter you received,' he said, lowering his voice. 'Someone had written on the sheet of paper above it and left an indentation.' He fished the printed e-mail from his inside pocket and began to read. '"Dear Jill, just a note to thank you for the lunch yesterday. Life has been so difficult since Jenny's disappearance and it was so thoughtful of you. With warmest regards, Tessa." Your London address is at the top.'

While he was reading she'd buried her face in her hands. But now she looked up, her eyes glazed with tears. 'I thought you'd forgotten about Jenny. I needed to do something to make you reopen the case.'

'We've never closed it, love,' Gerry said gently. 'It's just that there haven't been any leads. You really shouldn't have done this, you know. I could charge you with wasting police time.'

Her eyes widened in alarm. In her desperation, this possibility hadn't occurred to her.

'I could charge you but I won't. Not if you promise never to pull a stunt like this again.'

She nodded vigorously.

He touched her arm. 'I swear that we haven't forgotten Jenny. And if anything comes up you'll be the first to know.' He gave her what he hoped was a sympathetic smile and stood up. 'I'll put the kettle on shall I?'

As he made for the kitchen he was glad some of his colleagues hadn't been there to see him. There'd always be some who said he was a soft touch.

As Wesley had predicted, it was a soulless chain hotel in some anonymous suburb on the outskirts of Manchester and it was coming up to seven o'clock when they arrived at a reception which resembled a small regional airport check-in area. Two singles. Mr Peterson and Ms Tracey. The girl behind the desk didn't look much older than sixteen and she made the words sound almost suggestive.

Wesley was slightly surprised to discover that their rooms were adjoining and Rachel gave him a nervous smile as she unlocked her door. After agreeing to meet in the bar at eight, Wesley did likewise and shut his door behind him. He suddenly felt exhausted after a day of driving and interviewing the bereaved. Until now he hadn't realised how much emotional energy he'd used up.

He called Pam. She sounded cheerful. She'd seen his

sister, Maritia, and the new baby and Michael had spent the day at his friend's. It was impossible to move in town for the bloody festival but, apart from that, all was well in Tradmouth – in the Peterson household at least.

Gerry had called to say that Kassia's viol had turned up on the medieval ship moored up by the embankment and that the sailor who claimed to have found it – a man called Andre Gorst – had gone AWOL. He'd also pointed out that the ship had been in Tradmouth when Jenny disappeared. Gerry said he'd let him know the minute Gorst returned. It was a promising lead and Wesley wished he was there to follow it up.

Gerry also told him about Mrs Bercival's deception over the anonymous letters, making excuses for the woman, saying she'd done it out of desperation. He didn't intend to charge her with wasting police time, not under the circumstances. Wesley agreed with him, although he suspected Rachel probably wouldn't.

Rachel was waiting in the bar. To Wesley's surprise she'd changed her clothes, swapped her dark trouser suit for a short skirt and pink T-shirt. She already had a glass of white wine on the table in front of her, almost finished. Wesley brought her up to date with the latest developments in the case before asking if he could get her another drink. She didn't react as he'd imagined to the news about Mrs Bercival. She made no comment and he knew there was something on her mind. Once they had their drinks in front of them, he asked her if something was wrong. He reckoned he'd known her long enough for the question not to be interpreted as prurient curiosity. He was a concerned friend, that was all.

She took a long sip of wine. 'I don't know what to do, Wes.'

He waited for her to continue in her own time.

'I can't go through with the wedding. It's all got out of hand.'

He could see tears forming in her eyes. 'How do you mean?'

'I like Nigel. He's . . . ' She searched for the right word. 'Solid. Reliable.'

'Unimaginative?'

'I didn't say that.' She suddenly sounded defensive.

'You didn't have to. Nigel's a farmer. A practical man. What you see is what you get with Nigel and, believe me, that can be a good thing. I know he'll do his best to make you happy.'

She drained her glass. Wesley thought that she was drinking too fast. He'd never seen her do that before.

'Don't tell me it's just last minute nerves because—'

'I wouldn't dream of it,' Wesley said quickly. The last thing he wanted was an argument.

'I need another drink.'

'We should find somewhere to eat.' He stood up. 'There's a place down the road that looks reasonable.'

She didn't move. She looked up at him and held out her hand. 'Pam doesn't know how bloody lucky she is.' The innocent-sounding words carried an intensity that surprised him.

For a moment he searched for something to say, something to lighten the atmosphere. But everything he came up with either seemed trite or would be guaranteed to make matters worse. He eventually decided on, 'I'm sure she does. And I'm a lucky man,' said in a throwaway, half-jocular tone.

'You don't really believe that, do you?'

'Let's get something to eat.' He began to make for the door, hoping she'd follow. Maybe, he told himself, she just needed to talk things over. But her comment about Pam had made him uncomfortable. The fact that he had once been attracted to Rachel niggled at the conscience honed by the strict moral upbringing provided by his Caribbean parents. It was something he'd chosen to ignore over the years. Perhaps, he thought, he should have brought somebody else with him to Manchester.

He turned and saw that she was following, head bowed. He told himself firmly that he would provide a sympathetic ear. Anything else was out of bounds.

The restaurant, set in the middle of a row of shops, was Italian with laminated menus and Neapolitan love songs belting out from the speakers. The waiters appeared at first sight to be authentic but Wesley harboured the suspicion that once they finished their shifts the Italian accents would disappear and they'd revert to broad Manchester vowels. He ordered a cannelloni and Rachel a linguini dish. She hadn't taken much time to make her choice, almost as though she'd lighted on the first thing on the menu that caught her eye. She insisted on a bottle of wine to wash it down. As the waiter was hovering by the table, Wesley felt he had no choice but to agree.

Once their food was in front of them, Wesley attempted to return the conversation to work matters, moving on to speculation about the missing sailor Andre Gorst. Jenny and Kassia had an image of the ship tattooed on their shoulders and Gorst had been in possession of Kassia's viol. He had to be a serious suspect.

Rachel sat playing with her linguini, twisting it to and fro on her fork. 'He could even be William de Clare,' she said. 'We might have found our killer.'

'So you think Jenny Bercival's definitely dead?'

She didn't answer.

'Jenny and Kassia are both the same physical type,' he continued. 'And they both disappeared at the Palkin Festival so I'm becoming more and more convinced that there's a connection.' He paused. 'I get the feeling your mind's not on this investigation.'

She raised her eyes to his. 'I don't know what to do, Wes.'

'I can't make up your mind for you. But I'd say that if you're not certain about the wedding, you shouldn't go through with it.'

Her eyes lit up with fresh hope. 'You really think so?'

'It's not up to me. It's about what you want.' Rachel's words had sounded a warning. There had been a time once when he'd have found her assumption flattering, even desirable. But since then life had become more settled. He had changed over the years; and so had Pam. He suddenly realised with horror that he might be hurtling headlong towards smug, comfortable middle age.

Rachel pushed her plate away. 'Let's go for a drink.'

'I've had enough and we've got an early start in the morning. Don't forget we're taking Julie Darwell back to Devon. I'll get the bill.'

He stood up but Rachel remained seated, staring at her glass as though she was willing it to be filled by magic. He waited, uncertain what to do. It hardly seemed appropriate to pull rank. Anyway, it wasn't really his style.

He remained by the table, unwilling to leave her on her own in a strange place in the state she was in. He recognised the signs, the determination to drown your troubles in a bottle. He'd never seen Rachel like this before and it disturbed him. Eventually he left her sitting there and went to the bar to pay the bill.

When he returned to the table she looked up hopefully. 'I noticed a pub on the next block. Just one drink?'

Against his better judgement he agreed. Just one. He was about to say 'then bed' but he stopped himself, fearing the words would be misinterpreted. As they walked to the bar she linked her arm through his. He felt the pressure of her hand as she gave his arm a squeeze. The natural gesture between friends didn't seem right somehow. Or maybe it did, and that was why his heart was pounding.

Jason Teague felt resentful that there was still no sign of Den Dobbs. Someone had spotted the *Queen Philippa* near where the girl's body was found and Den had left him to deal with the fallout. It wasn't part of their agreement.

It was getting late and he'd tried Den's mobile number countless times, always getting his voice mail. He'd lost track of how many messages he'd left.

He left the comfort of the Tradmouth Arms and began to stroll along the embankment. News of the murder was everywhere but it hadn't disrupted the festival. Why should it? The festival-goers hadn't known her. She was nothing to them. But he'd seen the small pile of cellophane-wrapped flowers left at the embankment end of the jetty as a tribute. Somebody had noted her violent death. Somebody had cared.

His mobile rang and he stopped, taking it out of his pocket. His fingers felt clumsy all of a sudden and he almost dropped the thing.

He looked at the display and smiled to himself: this was the call he was waiting for. After a brief conversation he turned to his left and headed towards the Memorial Gardens, pushing his way through the crowd, making for his mate Jonathan's office. He needed to charter a boat for the next day.

Rosie Heffernan had begged her brother not to let on to their dad that she was staying with him. But Sam reckoned that if Rosie was in trouble then summoning help could hardly be a betrayal of trust. And their father was a DCI so he was used to sorting out problems.

However Sam decided to delay making the call until he heard what Rosie had to say for herself.

When he got back to the cottage at nine she was there in the living room, sitting on the sofa watching something inane on the TV. She looked round as she heard the door shut and smiled.

'When's Freya due back?'

'She's not. As from today she's on nights.'

'I thought I might have driven her away.' She didn't sound at all repentant about the possibility.

'Not at all. But when are you going back to your flat?'

'Maybe tomorrow.'

'Look, if someone's bothering you, you should let Dad know.'

'And have him fussing about? I can take care of myself.' She paused. 'Anyway, I went to a rehearsal today and everything was fine so I've probably been panicking for nothing.'

'What are you planning to do once half term's over and you're back at school? You can't hide forever.'

'I won't have to,' she said with confidence. 'He'll have gone by then. There's another Palkin's Musik concert tomorrow night. Will you meet me afterwards.'

Sam sighed. From childhood she'd always been able to persuade him to do things against his better judgement, playing on his fears and sympathy. He knew he'd do as she asked. He didn't have a choice because if anything happened to her he couldn't live with himself.

'Who is it, Rosie? Who are you scared of?'

For the first time in years he saw his sister burst into tears.

Chapter 10

John Palkin married his second wife, Alice Trencham, in 1386. Little is known about Alice other than that she was an heiress of considerable fortune whose father had died some two years before her marriage. I have seen contemporary documents of a domestic nature relating to her estate near Whitely which suggest that Palkin was entertained there on several occasions. On one of these occasions I imagine that he proposed marriage. To Alice, he must have seemed like a good prospect being Tradmouth's principal citizen and the holder of great wealth. When they married her inheritance was added to his fortune, money begetting money as it surely does, but after the wedding her estate was placed in the hands of a steward and Alice vanishes from the records until her death in 1388 when her will leaves her soul to Almighty God and all her earthly possessions to her husband.

A letter written by John Palkin states that his wife died of a fever at her house in Whitely. There is no record of her burial at the parish church there ... or indeed in any other nearby parish.

Neil had carefully uncovered the second skeleton the evening before, each stage being recorded for posterity by the photographer and an officer taking video footage. Colin Bowman had come to view the skeletons and in Neil's opinion Sacha Vale had been quite rude to him. She was full of herself, he thought. What was worse, she probably believed her own publicity.

Chris Butcher had stayed to watch, whispering to Sacha as if they were old friends sharing a secret. There was no mistaking the fact that he was flirting with her, and that she seemed quite pleased about it.

Dave had resumed work at the other end of the site with the rest of the team, leaving Neil to deal with Sacha and the bones. Neil felt slightly envious because they had found more nice medieval walls near the boundary with the road and some well-preserved coins dating to the reign of Richard II. He wanted to be back at the centre of things.

It was ten in the morning and now the circus of the crime-scene investigation had left for the time being, he had a chance to think. He was beginning to form a mental picture of what the site had looked like back in the Middle Ages. There would have been a tall house, probably three storeys if Tradmouth's surviving medieval houses were anything to judge by. It would most likely have been half-timbered with strong stone foundations and an upper storey jutting out over the street, and spacious, double-fronted with a small inner courtyard. A house worthy of Tradmouth's most prominent citizen at the zenith of the port's wealth.

The business side of the operation would have stood behind the impressive dwelling, hidden from the view of envious neighbours but accessible from the river. They had already found evidence of a jetty behind the warehouse building: stumps of ancient timbers protruding from the river bed at low tide. Palkin would have unloaded his ships there and the goods would have gone straight into the warehouse which had probably been constructed from roughly hewn stone.

But did the two bodies buried within the walls of the warehouse date back to John Palkin's day or were they far more recent? Once Sacha Vale had completed her work in the lab things would be clearer.

Wesley had told him about the missing girl. And they'd found two graves of uncertain vintage so no wonder the Forensic team were crawling all over the site like ants, getting in his way.

He was concentrating hard on uncovering the pelvis of the second skeleton so that it could be lifted when the sound of Butcher's voice made him jump. As Neil looked up he saw him standing on the edge of the trench.

'You seem to be getting on well with Sacha,' said Neil innocently.

Butcher squatted down, lowering his voice. 'Whatever you do, don't mention it to Astrid if you see her. I wouldn't want her to get the wrong idea.'

Neil shrugged and returned to his task. If Butcher wanted to play away from home, that was up to him. And he wouldn't wish Sacha on his worst enemy.

Butcher spoke again, louder this time. 'I never really expected to find them.'

'Find what?'

'The bodies.'

'You know who they are?'

Butcher gave a secretive smile. 'Let's just say I have my suspicions.'

Wesley was glad to be back in Tradmouth, relieved that he would soon be able to pass Julie Darwell on to someone else. Rachel had tried to speak to the victim's widow during the journey but had received only monosyllabic answers.

Once Rachel had taken Julie off to the B&B she'd managed to book for her – a fortunate late cancellation – Wesley had made for the police station, glad of the chance to stretch his legs after the long drive. The weather was dull outside, threatening rain, and the town seemed quieter now than it did a few days ago. But he was sure that come the weekend, the grand finale of the Palkin Festival, everything would step up a gear once again. After that the people of Tradmouth could get their town back until the holiday season began in earnest.

As he walked into the office Paul Johnson stood up to greet him, unfolding himself from an office chair that seemed slightly too small for him. He looked excited.

Before he could say anything, however, Gerry emerged from his office, beaming as if he was delighted to see him back.

'Wes. How did it go? Has Rach taken Mrs Darwell to the mortuary?'

'She's taken her to the B&B and then they're going to the hospital.'

'Good. Come and have a look at what I've got,' he said with a hint of mischief as he led Wesley into his office. On his desk lay a battered black instrument case swathed in clear plastic.

'Kassia Graylem's?'

'This Andre Gorst character I told you about had it hidden in his cabin on the *Maudelayne*. Claimed he'd just come across it in the bushes near the public lavs and helped himself. Sounds like a fairy tale to me. Gorst's gone missing but all patrols are on the lookout for him.'

'What about prints?'

'Only Gorst's and the other members of the crew who handled it.'

'Nobody else's? Not even Kassia's?'

He shook his head. 'I ran Gorst's prints through the database and he's got two convictions for assault. Both women. One in Bristol and one in London. Someone's spoken to the Bristol woman and she said Gorst's bad news. He lost his temper and knocked her about so she reported him.'

'And the London victim?'

'Couldn't trace her. I've got a feeling it won't be long before he turns up,' Gerry added optimistically.

'Anything else?'

'We've found three William de Clares who are in the right age range to be Kassia Graylem's lover but so far none of them fits with what you were told by Lisa up in Manchester. But there are a couple we haven't checked so don't give up hope just yet.' He paused. 'And I had the Shipworld website checked as you suggested and when it first started there was a character called William de Clare who was a handsome seducer of women.' He rolled his eyes. 'If it's not his real name then this bloke must really fancy himself. You didn't bring Kassia's granny down with you?'

Wesley shook his head. 'She didn't want to come. I think there's been a lot of bad feeling in that family. She said she didn't get on with Kassia's father and I got the impression she resented being landed with the girl after the parents' accident.'

'So how did she take the news?'

'I think it might take some time for the full implications to sink in.' Wesley sighed. 'Kassia Graylem's still a bit of an enigma. Even her friend, Lisa, didn't know much about her relationship with William de Clare. And if you don't confide in your friends . . . '

'We still have to find a link between Kassia and Jenny.' Gerry frowned.

'Well, they were both heavily into this Palkin thing and they had long auburn hair – the Pre Raphaelite look.' He thought for a moment. 'Maybe they had Andre Gorst in common.'

'He certainly spends a lot of time in London where they both lived and he was always here for the festival. The woman he attacked in Bristol was a redhead apparently so perhaps he goes for that type.'

'But why go to the trouble of wiping Kassia's prints off the viol case and leave his own?'

'I've given up guessing how the criminal mind works, Wes. Their logic isn't always the same as ours.'

'What about the similarity to the Shipworld story? Presumably Gorst has nothing to do with Chris Butcher or the website.'

'Not that we know of. But there must be lots of people out there obsessed by this Shipworld phenomenon. Like *Star Trek* or *Dr Who* – there are thousands of fans and they even have conventions.'

'If those bones Neil found do belong to Jenny, then who does the other skeleton belong to? Have any other young women gone missing round here in recent years who might fit the bill?'

Before Gerry could answer, Wesley's phone rang. The display showed it was Neil. He pressed the key to answer the call.

'Any news?'

It was a few seconds before Neil spoke. 'Still waiting for Sacha's verdict. It's frustrating to be so dependent on her say-so. She treats everyone like amateurs. I think even Colin was a bit miffed by her attitude. There's only one person she seems to get on with and that's Chris Butcher. He makes it so obvious he fancies her, it's embarrassing. Anyway, he reckons he might know who the skeletons belong to.'

Wesley pressed the receiver to his ear. 'Jenny Bercival and someone we haven't traced yet?'

'No. He thinks they could be Alice Trencham and Hawise Neston, the second and third wives of John Palkin. He says Alice vanished in thirteen eighty-eight and Hawise disappeared eight years later in thirteen ninety-six.'

Wesley said nothing for a while, taking the information in. If what Neil told him was right, it would ease their workload. Fourteenth-century murders were none of his concern. But this information came from Chris Butcher so who was to say it wasn't a smokescreen; diversion tactics to cover something more sinister.

'Can you do me a favour, Neil? Can you check out this story about Palkin's wives, just to make sure Butcher isn't having us on.'

Neil hesitated. 'I did a bit of research about Palkin before the dig began and I must say I didn't come across anything like that. He was married several times but that wasn't that uncommon in those days when people died of simple infections and women didn't survive childbirth. He might have just been unlucky.'

'Or he might have buried his unwanted wives under the floor of his warehouse.'

'Still doesn't explain why the ground seems to have been disturbed more recently.' He paused. 'Butcher says there's a book about Palkin written by a Victorian scholar called Josiah Palkin-Wright. I think he's got a copy so I'll have to ask him nicely.' He hesitated. 'I looked Palkin-Wright up on the internet and there were rumours that his wife disappeared in mysterious circumstances as well, as did her sister.'

'Let me know as soon as Sacha comes up with a date, won't you?'

Wesley heard Gerry clearing his throat impatiently. It was time to return to the present day.

It's good to have useful mates and Jonathan Petworth was as useful as they came, Jason Teague thought as he cast off from the jetty at Bloxham. At first Jonathan had told him that all the charter boats were booked up. It was always the same during Palkin Week, he'd said. Visitors come down to Tradmouth and decide to take a boat out because they see all the activity on the river and want to be a part of it. But today someone had changed their mind so one had become available.

The cabin cruiser was called *Freedom*, which seemed appropriate because if this came off, his share would give him the freedom to do whatever he liked. He could continue travelling, crewing on other people's yachts, preferably in the warmth of the Mediterranean. Or he could stay here in Devon as Jonathan's business partner and become a man of standing in the community. He had the choice. Control over his own fate without having to rely on his father's hand-outs.

He stood at the wheel and as the boat chugged across the harbour he could feel the cool breeze biting into his flesh. Not like the warm gentle winds of the Med.

He'd arranged to pick Den up at a small jetty near the sea wall. Den hadn't wanted to venture into the bustling main harbour because there were too many yachtsmen and fishermen about, and too many CCTV cameras hidden high up on buildings and lampposts. Den knew they were looking for him so he couldn't take any risks.

Jason spotted him waiting on the jetty, an old wooden structure jutting out into the water, hardly used these days. He looked more conspicuous there alone than he would have done mingling with the crowds on the quayside but Jason said nothing and helped him aboard the boat. As he jumped on to the deck Jason saw that his face was ashen, as though he'd spent the last few days in a windowless police cell. But Jason knew this wasn't so. Den had been lying low in some unspecified locality when he'd called – he hadn't told him where.

'Let's go,' Den said in a low growl Jason could barely hear over the wind and the noise of the engine. 'I've given you the position.'

Jason wanted to get this over with. He wanted his share. Above all, what he wanted was never to see Dennis Dobbs again.

He knew he had to take care as he rounded Fortress Point because the rocks below the waves were lethal and many a ship had come to grief here over the centuries. He needed to concentrate but he was aware of Den standing behind him, restless and jumpy.

'You sure you know where you're going?'

Jason didn't bother answering the question. He'd studied the chart and knew exactly where he was heading. But he couldn't banish the fear that some overenthusiastic local fisherman might have got there before them and claimed a catch that would keep him in comfort for the rest of his life.

They were further out now and Jason could see an oil tanker crawling over the horizon. Then he spotted the blue marker buoy bobbing on the waves.

He cut the engine and nodded to Den. He needed help to haul the thing on board. Den just stood there staring.

'Give me a hand then.' Jason said, irritated at the man's inactivity. He'd had enough of Dennis Dobbs with his big talk and big promises.

Reluctantly, Dobbs leaned over the side and began to pull. The boat was listing, dancing up and down on the waves as if she was trying to prevent them retrieving the thing in the water. It was coming now though: the first lobster pot. Jason could see plastic inside, glistening in the weak sunlight. After a great deal of effort they landed it on deck and Den stood looking at it, breathless and triumphant.

'One down, two to go.'

Jason restarted the engine before steering the boat thirty yards to the next blue buoy. They didn't speak as they repeated the process. One more to go then it was over.

But just as they reached the third buoy, Jason looked round and saw a dark-blue-and-white launch approaching fast. It looked very like the police launch he'd seen moored up in the harbour at Tradmouth.

Chapter 11

Written at North Lodge, Upper Town, Tradmouth this 28th day of February 1895

My dearest Letty

I have still had no word from you. Is it that Mama fears what would happen if you dared to reply and he discovered my treachery? For treachery is what he considers it to be.

This lack of communion with my fellow human beings is making me mad. Perhaps that is his purpose: to have me committed to some asylum so that he can control my fortune. And yet I feel there is more to his coldness than mere greed. I fear my husband is evil, Letty. I fear he sees me as a marionette to be controlled. A marionette without sense or feeling.

He has not visited my chamber with his cords

*and devices again for which I thank God. When
he was out of the house and Maud Cummings
was busy in the kitchen I crept to the locked door
at the top of the landing and turned the handle.
I swear I heard a low moan from within and I
was so frightened that I hurried back to my
chamber. Having considered the matter, I think
it may have been the wind in the chimney. I am
so much alone that I begin to imagine all
manner of horrors. Perhaps I will go mad.*

  *Josiah still works on his life of John Palkin. I
wonder if Palkin was as cruel to his wives as he
is to me.*

  *I wait to hear from you. I beg you, do not let
me down.*

  *Your most loving sister
  Charlotte*

'Remember you asked whether Chris Butcher was in
Tradmouth when Jenny Bercival disappeared?'

Wesley looked up and saw Trish Walton standing by his
desk. 'Well?'

'He was definitely here. He always comes down for the
festival.'

Wesley thanked Trish and rose from his seat, intending to
make for Gerry's office.

Normally Gerry flung his office door open as soon as he
arrived at work because he hated being isolated from the
heart of things. He liked to watch the team through his
glass windows and pick up on any developing ripple of
news. But now his door was shut which meant that he must
have slipped out. Wesley wondered where he was.

He sat down again and skimmed through the details of the Kassia Graylem case, looking for anything to connect her with Butcher, until his thoughts were interrupted by Gerry's return. As Wesley greeted him he noticed that the DCI's cheeks had turned an unhealthy shade of red as if he'd been rushing.

He put a hand on the back of a nearby chair to steady himself while he caught his breath. After a few seconds he spoke. 'A word, Wes. My office.'

Wesley followed him in and shut the door behind him. Whatever Gerry had to say, it wasn't for everybody's ears.

'I had a call from our Sam earlier.'

Wesley could see the strain on the boss's face. He was usually the first to make a joke of things, to lighten every situation with a quip. It was his way of dealing with the stress of the job and this new solemnity was out of character. He waited for him to continue.

'Our Rosie asked him to meet her from the concert last night – said she didn't want to go home alone. She's been staying at his cottage because she's been too scared to go back to her flat in Morbay. Sam says she's frightened of someone but she won't say who it is. Why hasn't she said anything to me, Wes?'

'Perhaps she doesn't want to worry you.'

'I am worried. I can't help it.'

Wesley was imagining how he'd feel if Amelia found herself in the same situation one day. He'd move heaven and earth to keep her safe from harm. Rosie Heffernan didn't make life easy for those who cared about her, and now it looked as if she'd got herself into some sort of fix.

Before Wesley could say anything, the phone rang on Gerry's desk. It was the Marine Unit. They'd taken two men into custody, one of whom CID had expressed interest in. The two had been taken to Bloxham police station and their boat had been impounded. Did Gerry want to come over and question them after the Marine Unit had finished with them?

Gerry put the speakerphone on so Wesley could listen in to the conversation.

'Have these men got names?' Gerry asked, slightly impatient.

'Dennis Dobbs and Jason Teague,' was the reply.

Gerry raised his fist in triumph. At least one of their lost sheep had come back into the fold.

There was a new report on Rachel's desk. Someone must have put it there while she'd been out taking Julie Darwell to view her husband's body. When she read it, she felt a new thrill of hope.

She hesitated before approaching Wesley, who was at his desk talking on his phone in a hushed voice. The conversation sounded private so she hovered there waiting for him to finish.

She heard him say, 'I've got to go now. A suspect's been picked up in Bloxham. I'll try not to be too late but you know how it is.' Then a hushed ''Bye,' in that way people do when they're reluctant to end a call. He was talking to Pam and she felt a stab of envy, so strong it surprised her.

'How's Mrs Darwell?' he asked as soon as he'd put the receiver down.

'She's gone back to the B&B with the family liaison officer,' Rachel answered, fingering the report in her hand. 'Someone's spoken to Kassia's tutor at London University. He says she was heavily into early music. Even blamed it for her dropping out.'

'No mention of a man? William de Clare?'

She shook her head. 'I've asked for a list of staff who were there at the time. Who knows, de Clare might be one of her tutors.'

'Good. Anything else?'

'Yes. Suffolk police have sent through the report on the Graylems' accident. It happened at the harbour in Southwold. The Graylems' boat had been moored there for about ten days. There was an investigation at the time and it looks as if a gas pipe came adrift so when Kassia's dad lit a cigarette the boat went up. They didn't stand a chance. Kassia should have gone aboard at the same time as her parents but she had a new camera and she stopped to take some pictures while they went on ahead. She was lucky not to have been killed.'

'Any suspicion that the gas pipe had been tampered with?'

'The investigation didn't rule it out but it was thought that in all likelihood it was a tragic accident. Luckily the boat in the neighbouring mooring had sailed off half an hour earlier or there might have been more casualties.'

'Who owned that?'

She consulted the report. 'The Wentworths – father and teenage son. They were traced and interviewed but they couldn't provide much information.'

'Anything there about the Graylems?'

'Seems they kept themselves to themselves and were described as being a bit New Age. But it was the school holidays and Kassia used to mix with some of the other teenagers.'

'What about witnesses?'

'The main witnesses were a middle-aged couple called

the Bethams. They had a boat nearby and they took Kassia in afterwards. They said the Graylems had taken their boat out that morning and before they left they'd heard some kind of argument. Raised voices.'

'Is that all?'

'That's all there is in the report.'

She handed the sheet of paper to Wesley who studied it for a few moments. 'The accident might have nothing to do with Kassia's death but I'd still like to trace all the people who were there.'

Rachel said nothing. Sometimes, in her opinion, Wesley could be easily sidetracked. She'd delegate the job to one of the most junior DCs: it would be good practice.

Suddenly she heard Trish's voice. 'Sir, it's the Shipworld website. You should have a look.'

Rachel watched as Wesley hurried to Trish's desk. She had been staring at her computer and now she pushed her office chair back so Wesley could get a good view of the screen.

After a few moments he summoned Rachel over and what she saw made her catch her breath. A shadowy grave dug in some large indoor space, possibly a cellar. The grave yawned to receive the dead woman who was lying beside the hole; a woman in a blue gown similar to the one Kassia was wearing when she died. She looked as though she was asleep with her hands folded neatly on her stomach and a long single plait of auburn hair arranged over her left shoulder. But it was the looming figure standing over her who caught Rachel's attention. It was certainly a man. Tall, with a long black cloak, and a face hidden behind a blank white mask with two dark holes for the eyes. Such an image would scare any child. It made her feel uneasy and she was a police officer.

There was a caption beneath the picture. *The Shroud Maker buries Alicia's body.*

So this creature with no face was the Shroud Maker, the villain of Shipworld. And whoever was in charge of the fantasy world had obviously used the grave she'd heard had been discovered at Butcher's house as a basis for the continuing story. Since the website was Chris Butcher's baby and he'd know all about what had been found at the dig, he'd probably passed the information on to his creative team; a team that included Miles Carthage. Even though the image was shocking, it hardly came as a surprise.

Wesley thanked Trish and Rachel watched as he went off to share the news with Gerry.

When Wesley and Gerry arrived in Bloxham they parked at the police station near the quayside. Bloxham was still a working fishing port and the scent of that morning's catch hung in the air.

Gerry made straight for the office of the Marine Unit on the ground floor and let himself in without knocking, introducing himself as he stepped into the room.

A uniformed officer who'd been sitting at his desk typing into his computer stood up and held out his hand. 'Gerry, long time no see. I believe we've got a couple of your customers down in the custody suite.' He sat down and invited the two men to do likewise.

'I don't think you two have met,' said Gerry. 'This is DI Wesley Peterson. Wes, this is Bob Nairn, Inspector in charge of the Marine Unit.'

The man shook Wesley's hand heartily. It was the kind of handshake that almost breaks your fingers and Wesley had to stop himself from wincing.

'So what happened?' Gerry asked as he made himself comfortable on one of the visitors' chairs.

Bob sat down and leaned forward as if he was sharing a confidence. 'We'd had intelligence to say there was going to be a drop from a Russian cargo ship. Heritage stuff. Religious mainly and undoubtedly nicked.'

'Why weren't we informed?' said Gerry. His tone was pleasant but Wesley had known him long enough to detect an edge of annoyance.

'Smuggling's more our concern than yours, Gerry. You know that.'

'Yeah drugs, arms and all that but old artefacts ... ' He looked at Wesley. 'Wes here's a bit of an expert. Used to be in the Art and Antiques Squad at the Met.'

'Well if we'd known that we would have informed you right away,' Bob replied with more than a hint of sarcasm. 'Look, if we hadn't had word you wanted to interview one of the characters we picked up in connection with your murder case, we might not even have got round to informing you at all so be grateful.'

Gerry raised his hands, a gesture of appeasement. 'OK, I get your point. What was this intelligence you had?'

'A lot of Eastern European antiques of dubious provenance have been appearing on the market and word had it the stuff was being brought in by ship and picked up by small boats at various parts of the coast. It was Falmouth last month but we heard they were moving on to Tradmouth. Probably because the Palkin Festival would be a good cover. Lots of strangers about and plenty going on to distract the harbour master and ourselves. A fisherman spotted some strange marker buoys some way out to sea and we've been keeping an eye on them. Then earlier on the pick-up was made. Statues and icons in waterproof packaging sitting in lobster pots. Neat operation.'

'What about Dobbs and Teague?'

'Dobbs says it's a misunderstanding but we're wise to him. His name's come up in several Met investigations, mostly drug-related, but they've never been able to pin anything on him.'

'What about Teague?'

'He's still protesting his innocence and swearing he didn't know what Dobbs was up to. He almost had me convinced. Guy deserves an Oscar. Nothing's known about him; he hasn't got a record. Mind you, that might just mean he hasn't been caught before.'

'Can we see them?' Wesley asked. Bob Nairn obviously saw himself as God's gift to policing and his attitude was beginning to get on Wesley's nerves.

Bob shrugged. 'We've finished with them for now so I don't see why not.'

Gerry led the way down to the custody suite, older and shabbier than Tradmouth's and regularly filled with fishermen who'd taken to settling disputes with their fists after overdoing the drinking on a Saturday night. The windowless interview room was lit by a strip light and there was a slight smell of fish, maybe drifting in from the quay nearby. After a few minutes Wesley found he no longer noticed it. They'd decided to start with Jason Teague and as he walked into the room with a uniformed constable he looked positively relieved to see them.

Teague gave them little apart from protestations of innocence. He'd known Dobbs was up to something but he'd no idea what it was or that it was illegal. Wesley thought that if he was telling the truth, he must be very naïve: unlikely for a man who spent his time working on rich men's yachts. Teague must have seen all sorts, even if he'd learned to ignore most of it in the interests of discretion.

They kept Dobbs until last and before they spoke to him, Wesley put in a call to an old friend at the Met to ask if they were aware of the antiquity smuggling operation. The friend was more than happy to talk and said the Met had heard whispers of what Dobbs was up to and would be delighted if he'd put a foot wrong at last. He was a slippery customer with some powerful mates who'd always managed to keep a few steps ahead of the police. Wes and his colleagues had done well, the Met officer said without resentment. Wesley didn't let on that he hadn't been responsible for the arrest and he wasn't sure whether this was because he'd taken a dislike to Bob Nairn or because he just couldn't be bothered with a long explanation. Either way, he didn't feel too guilty about the omission.

Dennis Dobbs looked defiant as he scraped the metal chair across the linoleum floor before sitting down.

'Nice to see you, Mr Dobbs,' said Gerry. He sounded jocular. But in Wesley's experience this was when he was at his most dangerous.

Wesley sat back and listened as Gerry began the questioning.

'So you've been smuggling antiques into the country.'

'No comment.'

'OK, you don't have to say anything about your nautical naughties. We're more interested in the murder of Kassia Graylem.'

'Who?'

'The young woman whose body was found floating in a dinghy on the river. Someone aboard your yacht, the *Queen*

208

Philippa, was spotted acting suspiciously near where she was found which means you're a suspect. Along with your mate Jason but he's got an alibi.'

The answer was a shrug, as if he was bored with their questions already and anxious to leave.

'Why did you kill Kassia? Did she know too much about your line of business?'

'She didn't know a thing because I'd never seen her before in my life.'

Wesley watched the man's face. He had a feeling he was about to make a revelation.

'Look, I just found her, that's all. I'd been up all night playing poker with some of the guys aboard that old ship that's in port – the *Maudelayne*. Some of them can't half drink. Anyway, I got back to the *Queen Philippa* around seven to make sure everything was ready for the pick-up when the call came. I needed somewhere to stash the stuff so there were lockers that needed clearing out and I wanted to do it while Jason wasn't there. He'd no idea what was going on, you see. Anyway, when I got on board I noticed a rope tied to the rail and when I looked down into the water I saw a little inflatable dinghy. She was just lying in it. Gave me the shock of my life. At first I thought she must be some bird Jason brought back who'd got pissed and passed out. But then I saw her eyes were open and her face was all ... twisted, and I realised she was dead. I mean, what was I supposed to do? The last thing I wanted was coppers asking questions and accusing me of something I hadn't done. So I decided to ...'

'You cast her adrift?'

'I went out on deck and noticed the *Queen Philippa*'s inflatable dinghy was still there so I knew the one she was lying

209

in couldn't be traced back to me. Anyway, I climbed down and threw a tarpaulin over her so nobody would see her. She was wearing this fancy dress, you see. Old-fashioned like some of the people at the festival. I thought that's where she'd come from.'

'Had you ever seen her before?'

'No. Never.'

'What did you do then?'

'I tried not to panic. I towed the dinghy out to the mouth of the river and once I'd pulled the tarpaulin off I set her adrift. The tide was turning so I hoped she'd be swept out to sea and she wouldn't be my problem anymore. Then I heard she'd been found.'

'So you're saying you just found a woman you'd never seen before lying in a dinghy tied to the rail of your boat?'

'It's true ... I swear. I'd never seen her before in my life. Look, anyone could have taken her there, killed her and dumped her. Tied the rope to my boat 'cause it happened to be handy.'

'The men you were playing poker with, will they vouch for you?'

'Yeah. Of course.'

'Was one of them called Andre? Andre Gorst?'

He shook his head. 'Don't think so. Why?'

Wesley caught Gerry's eye. Gorst was still in the frame.

'Are you familiar with a website called Shipworld?'

'No. Why?'

'It's just that the way Kassia was placed in that boat bears a resemblance to something on the website.'

'Was that her name ... Kassia?'

'Yes. Kassia Graylem. Name familiar?'

He shook his head.

'And I don't know nothing about no website,' he said quickly, turning his head away. 'I've never even heard of this Shipworld.'

'Has Jason ever mentioned it?'

'Don't think so.' He sounded a little disappointed, as if he'd been hoping to shift the focus of suspicion. There was a short period of silence before he spoke again. 'OK, I admit I tried to get this dead bird as far away from my boat as possible. You can't blame me for that, can you? But I had nothing to do with her murder. I swear that on my mother's life. You ask the blokes on the *Maudelayne*.'

'We will,' said Gerry with a threatening smile.

Gerry persuaded Bob Nairn to let them take Jason Teague over to Tradmouth for questioning. Wesley agreed with him that they probably couldn't trust Dennis Dobbs to tell the truth if his life depended on it. But they'd send someone to the *Maudelayne* to check his alibi. If, by any chance, his story about the discovery and disposal of Kassia Graylem's body wasn't a complete lie, they needed to pay more attention to Teague. Perhaps his open straightforward manner, the care-free young public schoolboy who lived on his wits and made his living from his love of sailing, was a mask. If so, was it a mask that hid a killer of young women?

Gerry decided to leave Teague for the moment. He reck-oned the delay would make him nervous and therefore more likely to slip up when he was questioned.

Wesley had just sat down at his desk to check if anything new had come in when his phone rang. The caller was a man but he refused to give his name. Wesley was sure he'd heard the voice before and he tried hard to place it but failed.

'What can I do for you?'

For a while the man didn't answer, as though he was making a difficult decision. Then eventually he spoke. 'That girl. The one who was murdered.'

'What about her?'

'Chris Butcher knew her.'

Wesley pressed the speakerphone button and, as he signalled to his colleagues to keep the chatter down, he saw Gerry emerge from his office and hover by the door, listening intently.

'How did he know her?'

'I saw them together on his boat early on Saturday morning. She had her viol with her.'

'How do you know all this?'

'I just know. You want to ask him what he did to her.' The caller's voice was breathless now, as if he was finding it hard to control his emotions.

'I'll need to talk to you and take a statement.'

The line went dead and Gerry walked over to his desk.

'Any idea who it was?'

'The voice is familiar but I can't place it. I'll get the call traced.' He paused. 'Whoever it was knew the instrument was a viol. Most people would have said violin.'

'Member of Palkin's Musik?'

Wesley thought for a few moments. 'There are two men in the group and it didn't sound like either of them.'

'Could it have been the bloke she lived with . . . Pixie?'

Wesley shook his head. He didn't know.

'Let's bring Butcher in anyway,' said Gerry.

'What about Jason Teague?'

'He says this is his first visit to Tradmouth but we've no way of confirming that. However, Kimberley Smith, the girl he claims to have spent the night with, has given a statement to the effect that he left her place around nine thirty on Saturday morning which puts him out of the frame for Kassia's murder. We just have to decide how involved he is with this smuggling business.'

Gerry grabbed his coat and signalled for Wesley to follow him as he made for the door.

They needed to ask Chris Butcher about the anonymous accusation and they couldn't forget his involvement with the Shipworld website. William de Clare had been a character in the Shipworld narrative and Kassia's death had been depicted on the website. Maybe Butcher himself was de Clare.

Wesley wanted to hear what Butcher had to say. In his opinion the whole Shipworld thing was getting out of hand. If the fantasy had such a hold over the lives of impressionable young people, whoever made up the stories should be careful. Very careful. Or maybe he was just hurtling towards staid middle age too rapidly, and didn't understand.

He made a quick call to Neil who told him that Butcher had just arrived at the bungalow for a meeting with the builders. Wesley told him he'd be right over and as he walked through Tradmouth with Gerry by his side the sun began to peep through the gathering clouds, luring the crowds out on to the streets again. Over on the embankment he could see groups of children sitting with their feet dangling over the wall, plastic buckets standing beside them on the cobbles. Then he remembered that today was the day of the festival crabbing championships. He saw the *Maudelayne* towering over the nearby boats and he was reminded that there was still no sign of Andre Gorst, who had to be their principal suspect. Perhaps the case was more straightforward than he thought and all this extra effort was a waste of time.

Gerry had phoned to ask for a patrol car to meet them at their destination as it would hardly be appropriate to walk back through the streets with a suspect in tow. When they arrived at Butcher's house Neil was busy in a trench scraping away at the remains of a stone wall. The white crime-scene tent was still standing over the place nearer the house where the bones had been found but there were no CSIs around today. Presumably they'd finished their mysterious rites and gathered all the available evidence from the earth.

Wesley remembered what Neil had said about Butcher's reaction to the discovery of the bones. If one of the skeletons did turn out to belong to Jenny, things would look bad for him. On the other hand, Wesley thought, if he'd known the skeletons were there, why would he have allowed Neil and his team to excavate in the first place? Unless it was some elaborate double bluff to throw them off the scent. Whatever Chris Butcher was, he wasn't stupid.

Neil looked up when he heard the gate bang shut and raised a hand in greeting. 'Butcher about?' Gerry's tone suggested that this wasn't a social call.

Neil nodded and pointed at the house. 'He's inside with the builder. They're both wearing hard hats so it must be serious,' he said with a grin.

Gerry marched to the front door first and pushed it open.

Wesley hadn't been inside the house before but he knew this was where Neil and his fellow archaeologists had been sleeping. The first room they entered was spacious and contained a couple of sleeping bags on top of airbeds as well as a large Victorian chest of drawers and built-in mirrored wardrobes. The makeshift bedroom looked fairly comfortable. Wesley had seen far worse.

The second room was slightly larger and contained three airbeds. This was clearly where the females slept as there were items of underwear dangling from a drying rack in the corner. The team had made themselves at home. In the spacious living room a huge window overlooking the sea provided a spectacular view and Wesley understood why Butcher had chosen this spot for his Devon retreat.

There were voices coming from the end of the wide hallway. They followed the sound and found themselves in a roomy kitchen that was an orange homage to the 1970s. Chris Butcher was standing by the back door talking to a swarthy man in an anorak and white hard hat. The two men turned as they entered the room.

'It's usual to knock,' Butcher said.

'We need to have a word, Mr Butcher,' said Wesley.

'I'm in the middle of a meeting. Can't it wait?'

'I'm afraid it can't.'

Gerry looked at the builder expectantly and the man took the hint and left, mumbling something about carrying on another time. Butcher's face was turning a dangerous shade of scarlet.

'We've had a call,' Gerry began.

'What kind of call?' Butcher looked worried.

'We asked you if you knew the girl who was murdered last Saturday morning but you told us you didn't. We'd like you to come to the station with us. And you might like to contact your solicitor and all.'

Butcher drew himself up to his full height and stared

ahead like a man on his way to the guillotine. 'Very well. I've got nothing to hide,' he said before following them out meekly to the police car that had pulled up outside.

When Wesley looked round he saw that someone was watching from the pavement, no doubt a local curious about the presence of a police car. Then he realised he'd seen the man there before. He was tempted to ask him why he was taking such an interest but before he had a chance, the man had disappeared. Wesley turned his attention back to Butcher. After all, rubberneckers come in all shapes and sizes.

Dennis Dobbs and Jason Teague were in custody and now Chris Butcher was down in the interview room awaiting his solicitor. They had thirty-six hours to decide whether to charge or release him and, as he was temporarily living on a boat that could sail away at any time, Wesley knew that once he was free it might be hard to get him back.

The solicitor had come from Exeter and it had only taken him an hour to get there. Wesley had expected Butcher to opt for an expensive London lawyer but it seemed he had a pragmatic streak. Once Wesley and DC Paul Johnson were settled in the interview room, the questioning began. Gerry hadn't joined him because he wanted to observe the proceedings from the viewing room next door, watching behind a two-way mirror along with CS Noreen Fitton who had expressed a desire to watch Butcher's reactions for herself. She was certainly more hands-on than her predecessor, who'd always been content to rely on Gerry's reports to bring himself up to date.

Even though Wesley was used to it, the thought of being watched by invisible eyes still made him feel a little uncomfortable, though not as uncomfortable as Chris Butcher who was sitting to attention in the chair opposite.

After the preliminaries were over and the tape machine was activated, he decided to come straight to the point.

'You were seen with Kassia Graylem the night before her death.'

'Who told you that?'

'Is it true?'

Wesley waited for him to speak. In his experience a suspect could never resist filling a vacuum of silence.

Butcher sighed. 'OK, I went to the Palkin's Musik concert and afterwards I saw Kassia walking down the High Street. I caught up with her and told her how much I'd enjoyed the concert. I asked her if she wanted to come back to the boat for a drink and she accepted.' He paused, a slight smile on his lips as though he was reliving an old, pleasant memory in his head. 'She had her viol with her. She played for me. My own personal concert.'

'Nice,' said Paul. His first word. He looked faintly embarrassed and said nothing more.

'How did she seem?'

'Fine. I had a good bottle of malt and we had a few drinks.'

Wesley nodded. This fitted with Colin's verdict on her stomach contents.

'You had sex with her?'

He gave Wesley a 'we're all men of the world' look.

'Did she spend the night on board?'

'She left just before six the next morning. I offered to call a taxi for her but she wouldn't hear of it. She said she needed some fresh air.'

'She lives out near Neston in the middle of nowhere. Did she say how she was planning to get home?'

'No. And I didn't ask. Look, I should have made sure she was OK and I'll regret it for the rest of my life, but I'd had a bit to drink and I reckoned I was still over the limit. I wasn't in a fit state to drive her anywhere.'

'You went up on deck to see her off the boat?'

'Yeah. I watched her walk away from the marina towards the town.'

'Did you see anyone around? Anyone who might have followed her?'

'I don't think so. I watched until she was halfway down the embankment walking toward the *Maudelayne*. Then I went down below so I didn't see where she went after that.'

'Had you arranged to meet her again?'

'I said I'd probably see her at the next concert. She knew the situation.'

'Ships that pass in the night?'

'Something like that.'

'Had you ever met her before?'

Butcher swallowed hard and Wesley knew he'd hit the target. 'We met a couple of years ago at a concert in London. We had a mutual interest in things medieval.'

'And?'

'I might as well come clean. We had an affair.'

'You wouldn't happen to be William de Clare?'

Butcher's cheeks reddened. 'There's no harm in a bit of role play.'

'You say you had an affair. Past tense.'

'That's right. Astrid found out and ... well, I thought it best to cool it. I told Kassia I couldn't see her for a while.'

'But you met up again and took up where you left off.'

'I'd no idea she'd be in Tradmouth. It came as a

surprise.' A smile played on his lips. 'A not unpleasant one as it happens.'

'But you didn't want to put your marriage at risk for her?'

'My wife put a lot of capital into my IT company,' he said with a knowing look. 'Besides, she's not a tolerant woman. I thought I was being discreet.'

'You don't seem too upset about Kassia's death.'

'I've had to come to terms with it.'

Wesley glanced towards the two-way mirror. He could picture Gerry behind it, willing him to push the man further.

'Was Kassia threatening to make trouble for you? You see, we've heard that she was infatuated with William de Clare.' He cleared his throat. 'I put it to you that she wanted to rekindle your relationship. Maybe she threatened to tell your wife.'

Butcher looked affronted. 'Absolutely not. She knew the score.'

'Infatuated people can delude themselves. You'd spent the night together. I'd be surprised if she didn't take that as a sign that the great romance was on again.'

'She'd changed. And she seemed to have something else on her mind.'

'What was that?'

'If I knew, I'd tell you. But she seemed . . . ' He searched for the right word. 'Preoccupied.'

'Did Kassia mention that she was afraid of anyone?'

'Can't say she did.'

'What do you know about her background?'

Butcher frowned, as if he'd found Wesley's last question disturbing in some way. 'She always said she had no past

219

and that everyone she loved had been taken from her. I thought she was just being pretentious, if you know what I mean. But she was deadly serious.'

'Anything else you can tell us?'

He thought for a moment before answering. 'When I first met her I knew she was studying history and when I asked her where she'd learned to play the viol so well, she just said in another time in another place.'

'Evasive?'

He looked at Wesley as though he was impressed. 'That's the exact word I'd use.'

'Have you ever met a man called Eric Darwell? He's a private investigator from Manchester.'

'No.'

'You sure about that?'

'Of course.'

'What about Jenny Bercival? She went missing last year.'

Butcher glanced at his solicitor. 'I might have met her.'

'Both Kassia and Jenny had tattoos of the Shipworld logo. The cog. Was that anything to do with you?'

Wesley saw panic in Butcher's eyes, there for a moment then swiftly suppressed. He was on the right track. 'Well was it?'

Butcher sighed. 'It's a Shipworld thing. The real John Palkin used to mark his property with the sign of the cog. It was his trademark, if you like.'

'So the girls were your property?'

Butcher shook his head. 'It wasn't like that. You don't understand.'

'Make me.'

There was a long silence before Butcher spoke. 'It was all about role play. I was William de Clare, Lord of the Lands

220

of Dart. Jenny was the Lady Morwenna, rescued from the old Lord of Pacifion, and Kassia was the Lady Alicia, de Clare's lover. It was fantasy. Fun. I spelled that out from the start.'

Wesley recalled Lisa's words. Kassia changed when she became involved with William de Clare. Whatever the relationship had been for Butcher, she had taken it seriously.

'Not much fun when they were killed.'

'I didn't think you'd found Jenny. How do you know she's dead? Her parents split up and she was going through a bad patch. I presumed that's why she'd chosen to disappear.'

'Two skeletons have been found on your property. We're waiting for them to be dated. If one of them turns out to be Jenny . . . '

Butcher raised his hands in a gesture of defence. 'Now look, that's absolutely nothing to do with me. I've only just bought the place. If I knew they were there, do you think I'd have let a load of archaeologists loose in the garden?'

'But you admit you were having an affair with Jenny Bercival at the time she disappeared?'

'We met in London and we used to get together when she came down here. It wasn't serious. Just a bit of fun.'

The fun word again. Something made Wesley think Butcher was trying to fool himself. Or the police. 'You didn't come forward when Jenny disappeared.'

'I only thought she'd gone back to London to get away from her mother's angst.'

'Were you upset when she went missing?'

He shrugged his shoulders.

'When did you last see her?'

'I can't remember.'

Wesley could tell he was lying.

221

'So you were involved with Kassia, who's now dead. And Jenny, who could well be dead. You're the common denominator. What have you got to say to that?'

'I had nothing to do with Kassia's death or Jenny's disappearance. I swear.'

Wesley made a great show of consulting his notebook. During the pause he glanced up at Butcher and saw that he was fidgeting with the empty plastic cup in front of him. He was nervous. The solicitor whispered something in his ear but Butcher appeared to ignore him.

'I've been looking at the Shipworld website. Who's the Shroud Maker?'

'The villain of Shipworld. Why?'

'He seems to be responsible for the deaths of various women. Is he based on a real-life character?'

Butcher shrugged. 'Not particularly.' His eyes flickered for a moment and Wesley suspected that the subject made him uncomfortable. So far he had delegated trawling the depths of the Shipworld website to others. Now he suddenly resolved to take more interest.

'I saw an image of the Shroud Maker. He has no face.'

Butcher raised his eyebrows. 'Nobody's supposed to know his identity. That's the whole point.'

'You're in charge of the website so you must know who he is.'

'That would be telling.'

'Don't play games with us, Mr Butcher.'

'Look, I'm not privy to the Shroud Maker's identity. Palkinson and his ilk deal with all that.'

'We still haven't traced this Palkinson. Any idea where we can find him?'

Butcher hesitated slightly before shaking his head.

'Sorry.' He suddenly looked up. 'Come to think of it, I did see Kassia talking to someone after the concert.'

'Who?'

'Miles Carthage. The man I told you about who does the illustrations for Shipworld.'

Wesley glanced at the mirror. This was a new development. 'You saw Kassia talking to Miles? He told us he'd never spoken to her.'

'I saw him stop her and whisper something in her ear. She gave him a strange look. Can't really describe it.'

'Try.' Wesley was growing impatient.

'As if she was excited about something. But I could be wrong.'

'Did she mention him while you were with her?'

'Can't say she did.'

The solicitor was looking hopeful that the attention was about to shift away from his client. There was, however, no getting away from the fact that Butcher had had sex with Kassia shortly before she died.

After another three hours of questioning, both Wesley and the solicitor knew they didn't have enough evidence to bring charges. As Butcher left the interview room he looked completely relaxed, as though he knew he'd got away with something bad.

Chapter 12

Written at North Lodge, Upper Town, Tradmouth this 5th day of March 1895

My dearest Letty

Josiah has gone to Exeter again and will stay there overnight so I will be alone in the house with Maud Cummings.

I still hear strange sounds from the locked room above my own. Shufflings and faint moans like those of some sorry ghost. I feel I shall go mad if I do not discover what those sounds signify. When Maud is asleep or away from the house I shall search for the key. You see, my dear sister, my fear has made me bold.

When I was at church last Sunday I overheard two sea captains' wives gossiping. They said a woman from Tradmouth is

*missing, the daughter of a common sailor, and
that in recent years two others have disappeared
in a similar fashion. I heard the captains' wives
say that the missing women had been in receipt
of charity at the home for fallen women where
they sometimes helped, doing their Christian
duty to the poor, and that the vicar is most
concerned. Then they lowered their voices and I
could hear no more of their conversation. When
my husband saw me listening, he almost
dragged me from the church.*

*How is Mama? My husband says she does not
wish to communicate with me but I am certain
that he lies. Does the Reverend Johnson inquire
about me?*

Please please send word soon.

Your loving sister

Charlotte

Pam had been waiting up for Wesley when he'd arrived
home at eleven the previous night. She'd greeted him with
a weary smile and a kiss, whispering in his ear that she'd
missed him. Then she'd asked him how Manchester was.

The day had been so full that Manchester now seemed
an age away but over a glass of wine he'd told her about
Eric Darwell's widow and Kassia's friend, Lisa, making
only a casual passing reference to Rachel. When Pam
asked how her wedding preparations were going he'd given
an evasive reply. As far as he knew they were going OK.
He hadn't really had time to ask. Pam had rolled her eyes
in despair at the male sex's lack of curiosity and let the
matter rest. But that night he'd found it hard to sleep and

when he arrived at the station the next morning he felt tired.

He sat at his desk and went through everything that had come in overnight. The anonymous phone call drawing their attention to Chris Butcher had been made from an unregistered mobile located in the centre of Tradmouth. Not much help there. Now they knew that Chris Butcher was William de Clare, he had to be their main suspect and Wesley felt frustrated that he'd been released pending further inquiries. Maybe the breakthrough would come when they discovered more about his exact relationship with Jenny and Kassia.

He'd asked one of the team to contact the witnesses to Kassia's parents' accident but the inquiries had produced nothing new. It was only the Wentworths, the widowed father and his son, who hadn't been traceable. Their contact number had been called and the Polish au pair who'd answered the phone said that her employers had bought the house from Mr Wentworth five years ago. She thought he might have gone to live abroad.

Rachel had phoned Kassia Graylem's grandmother to see how she was. It was unusual for somebody of Kassia's age to have so few relatives, she said to Wesley. Unusual and desperately sad. With her parents, two surviving grandparents, three brothers and their partners and any number of cousins, she found it hard to imagine being so alone in the world. Wesley agreed. Family was important.

As Rachel was about to return to her paperwork, Wesley perched himself on the edge of her desk. 'I'd like to have another word with Miles Carthage,' he said. 'Butcher says he saw him talking to Kassia Graylem. It might be a smokescreen to deflect attention from himself but when I interviewed Carthage before, I felt there was something he wasn't telling us.'

She raised her eyes. He could see tiny clumps of mascara on her lashes. 'I agree. He was odd if you ask me.'

'Want to come with me?'

After Manchester he knew it would be wise to keep his distance and he suddenly wondered whether he should have chosen her for the job. But it was too late to pick someone else now. She grabbed her coat and followed him out, looking as eager as a new recruit heading for her first interview, and his instinct told him he'd have to tread carefully.

As they made their way to Miles Carthage's flat, the early drizzle that had formed a fine mist over the hills across the river had stopped and the sun was doing its best to poke through the clouds.

When they arrived at North Lodge, Wesley was surprised to find the street door slightly ajar, as though the latch hadn't quite caught when it had been pushed shut. As they stepped over the threshold he heard noises coming from upstairs. Carthage was in.

He climbed the stairs with Rachel following and when he reached the first floor he rapped on the artist's door. It was answered promptly, almost as though he was expecting their visit, and the man stood in the doorway, outwardly calm, although Wesley had seen an unmistakable flash of panic in his eyes. When he asked if they could come in, Carthage said that he was working and it wasn't convenient.

'We can either talk here or down to the police station,' Wesley said reasonably.

At this Carthage shut the door in his face.

*

227

Gerry had put Tom from Scientific Support on to tracing Palkinson, the alleged provider of much of the Shipworld material.

Today there was a new instalment that featured a traveller who'd stumbled on the Shroud Maker's lair and so had to die. He was drowned in the Pool of Oblivion where the Shroud Maker disposed of the curious. And the Pool of Oblivion was an artificial azure blue – the blue of the outdoor swimming pool at Newlands Holiday Park. However, the papers had been full of the suspicious death in the pool, so it wouldn't have required first-hand knowledge to imagine the scene.

Tom had sat beside Gerry trawling through the website, both men reading in silence. When they reached the end, Gerry asked a question.

'Is there much of this sort of stuff on the internet?'

'Oh yes. It's very popular. Can be big business.'

'It is for Chris Butcher. He owns the website along with a fancy yacht and he's doing up a house on the waterfront.'

'Nice one,' said Tom with a hint of envy.

'He claims he doesn't do the day-to-day work on the site. Says most of it comes from this Palkinson you're looking for and the rest is sent in by fans. Any way of telling who's been writing the stuff that resembles the murders?'

'I'm working on it. Give me time.'

'Any chance Palkinson could be Butcher himself?'

Tom nodded. 'That's always a possibility.'

Wesley regretted that he hadn't been quick enough to put his foot in the door like an unwanted salesman. He could hear sounds coming from within the flat of footsteps and cupboards opening.

'Think we should get a search warrant?' Rachel whispered.

Wesley knew she was probably right. On the other hand, Carthage could be taking advantage of the delay to destroy evidence. They needed to get inside the flat before he had the chance.

When Wesley hammered on the door the noises ceased and after a few moments the door opened a crack. This time he was swift to step forward and Carthage backed away, eyes lowered, like a repentant child standing before the headmaster's desk.

'I'm sorry. You took me by surprise. I had some work to finish and I didn't want ...'

'I don't think that applies to us,' said Rachel, striding into the flat behind Wesley and shutting the door behind her.

'What do you want?' Carthage sounded frightened, like a man who knows he's facing defeat.

'We want to talk to you about the murder of Kassia Graylem. Last time we interviewed you, you said you'd never spoken to her. We now have a witness who says you were lying.'

'What witness?'

'Chris Butcher.'

Wesley wasn't absolutely certain whether Chris Butcher had been telling the truth and he suddenly felt he was taking a gamble. 'Did you speak to Kassia Graylem or not?' He took Kassia's photograph from his pocket and pushed it towards Carthage who picked it up and stared at it, his face clouding as if he was reliving bad memories.

'You told us she was just some woman you saw in the

street and sketched. That was a lie, wasn't it? Can we take a look around?'

Carthage sank down on to the tattered velvet sofa and put his head in his hands. Wesley had rarely seen such despair in an innocent man. But he'd often seen it in the guilty. He gave Rachel a nod and she left the room. Wesley followed her and they conducted a quick search of the studio where the sketch of Kassia had been found. There were more studies of people and the cog, but nothing out of the ordinary.

The bedroom was Spartan with a single bed covered with a pristine white bedspread. Here more cases filled with dead butterflies hung on every wall. The last thing Carthage saw before he went to sleep each night were his beautiful captives imprisoned around him. Did their tiny souls cry out in his dreams, Wesley wondered before telling himself he was letting his imagination run away with him.

As he left the bedroom he noticed an old screen in the passageway, browned with old varnish and decorated with Victorian scraps. He was about to pass it but something made him stop and shift it a little to peep behind. To his surprise he saw a door. He pushed the screen out of the way and tried the handle. It was locked.

He returned to the living room where Carthage still sat motionless, as though he hadn't moved a muscle in his absence.

'Do you have the key to that door behind the screen?'

Wesley saw Carthage's eyes widen in panic. He perched on the edge of his seat as though he was about to leap up and flee out of the door. But he'd have had to get past Wesley first. 'I can always call in some officers to break it down if necessary.'

The hinted threat at damage to his property did the trick. Carthage rummaged in the pocket of his trousers and drew out a large key. Wesley took it before calling Rachel back to the living room to keep an eye on him.

When he reached the door he almost dropped the key in his eagerness to see what was behind it. The lock clicked open smoothly as if it had been oiled recently and Wesley pushed the door open. The darkness beyond was relieved only by a chink of light where the heavy curtains covering the window on the far wall didn't quite meet. He reached in and felt for a light switch.

The light came on to reveal a spacious room painted a uniform white. A chandelier hung from an elaborate plaster ceiling rose and piles of stacked canvases leaned against the walls. Some were huge creations depicting epic subjects: battles and sacrifices; tragic lovers and dying heroes. The style was similar to that of the illustrations he'd already seen but these images were grander. And while the subject matter might have been dated, something, maybe the artist's skill, made them vibrant and alive.

One figure featured in every picture: a beautiful young woman who took the role of bare-breasted female warrior; of a human sacrifice on the receiving end of a druid's knife; of a weeping beauty cradling her dying lover in her arms. Kassia Graylem had played many parts in Miles Carthage's painted fantasies.

Wesley walked round the room slowly, examining each canvas. He knew what he was looking for. Somewhere amongst all these fantastic images of Kassia Graylem there might just be a depiction of her death.

But it wasn't there. Maybe Carthage had hidden it, or

perhaps he was still working on it, his greatest masterpiece. He had lied about knowing her. What if he had killed her and posed her lifeless body in the dinghy? The ultimate sacrifice for art: the model drawn in death.

He switched off the light, locked the door and returned to the living room. Carthage was still perched on the sofa, Rachel seated opposite him on a hard dining chair stained with old paint. She looked up as Wesley came in and gave a small shake of her head. Carthage had said nothing in his absence.

'I've seen the pictures,' he said quietly.

Carthage looked up. 'I want to tell you everything. Please.'

Wesley knew he ought to do things by the book and take him back to the station to be interviewed with the tape running but he decided to let him carry on rather than take the risk that the short journey to the interview room would break the spell.

'Kassia was my model. My muse. When I painted her I produced my best work. I make a good living from illustrations but sometimes I need to push the boundaries without being constrained by other people's ideas.' He looked at Wesley, desperate to make him understand. 'I keep the pictures of Kassia separate from my commercial work because they're special. Sacred.'

Wesley was tempted to point out that the very act of concealment made him look suspicious but he let the man carry on.

'As soon as I saw Kassia I recognised her.'

'You'd known her before?' Rachel asked.

Wesley gave her a critical look. Let him finish. She gave a moue of irritation and bowed her head.

'No, but I felt I'd known her for years. Like we'd met in some other life.'

'Tell us about her,' said Wesley gently.

'She was beautiful, inside and out. She didn't care about the conventions.' He swallowed. 'But I sensed she'd had her spirit crushed out of her by someone or something. I asked her what it was but she wouldn't say. She was so talented. A wonderful musician. She could have taken the world by storm.'

'Why didn't she?'

'She'd experienced a lot of pain in her life. She'd lost her entire family. Then she trusted someone who'd used her.'

'Was that Chris Butcher?'

His mouth fell open.

'We've spoken to Chris. He's told us all about his relationship with Kassia. It must have made you angry. He'd defiled your muse. Were you angry with him, Miles?'

'No.'

'Or were you angry with Kassia? Is that why you killed her?'

'I didn't kill her. I swear. I didn't want her to come to any harm.'

'You drew the picture of her lying dead in the boat.'

'That wasn't Kassia. That was Alicia.'

'And the one of her body in the grave?'

Miles looked exasperated. 'That wasn't her either. I was illustrating the story. They aren't my ideas.'

Wesley decided to try another approach. 'What did Kassia tell you about her family?'

'She said they were killed in a boating accident when she was fifteen. She never got over it.'

'Was your relationship sexual?'

Carthage shook his head.

'But you wished it was?' said Rachel.

'You don't understand. It would have ruined everything if we had sunk to the level of rutting farmyard animals.'

It was Wesley who asked the next question. 'You must have talked a lot while she was posing for you. What did she say about her affair with Chris?'

'She knew better than to chatter. It would have ruined my concentration. I needed her to stay completely still. I couldn't risk losing the moment I was trying to capture.'

Wesley didn't know why he should be surprised at the single-minded selfishness of the artist who claimed a woman was special to him and yet took so little interest in her life – if he was telling the truth.

'Did you send her notes?' He took out his notebook and read. '"I'll be waiting for you tomorrow. Don't be late. I need you. Palkin needs you. You must not betray him. Please don't let me down. If you do, I'll come and find you."'

Carthage nodded. 'She said she might not be able to come but I had to paint her. You do understand?' he said, a note of desperation in his voice.

'Was it you she was talking to in the porch of St Leonard's Church?'

Carthage looked puzzled. 'No.'

'Did you see her on the morning she died? Were you out early sketching?'

Carthage didn't answer. His eyes flickered around the room, as if he was seeking an escape route and Wesley knew the answer to the last question without him having to say it.

Suddenly Carthage began to speak, the words emerging in a rush. 'I didn't plan to follow her. I was out sketching the *Maudelayne* but then I saw her leaving Chris's boat. She was carrying her viol, you see, and it seemed strange.'

'She'd just spent the night with Chris Butcher,' said Rachel. To Wesley the statement seemed a little brutal.

Carthage looked away.

'She betrayed you with him. Were you jealous?' said Rachel. 'Jealous enough to kill her?'

Carthage shook his head vigorously.

'Was it you who called the police to say she'd been with Chris?'

Carthage nodded. 'I thought he'd killed her.'

'You were obsessed with your perfect muse,' said Wesley. 'You must have resented the fact she had a lover.'

'No.'

'We've only got your word for that,' said Rachel.

Wesley saw Carthage flinch. If he'd been in a position to give Rachel a covert kick, he would have done it. She wasn't normally so aggressive in her questioning. He could see she was putting Carthage on his guard and it was up to him to rescue the situation if they were to get at the truth.

'I can understand how you felt,' Wesley said. 'She was beautiful and while she was posing for you she was yours and yours alone. Then you saw her leaving Chris's boat and it was clear she'd spent the night with him. Maybe you spoke to her and she told you where she'd been. Maybe she even laughed about it.'

'I didn't speak to her. I was too far away.'

'Did you see where she went?'

Wesley held his breath, waiting for him to answer.

'No. I was upset. I walked away.'

'Why didn't you tell us all this when we spoke to you before?'

'I didn't want to get involved.' He pressed his lips together in a stubborn line, as though he knew he'd said too much.

Wesley made a call to the station. He needed someone there to go through Carthage's flat and have a look at his computer. Then he asked the artist to come to the interview room to make a formal statement, careful to make it sound like an invitation rather than a command. Artists, he knew, were sensitive souls.

Rosie Heffernan had picked up some clothes from her father's house on Baynard's Quay. He'd been complaining that she hadn't taken everything with her when she'd moved out into a flat of her own. Using the place as a ruddy warehouse, was how he'd put it. Not that she was worried. Her dad was full of bluster and noise but underneath it signified nothing. He was a pussycat. She often wondered whether he was as soft on the criminals who crossed his path.

She went down the back streets, avoiding the waterfront. When she passed the side street leading to the waterfront she could see the mast, furled sails and taut shrouds of the *Maudelayne*, reminding her of her foolishness.

Clutching the plastic bag full of clothes she hurried on towards the pub where she was due to meet the others. All the members of Palkin's Musik had arranged to have something to eat before the rehearsal for the following night's gig – or rather Dan Hungerford had arranged it for them. Maybe, she thought, he just wanted to make sure they were all present and correct. He'd been edgy ever since Kassia's death.

The light was fading and she could hear footsteps behind her, getting closer, ringing on the flagstones. She told herself that it was probably someone in a hurry and carried on, reluctant to look round. In a moment whoever it was would pass her without a glance.

The street was empty apart from a pair of giggling middle-aged female tourists wearing cardboard medieval headdresses which did nothing for their dignity. They were absorbed in their own concerns as they disappeared up the street leading to the church, leaving her alone except for her pursuer who seemed to have slowed his pace to match hers. Experiencing a sudden wave of panic she broke into a run, heading for the safety of the crowds at the boat float. That was when she felt the hand on her shoulder.

Before she knew it he had seized her arms and she winced at the pain of his grip as he dragged her down a narrow passage that ran between two shops. Once they were out of sight, he shoved her against the rough brick wall and she felt a stab of pain in her shoulder and his warm, beer-scented breath on her face. She was face to face with him now.

'Why don't you leave me alone?' Her words came out in a hoarse whisper. Terror had taken her voice away.

He released his grip a little. 'I'm in trouble. I need to stay at your flat for a while.'

No. I don't want anything more to do with this. If you don't go, I'm telling the police.'

That would be a stupid thing to do.' His hand went to her throat before slipping downwards towards her breast, and he swore as it caught on the locket she always wore, the one with her mother's picture inside. He tugged at the chain to free himself and Rosie heard a small metallic thud as the necklace fell to the ground. Her assailant's hand was plunging down the neckline of her dress, groping for her breasts, when suddenly his knees buckled and he collapsed to the ground.

Chapter 13

John Palkin had but one son from his four marriages. As far as I can tell this was not remarked upon at the time, childlessness being seen merely as a withholding of God's blessing which could be changed by nothing but ardent prayer.

Richard Palkin undoubtedly had a privileged upbringing and being the only son and heir there was nobody to rival his position in the household, apart from his uncle. John Palkin's brother Henry.

Richard was only thirteen years old when John's second wife, Alice, died at the estate in the village of Whitely she had inherited from her parents. If indeed she did die there. Richard himself died at the age of eighteen, shortly after he had started working at his Uncle Henry's ropeworks where he had been sent to learn every aspect of his father's business. There is an entry in the church records which states that Richard died at the ropeworks and that John Palkin paid for masses to be said for his son in perpetuity. The manner of his death is not specified.

In 1395, a year after Richard's untimely death, John Palkin's third wife, Hawise Neston, gave birth to a son who died after living but two days and was buried in St Margaret's Church. Hawise's fecundity was a threat to Henry who was now Palkin's heir. And threats must be dealt with.

I must mention, at this point, the nature of Henry Palkin himself. It seems from his will that he was a man given to jealousy, for he specifies that should his own wife marry again, she should be deprived of all the property and status to which she was entitled as a widow, effectively leaving her penniless.

From 'The Sea Devil – the story of John Palkin' by Josiah Palkin-Wright. Published 1896

'Look, mate, can I buy you a drink?' Gerry drew his wallet from his pocket. It was the least he could do for the man who saved his daughter's life, or at least that's how he put it.

Dan Hungerford looked embarrassed. 'I only did what anyone would do. Lucky I was passing when I did. I take it the man's been arrested?'

'He's been taken down to the station.'

Gerry looked at his daughter, who was sitting in silence. 'How did you come to know that toerag, love?'

Rosie looked down at the broken locket chain in her hand. She flicked the little gold heart open and gazed at her dead mother's face, unwilling to meet her father's eyes. Gerry recognised shame when he saw it. He'd just never thought to see it in his own daughter.

She took a sip of beer from her glass, delaying tactics. It was a while before she spoke. 'I met him in Tradmouth a couple of weeks ago. He was very charming at first, really fun. And interesting. He'd been all over Europe on the

240

Maudelayne. Then he started saying things that made me uncomfortable. And he ... he threatened me.'

Gerry hadn't yet broken the news to her that Andre Gorst was wanted for questioning in connection with the murder of Kassia Graylem and he didn't know whether to broach the subject. He didn't want to alarm his daughter by telling her that she might have been dating a murderer – flirting with death – so he said nothing.

'Why didn't you tell us about this, Rosie?' said Hungerford. 'Harry and I could have taken it in turns to see you home and—'

'That wouldn't have done much good, Dan. He'd managed to get hold of a key to my flat. I found him there one evening. He must have nicked it from my bag and had it copied. I've been staying at Sam's. I only went to Dad's place to get some of my things.'

'You should have told me, love,' said Gerry, suddenly feeling inadequate. 'I'd have sorted it.' He'd let her down – a senior detective, and he couldn't even protect his own flesh and blood. 'Sam should have let me know.'

'I asked him not to because I didn't want you fussing. I know what you're like.'

She drained her glass and looked at Dan. 'The rehearsal's still on isn't it?'

'If you're feeling up to it.'

'Course I am. Why don't we go and meet the others.' She looked at Gerry. 'I'll spend tonight at Sam's as arranged and move back into my flat tomorrow. Unless they let Andre out on bail.'

'They won't if I have anything to do with it,' said Gerry grimly. 'But you never know so I'll arrange for your lock to be changed.' He watched as Rosie began to put her coat on. 'This Andre . . . did he mention anything about finding Kassia's viol?'

Rosie's jaw dropped open.

'He had it?' said Dan.

Gerry nodded. 'It was found in his cabin. That's why we've been looking for him.'

Rosie buried her head in her hands for a moment. Then she looked up. 'Oh bloody hell, Dad, I could have been next.'

Gerry reached over and touched his daughter's hand. 'We've got him now, love.' He looked at Dan who picked up on the signal and stood.

'We'd better go and meet the others or we'll be late for the rehearsal.'

Gerry watched his daughter walk meekly out of the Tradmouth Arms with Dan Hungerford by her side.

It was time to have a word with Andre Gorst.

As Gorst was led down to the cells the officers on duty turned and stared, the stares turning into muffled sniggers. It wasn't every day that a man in medieval costume, complete with tights, turned up in the custody suite. The custody sergeant said that perhaps they should hold a fancy dress party down there. His underlings laughed dutifully.

Thanks to the Palkin Festival with its attendant pickpockets and bouts of drunken disorder around the pubs and fairground, the cells were full so it would be a matter of sharing. The custody sergeant felt uncomfortable about this but some things couldn't be helped.

He unlocked the gate and led Andre Gorst to cell number three. A lad already in there knew the score and could show him the ropes if necessary. Not that Gorst struck him as an intimidated ingénue. He had hardly uttered a word since he was brought down to the custody suite and there was something about his brooding manner the custody sergeant found unnerving. The man gave the impression of watching, notching up any minuscule error in procedure so he could use it later to wriggle out of any charges they brought against him. The sergeant had seen his type before. When a prisoner was lippy and straightforward at least you knew where you were. But DCI Heffernan had said he wanted Gorst left in the cells overnight to sweat so who was he to argue.

He unlocked the cell door and as he guided Gorst inside the man turned to face him. 'I know who killed that girl in the boat.'

The sergeant was quite unprepared for the revelation and the question left his lips automatically. 'Who was it then?'

'Let me out of here and I'll tell you.'

The sergeant rolled his eyes and locked the door. He'd been around too long to fall for that one.

The site had begun to produce all manner of interesting finds from medieval pottery to coins and even a seal bearing John Palkin's crest. Neil was rather relieved that no more bones had turned up.

It had also been a relief when the panoply of crime investigation had departed with the skeletons. He was still frustrated that there hadn't been any dating evidence in the trench to confirm how long the bones had been down there. Sacha Vale hadn't shown her face again to enlighten him. She'd probably be in the warmth of some lab now, supervising the tests. He shivered and felt a stab of envy. It was nine o'clock in the morning and a cold breeze was blowing in from the river, cutting through his combat jacket. The sun that had appeared first thing, promising a fine day, had now vanished behind a bank of grey cloud. Normal service had been resumed. Even the old man was there again, staring over the wall. They'd learned to ignore him.

One of the PhD students was standing a few yards away with a drawing board, recording the contents of the grave trench with earnest concentration. Not wanting to disturb her, Neil hurried over to the shelter of the house's porch to make his call.

Sacha answered after three rings. She sounded abrupt, as though she'd expected to hear someone else's voice; someone whose call would be more welcome.

'Any news?'

'I'm just about to ring the lab to see if the dating results have come in but I'm not holding my breath.'

'If they do turn out to be old, God knows how much public money will have been wasted on all that forensic stuff.'

'We could hardly take the risk, could we?' she said haughtily as though she'd taken his last words as some personal criticism. 'It might turn out to be a murder case yet. In my opinion the two women met violent ends.'

He heard the gate bang shut so he poked his head round the corner of the porch to see who had arrived. As soon as he recognised Chris Butcher his spirits sank. More interference. 'Hang on, Sacha,' he said, stepping out to greet Butcher who was carrying a briefcase and looking around as if he was searching for someone.

'Sacha about?'

244

Neil could tell the inquiry wasn't altogether casual. 'I've got her on the phone. No date for the bones yet.'

Butcher asked if he could have a word with Sacha and as soon as Neil handed his phone over, the man disappeared with it into the house to talk in private. He was so transparent, Neil thought. It was Astrid he felt sorry for.

Five minutes later Butcher emerged and handed the phone back to Neil with a muttered thanks. He looked flushed.

'I've got something to show you,' Butcher said, holding up the briefcase. 'Can we go inside?'

Neil led the way into the living room where he cleared a space on the cluttered dining table, dusting it down with a tea towel he fetched from the kitchen.

From his briefcase Butcher took out a box which contained a small tattered book in a dirty red cloth binding. 'This is the book I mentioned. *The Sea Devil* by Josiah Palkin-Wright. He lived in Tradmouth and became so obsessed with Palkin that he changed his name to Palkin-Wright. He claimed he was a descendant although there's no evidence to back that up. Judging by the book he had access to records I haven't managed to locate. I'll leave it with you. Look after it, won't you.'

'Sure.'

'The more I think about it, the more certain I am that those bones belong to Palkin's wives, Alice and Hawise.'

'You mentioned it before. What's your evidence?'

'In the book Palkin-Wright refers to a letter from John Palkin to a William Petrie in the village of Whitely.'

Butcher turned the pages carefully until he came to the right one. Neil took the book from him and read. From the tone of the correspondence he guessed that Petrie might be some sort of steward or bailiff. The letter asked whether his wife, the lady Alice, was still in residence.

The reply was there too. 'Most worshipful lord, you prayed and required me to tell you if my lady was still at the house. I fear that my lord has received false news for my lady has never visited here since last Martinmas.'

'Is there more?' Neil asked eagerly.

'Yes. A couple of pages later there's a reference to one from Palkin to the mayor complaining that there were scurrilous rumours circulating about the absence of his wife when he knew she had passed away at her manor at Whitely. The two strands of correspondence seem to contradict each other, don't you think?'

Neil sat back in his chair and looked at Butcher. 'So let me get this right. First of all Palkin's wife disappears and he puts a lot of effort into claiming that she died while she was at this manor in Whitely. But a few weeks before he'd written to Petrie to ask if his wife was there and receives a reply that she hadn't been there in months. Why would he do that?'

'The funny thing is, in thirteen ninety-three he marries for a third time and his wife, Hawise, has a son who dies. Then in thirteen ninety-six she disappears from the records too. According to Palkin-Wright there's no mention in any local church archives of masses being said for her soul, as would be expected for someone of her status.' Butcher looked out of the window.

'But if he did away with them and buried them under the floor of his warehouse, why would he write to Petrie? He sounds worried in his letter.'

'Trying to cover his tracks?'

'And don't forget the ground's been disturbed which

suggests the burials could be more recent.' He paused. 'These letters – do they still exist? Has anyone seen them?'

'I've spoken to a friend of yours who works in the archives in Exeter – a very helpful lady called Annabel.'

Neil grinned. 'How is she?'

'She sends you her love. I asked her about the letters and she says there's no trace of them anywhere. Which means they've either vanished since Palkin-Wright saw them or . . .'

'He made the whole thing up for the sake of a good story. What happened to him?'

'He became a recluse after his housekeeper died – according to rumours at the time, they were very close – and he died in nineteen eighteen during the influenza epidemic.' He glanced at the Rolex on his left wrist. 'I've got to go.'

As Butcher hurried away, Neil was left staring at the copy of *The Sea Devil*. But before he could open it he heard Dave calling his name. He was needed out on the site.

'The custody sergeant says Gorst's been asking to see you,' said Wesley. 'Says he has information about Kassia Graylem's murder.'

'Do I smell a confession?'

'You never know your luck. How's Rosie?'

'OK . . . I think.' Gerry stared at the paperwork on his desk. 'She's decided not to press charges, you know.'

'Why?'

'Says she just wants to forget the whole thing. Put it behind her.'

'If he's our man, she could have been his next victim.'

Gerry's hand formed a fist. 'I don't need you to tell me that, Wes.'

Wesley bowed his head. Perhaps he shouldn't have stated the obvious and reminded Gerry of his daughter's vulnerability. If things had gone differently, he might now be identifying her body in Colin Bowman's mortuary.

'Will you talk to Gorst, Wes? I don't think I can trust myself. Sorry to land you with the pleasure of his company but ... '

'No problem.'

Wesley looked through Gerry's window at the outer office. He could see Rachel watching him and it was hard to read her expression. When they'd brought Carthage back to the station to give his statement she'd hardly spoken, apart to share her opinion that the man was weird.

He rang down to the custody suite and requested that Gorst should be brought up from the cells before asking Rachel to sit in on the interview. She pushed her paperwork to one side and stood up, avoiding his eyes. Was it going to be like this from now on: the awkwardness; the embarrassed distance? He led the way down the stairs, saying nothing.

Gorst was waiting for him, having declined the services of the duty solicitor. Either he was confident of his own powers of persuasion or he knew a solicitor would make little difference. From his experience of the criminal mind, Wesley suspected the first. He looked up as they walked in and focused his eyes on Rachel, taking in every curve of her body.

To Wesley, the prisoner's medieval costume made the meeting feel slightly surreal, as if a ruffian from the age of Chaucer had been beamed forward in time and, instead of facing the pillory or the hangman, had become subject to the gentler justice of the Police and Criminal Evidence Act.

'I have to tell you that Ms Heffernan isn't pressing

charges,' Wesley said, the words sticking in his throat.

The response was a satisfied smile and a wink in Rachel's direction. She turned her head away.

'Why should she press charges? She never complained when things got a bit rough before. She enjoyed it,' he added with a knowing leer. Wesley glared at him, glad that Gerry had decided to stay out of it.

'You say you have some information.'

'That's right.'

'What is it?'

'It's about the instrument I found in the bushes. I saw someone dump it there.'

'Who?'

He didn't answer.

'So tell us what happened.'

'I was on my way back to the ship around eight on Saturday morning after spending the night with Rosie and I saw someone throw the case into the bushes. I brought it back to the ship because I thought I might be able to sell it. Make a bit of cash.'

'Who did you see?' Rachel asked.

Gorst looked from one to the other, aware of the power he held. 'It was just a dark figure. Might have been a man. But on the other hand it might have been a woman.'

Wesley glanced at Rachel. Neither of them believed a word of it. But as Rosie had confirmed that he'd been with her until seven thirty on the morning of Kassia's death and wasn't willing to press charges concerning the assault, they didn't have grounds to hold him.

'Can I go now?'

Wesley looked at his watch. Unless they applied for an extension they had to release him soon anyway.

'We might need to speak to you again. Don't leave town, will you?' he said as he stood up.

'No chance of that. We're in port until after the festival's over. Nice doing business with you.' He held out his hand but Wesley turned his back on him.

'What do you think?' he asked Rachel as they climbed the stairs back to the CID office.

'He's hiding something. Kassia was in Palkin's Musik so if he was involved with Rosie, who's to say he hadn't been trying it on with her as well.'

Wesley knew she could well be right.

Wesley made his way back to the incident room and found Gerry in his office.

When he reported his interview with Andre Gorst, he was careful to omit any mention of Rosie. But the fact that she'd provided Gorst with an alibi of sorts made the connection difficult to ignore, especially now he'd come up with this story about seeing someone drop the viol into the bushes. He'd said it could have been a woman; Wesley suspected this was an attempt at misdirection. On the other hand, if he was innocent, why lie?

'Pity about the prints on the viol,' said Gerry.

'Someone wiped it clean before Gorst touched it, which suggests his story might be true.'

Gerry snorted and began to fidget with a paperclip, deep in thought.

All Wesley's instincts told him not to trust Gorst. But perhaps he was just prejudiced. And prejudice clouds the judgement.

'If he's going back to the *Maudelayne*, we know where to find him,' Wesley said.

Gerry picked up a sheet of paper. 'I've just been looking at Miles Carthage's statement. What did you make of him?'

'Strange. He makes me uneasy.'

'Why?'

'I'm not sure that he's entirely in touch with reality.'

'Is he a possible for our murder?'

Wesley thought for a moment. 'I wouldn't rule him out. Kassia was his muse. He was obsessed with painting her. If she put a stop to it for some reason ...' He paused. 'He said he saw her near the jetty where the *Queen Philippa*'s moored.'

'Believe him?'

'It's worth following up.'

'In that case I think we should have another word with Jason Teague and Dennis Dobbs.' Gerry scratched his head. 'Dobbs is in custody over at Bloxham but Teague's out on bail, staying at his mate's flat in Tradmouth. Why don't we go and rattle his cage? I've asked someone to check on the mate, by the way. His name's Jonathan Petworth and he seems to be an upstanding member of society. Married to a farmer's daughter.'

Wesley glanced out of the window at Rachel. He caught her eye and she looked away. 'That doesn't mean he can't have criminal tendencies.'

'It means he's got a stake in local society so he has a lot to lose. And besides, we've got absolutely nothing on him. Not even a whisper of anything dodgy.'

They left the station and skirted the temporary fairground where parents and children sampled the shabby delights of the carousel and the helter-skelter. The scarier rides, Wesley noticed, were virtually empty but they'd come into their own in the evening when the teenagers poured in.

They soon found themselves at the offices of Tradmouth Charters Ltd which occupied the ground floor of a stone former warehouse. The building had once stood by the waterside before the citizens of Tradmouth had indulged in some major land reclamation during the reign of Queen Victoria, around the time Josiah Palkin-Wright was writing his biography of the man he claimed was his illustrious ancestor.

The warehouse Neil was excavating might well have resembled something like this in its heyday, overlooking the water with tall doors on each floor so that goods could be lifted straight off the ships. Whoever had converted this ancient warehouse into a modern office building had preserved the hoists which protruded from the upper floors. However all the doors and windows had been replaced with sparkling glass and the overall effect was pleasing.

Jason Teague was sitting at a pale wood desk not far from the entrance. He was typing something into a computer and he looked bored. Perhaps, Wesley thought, he was finding it hard to settle to a life ashore after his nomadic existence. Gerry had often told him how difficult it was for a sailor to settle for life ashore once the lure of the sea had seeped into the blood.

'Can we have a word?' Gerry said as he walked in.

Jason looked up and Wesley saw a flash of alarm in his eyes. 'I've already told you everything. I had no idea what Den was up to.'

'This isn't about Dobbs,' said Gerry. 'We want to talk to you about Kassia Graylem.'

'I told you, I never met her.'

'Your mate Dobbs found her body in a dinghy floating by

the *Queen Philippa* and we now have a witness who saw her walking near the jetty early on the morning of her death.'

Jason sighed. 'I don't know anything about that. I wasn't there. What about Den? What does he say?'

'That he spent the night playing poker aboard the *Maudelayne*. That's been checked out too. Trouble is, people sometimes lie to us.'

Jason Teague raised his eyebrows. 'That's hardly my fault, is it.'

DC Paul Johnson had heard it said that many cases were solved by routine paperwork; sifting through reports, statements and even CCTV; wading through irrelevant facts to get at the golden nugget. The knack was to recognise the nugget when it turned up on your desk amongst all the dross.

The e-mail attachment didn't appear too promising at first. A list of staff and students at London University while Kassia Graylem and Jenny Bercival had been studying there. As far as Paul could see, there seemed to be rather a lot of them and there were courses whose titles were a complete mystery to him.

It wasn't until he went through the list, searching for familiar names, that he noticed something interesting.

Jenny and Kassia were there all right, Jenny studying English and Kassia history as expected. But it was a name on the list of staff that stood out. Dr Daniel Hungerford, who now worked at Morbay University, had at that time been teaching in London.

With Kassia's musical talent, it was hard to believe that he hadn't come across her at some point, even if he'd never actually taught her. When Paul dug a little further he discovered that as a student she'd played in an early music group directed by Dr Daniel Hungerford, yet he'd claimed that he hadn't met her until he saw her busking in Neston.

It was a discrepancy. And Paul didn't like discrepancies. He hurried to Gerry Heffernan's office to share the news.

Chapter 14

Extract from a letter written at North Lodge, Upper Town, Tradmouth. 17th March 1895

My dearest Letty

   Josiah has been away in Exeter yet again, leaving Maud Cummings as my jailer. However, I discovered a weakness in his arrangements which has played to my advantage.

   Maud, I know, is fond of gin. I have caught her many times with a cup that does not contain the tea she claims it to hold. As soon as I smelled that sweet odour, like cheap eau de cologne, and knew it for what it was, my spirits were renewed at once. Maud Cummings had a failing. And I would use this failing to my own ends.

   So it was that I waited until she was slumped

in her chair in the kitchen, snoring like a pig.
With great care I searched her apron pocket for
the keys I have seen her withdraw from its
depths on many occasions. As I drew them out
she stirred and I was afraid that she would wake
so I stood frozen until she settled to her slumbers
once more. Now I had the keys, the means of
access to every secret part of the house, so I
gathered all my courage and ventured upstairs
to the door.

The previous night Dan Hungerford had been close to becoming Gerry's new best friend. His daughter's rescuer, Wesley knew, had shot up in the DCI's estimation for less than twenty-four hours before the status quo had been restored with Paul's new discovery.

Hungerford lived in Morbay, in one half of a nineteenth-century stucco villa on the hillside overlooking the harbour. Once the house had been home to a single family but after the Second World War it had been divided in two to accommodate the needs of the servantless classes. Hungerford occupied the less impressive half of the house while his neighbour enjoyed the grand front door and the sweeping oak staircase. The police pounded on the plain wooden door round the side of the building that used to be the servants' entrance.

Hungerford looked calm when he answered the door, as though he was expecting to give a routine statement about his rescue of Rosie Heffernan. And when the two uniformed officers told him that he needed to go with them to the police station to be interviewed, he seemed unconcerned. Anything to help the police put away the man who'd been making Rosie's life a misery, he said in the half-eager, half-nervous tone of the helpful citizen, but he had a concert that evening so he couldn't be long. The officers made no comment as they put him in the back of the patrol car and shut the door.

In view of his previous dealings with Hungerford, it was decided that Gerry shouldn't conduct the interview. Instead he watched from behind the two-way mirror while Wesley and Paul sat down opposite Hungerford and started the tape running. He had declined the offer of a solicitor. As far as Wesley could tell, Hungerford still had no idea what the interview was all about. He felt optimistic that the element of surprise would work in his favour.

Wesley placed the printed lists provided by the university in front of Hungerford, who stared down at them with a puzzled frown.

'You admit you taught at London University before you came to Morbay?'

'Of course. It's hardly a crime.'

'We've obtained a list of students who were at the university during the time you were there. There are two familiar names on the list. Kassia Graylem and Jenny Bercival.'

Hungerford froze for a split second. If Wesley hadn't been watching him so closely, he might not have noticed. 'I'll take your word for it.'

'According to university records, Kassia was a member of an early music group in her first year. A group you set up.'

Hungerford said nothing.

'So when you saw her busking in Neston you already knew her.'

'I've dealt with so many students over the years. I can't remember them all.'

'But Kassia was talented. And beautiful. Not easy to forget. Ever been married?'

Hungerford raised his eyebrows and shook his head. 'If you must know, I'm gay. My partner's abroad at the moment so I'm able to devote all my energies to Palkin's Musik.'

'When we first interviewed you why didn't you tell us you'd known Kassia before you met her in Neston?'

He bowed his head. 'OK, it was stupid of me but I didn't think it was relevant. And I didn't want to be a suspect. Palkin's Musik takes up all my time and I really can't afford to sit through hours of questioning. Besides, I don't have any information that might help you catch her killer. Look, for a few months she was in an early music group I set up but she left so I didn't get to know her that well.'

'Why did she leave?'

'I'm not sure. But there was talk that she'd become involved with some man.'

'Do you know anything about him?'

'No. But one day she turned up for a concert in the dress she wore for . . . the one she was found in. I overheard one of the other girls asking her where she got it and she said she'd met a wonderful man who bought it for her.'

'Did she mention the name William de Clare?'

He shook his head. 'As I said, I didn't know her well back then. When I met her in Neston I did ask if she was still seeing the man and she said sometimes. But I had the impression she didn't want to talk about it. Maybe he's married.'

'Did she ever mention John Palkin? Or Shipworld? Or Chris Butcher?'

'No.'

'Does the name Eric Darwell mean anything to you?'

'Isn't he the man who was found dead at that holiday park?'

'That's right. How come you know about it?'

'Because it's been splashed all over the local media. It's hard to miss.'

Wesley was aware that Gerry was watching behind the mirror. He could imagine him signalling frantically, wanting him to keep pressing.'

'You must have seen Kassia every day in the time leading up to her death. Did you get the impression that something was worrying her?'

'She did seem to have something on her mind. But don't ask me what it was.'

'Did she ever mention Miles Carthage? He's an artist. She was posing for him.'

'The name's not familiar.'

'Do you know anything about her tattoo? The one of the ship?'

'No.'

'I understand John Palkin used the symbol to mark his property. What about Jenny Bercival?'

'Who?'

'She was studying at London University when you were teaching there.'

'So were thousands of people. It's a big place. As far as I know I never came across her.'

'Where were you at the time of Kassia's death?'

'I've already given a statement and I've nothing to add to it. I didn't kill Kassia and I've no idea who did.' He leaned forward. 'And why would I kill her? I hardly knew her. And besides, she was a key member of Palkin's Musik and her ... absence has caused us major problems. Can I go now?'

Wesley looked at his watch. Hungerford hadn't told the whole truth about knowing Kassia before Palkin's Musik. And they only had his word for it that he was gay and his partner conveniently abroad. He gave the man a businesslike smile. 'Thank you, Mr Hungerford. You're free to go but we may need to speak to you again.'

'It's Dr Hungerford. Not Mr.'

Hungerford left the room without looking back, hurrying purposefully, as if he was late for another engagement. Maybe the man had been telling the truth; or maybe he knew more about Kassia's death than he was admitting.

Neil had decided to take a break from digging and, after washing his hands in the bungalow's brown-and-cream bathroom, he began to study the book Butcher had left with him. He had only just opened it when one of the student volunteers, a buxom lass with scarlet hair, poked her head round the door.

'Someone to see you, Neil. Wants to talk to the person in charge.'

Neil put the book down carefully. 'Who is it?'

'Old bloke. I've seen him hanging around. He says it's important.'

The girl vanished and returned a minute later with the man Neil had started to think of as the Ancient Mariner. Close up he looked older than Neil first thought; probably in his eighties with a gnarled face that spoke of a life spent out of doors in all weathers. The man took off his greasy Breton cap as if he was coming into the presence of royalty and shuffled his feet.

Neil stood up and stretched out his hand. The man looked surprised but took it. Although his hand felt cold his handshake was surprisingly firm.

'I'm Neil Watson, the site director. What can I do for you?'

The man didn't answer and when Neil invited him to sit, he perched on the edge of a dining chair, as if preparing to flee if necessary.

'I've seen you around . . . taking an interest,' Neil began. 'Would you like to see what we've found?' He was searching for a way to break the ice.

After a few seconds the man spoke. 'My dad built this place, you know. There was an old boathouse on the site and when the land was sold the new owners wanted a nice bungalow.'

'Where exactly was the boathouse?'

'Not sure. But it was quite big. Rickety old wooden thing it was. Must have been there for years.' He hesitated. 'That's where he found the bones.'

Neil sat forward, all attention. 'Go on.'

'He came across 'em when he were digging a drain and covered 'em up again right away. I read in the local paper that you'd found 'em.'

'That's right. When exactly did your dad find them?'

'A few years after the war it were. Didn't want no trouble, that's why he put 'em back.'

Neil was about to say that the police thought they might have uncovered a pair of recent murder victims but something stopped him. It had taken a lot for this man to reveal what he knew and, at his age, he didn't need a hard time. 'Why didn't you come forward earlier?'

'Didn't think you'd be interested. Not till I saw in the

261

paper that the coppers were asking questions. Then I didn't want to get into any trouble.'

'You're not in any trouble, don't worry.'

'Do I have to go to the police?'

'I'll see to that. Look, I don't know your name.'

'Jack Petigrew.' He looked around. 'My dad were proud of this bungalow. I've not been inside since it were finished. They'll not knock it down, will they?'

'I think he plans to modernise it.'

'Who?'

'Man called Chris Butcher. Made his fortune from the internet.'

Petigrew looked perplexed by the mention of modern technology.

'Did you follow in your dad's footsteps and become a builder too?' Neil asked, making conversation.

The man nodded. 'Yes, but I've been retired nearly twenty years. I'd better be off.'

'You've been very helpful. Thanks.'

Jack Petigrew shuffled out but when he reached the door he turned. 'This was the site of Palkin's house, you know. Makes you wonder what he was doing burying skeletons, doesn't it.'

Before Neil could answer he'd gone and Neil's phone was ringing. It was Sacha. She was talking in a low voice, almost husky. He had heard her speak like that before on TV when she said pieces to camera, taking the unseen audience into her confidence.

'I'm still waiting for the dating results and I've ordered stable isotope tests to be done on the skeletons' teeth to discover where the women grew up.'

'Good. I've just had some news. The skeletons were found

by a builder back in the late nineteen forties and reburied, which explains the disturbance to the ground. We can rule out the possibility that they're recent murder victims.'

There was a pause on the other end of the line, as though he'd just stolen Sacha's thunder. 'That's as may be,' she said peevishly. 'But I still stand by my original opinion that they were both murdered. There's dark staining to the facial bones of the first skull which suggests asphyxia and there's a nick in the ribs of the second skeleton, probably a knife wound.'

'I might have an idea who they are.'

'Well?' He'd like to think she sounded impressed but it was probably just surprise.

'According to a book Chris Butcher lent me, John Palkin had two wives who disappeared. They were supposed to have died in parishes some way away but there's no record of their burial in either place.'

He'd assumed that Sacha's antennae for publicity would tell her that this medieval murder mystery was a potentially good story for one of her TV slots. Who could resist? But she said nothing and it occurred to him that Butcher might already have shared this gem of information. It might be old news.

'You seeing Butcher tonight?' he asked before suddenly realising that he hadn't been meant to overhear the conversation. His question must have sounded impertinent. But he wasn't particularly bothered.

'Is that any of your business?' she snapped.

He didn't answer, and he was left listening to the dialling tone. She'd put the phone down on him.

The digging had just about finished for the day and some of the trenches had already been covered with tarpaulins

263

because rain had been forecast. A few of the team had headed into the centre of Tradmouth to get something to eat – fish and chips had been mentioned – giving Neil a chance to read Butcher's offering in peace. He turned the pages of *The Sea Devil* until he came to a section about John Palkin's will. Palkin-Wright had copied the will verbatim and it appeared that everything John Palkin owned had been bequeathed to his brother, Henry, apart from a generous legacy to St Margaret's Church.

Neil read on. He'd read many medieval wills in his time and they were all similar. Full of piety and ardent requests that the prayers of the faithful living should shorten the deceased's time in purgatory. Palkin's didn't vary from the formula, until the next to last sentence.

'And I pray my brother, Henry Palkin, will be relieved of that which is sent by Satan to torment him. May the Lord have mercy upon us. Amen.'

Neil frowned, pondering the kind of torment that might have afflicted the younger brother of this rich and successful man.

His thoughts were interrupted by a knock on the door. He ignored it at first, thinking it was one of his fellow diggers who was too lazy to fish the door key out of his or her pocket. But when there was a second, louder knock he stood up reluctantly and went to answer it.

He was surprised to see Chris Butcher's wife Astrid standing on the doorstep. On her previous visits she'd always looked immaculate in simple stylish clothes that had, no doubt, cost a fortune. Today her hair was loose around her shoulders and she wore jeans and an anorak. Neil thought she looked younger and more vulnerable.

'May I come in?' she said.

'It's your house. Be my guest,' he said, following her into the living room. She looked as if she could do with a coffee so he offered one, which was accepted gratefully.

'Is something wrong?' he asked once the coffee was made.

He hadn't expected her to confide in him, given that she'd hardly said two words to him before. So he was surprised when she sank down on to the sofa, warming her hands around the coffee mug as if seeking comfort, and asked him if he'd seen her husband.

'He was here earlier. Isn't he on the boat?'

She shook her head, then looked him in the eye. 'That woman, the one on TV. Is he seeing her?'

Neil didn't answer for a few moments. There was no way he wanted to get involved in someone else's domestic squabbles. 'What makes you think that?'

She took a sip of coffee and Neil could tell she was suppressing some strong emotion; jealousy probably, or simple anger.

'I don't think you've got anything to worry about with Sacha,' he said, trying to sound reassuring. 'She's only got eyes for one person, and that's herself.'

'Women like that don't know how much pain they cause,' she said almost in a whisper as she stood up to leave.

Neil tried to look as if he understood. But sometimes the human heart was a complete mystery to him.

After Hungerford had left the interview room, Wesley met Gerry out on the corridor.

'What do you think?' Wesley asked.

'He didn't tell us that he'd known Kassia before he met her in Neston. And it doesn't seem like the sort of thing that would slip your mind in the circumstances, does it?' Gerry looked at his watch. 'I'll get someone to confirm that the gay story holds water. Then I suppose someone should speak to Rosie again to try and break Gorst's alibi. And will you tell Trish to contact the Met and all to see if they have anything on Hungerford?'

'Already been done. There's nothing.' He sighed. 'And in a way I can understand why he didn't want to get involved. He's focused on his music and he doesn't want distractions.'

'Bit like Carthage with his art. This case is full of ruddy obsessives. What about Mrs Darwell? Someone keeping an eye on her?'

'The family liaison officer's still with her. She says she might go home to Manchester tomorrow.'

'Good. Pity Butcher was talking to us around the time of Eric's murder. And you and Rachel were interviewing Carthage that afternoon as well.'

'Butcher could still have made it up to the holiday park after we saw him. His car's parked in the Marina Hotel garage so he can't be ruled out yet. Same goes for Carthage, I suppose. Even without a car he could have caught the park-and-ride bus up there and walked the rest of the way.'

'The question is, why would either of them want to dispose of a private investigator from the Manchester suburbs? And why did Darwell tell his secretary that he intended to stay on here for a while to follow a lead. What was all that about?'

'If we knew that, Gerry, we could all go home.'

They'd reached the CID office. Wesley knew he'd have to call Pam to tell her he'd be late again.

As he walked in Rachel glanced up from a report she was

reading and gave him a questioning look. He hovered by her desk for a moment but when she said nothing he returned to his computer to check his e-mails. The awkward silence had made him feel uneasy; besides, he had work to do.

When he'd finished he looked at the noticeboard where pictures of Eric Darwell and Kassia in life and in death were displayed as well as ones of all the suspects whose names had come up in the course of the investigation – and also several of a smiling Jenny Bercival. Jenny's mother hadn't been in touch since her desperate attempt to make them take notice had been revealed as a deception. He wondered how she was doing and he was tempted to suggest to Gerry that they visit her. But what had they to tell her? Nothing.

He stared at the photographs, hoping for inspiration, for that elusive idea that would lead him to the truth. Kassia had definitely known Hungerford and there was always a chance that Jenny had too. Both women had unquestionably been under the spell of Chris Butcher, a wealthy and charismatic older man who'd involved them in his created fantasy world. But had this had anything to do with their fate? And where did Eric Darwell fit in? Because Wesley was as sure as he could be that his death was somehow linked to Kassia's.

A pile of witness statements taken from the guests and staff at Newlands Holiday Park lay on his desk. He picked them up and began to sift through them, hoping for inspiration. It had been raining on that fateful day so there hadn't been many people around, which meant that the statements seemed uniformly unhelpful.

However, near the bottom of the pile he came to one

which varied from the rest and suddenly he felt a frisson of excitement. An eight-year-old girl had been looking out of the window of a chalet near the pool where Eric Darwell's body had been found, waiting for the rain to stop. She told her mother that she'd seen a man in a suit walking towards the pool with somebody at his side. When she'd been asked to describe this person she'd done even better than that and named him.

The man in the suit had been walking through the holiday park in the drizzle accompanied by John Palkin himself.

Chapter 15

*Extract from a letter written at North Lodge,
Upper Town, Tradmouth, 17th March 1895*

*I was afraid, dear sister. I had the means to
discover my husband's secrets but my courage
almost failed me. I thought of Maud Cummings
asleep and snoring in the kitchen and I feared
that she might awake and discover my treachery
at any moment. And yet I knew I must proceed
as I might not have another opportunity.*

*I ascended the stairs on tiptoe and unlocked
the door but when the room beyond was
revealed, the scene that greeted me was so
terrible that I cried out. I fear to even set the
words down on paper, it was so dreadful.*

*Please, my dearest Letty, I beg you to come to
my aid. The Reverend Johnson, might help you.*

He is a good man, although I fear he will hesitate to interfere in matters between man and wife. But ours is no true marriage and I beg you to tell him this.

When Gerry told Wesley to go home and get some sleep because they had an early start tomorrow, he hurried eagerly out of the office. Gerry told Rachel to go too but she didn't move, even though her housemate, Trish, was putting on her coat. It was almost as if Rachel was reluctant to go home and the sight of her sitting there, tapping the keys of her computer, engrossed in her work, made Wesley uneasy. When he repeated Gerry's order that she should go and get some rest she didn't acknowledge him.

It was eight o'clock when he set off, his mind still on the child's strange statement. The man in the suit was walking towards the open-air pool with John Palkin. Mind you, there were any number of people in Tradmouth dressed as Palkin, disguising beard and all. Either the little girl had seen one of them, or she had an overactive imagination. He'd sent a woman DC to have a word with the little girl and he hoped she'd get at the truth.

When he arrived home he was surprised to find Neil in his kitchen, sitting at the breakfast table with Pam and the kids, tucking into a Chinese takeaway. Michael was listening with rapt attention to Neil's pronouncements about a community dig he was organising during the summer vacation and, in spite of an unexpected pang of envy at the sight of his wife, kids and best friend sitting there in such relaxed harmony, it was gratifying that his son was displaying so much enthusiasm. A few months ago he would have been more interested in hanging out with his mates, the ones

270

who'd encouraged him to take part in a shoplifting spree. Wesley said a silent prayer of thanks that his fall from grace seemed to be a phase; yet he knew that as the teenage years were approaching like an oncoming bulldozer, he couldn't relax. Perhaps parents never can.

Once the children had disappeared upstairs to their rooms, he opened a bottle of wine. Pam took hers into the dining room, saying she had reports to write before the new half term started. Wesley knew she was deliberately leaving him and Neil to talk.

'We weren't expecting you,' said Wesley.

'Something's cropped up and I thought you should know about it.'

Wesley felt a sudden twinge of panic. Perhaps he'd been too quick to put the discovery of the bones at Chris Butcher's house out of his mind.

'Is it the skeletons? Have you had the results of the tests?'

'Better than that. I've been talking to a witness … well, the son of one. There's this old guy who's been hanging around.'

'Breton cap?'

Neil nodded. 'I thought he was just interested in the dig but earlier today he plucked up the courage to speak to me. He told me his dad built the bungalow in the late nineteen forties on the site of a derelict boathouse and came across the skeletons when he was laying a sewer pipe. He didn't want a fuss so he reburied them, which explains why the ground was disturbed.'

'Thank God for that,' said Wesley. But the expression on Neil's face told him there was more to come. 'You look worried. What is it?'

'I've just had a strange visit from Chris Butcher's wife,

271

Astrid. She's worried that her husband might be up to something with Sacha.'

'And is he?'

'He's definitely been coming on to her and she's been encouraging him – flirty phone calls and all that. I thought you'd be interested, seeing as you've been interrogating him.'

'I'd hardly describe it as interrogating but thanks anyway.' He already knew about Butcher's inability to keep his trousers on and his double life as William de Clare so what Neil had just told him wasn't really news. As far as he was concerned, it was natural that Astrid should be concerned. Butcher was a charmer, a risk-taker who probably got his thrills from living on the edge of danger.

Wesley turned over the possibilities in his mind. Kassia Graylem had spent the night with Chris Butcher and Astrid was a woman scorned. Perhaps she hadn't been in London that night as she'd claimed. Maybe she'd returned to Tradmouth early and found them together. Maybe she'd followed Kassia and killed her. Colin said a strong woman could have done it. Perhaps the same thing had happened a year ago when she'd found him with Jenny.

He took a sip of wine. It tasted good as it slipped down his throat, warming and relaxing. He hadn't realised until that moment how much he had been looking forward to his small evening vice. He took a second sip. 'I'd like to speak to Astrid. Do you know if she's still on the boat?'

'She said she was sick of it so she checked into the Marina Hotel.'

Neil produced a slim cardboard box from his pocket. Wesley recognised it as the kind of acid-free box museums sometimes use to protect ancient books. Neil passed the box to him. Before he opened it he washed his hands at the sink and made sure the table was clear of any sticky remnants of the meal that might damage old paper. When he took the book out he saw the title. *The Sea Devil* by Josiah Palkin-Wright, the man who'd once owned the house where Miles Carthage rented a flat.

He turned the pages carefully, reading a passage here and there. 'I detect a strong whiff of hero worship,' he said as he neared the end of the book.

'It was his life's work. Butcher's been in touch with Annabel. She's found Palkin's will but none of the correspondence Palkin-Wright refers to in the book. I've given her a call and asked her to find out what she can – go through old local auction catalogues and all that. If the correspondence still exists, she's sure to unearth it.'

Wesley smiled to himself. Neil had always had great faith in Annabel, who worked in the archives in Exeter and was the daughter of an honourable who mixed in county circles. There had been times when Wesley thought that the pair might be made for each other in spite of the wide social chasm between them. Sometimes, however, sex can spoil things.

'There's an interesting bit at the end about Palkin's death,' Neil said, leaning over to turn the pages. 'Listen.' He picked up the book, held it in front of him and cleared his throat.

'"In 1404 John Palkin was sixty-six years old and had recently organised the defeat of a Breton army which mounted an invasion at Whitepool Sands in retaliation for Palkin's raids upon Breton ports. It is not known whether Palkin himself fought in the skirmish which saw hundreds of Bretons killed or taken prisoner with few English casualties.

King Henry IV himself congratulated him on his victory and gave tacit support to his continuing privateering activities. Later that year Palkin married his fourth wife, who was at least forty years his junior, and it was his bitter jealousy of his young bride that brought about his demise. His brother, Henry, told him that his bride was entertaining a lover in the bedchamber of his house by the waterfront. Palkin set up a ladder to look into the window and catch her in the act of lovemaking but he lost his footing and fell to the ground. He died but in the days following his funeral, which was conducted with great pomp in St Margaret's Church, several citizens of Tradmouth claimed to have seen his bloodied corpse walking the streets. His grave in the chancel of the church was opened and a stake driven through his heart. From that moment on all sightings of John Palkin ceased."'

Wesley raised his eyebrows. 'So Tradmouth had its very own vampire.'

'Amazing what rubbish people will believe.'

Wesley said nothing for a while. Then he spoke. 'What became of the widow and her lover? Any idea who he was, by the way?'

'Palkin-Wright doesn't say.'

'And it's possible that he only existed in John Palkin's imagination. Or his brother, Henry's. Maybe he was trying to stir up trouble.'

'Trust you to look for complications. I'll contact Annabel again and ask her what she can find out about Palkin's death,' said Neil as he poured himself another glass of wine.

After spending the previous night in the cells sleeping on a hard blue plastic mattress, Andre Gorst felt good walking down the embankment with the salt breeze on his face. After returning to the *Maudelayne* for a change of clothes, avoiding the captain who was prone to ask too many questions at the best of times, he had washed in the public showers next to the toilets in the park, thoughtfully provided by the harbour authorities for visiting yachtsmen, and spent the evening in the Star. Shortly after ten thirty he set off in the darkness to do the business that had been on his mind since his arrest. It would be easy money; and God knows he needed some of that.

He'd seen his quarry earlier that day, alone and vulnerable. It had only taken a few words and it was arranged. Gorst's silence would be assured for a sum of his choosing. A reasonable amount. He wasn't a greedy man.

A thin veil of drizzle meant that the embankment was almost deserted. This was the meeting that would buy him a few of life's luxuries: things to lure women into his web at his next port of call. Love them and leave them. Use them and leave them wanting more. He'd had a narrow escape with Rosie Heffernan and he cursed her for not telling him her dad was a senior police officer. Still, it had worked out all right in the end.

In the yellow light trickling from the lampposts that lined the waterfront he could see a figure approaching, carrying a plastic carrier bag as arranged. This was his chance.

Gorst planned to count the money there and then because you can never trust anybody, especially a murderer. He walked forward and held out his hand to take the bag but the figure hugged it protectively.

'How can I trust you?' The question was hissed.

Gorst didn't answer. 'Is it all there?'

The figure suddenly held the bag aloft and began to back

away, teetering on the water's edge. Even though the tide was high it was a long way down into the dark, oily water.

The figure turned and began to walk away and Gorst had no choice but to follow.

'If you don't pay up, I'll go to the police. I'll tell them what I saw.'

'Why would they believe you?'

'They will. I saw you put that violin case in the bushes.'

The figure began to swing the bag. It looked heavy – too heavy to contain the paper money that had been promised. The figure twisted the thin plastic of the handle around its hand, drew back its arm and, before Gorst could dodge out of the way, the bag made contact with his head.

Gorst fell to his knees, startled. Whatever was in that bag was indeed heavy and he felt something hot run down his face: his own blood. He raised his hands in defence against the onslaught.

But it was useless. The blows came fast, raining down on his knuckles and his skull, sending him sprawling, dazed, on to the cobbles. He was at the edge now, looking down into the black water.

The next blow sent him tumbling over the harbour wall. Then came the darkness.

Wesley awoke the next morning with a headache. He knew it was from simple lack of sleep because he'd lain awake thinking about the case; about the child who'd claimed to have seen Eric Darwell with John Palkin. The trouble was, searching for Palkin lookalikes in Tradmouth at that moment when the festival was about to reach its climax would be like looking for a blade of grass in a field. He took a couple of paracetamol tablets with his breakfast coffee and by the time he was ready to leave the house his headache was almost gone.

When he arrived at the station he found that Gerry had got there before him and was trawling his way through a pile of paperwork with a martyred expression on his face.

'Neil had a visit from Chris Butcher's wife last night,' Wesley began before going on to give Gerry a quick résumé of the previous night's events.

Gerry pushed the paperwork to one side and sat forward, interested. 'In that case it might be worth having another word with Mrs Butcher. Hell hath no fury and all that. If she's jealous of anyone her husband has a fling with, that could include Kassia and Jenny. Not that I'd blame her. Can't be easy being married to a Lothario.'

Wesley smiled. 'Lothario. That's a deliciously old-fashioned word, Gerry.'

'Good one though,' Gerry said with a wink.

'I have got one bit of encouraging news. The dating's not come through on those bones yet but there's evidence that they predate the late nineteen forties.' He went on to relate what Neil had told him about the builder's discovery. Gerry looked relieved.

'At least that's one less thing to worry about. I was afraid it might have been Jenny and some other poor lass.' He sighed. 'Doesn't help us find her though, does it.'

Wesley returned to his desk and sat staring at the picture of Kassia pinned up on the noticeboard, ignoring the pile of reports awaiting his attention. Suffolk police had concluded that her parents' death had been a tragic accident; even so, Wesley was still bothered by the report of the argument overheard by a couple on a nearby boat a few hours before the Graylems died. He searched round his desk for the file on the accident and when he found it he noted the couple's contact details. One of the DCs had already spoken to them but there were things he wanted to clarify.

When the phone was answered by a woman who confirmed that she was Mrs Betham, he apologised for bothering her again.

The first thing Mrs Betham asked was whether they'd caught Kassia's killer. She remembered her quite well. Such a pretty girl. Her and her father used to busk in the town centre sometimes. She'd had a beautiful voice.

'We're following a number of leads,' Wesley said noncommittally. 'You said you heard the Graylems arguing that morning. Did they often argue?'

'Oh no. I never heard them rowing with each other. They were very ... Bohemian, if you know what I mean, but they seemed to get on well.'

'So tell me about this argument you overheard?'

'It was about an hour before Jake Graylem took the boat out that morning. A few hours before the explosion. I heard raised voices and I'm sure one of them was Jake but I'm not sure who the other person was.'

'Could Mr Graylem have been arguing with his wife or daughter?'

'I'm sorry, I don't know.'

'Did you hear what was said?'

'Not really. I only caught a few words. I think he said something like, "I can't trust you. I don't want you on board." But I can't swear to it.'

'I believe a yacht belonging to a family called Wentworth was moored next to the Graylems' boat.'

There was a silence on the other end of the line. 'That's right. But they'd sailed off before the explosion.'

'Can you tell me about the Wentworths?'

'They had a very flashy yacht. I think the father was a barrister or something. He wasn't exactly friendly.'

'Who was on their boat?'

'It was just Mr Wentworth and his son. He was a good-looking lad. They didn't seem to have much in common with the Graylems but he used to chat up Kassia, which is hardly surprising, I suppose. I didn't really speak to the boy but . . .'

'But what?'

'I got the impression he was an arrogant little pup. Though I might be misjudging him. But I'll tell you one thing: the father had a hell of a temper. I used to hear him yelling at the boy and—'

'Could he be the one who was arguing with Jake Graylem?'

Mrs Betham hesitated before replying. 'I don't know. I'm sorry.'

'Can you remember the boy's name?'

Mrs Betham apologised again. She really couldn't recall.

Wesley thanked her and rang off. He was about to ask someone to make tracing the Wentworths a priority when Paul came rushing up to his desk.

'You know that kid said she'd seen Eric Darwell with Palkin? We've got someone dressed as Palkin on CCTV from a newsagent's near the holiday park at the relevant time. Come and see.'

Wesley followed him into the AV room where DC Nick Tarnaby was sitting going through footage; it was a tedious job but someone had to do it. He leaned over Nick's shoulder but the man didn't look round. The indistinct monochrome image on the screen was of someone striding past the shop in full medieval dress, the battered briefcase he was carrying striking an incongruous note. He looked portly but the costume could well have been padded and it was hard to gauge the height. He wore a velvet cap on his head and a false beard concealed his features.

This was no use at all. For all they knew, it could even have been a woman.

The young man aboard the ferry was crossing the river from Queenswear to Tradmouth dressed in a Robin Hood costume he'd acquired for a fancy dress party a couple of years before. He was leaning over the side, anticipating a boozy meeting with his mates at the Palkin Festival, when he spotted the body floating face downward.

As soon as the ferry reached the quayside the police were called and eventually the body was hauled into the launch to be taken back to dry land, watched by curious onlookers.

They assumed that it was somebody who'd been carousing at the festival, had too much to drink and fallen in. It happened every year. The river liked to claim a life, to feed on living flesh to keep up its strength.

Trish entered Gerry's office, brimming with untold news. Wesley stood beside Gerry and waited for her to speak.

'The captain of the *Maudelayne* called to say that Andre Gorst has gone missing.' Wesley could see her cheeks redden, as if she'd suddenly recalled Gorst's link with the boss's daughter and feared she'd said something tactless.

'Anything else?'

'The police launch picked up a body an hour ago. Man who fits Gorst's description. He's been taken to Tradmouth Hospital.'

'Suspicious?'

'Not sure yet.'

Wesley and Gerry looked at each other. 'We'll get some-one from the ship to identify the body and see what Colin has to say about the cause of death,' said Gerry. He went out briefly to give orders to a couple of the younger DCs who scurried off.

Wesley's mind was working. He hadn't believed Gorst's claim that he hadn't seen who'd dumped the viol. On the other hand, he couldn't think why he should lie. A possibility was forming in his head; even so, he'd wait to hear Colin's verdict before sharing it with Gerry.

Trish was still hovering in the doorway. She hadn't finished yet. 'There's something else. Scientific Support have found deleted e-mails about Shipworld on Miles Carthage's computer. They're from Palkinson, all about Lady Alicia in the boat and later being buried in Palkin's warehouse. There's also stuff about a Lady Morwenna being imprisoned for her sins in the Cave of Adron. The interesting thing is that it seems to be Carthage who's thinking up the plot, not Palkinson. He's just writing the text to Carthage's instructions and sending the material through for his approval.'

'That's not what Butcher told us. Do we have an address for Palkinson?'

'Yes. His name's Peter Joss.' She paused. 'The address is Bolton Hall. Same as Kassia Graylem's.'

Wesley raised his eyebrows. This was a complete surprise and there was only one possibility that he could see. Peter Joss was Kassia's housemate, Pixie. After all, nobody's christened Pixie and, as he hadn't come under suspicion, they'd never taken the trouble to learn his real name when they'd interviewed him.

'We'd better pay Mr Joss a visit,' said Gerry as he stood up. 'Then we'll have another word with Miles Carthage. He lied to us.'

Even this new revelation about Pixie's involvement with Shipworld couldn't take Wesley's mind off the accident that had killed Kassia's parents. As he drove out towards Neston with Gerry chatting and speculating beside him in the passenger seat, he kept visualising the explosion that had shattered the peace of the Suffolk evening and the distraught fifteen-year-old girl whose world had come to a terrible end.

When they reached Bolton Hall it struck Wesley that nothing much had changed since their last visit apart from the presence of a rusty yellow Skoda parked on the weed-infested gravel at the front of the house.

Scarlett Derringer answered the door wearing a short floral dress, baggy cardigan and flip-flops.

'What's new?' she said as she let them in. 'Have you got the bastard who killed Kassia yet?'

Wesley ignored her question. 'Is Pixie in?'

Scarlett looked a little alarmed. 'Why? He's got nothing to do with it. Anyway, he was here on the morning you say she died.'

'Where is he now?'

'In the garden planting carrots. He's still upset about Kassia so go easy, will you?'

'You're absolutely sure he was here on Saturday morning around six o'clock?'

Scarlett hesitated. 'He never gets up early.'

'What time did you first see him that morning?'

'When I was getting breakfast. About nine . . . nine thirty.

'So he could have already gone out and come back?'

'I didn't hear his car.'

'Would you have heard it if he'd gone out?'

She looked away. 'My room's at the back of the house so ... Look, Pixie always tells me if he's going out.'

'But you can't really be sure,' said Wesley like a cross-examining lawyer.

Scarlett looked horrified, as if she feared she'd just landed her friend in deep trouble.

'We need to speak to him,' Wesley said more gently. 'Please.'

All of a sudden they heard a car engine start up. 'Is that his car outside? The yellow one?'

Scarlett hesitated for a moment then she gave a small nod. Wesley opened the front door and rushed out, only to see the Skoda disappearing down the drive. Not being one for the drama of car chases, he made the call ordering all patrols to be on the lookout for Pixie's vehicle. The state the car appeared to be in, it probably wouldn't get far.

'Do you know Pixie's real name?' he asked.

'It's Peter but nobody ever calls him that. Apart from his dad who he can't stand. His mum used to call him Pixie when he was little. He prefers it. She died when he was fourteen,' she added in a matter-of-fact voice.

'People in this house don't seem to have much luck with parents,' said Gerry. 'Yours are dead, so are Kassia's. And now Pixie's mum ...'

'Maybe that's why we found each other. Orphans of the storm.'

'What about Pixie's dad?'

'He says he's a bastard who's only interested in women and money. They don't get on.'

'Does Pixie work?'

'He does a bit of computer stuff and some freelance copywriting I think. He's really into all that fantasy stuff.'

'I thought you didn't have a computer here,' said Wesley.

'I don't and neither did Kassia. But Pixie does. Like I said, he needs it for work.'

'What kind of fantasy stuff does he work on?'

'Search me. I hate anything to do with computers.' She looked Wesley in the eye. 'I started off life as an IT specialist and had a breakdown. Not touched the things since.'

'Mind if we have a look at Pixie's room?'

'It's not for me to say, is it? But if I refuse, I suppose you'll get a warrant and search anyway. Up the stairs, turn right. Last door on your left. And don't make a mess.'

When Wesley and Gerry reached the room it was in virtual darkness. The threadbare curtains were drawn against the sunlight and the first thing Gerry did was to fling them open. A cloud of dust billowed down, making Wesley cough.

'Right then,' said Gerry as Wesley recovered his composure. 'Let the dog see the rabbit.'

Gerry took the chest of drawers and Wesley the wardrobe. It wasn't long before he found something that looked out of place amongst the frayed jeans and faded T-shirts. He took the cardboard folder off the wardrobe shelf and opened it.

Nestling in the file beside Miles Carthage's lavish illustrations, Wesley saw a wad of A4 sheets typed with text, scarred with scribbled notes and amendments. He began to turn the pages and realised that it was the same text they had read on the Shipworld website. Nothing they hadn't seen before. Without a word he passed the file over to Gerry.

'Give Traffic Division a call will you, Wes. We need Pixie

picked up as soon as possible. And tell the lazy buggers to get their fingers out and treat it as urgent.'

Wesley did as he was asked, then finished searching the wardrobe and made for the door.

Gerry turned his head. 'Where are you off to?'

'Kassia's room.'

'It's already been searched.'

'I know. But I saw a photograph album in there. I'd like to have another look at it.'

He crossed the landing and opened the door to Kassia's room. Once inside he could tell things had been disturbed by the search team, little items out of place and the duvet turned back.

He took the pink album from the drawer where he'd found Lisa's card and the notes from Miles Carthage and flicked through the photographs of Kassia and her parents with their boat until he came to the empty space where one had been removed. *Me, Dad, Mum and R.*

When he came downstairs, he told Scarlett he was taking the album back to the station and gave her a receipt which she stuffed into the pocket of her cardigan as though she didn't know quite what to do with it. Over the years he'd learned it was as well to do things by the book whenever possible.

They were about to leave Bolton Hall when a call came through to say that Peter Joss, a.k.a. Pixie, had been picked up on the main road into Tradmouth.

'Now that's perfect timing,' Gerry said as he settled down in the passenger seat looking pleased with himself.

Captain Garcia of the *Maudelayne* had arrived at the mortuary, still in costume which caused some raised eyebrows amongst the staff. He'd been taken to the viewing room where he confirmed that the dead man was his crew member, Andre Gorst.

Colin Bowman's first thought was that the head injury could have been accidental or caused postmortem, but on closer examination he concluded that it looked suspicious.

He went to his office and made himself a cup of Earl Grey before calling Gerry Heffernan to tell him the news.

Andre Gorst had been identified and it was possible that he'd been murdered. But then, Gerry observed, a man like that was bound to make a lot of enemies.

However, Gorst wasn't going anywhere. And Peter Joss was waiting in the interview room. When Wesley and Gerry joined him he looked up, almost as if he was pleased to see them.

'You create the text for Chris Butcher's Shipworld website?' said Wesley once the introductions had been made for the tape.

'It's gainful employment – better than benefits. And I worked as a copywriter in London in another life so I'm bloody good at it,' he added with a hint of pride.

'I thought it was fans who sent in material,' said Wesley.

'They sometimes do.' He smirked. 'But most of it needs editing or completely rewriting. That's why I'm needed. To keep the story on track.'

'What about the death of Alicia?'

'What about it?'

'You described Kassia's death. Almost as though you'd been there.'

'I didn't need to see it to describe it. I knew what she was

286

wearing 'cause she always wore that blue dress for concerts and I knew she'd been found in a boat. All it needed was a bit of text description.'

'Didn't you think it was in bad taste?'

For a moment he looked uncomfortable. 'All writers are vampires living off other people's misfortunes,' he said. 'Anyway, it wasn't my idea.'

'Whose was it?'

'Miles Carthage. Now there's a weird man.'

'What do you mean by weird?' Wesley asked.

'He's . . . obsessive.'

'Think he's capable of murder?' Gerry asked.

'Wouldn't surprise me.' He paused. 'But what would I know?'

'We've found the e-mails you exchanged.'

For a second Pixie looked worried. 'So?'

'He gives you the instructions. Thinks up the storylines.'

'He's well in, isn't he.'

'How do you mean?'

'He's related to Chris Butcher . . . not that he doesn't have talent.'

This was something new. 'How is he related to Butcher?' asked Wesley.

'I don't know exactly. All I know is that he's family.'

Wesley and Gerry exchanged looks.

'Did you know Kassia used to pose for him?'

'Yeah. He told her she inspired him and she was flattered.'

'You never thought to mention it to us?'

'I didn't think it was important.'

'Why did you run when we came to Bolton Hall?' Gerry asked.

'I didn't. I needed to go to Neston from some bird netting. The buggers are destroying my veg patch.'

'Have you been in touch with Miles recently?' said Wesley.

'Yeah. He's come up with a big new storyline. A huge battle between Palkin's forces and the Devil Elves of Bretania. Look, you don't think he's got anything to do with Kassia's murder, do you? Because if he did, I feel bad about not doing more to stop her going there. I thought he was harmless but ... '

'Ever heard of Jenny Bercival?' said Gerry.

Pixie shook his head. 'No. Who is she?'

Wesley believed him.

'We need to talk to Miles Carthage,' said Wesley as they walked back to the CID office.

Gerry sighed. 'We've got an appointment with Andre Gorst first. Apparently dead men can't wait.'

The postmortem confirmed Colin's suspicions. Andre Gorst's lungs, now sitting in a steel dish, had been filled with river water. He'd drowned but, like Eric Darwell, he'd been rendered unconscious before falling or being pushed into the River Trad.

Gorst's head injury, Colin reckoned, had been caused by some sort of cosh, not a baton or anything like that, something more shapeless. Maybe a sandbag, or another equally heavy object. He had met his death sometime last night, probably between ten p.m. and two in the morning. Colin apologised for not being more specific.

Gerry had sent a team out to seek potential witnesses amongst the yachtsmen whose vessels were moored by the embankment and the Palkin Festival revellers. It had been raining last night but he still hoped someone had seen something.

'Well, one thing's for sure,' Wesley said as they walked towards Albany Street, pushing their way through the crowds lured out by the early afternoon sun. 'He did see who dumped that viol and I think he tried to blackmail them.'

'I knew he was lying to us,' said Gerry. 'If he hadn't been, he'd still have been alive.' There was no regret in Gerry's voice, just a simple statement of fact. 'After what he did to our Rosie, maybe the bastard deserved everything he got.'

Wesley said nothing.

There was no answer at Miles Carthage's flat so Wesley and Gerry returned to the police station. They'd try again later. Wesley tried to call Chris Butcher to ask about Pixie's claim that Carthage was a relative, but all he got was his voice mail.

When Wesley sat down at his desk he saw Rachel watching him.

'What's that?' she asked.

It was a few seconds before he realised what she was talking about. The bright pink photograph album decorated with kittens that he'd taken from Kassia's room was sitting on the edge of his desk, looking out of place amongst the files and reports.

'I found it in Kassia's room. It contains pictures of her and her parents at their boat.'

Rachel raised her eyebrows. 'It survived the explosion?'

Wesley picked up the album and flicked through the pages. 'According to the report, Kassia had a new camera with her when it happened, along with the viol which she was carrying because her and her dad had been busking in the town. If she hadn't stopped to take some pictures she would have been killed. It's my guess that these pictures were already in the camera and she had them printed later. I was intending to go through them but then Peter Joss was brought in.'

'Want me to have a look?' She was looking at him hopefully.

'No, it's OK. I'll do it later.'

She turned away. For everybody's sake, he needed to get this sorted once and for all.

Nobody had seen anything suspicious on the night of Andre Gorst's death, or at least nobody was admitting to it. But they'd keep plugging away, asking questions and checking CCTV footage. It was often the tedious routine stuff that produced results.

Wesley sat at his desk, turning the pages of the photograph album. Maybe he was wasting his time and it was irrelevant. But he still wondered why that one picture was missing. *Me, Dad, Mum and R.*

He pushed the album to one side and caught sight of the photographs on the office wall. There was Jenny Bercival smiling down at him and he couldn't help thinking of her mother. She was still in Tradmouth, still venturing out every day to the Palkin Festival studying the face of every young woman in the desperate hope that she might be Jenny.

As yet there had been no sightings of Jenny. And the ever-present possibility remained that the hungry river had claimed her on that night a year ago. Her disappearance might have been tragic rather than sinister, but before she'd vanished she'd been seen in the market square and at the edge of that square there was a flight of steps which led up to Albany Street where Miles Carthage lived. Carthage who not only illustrated Shipworld but who also devised the storylines and regarded Kassia Graylem as his muse. And then there was Pixie's claim that Carthage was related to Chris Butcher. They needed to speak to Butcher as soon as possible.

He looked up and saw Rachel standing by his desk.

'Scientific Support have found more stuff on Peter Joss's computer. More e-mails from Miles Carthage telling him the storylines. Look at these. They're dated a year ago.'

The sheet of paper she handed him was filled with extracts from e-mails. Someone, probably Rachel herself, had picked out the juicy bits so he wouldn't have to plough through them and he felt grateful. He began to read.

'The Lady Morwenna is coming to the Shroud Maker tonight and he must keep her safe so that she cannot betray Palkin.' He looked at the date – the day Jenny Bercival had vanished. He read on. 'The Shroud Maker will keep the Lady Morwenna secure and feast upon her beauty. None must know she is held in the Cave of Adron.'

There were more story outlines: elves, battles, beautiful wraiths who were once maidens in thrall to the Shroud Maker. All things that Gerry would have dismissed as nonsense. Then about ten days ago a message had been sent saying that another maiden was in need of protection, one beautiful enough to tempt any man. Her name was Alicia and she wore a gown of blue velvet.

'These e-mails weren't on Carthage's computer.'

'He must have deleted them, which is suspicious in itself, don't you think? We can get Scientific Support to have a look.' She looked rather pleased with herself. 'There's something else. I asked someone to run a check on Carthage and it turns out he actually owns that house on Albany Street. He inherited it from a great-uncle four years ago. The great-uncle was a recluse who was related to Josiah Palkin-Wright. The house has been in the same family for over a century.'

Wesley turned round to face her. 'Carthage led us to believe that he just rented the first-floor flat. Wonder why that was.'

'I'll organise a search warrant for the house shall I?' said Rachel.

As soon as Wesley had nodded his assent Rachel made for Gerry's office and he watched as she broke the news. Gerry took his feet off his desk and straightened his back, all attention. Wesley knew he'd be impatient to question Carthage and search his house. But they had to follow procedure. One slip-up could ruin everything.

Chapter 16

Extract from a letter written at North Lodge,
Upper Town, Tradmouth, 17th March 1895

I stood in the doorway, stunned at the sight of
the woman, half-naked, filthy and chained to
the wall. The poor creature was barely
conscious of my presence and I thought her
close to death. Then I understood. The
humiliation that my husband had heaped upon
me had been heaped upon this unhappy woman
a hundredfold.

I surmised that my husband and his creature,
Maud Cummings, had imprisoned this
unfortunate and I resolved to set her at liberty
and bring the wrongdoers to justice.

I approached her and saw the terrible wheals
upon her bare flesh. 'Who are you?' I whispered,

robbed of my voice by the horror of my new situation.

She opened her eyes and I could see that, against the grey filth on her delicate face, they were the vivid blue of cornflowers.

'Help me,' she gasped. As she shifted I could hear the rattle of her chains and I began to investigate her restraints to see how I could free her. The chains were secured with strong locks and, recalling Maud Cummings' keys, I searched amongst them for one that might bring about this woman's release. As I tried one key after another, I asked her how she had come to be in this dreadful situation.

The woman bowed her head as if in shame, and when she began to speak, her voice was barely audible.

Neil sensed that Chris Butcher was losing patience with the excavation he'd seemed so keen to encourage a few weeks before. He'd announced that morning that he was anxious for the builders to make a start so that the work could be completed before the weather deteriorated. The implication was that he wanted Neil and his team out. Maybe the novelty of buying a house on a site occupied since the Middle Ages had worn thin.

Since the night she'd visited the house Astrid had treated him with a distant coolness, as though she found the memory of her confidences embarrassing. Neil, however, was too busy recording the site for posterity and making sure the correct procedures were followed to worry too much about Butcher's domestic life.

Sacha had been in touch at last with the dating results for the skeletons. The young females had both died between the years 1870 and 1915, which raised as many questions as it answered. Neil hadn't heard from Sacha again since her call, which didn't particularly worry him. He didn't like the woman and it wouldn't bother him if he never worked with her again.

But he was curious about those bones, about why they were there and who was responsible for the deaths, because Sacha was certain that they were murder victims. For a while he'd thought they might be Palkin's two missing wives, the ones mentioned in *The Sea Devil*. Now it seemed the mystery was more recent.

He'd made some calls and discovered that, at the time the women were buried, the land and the boathouse had belonged to Josiah Palkin-Wright, the author who had claimed descent from the great man. He needed to find out more about Palkin-Wright, to know whether he was linked to the bodies or whether they'd just been deposited in his disused boathouse by an opportunist.

Most of the evidence for John Palkin's life, the evidence that inspired the Shipworld website and the festival, had come from Palkin-Wright's work. He'd been a man with an obsession who'd regarded John Palkin as some sort of hero. And he'd delved into the minutiae of the medieval Mr Big's life, obtaining source material that, as far as Neil – and even Annabel – knew hadn't been seen or referred to before or since. Somewhere, Neil thought, these documents might still exist. Or had they only existed in the mind of the author?

On his way back from visiting Wesley the previous evening he'd walked past North Lodge and stopped to read the plaque beside the front door. Although the house appeared to have been split into flats at some point in its history, it didn't seem to have undergone any violent modernisation over the years. Palkin-Wright's possessions would probably have been disposed of a century ago but there was always a slender chance that some trunk might have been overlooked and abandoned in some forgotten corner of a dusty attic. Now the dig was coming to an end he was feeling restless; and he was eager to see inside that house.

He walked through streets that were virtually deserted and when he reached the house he tried the bell with the name M Carthage printed neatly beside it. If, by any remote chance, anything had been left behind, it would probably be in the attic and there was a chance the tenant might have access.

When there was no answer he pressed the unlabelled bottom bell and heard it sounding somewhere in the depths of the building. He waited a while but when nothing happened he started to walk away, turning to look up at the two small dusty windows just below the roof.

He was imagining the things that might still be nestling in the tall white house, things that could lead him to the truth about John Palkin, when he almost collided with a man who was approaching the front door. He was probably in his thirties, pale with black hair, and he had a leather bag slung over his left shoulder'

'Do you live here?'

The man looked wary, as if he suspected Neil was about to rob him. 'Why?'

Neil began to explain about the excavation and the bones. Most people, in his experience, were only too happy to help solve a historical mystery – even to the point of sharing his enthusiasm. But the man listened, expression-less, his eyes focused on something in the distance.

'I notice there's an attic. Probably the old servants' quar-ters. I know it's a long shot but I was wondering whether the former owner, Josiah Palkin-Wright, left anything behind.'

He shook his head. 'I don't know anything about that. I just rent the first-floor flat.'

'Does anyone live in the attic?'

'No. It's empty.'

'Who's the landlord?'

The man had taken a key from his pocket and was about to unlock the door when he froze. 'Someone from London. Can't remember his name.'

This wasn't much use. But Neil wasn't giving up. 'You must have his details. If I can get his permission to see up there ...'

'I'm sorry, I'm busy.' The man opened the door and slipped inside, leaving Neil standing on the doorstep feeling foolish.

He turned to go. Now that he thought about it, it seemed increasingly unlikely that anything from Palkin-Wright's era remained in the house, especially if the place had been bought as an investment by a London landlord.

He reached the bottom of the road, heading back to the dig, when he saw a couple of familiar figures walking towards him. Wesley and Gerry were followed by a brace of uniformed constables, one tall and one small.

As they approached Neil waited in the centre of the road. He saw that Wesley's face was serious with no smile of greeting.

'Not at the dig?' Wesley asked.

'I'm on my way back there. I've just been to Josiah Palkin-Wright's old house. That book I showed you last night – remember I said he must have had access to original documents? Well, I wondered whether they'd been squirrelled away in some forgotten corner of his attic. I called but the guy in the first-floor flat says the place belongs to some landlord in London, which means that if there was anything, it was probably disposed of years ago.'

Wesley and Gerry looked at each other. 'What did this man look like?' Gerry asked.

Neil provided a description of Miles Carthage. He had lied to Neil about the landlord, and Wesley wondered why.

'We're going there now,' Wesley said.

'If you get in, can you have a look in the attic?' Neil said, half joking.

'We've got a search warrant so we'll be looking everywhere,' said Gerry.

For once Neil was lost for words. Should he hang about in the hope of seeing inside the house? Or would the police think he was cramping their style or committing some technical crime against procedure? As it was Wesley and Gerry, he decided to take the risk and when they made for North Lodge he followed a little way behind and hovered on the pavement as they climbed the front steps.

Gerry rang the bell and hammered on the door but there was no answer. After a full minute, he gave up and turned to Neil. 'You're sure he's in?'

'He went in ten minutes ago but he could have slipped out again and headed the other way.'

'Do we break it down, sir?' said the smaller constable, eager for action.

Gerry shook his head and to Neil's surprise he took a

leather pouch from his jacket pocket and held it up tri-
umphantly. 'A present from a grateful ex-con,' he said
before emptying the contents of the pouch into the palm of
his hand. 'He was kind enough to teach me the fine art of
lock-picking.'

He dangled the skeleton keys from his fingers and turned
to Neil. 'You can wait for us to give you the all clear then
you can have a look for your old papers.' He grinned at
Wesley as if delighted by his own generosity, then started
fiddling with the lock.

If Gerry was up for it, Neil wasn't going to argue.

Wesley stood at the foot of the attic stairs and looked
upwards. It was dark up there and the single panelled
wooden door at the top was in deep shadow. He had a
sudden sense of evil which he swiftly dismissed as nonsense.
An overactive imagination.

Gerry was already at the top, trying the skeleton keys in
the lock. Wesley held his breath. Then he heard a telltale
click.

To Gerry's surprise the door swung open smoothly, as if
the hinges had been oiled. Wesley climbed the stairs to join
him. Beyond the door was a spacious room and in the light
streaming in from the two windows, filthy with years of
grime, he could see it was unfurnished, the floorboards
dusty and bare. There was a cast-iron fireplace on the far
wall with a built-in cupboard to the right. Wesley's first
thought was, that if Carthage owned the place, he was
wasting money by not making it into a self-contained flat
and letting it out to holiday visitors. The room was empty
and he knew Neil would be disappointed that there was
nothing here that might move his research forward.

Neil wasn't the only one who had in interest in what they might find from Palkin-Wright's day. Palkin-Wright had owned the boathouse where those murdered women had been buried during his lifetime. The skeletons were too old to concern the police but they remained at the back of Wesley's mind.

'There's a door over there,' Gerry said, nudging his arm.

When Wesley opened the door he found more of the same. The room was completely empty. Another door led on to a tiny bathroom, unmodernised and lined with cracked white tiles.

'Nobody's lived here for years,' Gerry observed. 'Let's go and see what the uniforms have come up with.'

He was about to make for the door but Wesley stood blocking his way. 'It might be my imagination but is this attic much smaller than the floors downstairs, even allowing for the pitch of the roof?'

'Maybe next door has the space.'

'This house is detached.'

Gerry rolled his eyes. 'Just shows how observant I am.'

'Easy mistake to make.' Although North Lodge was detached, the closeness of the old houses on the narrow street gave the illusion of them being joined together.

Gerry stood and watched as Wesley circled the room, opening the cupboard by the side of the fireplace and closing it again. When he returned to the other room Gerry followed.

Wesley had noticed the door in the corner which he'd assumed was a closet, the sort found in thousands of Victorian bedrooms. But now he saw that the door had a modern lock.

'Seen that?' He pointed at the door.

Gerry stared at it for a few seconds. Then he jangled the skeleton keys and went to work again, concentrating on his task.

Once the lock clicked, Gerry stood back and left it to Wesley to turn the handle and push the door open.

It was the smell that hit him first. Excrement and urine. And something else. Death maybe.

In the pale light seeping in through a small barred sash window, he could see that the room was cluttered with dark, heavy furniture. A dressing table, worn plush armchairs clustered around a small iron fireplace. Piles of artist's canvases leaned against the walls and a threadbare Turkish rug covered the floor. A large iron-framed bed stood at one end of the room, so deep in shadow that he couldn't make out what was beneath the undulations of the blood-dark eiderdown. He could see that the source of the foul smell was an unemptied chamber pot near the bed.

An easel had been set up near the bed but in the dim light Wesley couldn't make out what was painted on the canvas it held. If it wasn't for the smell and the gloom the room might have been almost cosy, until he noticed the chains attached to the wall to the far side of the fireplace.

He focused his eyes on the bed. Something shifted beneath the covers and he stood frozen in horrified fascination as a skeletal arm slowly emerged, the thin grey hand clutching weakly at the air like some starving animal in its death throes. He caught his breath for a moment, his heart hammering. Then, without taking his eyes off the bed, he took a step forward, dreading what he might see.

Her face was parchment-pale, the lips as light as the thin

flesh stretched tight across the skull. Unbrushed, filthy hair, the colour of rope, drooped limply around the face. She looked like a corpse.

Then he heard a whisper, frail and shaky like the rustle of dead leaves. He could just make out the words. 'Help me.'

'What happened up there? Nobody'll tell me.'

Albany Street was too narrow for vehicles so the paramedics had been forced to take the stretcher over the cobbles down to the ambulance parked on the wider part of the old street. Wesley stood at the door to North Lodge and watched them, so preoccupied that he'd almost forgotten Neil was waiting downstairs. Neil repeated the question and this time Wesley answered.

'We found a girl. Her name's Jenny Bercival. She went missing at last year's Palkin Festival.'

'She's been up there all this time?'

'That's what we need to find out.'

'She is still alive?'

'Yes, but she's in a bad way.'

'Any idea where the guy's got to?'

'Not yet.' Wesley had already put out the call so all patrols were on the lookout for Carthage. He was impatient to interview him, to discover why Jenny had been kept up there, a terrified prisoner in that stinking hidden room. It was certain that Carthage was responsible, which meant he had probably killed Kassia too. Gerry had returned to the station to co-ordinate things from there. When the press found out about Jenny, all hell would break loose.

'Sir.'

Wesley looked round and saw Paul Johnson standing in the doorway of North Lodge. He was supervising the detailed search of the premises and there was an anxious look on his thin face.

'You should see this,' Paul said, the words loaded with meaning.

Neil tapped Wesley on the shoulder and said he'd be off and if they found any documents, would Wesley let him know. Wesley said an absent-minded goodbye, amazed that his friend's mind was still on his work after everything that had happened in that house.

CSIs in crime-scene suits were trudging up and down the stairs to the attic and Wesley expected Paul to go there. But instead he made for an open door beneath the stairs, presumably the door to the cellar, a part of the house he hadn't yet seen. As he stood at the top of the stone steps he could see a group of CSIs down there, the lights they'd set up illuminating the gloomy basement like a stage set. They were clustered in the far corner around what looked like rolls of rotting cloth lying on the cold flagstone floor.

He followed Paul down and when he reached the bottom of the steps one of the CSIs turned to him.

'We've got human remains. They were in front of an air vent so there's quite a good state of preservation. Come and have a look.'

Wesley hesitated for a moment, preparing himself for yet more horrors. When he approached, he saw a body lying on a roll of faded cloth, probably some kind of curtain material with a large floral pattern. Scraps of clothing clung to the desiccated flesh and the long hair on the skull had turned grey with dust and decay. But Wesley's eyes were drawn to the mouth, to the decayed lips which were drawn back over the teeth to form an eternal, silent scream.

'There's two more over there but we haven't examined them yet.'

'Has Dr Bowman been called?'

Before Paul could answer, Wesley heard Colin calling a greeting. He wondered whether he'd sound so cheerful once he saw what they'd found.

The pathologist began to examine the first body. Then, at his request, the other two rolls of cloth were unwrapped carefully. Two more bodies, women in the same state of decomposition, their long clothing rotted into strips of uncertain colour.

It didn't take long for Colin to admit that he couldn't really give any accurate verdict without tests and a thorough examination. Wesley knew that if they were old, they were none of his concern. If they were recent, there was only one person who could be responsible. He left Colin to his work; he had to get down to the hospital to see how Jenny Bercival was and if she was able to throw light on the ordeal she'd undergone for the past year.

And they needed to find Miles Carthage. He was the key to everything.

Jenny Bercival had been taken straight to Tradmouth Hospital and when Wesley called he was told that she was comfortable. At least she was alive. A mother had got her child back and that was a cause for rejoicing, although he couldn't begin to imagine how damaged that child would be by what she'd had to endure.

When he'd called Gerry to tell him about the mummified bodies in the cellar, the DCI had ordered more back-up and all patrols were on the lookout for Miles Carthage.

Wesley had thought Carthage strange and obsessive.

Now all the evidence pointed to him being a prolific killer who'd probably ended the lives of Kassia Graylem, Andre Gorst, Eric Darwell and possibly those three unknown women in the cellar of North Lodge. Jenny would have died too if they hadn't found her in time. Wesley hadn't considered him seriously as a murderer when they'd met, so it disturbed him to think that he'd been in that house, quite unaware that Jenny was imprisoned in the attic above his head. There were times when he doubted his own judgement.

He was heading for the hospital, walking down the embankment near where the *Maudelayne* was moored, when the insistent ringing of his phone interrupted his negative thoughts. Someone answering Miles Carthage's description had been spotted by a patrol up near the castle. He gave the order to seal off the area and get the team up there, although they weren't to approach Carthage without his say-so. He called Gerry to tell him what was going on and asked for one of the patrol cars to pick him up. His visit to Jenny would have to wait. Besides, Rachel was keeping vigil at her bedside and she would call if there was any news.

As he waited for the car, staring out at the river, his mind kept returning to that cellar. Even now when he closed his eyes he could see those grey, dead faces, those crumbling masks of horror. That and the discovery of Jenny would probably be the subject of his nightmares for months to come. Miles Carthage, who'd used his talent to produce images of such beauty and sensitivity, had also been capable of horrific cruelty. He found the notion disturbing.

He'd already asked Trish to check on all the people who'd ever lived at North Lodge and the answer confirmed what he'd already been told. It had been in the same family for a century or more, kept by them as a holiday home for a while and never rented out to strangers. He wondered how he could have got it so wrong. He should have dug more deeply when he'd discovered that Kassia had posed for Carthage. Now it appeared as if the manner of Kassia's death had been part of Carthage's twisted quest for the ultimate inspiration. Perhaps he planned to paint Jenny in extremis as an accompaniment to a Shipworld storyline about a fair maiden imprisoned in the Shroud Maker's attic, a maiden who is punished by suffering a slow and unpleasant death. If this was his intention, Wesley thought, Carthage was an exceptionally sick individual.

The patrol car drew up beside him and as he climbed into the passenger seat his phone rang again. It was one of the team telling him that the area around the castle had been cleared. Carthage was sitting on a flat outcrop of rock below the cliff path, a place once popular with sunbathers which had been closed a while ago for health and safety reasons because of rock falls. There were signs up there telling the public to keep out but it seemed that Carthage had ignored them as so many people did. This meant that Wesley had to take the safety of his team into account. Or maybe they could sit it out and wait for Carthage to come to them. He couldn't stay there forever.

The car drove through the barrier of police tape where curious onlookers had gathered, craning their necks to see what was going on, and screeched to a halt outside the castle entrance. The cliff path lay to his right, just below the ruined walls of the castle John Palkin had built to defend the port back in the late fourteenth century. Now a man who claimed to be his descendant was there in the shadow of those walls and Wesley wondered how it was all going to end.

He was given a stab vest and once he'd put it on he followed a uniformed sergeant on to the path. The team had obeyed his initial instruction and kept back out of sight. The element of surprise was crucial.

The sergeant stopped and pointed. Standing on tiptoe, peering over the hedge that lay between the path and the sea, Wesley could see the artist on a flat plateau of rock fifty feet below. Once a wooden walkway had led from the footpath to the plateau but that had been washed away and now the only way to reach it was to go down to the beach and clamber over the rocks. Wesley wished he was wearing different shoes, but he had no choice. He needed to talk to Miles Carthage. He had to discover the truth.

He made his way down to the beach, going carefully down the steps and steadying himself by holding on to the rough cliff wall. When he reached the sand he signalled the sergeant to stay where he was. The man looked concerned but Wesley knew that going in mob-handed would only make their quarry jumpy. And a jumpy man might do anything.

Wesley began to climb. He could see Carthage gazing out to sea, sketching frantically, oblivious to anything but the seascape before him. He had no idea what had happened at North Lodge in his absence, and this was to Wesley's advantage.

Although it was a relatively easy ascent his unsuitable shoes kept slipping on the rocks and, after a couple of near misses that set his heart thumping, he decided to take them off, tucking his discarded socks neatly into each shoe before leaving them on a ledge of rock to collect later. Once barefoot, it was easier to grip although the pain of jagged rock against flesh made him wince.

Carthage was engrossed in his work and his face was a mask of concentration bordering on obsession. From where he was standing Wesley could see what he was drawing, an elaborate seascape encompassing the surrounding beach, cliffs and trees. But it was time to break the spell.

'Mr Carthage.'

Carthage started at the sound of Wesley's voice and twisted round to face him, a flash of alarm in his eyes.

'I need to talk to you.'

'You're talking to me now.'

Wesley forced himself to smile. 'It's not very comfortable here. Can we go somewhere else?'

'No. I have to finish this.'

Wesley had no choice. He sat down beside Carthage on the rock, the damp seeping through his trousers. Carthage began to sketch frantically. Wesley wondered whether the shock of what he was about to reveal would still his busy fingers.

'We've found Jenny.'

Carthage stopped sketching for a second, his hand hovering above the paper. Then he continued shading in cliffs with heavy strokes of his pencil.

'What was she doing up there?'

Carthage stopped drawing again and stared out to sea. Then he shook his head. 'Her name's not Jenny. She's the Lady Morwenna. I can't allow her to leave the Cave of Adron. She belongs with me.'

'You locked her in your attic.'

'She tried to escape. She didn't understand.'

'What didn't she understand?'

'That her beauty has to be preserved.'

'I thought Kassia was your muse.'

He shook his head vigorously. 'She was the Lady Alicia. She died and was laid to rest in a boat.'

'Do you tell Palkinson what to write?'

'Yes.'

'Does someone else give you instructions?'

He nodded. 'Yes. The Shroud Maker. But nobody knows his identity. He has no face.'

In spite of the warmth of the day and the sun beating down on the bare rock Wesley shuddered. 'But you know who he is.'

Miles gave a small, closed smile, as if he had a precious secret he wasn't about to share.

'What did you give Jenny to make her stay?'

'Give her?'

'You must have given her something to make her drowsy.'

'When she gets upset I let her have the pills the doctor gives me. They help her sleep.'

'What about her food?'

'She has what I have. Unless she's asleep. Or she doesn't behave herself.'

The last statement sounded petulant and Wesley hardly liked to think of the truth behind it. Still, he had to ask. 'What do you mean?'

'Sometimes I have to punish her.'

'Does that mean you don't give her any food?'

Carthage nodded, his eyes still fixed on the horizon.

'I saw Jenny. She's very ill. You should have called a doctor.'

'She doesn't need a doctor. I look after her.'

'Did you kill Kassia? Put her in the dinghy?'

Carthage shook his head again. 'I've never killed anybody.'

'Then who did?'

'I don't know. It might have been the Shroud Maker.'

'Who is the Shroud Maker?'

Carthage didn't answer.

After a long silence Wesley spoke again. 'I like the illustrations you do for Shipworld.' He paused for a moment. 'I believe you're related to Chris Butcher.'

Miles looked up. 'That's wrong. It's not Chris.'

'Who is it, then?'

Miles gave a secretive smile and said nothing.

It was time to get Miles to the station and Wesley knew he'd feel safer once he was off that outcrop with the sea swirling a few yards below like a hungry beast.

Wesley put a hand under the man's elbow to help him up and, as Carthage seemed to be co-operating, he took the opportunity to ask another question. 'I went down to the cellar. I saw the others. Who are they?'

Carthage looked round, alarmed. 'They're nothing to do with me. They're Josiah's women. They were in the attic but I moved them when the Lady Morwenna came.'

'What do you mean, they're Josiah's women?'

'He wrote it all down. His notebooks are in the trunk.'

'Trunk?'

'There are letters in there that Josiah's wife wrote to her sister. He hid them before they could be sent.' Carthage turned calmly and looked at Wesley. 'I swear I didn't kill Kassia. I'd never do a thing like that. Can we go now?'

Wesley watched while the artist packed his sketch pad and pencils away in his leather shoulder bag. Then he stepped back so Carthage could go ahead of him down the rock, taking his phone from his pocket to alert the others that he needed help.

Without warning he heard a thud, leather on rock. Carthage had thrown his bag down and was dodging forward. Wesley put a hand out to grab his arm, the action instinctive and a little too late. The cloth of Carthage's shirt slipped from his grasping fingers and he could only watch as the suspect hurtled towards the edge of the plateau like a sprinter intent on the finishing line.

Afterwards Wesley could remember yelling something at the top of his voice. Probably the word 'no', swallowed by the wind and the crash of the waves. But whatever it was he shouted it had no effect. A thousand words of persuasion probably wouldn't have stopped Carthage hurling himself off the edge of the flat rock into the foaming sea below.

The shock paralysed Wesley for a while as the waves roared in his head, relentlessly, without pity, swallowing the living and the dead. He stood there on the edge of the rock, searching desperately for any sign of Carthage in the water below. There was none. The man had gone and he knew there was nothing he could have done to stop him, even though he'd blame himself for the rest of his days.

A voice, one of the officers waiting on the path, jolted him back to the moment and, without thinking, he picked up Carthage's bag. The sketch book tumbled out and fell open on a picture of a face concealed by a blank white mask. Underneath were three words: The Shroud Maker.

Chapter 17

Extract from a letter written at North Lodge, Upper Town, Tradmouth, 17th March 1895

Her name was Jessie and she was, dear sister, a woman of the streets who lived in dire poverty in those coal lumpers' tenements I saw in Tradmouth. Her body and her undoubted beauty were, no doubt, the only commodities the unfortunate creature had to trade.

I had heard of such fallen women, sister, but I had not known them to be such tragic beings. Jessie told me how my husband had taken a liking to her and treated her well at first, buying her gifts and paying her generously for her favours. Then one day he saw her in the company of a sailor, and it was then he invited her to this house and imprisoned her, saying she would

*never betray him again. She spoke of the things
he did to her, things I would never repeat to you,
dear Letty. Suffice it to say that he is the Devil
himself and I knew I had to free this poor,
pathetic Jessie from her terrible situation. She
told me too that he had been seen with other
women, perhaps those women who had vanished,
never to be found again. I am so afraid.*

*Sister, I beg you to go to the Reverend
Johnson and show him this letter. He will know
what action to take.*

*Your most loving sister
Charlotte*

There was no sign of Miles Carthage but the consensus of opinion was that, unless luck was on his side or he was a very strong swimmer, he was unlikely to have survived the currents in that particular part of the English Channel. Bodies could be swallowed up by the billowing waves and washed up months later further along the coast.

Wesley knew it was inevitable that there would be an inquiry. The officers watching from the cliff path above were bound to back up his story so Gerry reckoned he had nothing to worry about. In spite of this he still hated being treated like a guilty man.

When he'd returned home that night Pam was filled with righteous anger at the prospect of questions being asked. If she'd thought it would do any good she'd have confronted the investigators and rubbed their smug noses in copies of her husband's exemplary record. The doctors said that Jenny Bercival had been in a bad way. If she'd been left there much longer, she might not have survived her ordeal which meant that Wesley had just rescued a young woman from certain death and brought a murderer to justice. Wesley had never seen his wife so incensed. It was a side to her that was new to him and he rather liked her imitation of a tigress defending her young.

It looked as if the man who had killed Kassia Graylem and Andre Gorst and kidnapped Jenny Bercival was now dead. And even though his responsibility for Eric Darwell's death wasn't certain, the case was closed. All that remained was to complete the paperwork.

But Wesley had heard that heartfelt statement – *I didn't kill Kassia. I'd never do a thing like that.* The words echoed in his head at night, robbing him of sleep. Gerry had dismissed his claim that some mysterious individual who called himself the Shroud Maker was responsible as the ramblings of a sick mind, an inability to divorce fantasy from fact. He reckoned the only way Carthage could deal with what he'd done was to shift the blame on to a creation of his imagination: simple really when you thought about it.

The mystery of the bodies in the cellar had lost its urgency since Colin and a forensic anthropologist had confirmed that they had most likely been there for around a hundred years. Neil's usual bone specialist, Margaret, had done the honours as Sacha Vale had departed for London to work on a new TV series. Wesley wondered whether she would keep seeing Chris Butcher. If she did, it would upset Astrid. Strange, he thought, that both Jenny and Kassia had been involved with Butcher. An idea began to take shape in his head. But it was nebulous, half-formed. And perhaps it was as far into the realms of fantasy as Shipworld and the Shroud Maker.

*

It was Sunday, the final day of the Palkin Festival, and the embankment was packed as Gerry made his way to the hospital where he'd arranged to meet Rachel at the entrance to Jenny Bercival's ward.

He'd already been working hard that morning to reassure Wesley that what happened wasn't his fault, even though the powers that be were harrumphing that he hadn't followed the correct procedure. Gerry told him that if he'd gone on to that rock with back-up, Carthage would have jumped even sooner. At least he'd had a chance to discover the truth. Wesley had responded by saying he wasn't sure they had the whole truth just yet. Somehow he couldn't see Carthage killing Andre Gorst like that. It didn't seem to be his style. Gerry knew he could be right, but it was something he didn't like to think of just at that moment.

'Is Jenny expecting us?'

'Oh yes,' said Gerry.

Rachel began to walk ahead, religiously using the antiseptic hand gel on the wall before opening the door to the ward, shaming Gerry into doing likewise. His late wife, Kathy, had been a nurse and she'd have insisted on him obeying the rules. Being in a hospital, especially Tradmouth Hospital where she'd worked, always reminded him of her and caused a nagging feeling of deep loss. He was glad he had work to distract him.

Gerry let Rachel enter Jenny's side ward first, standing behind her like a shy suitor. Maybe, he thought, she'd be afraid of men after what she'd experienced. Luckily her mother was with her, sitting protectively by the bed. As Mrs Bercival greeted them Jenny shifted back against her pillows, a wary look on her ashen face. Gerry asked her how she was feeling, trying his best to sound avuncular and unthreatening. For a man used to the blunt approach, he didn't find it easy.

Jenny was thin to the point of emaciation and she kept coughing, as though the dust of that attic was still lodged in her lungs. When she spoke it was in a hoarse whisper, like someone whose voice had failed after a prolonged bout of screaming.

As they'd arranged, it was Rachel who began the gentle questioning and Gerry could see the strain on her face. Maybe it was their increased workload, or pre-wedding nerves. Or perhaps coming face to face with the reality of Jenny's ordeal disturbed her, reminding her that life could hold hidden horrors; things that made joy and optimism seem naive.

Mrs Bercival clung on to her daughter's hand as if she was reluctant to let go. It wasn't only the daughter who was in need of comfort, Gerry thought. Their ordeals had been quite different but they'd both been through hell over the past year.

'Are you up to talking about what happened, Jenny?' Rachel asked.

Jenny glanced at her mother. 'Mum, I'll be OK if you want to go and get a coffee or ...' Her voice was weak, barely audible.

For a few moments Mrs Bercival stayed put until she realised the meaning behind her daughter's words, when she gathered up her handbag and left the room reluctantly. Gerry was glad she'd taken the hint. Jenny might be more open about what had happened to her without her mother listening.

Jenny sat against the pillow, staring ahead, her flesh almost as pale as the white bedding.

'This can wait if you're not feeling up to it, love,' said Gerry softly.

She cleared her throat. 'No. I'll be all right.' Her voice shook a little. They'd take it slowly.

'Can you tell us how you came to be there?' Rachel asked cautiously, as though she feared the question might cause distress.

Jenny turned her head slightly to look at her. 'I was into Shipworld – I mean, really into it – and I met Chris Butcher at the festival the year before last. He called himself William de Clare.' She gave a weak smile. 'He wanted to be my gallant knight and I guess I was flattered. We used to meet up in London. I knew he was married but that didn't matter. He said his wife didn't understand all the things he liked to do. Playing parts and all that.'

There was an awkward silence before Rachel asked the next question.

'And the tattoo?'

A slight flush of colour appeared on the girl's cheeks. 'I did it to please him.'

'Tell me what happened last year,' said Rachel.

'I met a guy at the festival. He worked on the Shipworld website and he knew all about me and Chris. He did brilliant illustrations.'

'This was Miles Carthage?'

'I thought it was amazing to meet someone who had talent like that and he said he wanted me to model for him. He seemed a bit odd. A loner. But he was an artist so I thought he was just a bit . . . eccentric.'

'You modelled for him?'

'He said Chris had asked him to do a portrait of me. I mean, Chris had said our relationship was just a bit of fun but I thought this meant he wanted to get more serious. The painting Miles did was brilliant and he said he was going to use some pictures of me on Shipworld. I was going to be part of it. I was going to be the Lady Morwenna.'

'So what went wrong?'

'One night I went to Miles's house as arranged. I didn't tell my friends where I was because he said Chris didn't want anybody to know. Before he started working we had some wine but he must have put something in it because when I came round I found myself in that room.' She shuddered and looked away. 'He told me he was going to keep me there. He loved beautiful things and he didn't intend to let me go.'

'Did he ... assault you?' Rachel asked carefully.

Jenny shook her head. 'He said he wanted to keep me there like a manikin and he came to me when he wanted to draw or paint me. Nothing else.'

'Did you try to escape?'

'Yes but he'd made sure the place was secure. He used to bring me food. And things to read. Books about medieval life. And there was this old book by Josiah Palkin-Wright. He said he was his great-great-uncle or something. He said Josiah used to keep women in the attic but they died. There was always that threat. If I didn't behave myself I'd end up like Josiah's women. He used to bring me wine every night. I knew it was drugged and a couple of times I tried not to drink it but he forced me.' She shuddered at the memory and tears began to fill her eyes.

'You must have been terrified,' said Gerry.

Jenny looked straight at him. Her glistening eyes seemed huge against the thinness of her face. 'He said he wanted to collect beautiful things and I was the first thing in his collection. I was just an object to him. Hardly human.' The panic began to rise in her voice. 'I didn't think I'd get out of there alive.'

'Did you ever see anyone else with Miles?' Rachel asked.

Jenny's eyes widened. 'I saw him with Chris's wife once. But that's not surprising because he's her brother. That's how he got the job illustrating Shipworld. He told me all about it.'

Gerry and Rachel looked at each other. Pixie had been right all along. Miles and Chris were related. By marriage.

'Did Chris's wife know about you and her husband?'

'We were very discreet. As far as I know Astrid just thought I was Miles's model.' She closed her eyes. 'I'm tired. Can we do this another time?'

Gerry stood up. 'We'll leave you in peace, love. Thanks for talking to us.' He nodded to Rachel. They'd learned enough for now.

'Do you think Astrid manipulated Miles Carthage?' Rachel asked as they walked down the corridor. 'Was she pulling the strings all along?'

'It's something we'll have to look into. On the other hand his behaviour was hardly normal, was it? Who's to say he saw nothing wrong in holding a woman captive just because he wanted to paint her.'

'He painted Kassia Graylem too. I wonder if he feared Jenny would die on him and he was preparing Kassia as her replacement with his sister's encouragement.' She paused. 'Strange to think that if he had imprisoned her, she might still be alive.'

Gerry raised his eyebrows. 'The lesser of two evils. Although I'm not sure Jenny Bercival would agree with you.'

'But something went wrong and Kassia died. We just have to find out why.'

Astrid Butcher had told herself that Chris stayed with her because she was different from the others, those girls with their russet tresses and simpering faces who were so devoted to Chris's weird fantasy world that they were willing to disfigure their flesh with tattoos. But the fear that he might abandon her for one of them was always there, and life without him would be a kind of death so she'd taken steps to protect herself. Self-preservation is no crime whatever the law might say.

In some ways she'd felt responsible for her little brother since they were children – Miles with his obsession with beauty and their family connection to Josiah Palkin-Wright.

It had started when he was fifteen and he'd become fixated on a girl called Laura who'd been a year his senior. Laura with her long copper hair and cat's face. At first their parents had imagined that his obsession was connected with his prodigious artistic talent ... combined with the natural preoccupations of an adolescent boy.

Then there had been the incident. Laura had agreed to meet him and he had locked her in a shed, saying he wanted to keep her for himself. The girl had been frightened but unharmed and Astrid had leaped to her brother's defence, saying it had been a harmless prank, although Miles himself had been unable to see that he'd done anything wrong.

Their parents had managed to persuade Laura's family not to take things any further and nothing more had been said. Much later on, when Chris's infidelities grew too much for her to bear, she remembered Laura and wondered if she could turn Miles's obsession, his lack of empathy with the human beings he chose to collect, to her advantage.

Miles had left home to go to art college in London and later he'd moved to Tradmouth to the house he'd inherited from their great-uncle – the house that had once belonged to Josiah Palkin-Wright. Astrid had persuaded Chris to give him work but she'd always known that one day he might be useful to her. Poor damaged Miles was like a loaded gun. All Astrid had to do was to provide the ammunition and let him take her revenge for her.

She heard a knock on the door of her hotel room and hurried to answer it. There was nothing they could accuse her of. If Miles had chosen to deal with the girls who were making his sister's life a misery, that was nothing to do with her.

It was the big Liverpudlian DCI and the cool blonde. At least she wasn't Chris's type, she thought as she invited them to sit.

'We'd like to talk about your brother, Miles Carthage.'

'I don't have much to do with him. We fell out when he inherited my great-uncle's house and I was left nothing. You know what families are like,' she said, confident that she had taken the wind out of DCI Heffernan's sails.

He went on to outline what they'd found at North Lodge and what Jenny had told them and Astrid put her hand to her mouth, feigning horrified amazement.

'Miles was always obsessed with collecting beautiful things. When we were growing up he had problems but I never realised . . . ' She shook her head, hoping she sounded convincing. Then it suddenly occurred to her how fool-hardy her plans had been. How had she imagined it would end? With the girls' deaths? With Miles in jail? Perhaps she'd been so blinded by jealousy that she hadn't thought beyond that first, glorious revenge.

'Where's Miles now?' she asked.

'I'm sorry,' said the blonde. 'He jumped into the sea. The lifeboat was called out but there was no sign of him. I'm sorry,' she repeated.

Astrid put her head in her hands. Sometimes collateral damage was inevitable. Besides, she was sick of feeling responsible for her brother. And, although she'd placed the ideas in his head and fed his fantasies, she could never be blamed for what happened if he wasn't in a position to point the finger.

But she was puzzled by some of the accusations the police appeared to be making against him. The Miles she knew was incapable of strangling Kassia and there was no way he'd have murdered the sailor from the *Maudelayne*. Or the man in the holiday park swimming pool. Miles had only wanted to look, to collect and possess.

'Miles wasn't a killer,' she said. 'He didn't do the things you said.'

'Tell that to Jenny Bercival,' said the blonde with a look of sheer contempt.

Wesley had left the search and returned to the station. There was nothing he could do, and even though it looked as if the case was solved he wasn't inclined to celebrate. Miles Carthage was probably dead and Wesley kept asking himself whether he'd really been responsible for his actions. The news that he was Astrid's brother had come as a surprise, although he did recall Butcher saying something about his wife having relatives in Tradmouth. He just wished he'd made the connection.

There was always the possibility that Miles had been manipulated by his sister but, without Miles's evidence, that would be almost impossible to prove in a court of law.

Gerry and Rachel had gone to talk to Astrid Butcher and they'd probably bring her in to conduct a formal interview. After the events of the day, Wesley didn't want to see her. Fortunately there was plenty to do in the CID office, plenty to take his mind off the memory of Miles Carthage running headlong down that rock and plunging into the swirling water below.

He had just returned to his desk when his phone began to ring. When he answered the caller's voice was unfamiliar.

'DI Peterson? Do you remember you asked if there have been any similar murders to your girl in the boat, here or abroad? It's taken some time for the various forces to get back to us but now information's come through that there've been several similar cases in France. I'll get the details together and e-mail them to you.'

Wesley thanked the caller. Now that it looked as though they had their killer, the matter lacked urgency, but he was curious all the same.

He noticed a yellow Post-it note stuck on the edge of his computer screen. Ring Mrs Betham. Someone must have left it there while he was out of the office.

While he was waiting for the information about the French cases to appear in his in-box he dialled Mrs Betham's number, wondering what she had to tell him. In a short conversation he learned that she'd found some photographs her husband had taken of the Graylems and the Wentworths shortly before the terrible accident. Would he like her to e-mail them through? Wesley had said yes, he'd be grateful. Then she'd told him that her husband had remembered the Wentworth boy's name. Rory.

When he saw that the e-mail from Mrs Betham had arrived, he opened the attachment. He scrolled through the photographs, concentrating on the faces. Then he called Trish over to his desk.

'Does he look familiar to you?'

Trish stared at the screen. Then she studied the pictures arrayed on the noticeboard at the far end of the room.

'It certainly looks like him.'

'Only in those days he called himself Rory Wentworth.'

Wesley studied the image on the screen more closely. The face was younger, fuller, and the hair was shorter, but the smile was the same as he stood on a quayside for posterity, stripped to the waist.

'I take it he's still in Tradmouth?'

Trish nodded. 'As far as I know.'

'I think we should have a word.'

He could see from the keen look on Trish's face that she was longing to go with him. Nevertheless he wanted to be sure of the facts before he acted.

'I need to have another look at the report into the accident that killed Kassia's parents.'

'I'll dig it out again.'

'Thanks,' he said. He had always been able to rely on Trish.

The Palkin Festival was reaching its climax and the town was packed in anticipation of a fly-past by the Red Arrows followed by a grand firework display as soon as darkness fell, all in honour of John Palkin.

The report on the boating accident which had resulted in

the deaths of Kassia Graylem's parents raised some interesting questions, as did the death of a young girl in a
boating accident on the south coast the year before – a girl
who went out alone in a sailing dinghy and disappeared,
her body swept away by the tides, never to be found. A
witness speculated that she'd probably hit her head on the
boom of the boat and fallen into the sea and the story
had been accepted at the time because that witness had
been Carlton Wentworth, a widowed barrister on holiday with his teenage son. Unimpeachable. Wesley googled
Wentworth's name and when he saw the results he smiled.

He'd also read the e-mails forwarded from police forces
in France after he'd contacted them to request an e-fit of
their suspect; when the information came through he
cursed himself for not checking sooner.

When Gerry returned from his interview with Astrid
Butcher, he told him not to worry about it. However,
Wesley, a natural worrier, couldn't help it.

Wesley hurried to the office of Tradmouth Charters, and after
he found it closed and empty he made a couple of phone calls
and obtained the number of Jonathan Petworth, the owner
of the business.

Petworth sounded surprised when Wesley introduced
himself and explained that he'd decided to close the office
for the final day of the festival, same as he did every year.
They hardly did any business with all the commotion going
on and besides, he always joined in on the final day. It was
a sort of tradition.

'Do you know where we can find Jason Teague?' Wesley
asked.

'He said something about going to the festival. Why?'

'Have you known him long?'

'We were at school together.' Wesley detected something guarded about the answer, a caution which suggested there was something behind the simple statement. He wished he could see the man face to face.

'You must trust him if you're going into partnership with him.'

There was a short silence on the other end of the line before Petworth spoke again. 'Is that what he told you?'

'Isn't it true?'

Petworth hesitated. 'He said it suited him to stay in Tradmouth for a while and he asked if I had any work for him. I said he could make sure everything was OK when the punters returned the boats. That's it.'

'He was in your office when we called a few days ago.'

'He'd come in to return some keys.'

'You sound as though you don't trust him.'

Another silence.

'I think we should have a word, Mr Petworth.'

Petworth agreed meekly to come down to his office to meet him. He lived nearby and he'd be there in two minutes. As Wesley waited by the entrance to the converted warehouse, those two minutes seemed to pass slowly. He needed to speak to Jason Teague's school friend in order to learn all he could about the man. After all, knowledge was power.

When Petworth appeared he was slightly breathless, brandishing a bunch of keys. Tall, with a long face, he was dressed in a Palkin costume, padded around the middle to give him the appearance of the portly sea captain, his face half concealed by a bushy false beard.

'Sorry about all this,' he said, embarrassed, tugging off

the beard. 'My wife likes me to join in with the spirit of the thing and at least I'm not the only one who looks like a prat.' In spite of the jocular words he looked worried. 'What's this about?' he said as he unlocked the door.

'I need to talk to Jason. You must know him well?'

'Not that well.' He sounded as if he was trying to distance himself and Wesley wanted to know why.

'What school did you and Jason go to?'

'Pridewell House in Surrey. Why?'

'Ever heard the name Rory Wentworth?'

Petworth's face turned a deep shade of red and he didn't answer.

'Did your friend Jason ever mention a family called the Graylems? They were killed in a boating accident.'

Petworth looked puzzled. 'No. Who are they? Any relation to that poor girl who . . . ?'

'She was their daughter. Rory Wentworth met them on holiday in Southwold in Suffolk and, from what I can gather, there was some sort of falling out. Later that day there was an explosion and their boat was destroyed, killing Mr and Mrs Graylem and leaving Kassia orphaned. Rory and his father had left just before the explosion and nothing was ever proved.' He paused to let the statement sink in. 'Only Rory Wentworth went and changed his name to Jason Teague, didn't he. Why didn't you tell us?'

When Jonathan didn't answer Wesley continued. 'More recently four women have been murdered in French coastal towns, mostly in the south and west where Teague told us he worked on the yachts of the wealthy. The murders occurred in different regions so the police there didn't notice a pattern until recently. Some of the women were seen with a man answering Teague's description and the

327

murders all bear a remarkable similarity to the death of Kassia Graylem.'

Jonathan Petworth sank down into the nearest office chair and put his head in his hands. After a few moments he looked up. 'Honestly I had no idea. If I had . . .'

'What can you tell us about Teague . . . or Wentworth?'

Petworth lowered his eyes. 'OK, Rory and I were at school together but I'd never have described him as a friend.'

'Where did he get the name Jason Teague from?'

'There was a lad of that name at school. He was very religious; wanted to be a vicar and I presume Rory decided to use his name as some sort of joke. I believe the real Jason ended up in Scotland. Rory stole his identity. Look, I was shocked when he contacted me to ask for work. He was somebody I always steered clear of if you want the truth.'

'That's exactly what I want,' said Wesley.

Petworth looked rather grateful that he'd been given permission to abandon his natural reticence. 'I think Rory Wentworth is a psychopath. Or is it a sociopath? I'm not sure which. Not that I ever witnessed anything, you understand, but there was talk that he once hanged a rabbit, just to watch it die. And if he didn't get his own way . . . He didn't lose his temper but things happened to people who crossed him. One boy in our class who had a big mouth told Rory where to go and later he fell down the stairs. Swore he was pushed but there was never any proof. And one of the teachers received a parcel that blew up in her face. She'd been scathing about one of Rory's essays and showed him up in front of the class. There was an investigation but again nothing was proved and I'm afraid the school hushed it all up for the sake of its reputation. Rory was asked to leave but his dad managed to sort things out for him and get him out of trouble so the school kept him on in the end. His dad was a barrister – very persuasive. He'd lost his wife and Rory was his only child so I suppose he felt the urge to protect him whatever he did.' He looked at Wesley as if he was desperate for him to understand. 'You can imagine how I felt when he turned up here asking for a job. I didn't like to say no. I've got a business to run and ...'

'And what?'

'He hinted that boats were vulnerable. Said he'd heard about a fleet of charter vessels tied up in a harbour in France being set on fire. He dropped it into the conversation casually but I knew what he meant.'

'You should have told us.'

'What proof did I have?'

Wesley felt sorry for the man. Rory Wentworth's brand of terror had been subtle. Too clever to do anything that would bring him to the attention of the authorities until he got involved with Dennis Dobbs in order to earn a passage home, and even then he'd wriggled out of any charges. He was expert at playing the innocent.

And then there'd been the girl who'd disappeared aboard the boat on the south coast the year before the Graylems died; the girl seen sailing out alone by Rory Wentworth's father. How far would a father go to protect his son? Wesley thought he knew the answer.

'Did he ever borrow that costume you're wearing?'

Jonathan looked surprised. 'Yes, he borrowed it the other day because he wanted to go to the festival.'

'Which day was this?'

He thought for a few moments. 'Monday I think. Why?'

Wesley didn't answer the question. Monday was the day Eric Darwell had been murdered, Darwell who had been seen in the company of a John Palkin lookalike.

'Any idea where we can find him?'

'Like I said, he mentioned going to the festival.' Jonathan glanced nervously towards the steel staircase at the back of the open-plan room. 'I've been letting him stay in the flat above here while that boat's been sealed off. You can have a look up there if you like. I've got the key.'

He took out a key from a desk drawer and handed it to Wesley, who without a word made for the staircase. When he reached the flat he found it immaculately neat, as if all evidence of habitation had been removed. Even the towels had been stripped from the rail in the bathroom and placed in the wooden linen basket.

Rory Wentworth, alias Jason Teague, had gone.

The checks they'd already done on the names Rory Wentworth and Jason Teague had failed to come up with much. But they hadn't been asking the right questions and, as far as the French police were concerned, their murder suspect had vanished without trace and had given a number of false names to what few witnesses there had been.

Wesley had put the team to work on contacting other forces to see whether anything was known about what Rory Wentworth had been up to since the Graylems' boating tragedy. Each inquiry hit a brick wall and it seemed that, from the age of eighteen, Wentworth had succeeding in slipping off the radar, living a nomadic existence, probably cushioned by funds from his wealthy father who, they discovered, was now living abroad in some unspecified tax haven.

From what they now knew about him, Gerry reckoned there was only one place he would feel truly at home: aboard a boat. The *Queen Philippa* had been left unguarded for several days now, and Gerry suspected that was where he'd head for.

They made their way to the embankment. After the revelations of the past hour Wesley feared that if they were to corner Wentworth and make an arrest things might turn nasty so he'd put more officers on standby. If the suspicions of the French police were to be believed, Rory Wentworth was a prolific killer and a more credible one than Miles Carthage. Wentworth would have thought nothing of disposing of Andre Gorst when he'd attempted to blackmail him or killing Eric Darwell when he'd come to Tradmouth asking awkward questions. Carthage, on the other hand, would have retreated into his own sad, twisted world of beauty and fantasy.

Now everything was becoming clearer. The quarrel before the Graylems' accident. The possibility that a gas bottle had been tampered with to cause the explosion. The boy who showed no emotion other than a cold, carefully controlled fury when his desires were thwarted. The boy could use charm to get what he wanted. And if charm didn't work he would take cool revenge on anybody who crossed him. He had derived pleasure from killing, just as he'd killed that rabbit as a schoolboy. Hanged it and watched it slowly strangle to death.

He recalled the Bethams' account of the row Kassia's father had had with someone on the morning before the explosion and guessed that the Graylems had thwarted Rory in some way. They had died because they hadn't realised that the boy they'd befriended was dangerous. He wondered why Kassia had kept quiet about it all these years. Perhaps it was the lack of proof. After all, even the police had accepted the explosion was an accident.

Wesley wished he'd checked the background of the man who'd called himself Jason Teague more thoroughly rather than allowing himself to be sidetracked by Dennis Dobbs's smuggling activities.

He suppressed this nagging twinge of self-doubt and pushed his way through the crowds with a new determination, ignoring the dirty looks and exclamations. They had to find out whether the *Queen Philippa* was still there at the end of the jetty where Kassia Graylem had last been seen alive. If their man had made his escape by boat, they'd seal off the whole area until he was found, Palkin Festival or no Palkin Festival.

Even if the crowds didn't part for Wesley and Gerry, they parted for their uniformed back-up who were following behind. They'd reached the embankment now. The river was alive with small craft, decked with bunting, swarming around the Royal Navy frigate moored in the centre of the water like flies around a corpse. Gerry surveyed the scene and mumbled something about needles and haystacks.

When they saw the *Queen Philippa* wasn't at her mooring, Gerry swore under his breath and shaded his eyes, scanning the river in the hope that the boat would have just cast off and be within hailing distance of the bank. But she was nowhere to be seen. Rory Wentworth had gone, lost amongst the crowd of vessels.

'Can you see it?' Wesley asked, realising as soon as the words had left his mouth that it was a stupid question. If Gerry had spotted the *Queen Philippa* he would have shouted in triumph and called out the river patrols. 'I thought it was still sealed off.'

'Depends what you mean by sealed off. There was some crime-scene tape saying "do not cross" but we've hardly got the manpower to mount a twenty-four-hour guard.' Gerry reached for his phone and put in calls to the Marine Unit and the harbour master. They needed help.

Chapter 18

*Written at Younger Road, Exeter this
14th day of March 1895*

My dearest Charlotte
*Why do you not reply to my letters? I am
sorely worried and yet I am reluctant to tell
Mama of my concerns. Please, please write and
tell me your news for I cannot bear to think of
you being unhappy.*

*I saw the Reverend Johnson yesterday and he
asked after you. He said that he will call upon
Mama on Thursday. How I look forward to his
visit. I find it so hard to think that you rejected
that dear, gentle man for Josiah — or at least
that is what Mama told me. It may be that he
will make do with the younger sister. As a*

*married woman, surely you cannot envy
me.*

Please, sister, send word of how you fare.
With all my affection, your loving sister
Letty

*Written at North Lodge, Upper Town, Tradmouth
this 21st day of March 1895*

My dear Letty
I write with news that your sister,
Charlotte, is unwell and has been asking for
you. If you take the train to Queenswear
and send word, I will meet you at the
station.
Your loving brother-in-law,
Josiah Palkin-Wright

Gerry stood on the deck of the police launch as the agile craft wove through the sea of bobbing vessels in a mist of salty spray. He ignored the people on the leisure craft who waved to them merrily, glasses in hand, out for a day of pleasure on the water.

The crew were on the lookout for the *Queen Philippa*. Once patrols had made sure that she hadn't sailed upstream to hide in one of the creeks between Tradmouth and Neston eight miles inland, they'd contacted the harbour master, who was having his work cut out on the busiest day of his year. He handled this new burden with calm resignation and informed them that the *Queen Philippa* hadn't made contact to say she was leaving the river. Someone was stationed in his office with binoculars and he promised to call if the vessel was spotted amongst the hectic assortment of river traffic. It was the best he could offer.

The coastguard had been alerted too as, during the chaos of the festival, it would be all too easy for a yacht to slip out of the river into open waters and make for another port – or even the French coast – unhindered. And Rory Wentworth was an expert yachtsman who made his living from the sea and knew it like a lover.

Everything seemed to fit together now. Kassia died because she'd recognised the man who had probably killed her parents. Wesley wondered if she'd challenged Rory, maybe threatened to get the case reopened. Or perhaps she'd just seen him aboard the *Queen Philippa* and approached him out of curiosity or a desire to get to the truth, unaware of the reality behind his amiable mask. He'd have taken pleasure in disposing of her as he'd taken pleasure in killing those women in France.

Wesley guessed that Kassia had given Eric Darwell the photograph missing from her album – *Me, Dad, Mum and Rory*. At her request Eric probably set to work finding out the truth about him, relishing the prospect of a few extra days in the Southwest and not realising for one moment that he was placing himself in danger.

Then there was Andre Gorst. The cog had been moored there for a while so he would have recognised the man from the *Queen Philippa* when he'd dumped Kassia's viol in the bushes. Then he'd made his clumsy attempt at blackmail, assuming that he was dealing with a man who'd killed a woman in a fit of passion. It probably never occurred to him that he was entangling himself with someone who thought nothing of taking a life, who even took pleasure in it.

Wesley sat in the shelter of the cabin, his guts churning, praying silently that he wouldn't bring up his breakfast and make a fool of himself. The words of 'For Those in Peril on the Sea' began to whirl through his head as he yearned for dry land. They were at the Bar now, the hinterland between the haven of the river and the vast open sea. From the spray-spattered porthole he could make out the castle on his right, perched on the towering cliffs guarding the river mouth. His stomach lurched as the boat shot over the waves with all the instability of a fairground ride but he tried hard to concentrate on what was going on around him.

One of the Marine Unit officers was talking on the radio and above the noise of the engine Wesley strained to hear, fingering the unfamiliar bulk of his life jacket. He could just about make out what was being said. A yacht answering the *Queen Philippa*'s description had been spotted half a mile away rounding the headland, sailing in the direction of Bloxham. The port authorities at Bloxham were being alerted in case Wentworth decided to head there. Wesley suddenly felt hopeful that his ordeal might soon be over.

He decided to venture out of the cabin, hoping the fresh air might make him feel better. The nausea rose with each movement of the boat and he couldn't help envying Gerry who was now striding around, sharing grim quips with his fellow sailors.

They were travelling fast across the water, steering past dark glistening rocks protruding from the waves like lethal obstacles in a computer game. One false move, one overzealous turn of the wheel, and the rocks would tear through the hull like a knife through flesh.

Wesley closed his eyes for a moment but that seemed to make the sickness worse. When he opened them again he could see a white vessel ahead, in full sail, cutting through the water. The launch was slowing now as it approached and Wesley heard one of the officers call out an amplified order to stop. He could see two men on the deck, standing, ropes in hand, frozen with astonishment.

But the men were both middle-aged, most likely professional men indulging their expensive hobby. Neither of them bore the slightest resemblance to Rory Wentworth, and one look at the name of the yacht confirmed that this wasn't the *Queen Philippa*, although the two vessels were remarkably similar. As soon as the error was realised radio contact was made, apologies given and inquiries made as to whether the *Queen Philippa* had been spotted. To Wesley's surprise, the answer was yes. She had passed the unsuspecting sailors about half an hour before, heading in the direction of Morbay. She'd sailed very close and when they'd tried to hail her and make radio contact this was ignored.

At least now they knew they were on the right track.

Wesley returned to the cabin and sank down again, taking deep, gulping breaths, the only thing that seemed to ease the nausea. He looked up and saw Gerry descending the steps, a determined look on his face. Dressed in weatherproof gear, he resembled a giant orange. Wesley suspected he was rather enjoying himself.

'How you feeling, Wes?'

'Not good.'

'They've just radioed the harbour master at Morbay and he says the *Queen Philippa*'s just entered the harbour. Back-up's being organised but I've told them to lie low. The last thing we want is to scare him off before he moors up and sets foot ashore.'

They were shooting round the headland now and through the porthole Wesley could see Fortress Point lighthouse up to his left. The towering grey cliffs gave way to stretches of red sand and the land of a thousand childhood holidays. There were funfairs and caravan parks on this part of the coast and today the sunshine had lured bathers on to the beaches and into the sea. He summoned the courage to follow Gerry up on deck and shielded his eyes against the glare of the sky. Soon the golden sands of Morbay itself came into view. They were approaching the harbour, once home to a substantial fishing fleet but now largely used for leisure craft. The launch slowed down as it glided into the haven.

'Any sign?' Gerry called out as the radio crackled to life.

After a few moments one of the Marine Unit team called out. 'Harbour master says the yacht's just moored up near the landing stage. Hasn't made contact yet.'

Now they'd reached calm waters and the launch was cruising slowly into the harbour, Wesley's nausea abated. The engine slowed to a stately pace and they chugged up to the harbour wall, just out of sight of the landing stage. Gerry had been hoping to take Wentworth by surprise but Wesley thought this was optimistic in a marked police launch.

One by one they climbed up the metal ladder fixed to the sheer harbour wall. Wesley had ascended the sides of a trench at an archaeological dig dozens of times but the thought of all that deep water beneath him made him nervous. As he stepped on to the quayside he felt a little unsteady and Gerry took his arm, muttering something about sea legs. Wesley said nothing: he wasn't going to lose his dignity now.

They'd arranged to meet the uniformed back-up who were waiting for them some way off. Gerry hurried over to where they were gathered, Wesley following in his wake. If Wentworth hadn't spotted them, it'd be a miracle.

Gerry seemed to have read his thoughts. 'Looks like the bloody policeman's ball around here. Couldn't you get any high vis jackets, just in case he's short-sighted?'

The uniforms exchanged puzzled looks. Clearly the dose of Liverpudlian sarcasm was wasted on them.

After instructing the back-up to stay where they were till Gerry gave the signal, the two detectives strolled over to the landing stage fifty yards away. The *Queen Philippa* was tied up there at the end, nestled between two larger vessels. As they approached, Wentworth emerged from the cabin and stepped out on to the deck. He was dressed in shorts and a blue polo shirt and he looked completely relaxed, which was just how they wanted him. Unprepared.

'Do we go in now?' Wesley whispered as he saw Wentworth retreat into the cabin.

'We wait.'

A chill wind had started to blow in off the sea and for a while the only sounds Wesley could hear were the lapping of the water and the crying of the seagulls overhead, punctuated with the metallic clinking of halyard against mast and the odd distant splutter of an outboard motor.

The wait couldn't have been more than fifteen minutes but it seemed a lot longer. Then, just as Wesley's patience was starting to wear thin, Wentworth appeared on deck again. Wesley watched, holding his breath, as the man jumped from the deck on to the jetty, sure-footed as a cat, as at home on the water as Wesley was on dry land. He began to saunter towards the harbour office, hands in the pockets of his shorts. As soon as he reached the entrance, they'd take him.

But then he changed direction and started to head for the street. Wesley wondered why he was surprised that the man wasn't doing things by the book. After all, he'd broken the ultimate law. He'd killed.

Gerry signalled to the officers who were waiting at the other side of the harbour office before breaking into a run. Wesley followed but, being younger and fitter, he soon overtook him. He could see Wentworth walking purposefully towards the promenade which was crowded with half-term holiday-makers, families with buckets and spades heading for the sand. Catching up with Wentworth had suddenly become urgent.

They were closing on him but Wentworth didn't appear to have noticed them.

'We've got to stop him before he gets lost in that crowd,' said Gerry, who was panting a few yards behind. The other officers had caught up now so he gave the signal and they began to run, their boots pounding on the promenade like drumbeats.

Wentworth swung round. Wesley was now close enough to see his face but where he'd expected to see panic, instead there was cold calculation. He saw Wentworth reach into his pocket and draw out something small and dark. It took a few seconds for his brain to register that it was a gun and he was pointing it straight at them.

Wesley stopped, putting out a hand to warn Gerry and the others. The gun looked small, almost like a toy. This had to be stopped before it got out of hand. He heard one of the back-up team on the phone to the Armed Response Unit. But it would take a while to arrive.

'Don't be daft,' Gerry said, raising his voice to be heard over the raucous seagulls wheeling overhead. 'Don't make this any worse than it already is.'

'Stay back.' Wentworth sounded jumpy now. Wesley knew that nerves and firearms were a lethal mixture.

'This can only end one way, Rory,' he said. 'Place the gun down on the ground and put your hands on your head.'

Wesley heard an ominous metallic click. Wentworth's expression was blank, devoid of emotion. The man wasn't panicking. He was preparing to kill with the cool efficiency of an executioner.

For a moment there was a silence when even the circling sea birds made no sound. Then the air exploded around him. Wesley fell to his knees and felt a heavy weight pushing his body to one side.

He hadn't been aware of closing his eyes until he opened them and saw Gerry slumped on the ground beside him, clutching his chest.

'Officer down,' they'd shouted as Wesley knelt beside Gerry praying for the paramedics to arrive. Gerry was murmuring but he couldn't make out the words. He could feel something warm and sticky seeping on to his arm. Blood.

The Armed Response Unit had descended on the scene with a squealing of tyres. But Wentworth had got away, dodging down the promenade through the throng of unsuspecting families. The back-up team had followed at a distance and lost him because they hadn't wanted to risk getting too close with all those kids about. The last thing they needed was a hostage situation.

Wesley was trying his best to stay calm and professional.

But it wasn't easy when the man who was not only his boss but also his friend was lying in his arms, dying for all he knew. He looked round and saw people standing there, frozen like statues. He shouted to them, asking where the ambulance was. Aware of his own voice cracking with emotion, he suddenly felt lost.

It seemed an age before he heard the welcome wailing of the ambulance siren. He heard himself talking to the green-clad paramedics, explaining what had happened and functioning on some automatic level that he hoped was making sense.

It wasn't long before they had Gerry in the ambulance, wires sprouting from his chest and an oxygen mask hiding most of his face. As he was lifted in on the stretcher, he managed to talk after a fashion. Wesley couldn't quite make out what he was saying but it sounded like one of his jokes.

When the ambulance had driven away, Wesley was left there alone. The Armed Response Unit was out looking for Wentworth and everyone had been issued with bulletproof vests. Pity they hadn't thought to give Gerry one; nobody had considered the possibility that Wentworth had acquired a gun on his travels.

He stood there, a hollow feeling in his heart. Maybe he should have gone in the ambulance with Gerry. On the other hand someone had to co-ordinate the search and Gerry would have told him not to be a sentimental idiot; but the last thing he felt like doing at that moment was carrying on.

A crowd had gathered behind a hastily erected barrier, staring like curious sheep under the gaze of a trio of uniformed constables from Morbay nick. There were children in the crowd and Wesley felt like yelling at them. Didn't they realise there was a dangerous man at large? Didn't they realise he had a gun and thought nothing of killing?

His phone rang. Wentworth had been cornered in an amusement arcade on the promenade. Shots had been fired and an onlooker, a young lad, had been injured although not seriously as far as they could tell. Wentworth had then made a run for it, dropping his gun on the arcade's grubby carpet to be retrieved swiftly by the surrounding officers. He was now heading back to the harbour area.

Wesley retraced his steps. There was a chance that Wentworth might try to return to the *Queen Philippa* and make his escape by water. All available officers would be making for the harbour but he wanted to get there before them.

He ran along the embankment. He could see the *Queen Philippa* at the end of the landing stage and he caught sight of a movement aboard. Someone was on deck, bent down as if playing a game of hide-and-seek. As Wesley drew closer he could see that it was Wentworth and that he was opening a locker, delving inside, searching for something.

Confident that the sound of the gulls overhead would mask his approaching footsteps, Wesley ran down the landing stage and stepped aboard gingerly, steadying himself on the rails. He turned his head and saw that half-a-dozen officers were several yards behind him, making for the same spot. Wentworth wouldn't stand a chance now.

'Rory Wentworth. You're under arrest,' he said, taking his handcuffs from his pocket as he began to recite the familiar words of the caution.

Wentworth turned slowly and straightened himself up. There was something in his hand; something brightly coloured and the size of an old-fashioned police truncheon. And he was grinning; the merciless grin of a death's-head.

'It's all over,' Wesley said quietly. 'You'll have to come with me now, Rory.'

'I don't have to do anything.' Wentworth held the thing up and pointed it at Wesley. 'This is a flare. If you don't want your face burned off I advise you to get ashore and let me cast off.'

'Don't be stupid.'

Wentworth began to unfasten something on the flare. Then he stepped forward, brandishing it like a sabre, his eyes alight with amused hatred.

'This won't do you any good, Rory.'

As Wentworth took another step forward, his foot came into contact with a coil of rope and as he stumbled there was a sudden roar and a blinding flash of light as the flare ignited, engulfing him in a red flame. Wesley watched, mesmerised, as the man staggered to the edge of the deck and hurled himself into the water, blazing like a fireball.

Wesley knew he should have been pleased about the arrest of Rory Wentworth and the fact that he'd been rushed to the burns unit at Tradmouth Hospital. But he kept thinking of Gerry and experiencing a pain that verged on the physical, a sort of aching in the heart and the stomach. He called the hospital but they would only say that Gerry was being assessed. When he eventually got through to Rachel she fell silent on the other end of the line before promising to make the necessary calls to Rosie, Sam and Joyce.

As soon as he'd seen Wentworth into the ambulance he'd walked back to the *Queen Philippa* which had now been dressed overall in crime-scene tape. He felt numb. Unable to think. Unable to pray for Gerry's life.

*

That evening Wesley stood at the window of the CID office watching the fireworks light up the sky, a fine display to celebrate John Palkin's life. In other circumstances he'd be enjoying the spectacle. But as it was the brilliant fountains of light, reflected like flashing diamonds in the smooth, dark river, only reminded him of Rory Wentworth who was now conscious and, according to the hospital, not in any danger. Rarely had Wesley felt so much hatred for a suspect and he feared that he'd find it hard to maintain the necessary professional distance. On the other hand he needed to speak to the man. He needed to get him put away where he could never hurt anybody ever again.

He heard one of the DCs say that he'd like ten minutes alone with the suspect. Wesley half-heartedly scolded him, saying he could understand his anger but everything had to be done by the book if they were to secure a conviction some clever lawyer couldn't help him wriggle out of.

He'd rung Morbay Hospital twice but they were noncommittal. Mr Heffernan was stable and about to undergo surgery. Wesley didn't derive much comfort from the news. He knew that stable could mean anything.

When the call came to say that Wentworth was up to being interviewed, he stood up, his hands tightened into fists. Rachel said something he couldn't quite make out and when he turned round he saw that she was looking at him. Her eyes were puffy, as though she'd been crying.

'Do you want me to come with you to interview Wentworth?' she asked, her voice hushed, as though she was in a place of mourning.

'Thanks.' He'd been about to ask Paul but Rachel's gender might give them an advantage. Wentworth had killed women and her presence might lower the man's defences.

'Do you think the boss'll be OK?' she asked as they walked down the stairs.

'He's in good hands.' He knew this was a cliché but he needed to believe it.

When they reached the hospital a nurse showed them into the room where Wentworth was lying with a police guard stationed outside. His injuries, the nurse said, weren't as bad as they could have been because he'd had the presence of mind to jump straight into the water although he'd still suffered burns to his face and would bear the scars for life.

When Wesley opened the door he saw Wentworth propped up against the hospital pillow, swathed in bandages, faceless. But Wesley could see his eyes staring at him, unrepentant and filled with contempt.

It was to be an informal interview. A chat. The official statement with the tape running would follow later. Meanwhile there were things Wesley needed to know so he decided to come straight to the point. 'Why did you kill Kassia Graylem?'

'Is it any use saying I didn't?' Wentworth's muffled words were casual, as if Wesley had been inquiring about some minor misdemeanour. Wesley had never been a violent man but he knew he'd need all his self-control to get through the interview.

'We've been in touch with the police in France.'

Wentworth said nothing.

'Two women were murdered on the west coast last year and two on the Riviera recently. We've also heard from the Italian police that there were three similar murders on the Amalfi coast a couple of years ago. All the victims were strangled and put into inflatable boats.'

347

'Inflatables capsize,' Wentworth said simply.

'An Englishman answering your description was seen with two of the French victims before they vanished. Last month another woman went missing in Antibes where you met up with Dennis Dobbs.'

'Really?'

Wesley felt a slight pressure on his arm. Rachel had touched him as though she sensed that he was almost at breaking point.

He asked the question again. 'Why did you kill Kassia Graylem?'

'Who says I did?'

'We've got a picture of you with Kassia and her parents taken seven years ago in Suffolk.'

Wentworth shrugged. 'That proves nothing.'

'She recognised you and said she was going to prove you killed her parents. We've spoken to your alibi, Kimberley Smith, again, and she's changed her story. On Saturday morning she had to start work at the hotel early so she left her flat near the market at five thirty. She told us that you asked her to say she was with you till later; spun her some yarn about being involved in a burglary and told her she was the love of your life. She wasn't too pleased when she learned the truth. We couldn't stop her talking after that.'

Wentworth said nothing.

'Kassia had just spent the night on Chris Butcher's yacht and when she was walking along the embankment she spotted you. She'd seen you before and recognised you but she hadn't been certain. You must have had a hell of a shock when she approached you.'

'Who says she approached me? You've got no evidence.'

'Killers always leave traces,' said Rachel. 'A hair or a

348

flake of skin. Some invisible sign of contact. We found a leather belt on board the boat. We've sent it to the lab. If it was used to kill Kassia, we'll soon know.'

Wentworth stared at her for a few seconds and Wesley could see the hatred in his eyes. She'd defied him. If they'd been alone in some isolated spot, he'd probably have killed her. But instead he nodded calmly, as though he was tired of keeping up the pretence.

'This isn't an official interview and I've got no legal representation so nothing I say now will stand up in court. Is that right?'

Reluctantly Wesley said yes.

'OK. I admit it. I killed Kassia. She was being a pain, going on and on about her fucking parents. I snapped.'

'And her parents?'

'Her dad made me angry. I'm getting sick of this,' he said. 'I want you to go. Nurse,' he shouted, his voice still muffled by the bandages.

Wesley ignored him and hoped the staff hadn't heard. 'What about Eric Darwell?'

Wentworth gave a derisory snort. 'The little private eye in the cheap suit. He came sniffing around. Kassia told him she was sure I'd killed her parents. Said she thought she'd seen me and she wanted him to confirm it. She'd even given him a photo of me with her and her parents. He came to the boat on Monday morning and said he'd heard on the news that a girl answering Kassia's description had been found dead. I told him it couldn't be her 'cause I'd seen her on the embankment the previous evening. I couldn't have him going to the police with his story, could I?'

'What happened?'

'I knew I had to get rid of him so I told him I couldn't talk then 'cause I was expecting Den back but I said I'd meet him later at the holiday park where he was staying. I went there in Jonathan's fancy dress and pretended I wanted to look round the place. He took me to this scruffy old swimming pool. He was wearing a suit and carrying a briefcase 'cause he thought of it as a business meeting. You had to laugh.'

'You took his briefcase.'

'Sure. He said he'd brought the evidence in it – the photo and his notes. If you're looking for it, you'll find it at the bottom of the river.'

'Did Andre Gorst see you putting Kassia's viol in the bushes? Did he blackmail you?'

'He was a stupid greedy nobody. I did him a favour,' he said with contempt.

'Where did you get the gun?' Wesley asked.

'Marseilles. You can pick up all sorts of things in Marseilles.'

'You haven't asked about the officer you shot.'

Wentworth didn't answer.

'Why did Kassia's father make you angry?' Rachel asked. 'I want to understand.'

The man with no face turned his head towards her. 'I wanted to go sailing with them and he said no. He called me a spoiled little posh kid and told me to keep away from his daughter. Nobody speaks to me like that. I caused the gas leak and waited. The stupid bastard smoked like a chimney so I knew it was foolproof. As soon as he set foot on board, bang. I taught him a lesson, that's all.'

'And your father saw to it that you got away with it,' said Wesley.

'I always get away with it, as you put it. I'm untouchable.'

'And the women you killed in France and Italy?'

Wentworth hesitated. 'They weren't important. Look, you're not recording this so I'll just deny everything I've just told you. I'll say the gun belonged to Den and I waved it around when I panicked and I'd no idea it was loaded. My dad'll fix everything, you'll see.'

Wesley caught Rachel's eye. If they didn't have the upper hand, he would have found the man's confidence frightening.

When they reached the door Wesley glanced back and suddenly he knew why the sight of that featureless face masked in white bandages seemed so familiar.

It was the face of Shipworld's Shroud Maker. Bringer of darkness into a light, colourful world.

The doctors at Morbay Hospital reckoned Gerry was lucky. The bullet had only damaged his shoulder without penetrating any vital organs. The operation to remove it had been a success and when Wesley visited him he was sitting up in bed, claiming that his new bullet scar would give him some welcome credibility amongst the villains of the area. Wesley laughed dutifully, but the thought of what might have been still left him with a nebulous feeling of dread, as if he'd been robbed of some of his certainties and life would never be quite the same again.

Sam called in to sit beside his father's hospital bed whenever work allowed and a tearful Rosie had been visiting every day. Sometimes she'd been there at the same time as Joyce and it seemed that some kind of pact had been reached. A truce of British politeness. Joyce even expressed enthusiasm for attending one of Rosie's concerts but Rosie had responded bluntly, saying the concerts were over until the next Palkin Festival – adding that if Dan Hungerford felt inclined to re-form Palkin's Musik for the next festival in a year's time, she probably wouldn't be available. Joyce had smiled and said nothing. Now Gerry had been released from hospital and was recuperating at home. Wesley hoped it wouldn't be too long before he returned to work.

Rory Wentworth too was out of hospital, his once flawless tanned features now a mask of mottled scar tissue. He had been questioned formally, charged and remanded in custody until his trial. This was in spite of the intervention of his father who'd been reluctant to acknowledge his son's nature over the years; who'd denied the truth until it could no longer be ignored. Wesley found himself feeling a little sorry for Carlton Wentworth. It was a terrible thing to have so much materially and yet to bear a terrible, unacknowledged burden; a time bomb that could blow your comfortable world apart at any moment. Nobody knows what goes on in other people's lives, Wesley thought. Sometimes envy is the most pointless of the deadly sins.

There was only the paperwork to sort out, including that generated by the European police inquiries. Then there was a new spate of burglaries at holiday cottages. Standard fare for this time of year with the main tourist season just beginning. Jenny Bercival had been reunited with her mother and had now returned to London to recuperate from her ordeal. She was having professional help to come to terms with what had happened but Wesley feared that she might never fully recover.

At least the Palkin Festival with its accompanying problems was over for another year and the *Maudelayne* had sailed off into the sunset minus one of her crew. Captain

Garcia had allowed a short service of remembrance to be held for Andre Gorst, although in view of his behaviour with Rosie Heffernan, if the man hadn't been murdered, it was doubtful whether he'd have welcomed him back on board.

Wesley was sitting at his desk. He'd felt uncomfortable about usurping Gerry's office in his absence. Even though he was acting DCI for the time being, it just hadn't seemed right. He was checking over the budget reports with a nagging feeling of resentment and the recurring thought that if he'd wanted to be an accountant he would have gone to work for a large firm in the City and be earning a good deal more than his policeman's salary. As the figures swam in front of his tired eyes, he was relieved to hear Rachel's voice.

'Can I have a word?' she said. 'In private.'

'OK,' he said as he stood up. 'We can go into Gerry's office.'

In Gerry's absence Rachel was acting DI reporting straight to CS Fitton. She'd postponed her wedding to Nigel until later in the year because of her new workload and Gerry's incapacity. Wesley wondered whether this was the real reason. Sometimes, though, it was best to accept things at face value.

She followed him into the glass-fronted office and after he'd shut the door he sat down on one of the visitors' chairs. Gerry's worn swivel chair was standing empty at the other side of the desk.

Rachel sat down a few feet away, crossing her legs neatly. Recently they'd hardly had a chance to be alone because they'd been so busy. But there was no backing out now.

It was Rachel who spoke first. 'Look, I know we haven't talked about . . .'

'There's no need. It's forgotten,' he said quickly.

She looked down at her hands. 'I've been feeling like an idiot, coming on to you like that. I'm supposed to be getting married, for God's sake.'

Wesley said nothing. That night in Manchester was still etched on his memory. The soft knock on his bedroom door. Rachel pushing her way inside and kissing him. He was ashamed when he recalled that he'd responded to her kiss until some inner voice, whether born of his strict upbringing or his love for Pam and his children – he wasn't sure which – had made him pull away and tell Rachel it would be best if she left. But he had felt her body pressed close to his and smelled the perfume she wore. He'd been tempted, and the memory made him feel uncomfortable.

'You're sure about going ahead with the wedding?'

'Is that any of your business?'

'I'd ask the same question if I thought any friend was having second thoughts. And I hope we're friends.'

'I've postponed it but Nigel's going on about setting a date in the autumn. A wedding's like a steamroller. It's a difficult thing to stop.'

'But you want it to stop?'

'I didn't say that.'

'It's better to say something now before it's too late.'

'Is that what you want? Do you want me to tell Nigel it's off?'

'No.' He was aware that the word had sounded too emphatic. And he didn't want to hurt her feelings. He never wanted to hurt anyone's feelings. 'I'm thinking of you, that's all.' He paused for a few seconds, searching for the right words. 'Nigel's a decent man and I'm sure you'll be happy together if ...'

It came as a relief when his phone started to ring. He looked at the caller display and saw that it was Gerry. 'I'll have to take this,' he said to Rachel, who stood up and left the room. Wesley waited until the door was shut before he spoke.

Gerry's small whitewashed cottage on cobbled Baynard's Quay stood at the end of a row of much grander houses, set back slightly behind a tiny front yard. He'd bought it many years ago when he and Kathy first married but nowadays the desirable property would be well beyond a policeman's pocket. Sam and Rosie had been raised there and when Kathy died Gerry had stayed put because he loved the house with its spectacular view of the river and the passing boats. Besides, it held too many memories for him to uproot himself and move.

Wesley opened the salt-air-rusted gate that separated Gerry's sanctuary from the tourists strolling up and down the cobbles, enjoying one of Tradmouth's most picturesque spots. He knocked on the door and after a few moments Gerry answered, his face lit up by a wide grin as though Wesley had rescued him from the terrible fate of tedious inactivity. Gerry's normally round face looked gaunt and he was thinner in general; there were some who would have said that wasn't a bad thing.

'How are you feeling?' Wesley asked as he stepped over the threshold.

'All the better for seeing you, Wes.' He led the way into the living room and Wesley offered to make coffee. Gerry waved the offer away. He wasn't an invalid. Wesley, feeling

355

bad about pricking Gerry's pride by making the assumption, sat back and waited for the coffee, listening to Gerry crashing about in the kitchen.

'Any developments?' Gerry said as he handed Wesley the steaming mug.

'Wentworth's in custody awaiting trial.'

'What about Miles Carthage? Body turned up yet?'

Wesley shook his head.

Gerry put his mug down heavily on the coffee table, spilling some of the brown liquid. He made no attempt to clear it up. 'Think he could still be alive?'

'Do you?'

'I've been wondering about that. There's always a possibility that he survived, you know. How's his sister, Butcher's wife?'

'She's pleading ignorance. Says she had no idea what Miles was up to.'

'Believe her?'

'No. But it's a hard thing to prove. Apparently the Butchers have decided to rent a place here for the summer until their new house is ready.'

'I called Rach first thing and she sounded stressed,' said Gerry. 'Shame about the wedding.'

Wesley said nothing. He and Gerry were close but there were some things he couldn't share.

'I'm going to the hospital for some physio this afternoon; they want me to get more movement back in this arm.' Gerry sighed. 'I need to get back in harness. I'm crawling up the walls stuck in here.'

Wesley looked at the boss and realised that he reminded him of a child standing outside a locked sweet shop with his nose pressed up against the window.

His phone began to ring and when he looked at the caller display he saw that it was Neil. He muttered an apology to Gerry who turned his attention to his coffee.

'You know you said there were some old notebooks and letters in a trunk at North Lodge?' Neil began.

Carthage had mentioned the documents just before he'd flung himself off the rock into the hungry sea. Wesley had ordered the trunk to be taken downstairs and he'd been intending to look at them. But the arrest of Wentworth and Gerry's brush with death had driven them from his mind. 'Yes. What about them?'

'Chris Butcher wants to see them. He's keen to develop a new website. Not fantasy this time. The story of Josiah Palkin-Wright and his crimes.'

'Very appropriate.'

'I think I might have identified those skeletons at Butcher's place. I went to the offices of the *Tradmouth Echo* and found reports of three women going missing in Tradmouth. One in eighteen ninety-three, one the year after and the last in eighteen ninety-five. All prostitutes from the slums in Low Street. There used to be medieval houses there that had deteriorated into tenements. They were pulled down in the nineteen twenties by some vandals from the council.'

'Have we got names for these women?'

'Jane Carr, Nelly Trelawny and Jessie Allson. Nelly was seen in the company of Josiah Palkin-Wright shortly before she vanished but he denied all knowledge – claimed she'd just asked him the time. The boathouse that used to stand on the site of the burials belonged to Palkin-Wright so it looks like we might have ourselves a serial killer.'

'Not my problem,' said Wesley with relief.

'I'm dying to have a look in that trunk. Is the house still a crime scene? Have you still got access?'

Wesley said a cautious 'Yes.' He knew what was coming. 'The CSIs have finished in there so it can't do any harm. As long as you provide a receipt for anything you take.'

He glanced at Gerry, who took another sip of coffee. 'You're in charge now, Wes. It's up to you,' he said with a casual wave of his hand. Wesley thought he detected a slight hint of sadness in his voice, the melancholy of an old king who'd just been ousted by a younger pretender, though Gerry had never been the bitter type.

Wesley told Neil he'd meet him in an hour's time at North Lodge and stood up to leave. Gerry seemed reluctant to let him go, as though he craved company and saw a lonely afternoon stretching ahead of him. But Wesley had things to do.

The thought of entering North Lodge again made him uneasy. Even though it had been confirmed that those bodies in the basement were none of his concern, they'd been on his mind since they were found. And in his dreams he still saw those faces, those desiccated masks with hollow eyes that had seen the terrors of hell.

He picked up the keys from the station and when he arrived at the house Neil was waiting for him, a keen expression on his face. They were at the recording stage of the dig, he explained, and Butcher was financing an exhibition of the finds at the Museum.

As Wesley entered the silent hall he had an uncomfortable feeling that somebody was standing at the top of the stairs watching them. For a split second it crossed his mind that Miles Carthage might have survived and returned home. However, when he looked up, there was nobody there.

The trunk had now been moved to the bare front room and Wesley watched as Neil opened it, removed the contents and spread them out around him on the dusty floorboards, gloating like a miser counting treasure. Then Wesley saw a look of disappointment on his face.'

'I was half expecting to find medieval stuff, primary sources he'd used for his book that should be in the archives,' he said after a while. 'But all this is more recent.'

'So where did the material for his book come from?'

'God knows. Annabel's been looking into it and she hasn't found any of the documents referred to in the book, apart from Palkin's will which is safe in the cathedral archives. She's managed to confirm that the story in *The Sea Devil* about Palkin dying while he was spying on his fourth wife is a load of rubbish. According to church records, he died in his bed. And there was no fourth wife. He'd also got it completely wrong about the second and third wives disappearing as well. They were both buried at local churches and Palkin paid for masses to be said for them at St Margaret's. It makes you wonder what else he made up. The story about a stake being driven through Palkin's heart wasn't true either. Although the parish records of St Leonard's say that his brother, Henry, was thought to have taken his own life and was buried in unconsecrated ground.'

'No stake?'

'There's no mention of one. Palkin-Wright was a lousy historian.'

'It sounds as if he lived in a fantasy world like Miles Carthage,' said Wesley.

'Must run in the family.'

'What did Annabel manage to find out about Henry?'

'Not much. The town records say he ran the ropeworks. He inherited Palkin's fortune but he killed himself a year later. That's all there is in the parish records. He died by his own hand and he left a widow and a son.'

He began to sort through the papers in the trunk. 'Most of this is Victorian. Contemporary with Palkin-Wright. Hang on.'

He picked one document out with exaggerated care. It looked considerably older than the rest – ancient parchment. He frowned with concentration as he studied it, deciphering the unfamiliar script. After a while he spoke in awestruck tones. 'Now this is the real thing. It appears to be from John Palkin to his son, Richard. He's sending him to work in Henry's ropeworks but it doesn't sound as if Richard's too happy about it.' He read. '"Fear not thine uncle, though he envies me greatly and is ever in an ill humour. He desireth my fortune and yet thou shalt inherit all upon my death. Thou must make amends with him so that we may live in amity together. This is my earnest desire."' Neil looked up. 'Well, he was wrong about Richard inheriting everything. Poor lad died at the age of eighteen. Makes you wonder.'

'What?'

'Whether Wicked Uncle Henry was responsible. After all, with Richard gone, he became his brother's heir.' He thought for a few moments. 'John Palkin's will mentions that Henry is tormented by Satan. I suppose that could mean anything. Jealousy? A bad temper?'

'A tendency to violence? Or some kind of mental illness that wasn't understood in those unenlightened times?'

'Richard died at the ropeworks. Maybe Henry was responsible and killed himself later out of remorse.'

He handed the delicate parchment to Wesley who cradled it like a newborn baby, squinting at the faded handwriting.

'There's a bit here about Henry being a maker of shrouds.' Wesley smiled to himself. 'In Shipworld the villain is known as the Shroud Maker so I wonder if this is where the idea for the character came from.'

'It's possible, I guess.' Neil delved into the trunk again. 'As far as I can see, that letter's the only genuinely old thing in here. Wonder where Palkin-Wright got it.'

'Don't suppose there's any way of finding out.'

Wesley set the document to one side carefully and joined Neil, kneeling by the trunk and sorting through the papers.

'There are some letters in here.' Wesley pulled out a bundle of envelopes with copperplate writing, faded to a sepia brown.

They were all addressed to the same person – a Miss Letitia Ventnor, Younger Road, Exeter. It looked very much as if they had never been posted so Miss Ventnor, whoever she was, had probably never received them.

He opened one and handed a couple to Neil. They read them and opened more, noting the writer's increasing desperation. They were from a woman called Charlotte who was obviously Josiah Palkin-Wright's wife. And it seemed that her marriage was no ordinary one.

Neil put his hand in the trunk and pulled out another bundle of letters, this time addressed to Mrs Charlotte Palkin-Wright at North Lodge. He opened the first, read it and passed it to Wesley. It was from Charlotte's sister,

Letitia, asking why she hadn't been in contact. As Wesley read another, he experienced a feeling of dread. Charlotte's letters had clearly never reached her sister. In the final letter Letitia announced that she was coming to Tradmouth and that she would call on Charlotte to see what was happening. There was nothing more after this date.

Wesley looked up. 'Charlotte complains to Letitia that her husband keeps her prisoner and that she hears strange noises in a locked room, presumably the one upstairs.' He opened another of Charlotte's letters and studied it before speaking. 'Yes. In this one she says she's found a girl called Jessie imprisoned up there.' He shook his head in disbelief.

'That fits with the newspaper reports I found,' said Neil. 'One of the missing girls was called Jessie Allson.'

'Charlotte's begging her sister for help and she asks her to contact someone called the Reverend Johnson.'

There were more papers in the trunk; mostly notes Josiah Palkin-Wright had made for his book on the life of his illustrious ancestor. Then Wesley spotted a notebook with a marbled cover and pulled it out. It was filled with Palkin-Wright's cramped handwriting and he began to read, flicking through the pages.

Once he'd finished he passed the book to Neil who read in silence, frowning with disgust. Eventually he looked up. 'He persuaded prostitutes to come to the house then he held them prisoner in the attic. He tied them up and watched them die and his housekeeper, Maud Cummings, helped him. Bloody hell, Wes. This is sick.' He turned another page. 'He says he buried them under the boathouse by the water. There's our confirmation. As far as I can make out it was Jane and Nelly who were buried there.'

'So it was probably the third girl, Jessie, who ended up in the cellar with Charlotte and Letitia.'

'Do you reckon Josiah was sick or evil?'

Wesley considered the question for a few seconds. 'In the past they often couldn't tell the difference.'

'Do you think this is where Carthage got the idea of locking up that poor girl?'

'It wouldn't surprise me.'

Neil pointed to a large brown envelope. Compared to the rest of the documents in the trunk, it looked new and out of place. 'What's that?'

Wesley picked it out, opened it and extracted the contents – a wad of A4 sheets covered in close neat handwriting. He examined them a while before speaking. 'These are story outlines. No, they're more like instructions. "The Lady Morwenna must be held in the Cave of Adron. Feed her the Shroud Maker's potion so that she will slumber."' He selected another. '"The Shroud Maker will lure the Lady Morwenna to the cave with the promise that her beauty will be immortal. She must not suspect that he wishes to preserve her loveliness for himself." There's another here. "The Lady Alicia is dear to Palkin so she must be kept safe. Her beauty must be recorded lest the Shroud Maker captures her."'

'So Carthage couldn't tell fantasy from reality.'

Wesley studied the papers in his hand. 'I've seen his handwriting and this is completely different.' He pushed them back into their envelope. 'I'm going to take these to the station. I need to compare this writing with some of the signatures on our statements.'

'Fine,' said Neil, his mind on other things.

Wesley wanted to get out of that house where so many

bad things had happened. He told Neil he'd leave it to him to arrange for the ancient document in the trunk to be taken to Exeter. He knew his words seemed distant but there was a lot on his mind.

Chapter 19

Journal of Josiah Palkin-Wright

22nd March 1895

Women are betrayers and deceivers and my so-called wife is the most perfidious of all. When Maud, who has ever been loyal to me — more loyal than my own mother who betrayed my father with another — found that Charlotte had discovered the whore Jessie in the attic I knew she deserved the harshest of punishments. How angry I was when I dragged her up to the attic by her hair and bound her. If she wishes to share Jessie's punishment, I shall let her have her will.

I wrote a missive to her sister, the one she

would have revealed all to, had I not had the foresight to intercept her letters. I have invited her to visit her sister here and when she comes I will deal with her. As I will deal with my wife and the whore Jessie. As I dealt with the other whores who required chastisement.

28th March 1895

Today I went up to the attic room and placed my hands around the throat of the whore Jessie while my wife watched, her eyes bulging with terror, too weak to scream. When I had finished I chastised Charlotte in the same way for her deception. I felt such pleasure as I squeezed the life out of their frail bodies and such ecstasy at the power I held and the rightness of my vengeance.

Maud helped me to wrap the carcasses and shut them in a room that is never used. Maybe I will bury them with the others at the boathouse, at the place where my ancestor built his great warehouse.

Now I must prepare for the arrival of Letty for she has sent word that she will be arriving on the afternoon train. I am become the destroyer of those who would betray me. Those who deserve death.

Tragedy of Drowned Curate

The body of a young man found drowned in the River Trad has been identified as that of the Reverend Charles Johnson. The Reverend Johnson was visiting Tradmouth when he is believed to have met with a tragic accident, there being no witnesses to this unfortunate event. His family and friends say that he was a fine and devout young man who will be sadly missed by those who knew him.

Astrid took the BMW to the meeting place. It was an empty cottage with half its roof missing some fifteen miles from Tradmouth, overlooking the sea near Monk's Island. It was a place where nobody went, standing on the edge of a tall cliff separated from neighbouring farmland by woods and brambles.

Miles had always been a strong swimmer. He'd often swum in that cove as a child and the sea held no terror for him. But Astrid had told the police that he couldn't swim. She had lied to them.

Once Miles had recovered a little and his clothes were dry, he'd ventured up from the tiny cove where he'd come ashore and found a working phone box on the edge of a village. He'd called her, reversing the charges, and she'd found the hiding place and provided him with the necessities while she decided on the best course of action.

She'd loathed those women, the ones Chris had betrayed her with, hated them with such a passion that she'd longed to see them punished. Poor, unworldly Miles had always been under the spell of his big sister so it had been easy to make him do whatever she wanted. And when he had started to work on the Shipworld website, her plan had come together.

She fed him the storylines, planting the seeds in his head, always pointing the way, using her husband's creation against him without his knowledge. Obsession had always been in Miles's nature and all she'd had to do was whisper her orders in his ear to tip him over the brink. She'd told him they had to be kept secure so that he could keep their beauty to himself and capture it for eternity on canvas and paper, just like the Shroud Maker in Shipworld. She'd convinced him that they didn't suffer, or if they did it was for beauty's sake. Hatred and envy had consumed her like a poison. She had punished them through Miles. And Chris had known nothing about it.

She stood outside the cottage on the edge of the cliff. Even on a perfect day like this there was a strong breeze blowing off the water, sending her scarf fluttering behind her like a pennant.

She felt a hand on her shoulder.

'I need to send the last illustration to Palkinson.'

Astrid took his hand and gave it a squeeze. 'I've got to work out how we're going to get you out of here first. I need to think.'

'I didn't do anything wrong, did I? I looked after them.'

'Of course you did. But it'd be best if you went away for a while until the fuss dies down.' She kissed her little brother on the cheek, as she used to do when she was comforting him after the nightmares that plagued him throughout his childhood.

'When I come back I'm going to tell them I didn't hurt them. I'm going to say that you made me do it.'

Astrid flinched. 'No, you mustn't do that, Miles.'

'Why not? I left my pictures at the house. I need to go back to Tradmouth.'

'It would cause trouble if you turned up there now. If you stay here for a while until I can arrange things, everything will be fine.'

The body, later identified as that of Miles Carthage, had been washed up near Monk's Island. This mystified Gerry as he was sure the tides wouldn't have carried him that way. Colin Bowman was also puzzled about the time of death which he estimated to be at least a week after his disappearance. But, as there were so many factors to take into account, he admitted that these things weren't always easy to calculate.

The signs of violence on the body could have been due to rocks and tides. Even so, Colin wanted to do more tests.

Wesley would have to be patient.

Chris was out. He'd been out a lot recently. He'd told her he had meetings in London, but she didn't believe him. He was at it again, seeing some woman. While she'd had ways of dealing with it before, now things were different. She didn't have Miles any more.

She was sure she knew who his latest woman was – that bitch from the TV archaeology programme. Sacha Vale. Long auburn tresses. Beautiful. His usual type. However, it was when he persuaded them to be tattooed that she really had to worry and Sacha looked as if she had a mind of her own, so she might not be willing to play his little games.

Maybe this time she'd get in early and deal with the situation herself, although she wasn't quite sure how. Still, there were many ways to punish the wrongdoer – as many punishments as there were sins.

The doorbell rang and when she hurried to answer she was shocked to see that the man standing on the doorstep was holding up a police warrant card for her inspection.

'Mrs Butcher,' said Wesley Peterson. 'I need to talk to you? It's about your brother.'

It had taken courage for Jenny Bercival to face her fears as her psychiatrist recommended, and look at the Shipworld website on the expensive new laptop her estranged father had just bought her.

Once she had stopped shaking, she was surprised to see that Palkin had enjoyed a great victory. He had defeated the forces of the Devil Elves of Bretania. And the Shroud Maker, Palkin's greatest enemy, was dead.

Author's Note

One of the most noteworthy events in the history of Dartmouth in Devon was a visit to the port by Geoffrey Chaucer in 1373. The author of *The Canterbury Tales* was a trusted customs official of Edward III who was sent by the king to inquire into the seizure by Dartmouth's mayor and bailiffs of a ship belonging to a Genoese merchant.

Dartmouth had a terrible reputation for piracy at the time and, no doubt, it fell to Chaucer to make sure that the merchant's property was returned to him. Twelve years later, between 1386 and 1389, Chaucer wrote his most famous work which featured a character called the Shipman: a seaman from 'Dertemouthe' who was little better than a pirate, stealing ships' cargos and drowning the prisoners he captured.

It is highly likely that the Shipman was a composite character, based on the many tales of lawless Dartmouth sailors that must have reached the ears of London courtiers. However, over the years some have assumed that the

Shipman was a caricature of one of the port's principal citizens of the time – a man called John Hawley II, a wealthy merchant and shipowner who was among the town's leading burgesses and served as mayor fourteen times. Chaucer probably met Hawley during his visit but it unlikely that he used him as his model, even though the merchant was almost certainly engaged in what would be considered today as piracy.

This was the time of the Hundred Years' War between England and France and in 1379 John Hawley was granted a licence to 'go to sea for a year with seven ships at their own expense to attack and destroy the king's enemies' – the standard wording for a privateer. By 1386 he was directing the operations of a fleet of privateers who attacked French and neutral shipping off the coast of Brittany. In 1389 Dartmouth was granted the sole right to the export of tin in recognition that the town 'has brought great havoc on the king's enemies in time of war.'

The town also grew rich on the Bordeaux wine trade (Bordeaux belonging to England at that time) and great wooden ships called cogs were the workhorses of both commerce and war. Cogs had one large square sail and were steered by a rudder attached to the stern post. They were also built up at bow and stern into 'castles' in which sailors could take refuge and shoot arrows during the frequent sea fights. Even to this day the arms of Dartmouth feature a cog, a potent symbol of the port's power back in the Middle Ages.

Although my fictional character John Palkin is (like Chaucer's Shipman) not based on any one person, I suppose there are similarities between him and Hawley. In homage to Chaucer I have named the replica cog that visits

Tradmouth during the Palkin Festival the *Maudelayne* after the Shipman's vessel.

During the nineteenth century there was a huge resurgence of interest in the Middle Ages. Gothic architecture became the height of fashion, both in the domestic sphere and for great public buildings such as the Houses of Parliament, designed by Charles Barry and Augustus Pugin who were influenced by the work of their medieval predecessors. The medieval period was widely regarded as a romantic golden age and artistic movements such as the Pre-Raphaelite Brotherhood frequently used medieval art, literature and legend as their inspiration: in this book I have referred to Alfred Lord Tennyson's poem, *The Lady of Shalott*, which draws on Arthurian legend.

Perhaps this fascination with all things medieval was a reaction against the increased and dehumanising mechanisation of the Industrial Revolution and the Victorians tended to ignore the fact that life in the distant past was usually, to quote Thomas Hobbes, 'nasty brutish and short' for the majority of people. My fictional writings of Josiah Palkin-Wright, therefore, reflect a common preoccupation of that particular time.

As for Shipworld and fantasy fiction in general ... well, with the influence of authors such as the great J.R.R. Tolkien going from strength to strength, it's as popular today as it ever was.

Do you love crime fiction?

Want the chance to hear news about your favourite authors (and the chance to win free books)?

Kate Brady
Frances Brody
Nick Brownlee
Kate Ellis
Shamini Flint
Linda Howard
Julie Kramer
Kathleen McCaul
J. D. Robb
Jeffrey Siger

Then visit the Piatkus website and blog
www.piatkus.co.uk | www.piatkusbooks.net

And follow us on Facebook and Twitter
www.facebook.com/piatkusfiction | www.twitter.com/piatkusbooks

piatkus